Cassandra's Turn

CASSANDRA'S TURN

PATRICK JONES
AND THE ELSINORE QUILLS

Dragon Gems
An Imprint of The Grumpy Dragon

The Grumpy Dragon
1818 Whitman Road
Colorado Springs, CO 80910
www.GrumpyDragon.com

Cover Design: Teri Stearns

Photographer: Teri Stearns

Editors: Spring Lea Henry, Teri Stearns. and
The Elsinore Quills

Copy Editors: Cathi Dunn Macrae, Victoria Hanley

Dynamic Folds: Paul Baxter

Dragon Gems Logo:
Spring Lea Henry, Jordan McMullen, Ray Henry

Dragon Gems is an imprint of The Grumpy Dragon and indicates
books containing partially or entirely teen created content.

Publisher Cataloging-in-Publication Data

Cassandra's turn: A tear collector novel. / by Patrick Jones and the Elsinore Quills.
   334 p. 22.86 cm.
   ISBN 978-0-9881880-2-0
   1. Supernatural—Fiction. 2. Sympathy—Fiction. 3. High Schools—
Fiction. 4. Schools—Fiction. 5. Identity—Fiction. 6. Family life—Michigan—Fiction. 7. Michigan—Fiction.
I. Jones, Patrick, 1961- . II. Elsinore Quills. III. Title.
   PZ7.J7242Cas 2013
   [FIC]

Library of Congress Control Number: 2013934823

In memory of Dorothy Broderick,
the original voice of youth advocates

Acknowledgements

Thanks to Emily Easton at Walker Bloomsbury Books for first bringing Cassandra to life in *The Tear Collector* and then letting her go to find a new home at the Grumpy Dragon. This book wouldn't exist without Grumpy Dragon editor/publisher Spring Lea Henry taking this bold step bringing youth participation to a new level. Thanks to the other involved adults: Teri, Cathi, Diane, Dori, Sue-Ellen, and Ray. Nor would this book exist without the Elsinore Quills, the five young editors-in-training, who brought so much to this project—both as a collective as we sat around the table in Colorado one Saturday and with individual assignments. Kudos too for Cydney Heed, an honorary Elsinore Quill who read an early draft of this book and wrote the letter featured in chapter 26. As always thanks to my partner, Erica Klein, who suggested the first scene in the first book (of we hope many) set in the Tear Collector world.

Thanks to Nicole Hagstrom, whom I met at the most terrific Teen Book Festival in upstate NY, who read and commented on an early draft of this manuscript.

Things fall apart; the centre cannot hold;
Mere anarchy is loosed upon the world
The blood-dimmed tide is loosed, and everywhere
The ceremony of innocence is drowned;
The best lack all conviction, while the worst
Are full of passionate intensity.

—William Butler Yeats, "The Second Coming"

To be, or not to be—that is the question;
Whether 'tis nobler in the mind to suffer
The slings and arrows of outrageous fortune
Or to take arms against a sea of troubles....

—William Shakespeare, *Hamlet*, 3.1.

"There is a sacredness in tears. They are not thee mark of weakness, but of power. They speak more eloquently than ten thousand tongues. They are the messengers of overwhelming grief, of deep contrition, and of unspeakable love."

—Washington Irving

"All you need is love."

—John Lennon and Paul McCartney

Prologue

ten years' earlier

Good Friday

*S*he watched in silence. Her six-year-old eyes took in the sights; her other senses were overwhelmed. On the wet grass, family members sat in anticipation. The little girl sensed their eyes boring through her body and into her soul. They were waiting for her moment to rise.

She gulped. Small hands clenched into fists while she tried to control her labored breathing. So much pressure. So many expectations, and she didn't know why. Her chest tightened. She felt different, but that was not uncommon. The girl knew she was different than the other children at school. They laughed; they cried. She did neither, and she didn't know why.

As a small hand slipped into her own, she jumped lightly, heart beating faster than she could imagine possible. Even after swimming with her female cousins, she never felt this way. She turned her head, eyes meeting the crystal blue ones of her cousin, who was just about a year older. He smiled, almost shyly, and nodded. Immediately her heart calmed to a normal pace, and her breathing evened. Today, she was told, was her cousin's coming of age as well.

His hand let go, and he stepped away, the sun casting an eerie glow on his dirtied tunic and pants. In her eyes, he looked like an angel. Although she'd seen the ceremony every year since her birth, never once had she understood—really understood—what was going on. Rather than dressing in normal clothes, everyone changed into costumes from olden times, like she'd seen in her illustrated Bible at *church or in pictures at home. The yellow sun shone on the green grass, but everyone's dress was muted.*

"Just follow the story," her mother told her that morning. "You know the story, my little Di'mah. Just follow it, and you'll understand."

She knew the story very well. Every night her mother told it in a soothing voice. She'd heard the story of her past and of her ancestors many times, but today they would re-enact it.

A scent of lilies wafted through the air, and she closed her eyes, breathing it in. Beneath her leather sandals, the grass peaked up and tickled her toes, and she shifted, even though she wasn't supposed to move. She knew but one emotion, lodged deep in her chest. Fear.

The girl watched her cousin, wondering if he felt uncomfortable in his outfit. Her own clothes were heavy and hot. All the women wore white veils, but she wore a violet veil that belonged to her great-grandmother. The veil covered the girl's long dark hair that slipped down on her sensitive shoulders, just like the dress draped across her body. Underneath she felt so insignificant. The ceremony, so vital. The clothes, so important. Her role, so central. But her. . .?

There was a commotion, and all the people—at least a hundred or so—rose and focused their attention. Her cousin returned to the other side with the rest of the males, walking toward the noise.

The girl's mother pushed her to the front. Behind her, relatives shouted loudly as a man walked down the path in front of them. He carried a wooden cross on his shirtless back.

Her eyes closed, and she took a deep breath. Only a little longer, and this would be over.

When her eyes opened once more, she stared at the two males about five or six feet down the path. An old man held the cross, a smile of grace plastered on his face—a twisted smile nonetheless. Outside he reenactment, she had never seen him do anything but snarl. Of course, outside the reenactment she rarely saw him anyway. The boy, her cousin, despite having comforted her earlier, was shaking. Was it from fear or excitement? Maybe both. Whatever it was, they had something in common.

The old man with the cross fell to one knee. Her cousin stepped forward from the crowd. He tried to pick up the cross, but it was too heavy. The old man instructed her cousin to take off his tunic, which he did. The girl strained to see, but others blocked her view. She struggled to the front and was surprised when she saw her cousin carrying the heavy cross for the old man and walk toward her. Her cousin's eyes looked as if a fire blazed behind them.

When the two stood before her, the old man took the cross back for himself. Before her cousin returned to the other side of the path—for always it was males on one side, females on the other—he stood directly across from her and reached out his hand. The tips of their fingers touched, and she felt something new as she stared into his blue eyes. She'd heard other people talk about the feeling of love in their family, but whatever that meant, she knew it was not what was within her heart now. It was darker, deeper. Fear.

Her cousin retreated to his side of the path, not once taking his eyes off of her.

"It's your turn," three voices whispered quietly in the wind. She turned around; her mother, grandmother, and great-grandmother stood behind her. Although her great-grandmother was the oldest, she always appeared to be the strongest. Everyone bent to her will.

"Go." Her mother waved her hand, shooing the little girl off toward the old man. She stumbled her way to center stage, nearly tripping over her garb in the process.

There were a few giggles from the audience and a couple of hushes. Everyone's eyes judged her, as if waiting for her to mess up. Although her cousins were nice to her, she knew they thought of her as spoiled, and always had. Even among her family, she felt different.

"There's no need for fear," the old man said, flashing that twisted, snarling smile. She didn't trust his words because she was afraid of him. Now. Always.

Her cousins handed the man a small vial. He placed two drops of the fluid under his eyes so they looked like tears. Tears she'd seen on others—tears she'd never seen in her own family.

"Wipe his face with the veil," her mother said, and she obeyed as always, wiping the tears from the man's face with her great-grandmother's violet veil.

After she finished, the veil—and her heart—felt heavier. She held the violet cloth in front of her and almost fainted which she saw the image of the face of Jesus, the son of God.

"This is how we became what we are," her mother said.

"What we are?"

As she stared at the face of Jesus, her mother touched her shoulder gently. When her mother removed her hands, the girl felt exposed and afraid. "We are not human like those around us," her mother whispered. "This is how we came to be. We are tear collectors."

With the false smile on his face, the old man muttered something in a language she didn't understand. Hebrew, she guessed. Sometimes her family would speak it to her, even though she knew only one word, "di'mah," which meant teardrop.

"Do you accept these tears?" the old man asked. She nodded slowly. Out of the corner of her eye, she saw her cousin mimic her action. The man closed his eyes, lifted off the lid of the vial, and held it high for all to see. Then he brought it down, his face oddly gentle and kind.

She took in a deep breath and held it as he tipped the vial over her.

All it took was a drop on each shoulder. One drop of liquid. Like a raindrop. Like a tear.

Her shoulder burned with an agonizing pleasure, and her eyes rolled back in her head, a white flash filling her vision. Shivering tingles raced through her entire body, nearly stopping her heart, trickling down to the very tips of her tiny fingers. Even though she tried her best to breathe, the pressure on her chest made it difficult, making her gasps shallow and painful.

But through the pain, she felt pleasure. Power coursed through her veins, tickling her every nerve.

Although it seemed like forever, only a few seconds passed be-

fore her body returned to normal. Her previously erect back collapsed, leaving her hunched over, and gasping for air. Her vision was fuzz-blurred by the rush of adrenaline. As if her body couldn't take any movement, she sat in silence until she fell into her great-grandmother's arms.

When she woke again, she heard screaming. She sat up with a terrified gasp and swiftly turned her head. It was now early evening. Her cousin lay next to her. He rose as well.

More screaming, followed by shouts.

Shaking her head, she followed the now deserted path toward an open area in the grassy park where her grandmother and mother stood arguing. Her mother's hands hid her face.

"Mother?" she called in a small voice. Her earlier energy still resided beneath her skin, but it was fading fast.

"Go back to sleep," her mother snapped. Her face was scrunched up, eyes narrowed. Was she in pain? The little girl cocked her head before she grabbed her mother's hand and leaned against it. The warmth couldn't compare to the earlier heat. "You need your rest."

"She should see this; she is one of us now," the little girl's grandmother said.

"Not this! Anything but this!" Her mother's words were cloaked in fear.

Before the child could react, her grandmother grabbed her hand and steered her deeper into the woods, ignoring her mother's screams begging her to stop.

Reaching a heavily wooded area, the girl saw her closest family members organized in a circle surrounding one lone figure. The red clothing proclaimed him a male, but she couldn't see his face, which it was covered with a mask—black except for six small, violet, tear-shaped marks over the eyes and five small, red tear-shapes by the mouth.

As a cold breeze blew, the girl shuddered and huddled against her grandmother.

"You have threatened our way!" The old man who had anointed her with tears stood over the masked figure. Dressed in a blood red tunic, he had lost all trace of his former smile. His black eyes reminded the little girl of a vulture. "You are breaking our laws."

"You know I don't care," the masked man said, chuckling.

How could he laugh at a time like this?

The man in the mask continued, "Your rules. Your laws. They are not the true old ways. You have perverted—"

"You insolent—" the old man growled, but stopped when the masked man held up a pale, smooth hand.

"I know, I know. I'm a failure. I'm leaving now. You have your precious one to take my place. He has felt the energy of our Savior's tears. He'll be a perfect replacement for me. And for you." He stood up, pushing back the old man in the process. "I don't need your rules or the family. I see what we've become, and it sickens me. We must return to the ways of—"

"Silence!" the old man shouted five times.

From across the way, the girl saw her cousin staring at the masked man. His crystal blue eyes never left the figure as an eager smile came over his face.

She whimpered and hung onto her grandmother. She wanted her mother, who hadn't followed them into the circle. Her grandmother's tightening grip terrified her.

"Do you see what's happening?" her grandmother whispered.

"Yes, grandmother."

"Do you understand?"

"No."

"Don't worry, you will one day."

The girl watched as the argument continued. The old man yelled for silence again, then motioned for her cousin and an older boy with dark blue eyes and a shock of brown hair to come forward. She had never noticed this teenager before, yet when she looked at him, she seemed to know him. How could that be?

The two young men held the arms of the man in the mask. At first, he tried to resist, but then surrendered. How could two such young men hold him? Had they been made stronger somehow?

The old man stepped forward. He reached into his tunic and took out a small, brown bottle. The man in the mask made a sound like the whimper of a hurt dog.

The circle gave a collective gasp. A look of fear washed over the faces of her cousin and the other young man—a teen boy who was also a cousin, part of this family, part of this ritual.

"For your sins you suffer," the old man said.

He ripped open the man's tunic so that his shoulders were exposed. Then he unscrewed the black cap on the bottle. The males edged forward to get a closer look. Many women covered their eyes. Just before the little girl did the same, she noticed her grandmother—who didn't cover her eyes, but closed them tightly—sticking her fingers in her ears to block out sound.

For just a second, the girl heard a sizzling sound, like burgers on the grill. She started to open her eyes, but the man's screams scared her. She focused on the scent. Like candles at church, something was melting under intense heat.

"Enough! It is over now," the old man said.

She opened her eyes. Her two cousins man dragged the man around the circle. The girl saw the skin on his shoulders, or what was left of it.

She heard a loud gasp. Turning toward the sound, she saw her mother fainting into her great-grandmother's strong, old arms.

The old man proclaimed, "Leave us, and never return!"

"Is everything all right?" her cousin asked.

Now it was only herself, her cousin, and her great-grandmother, whom she feared and obeyed. The three sat in circle under a nearly full moon. The rest of the family celebrated in the woods, although the little girl didn't know why they'd celebrate such a horrible occurrence. So much she didn't understand, but knew better than to ask. A lesson taught early in her family was to accept what was said and done, not to question anything.

The girl glanced at her cousin. Like her, he was still wearing his earlier outfit. At first she smiled, glad to have him there, but his eyes were cold. He hadn't been asking if she was okay; he had been asking if he was in trouble.

The old woman started to speak, first to the boy. "Your great-grandfather is tired, so I will tell you both the rules."

"The rules?" the girl asked, but the boy said nothing.

"I will tell you why you'll never see that man again. He's been exiled from the family."

"Forever?" her cousin asked. The older woman nodded, and motioned them closer.

"We are special creatures, but with our powers comes a secret life we must uphold, and to do that we must—and I mean **must**—live by a set of rules, important rules you must ingrain into your memory for the rest of your lives. First, you must always follow your role. Family comes first. It is your duty to serve the generations above you, no matter how hard. Understand?"

The cousins nodded. The old woman motioned for the girl to put out her hand. In the girl's hand, the old woman placed a six-sided, white linen handkerchief with one violet thread.

"What is this for?" the girl asked.

"It is your duty to serve the generations above you, no matter how hard," she repeated.

"I don't understand."

"You are a tear collector, and you will use this handkerchief to collect tears for your family. No more questions, understood?"

The girl nodded again.

The old woman spoke more softly, as if telling a secret. "Second, we are not human, and therefore we shall not mate with humans, only with each other. Third, you will not kill one of our kind. We are blood and too important to kill each other. We are few in number by purpose, but only the elders select who lives and dies."

For a second, the girl tuned out her great-grandmother. Which of these rules had the man broken to have deserved such a horrible fate?

"Fourth, do no harm." As she spoke these words, she stared at the boy. "To collect tears for your elders and for the greater good, you will manipulate the emotions of humans, but you will not cause direct harm. You may never take a human life, except in self-defense. Understand?"

The boy nodded as did the girl, to show she understood. But that was a lie. She was a tear collector, not a human, and had to live by a set of rules. The realization washed over her like a giant wave at the beach, and she felt as if she were drowning. Yet she nodded as if she agreed.

Her nodding stopped when the old woman clutched her face between her hands. At first it hurt, then her great-grandmother stroked the back of her cheek as if to comfort her.

"And finally," the old woman whispered, "you must never, ever fall in love."

Chapter I
Monday, April 20
early evening

"Becca, are you awake?" I whisper to no response. I force myself out of these memories and focus on life-and-death decisions about the future for Becca, my boyfriend Scott, and myself.

For now, Becca is sleeping, but soon she'll be dead, if not by my hand, then by the tumor eating away at her eight-year-old body. Becca's room is filled with the toys of a happy child; the air of the Berrys' house is filled with the moist misery of a family in crisis. Becca's big, pink bed is too large for her small body. Her pain is too much for her parents, reeling from the death of their older daughter Robyn, my best friend, who was killed in a car crash. Everyone thinks it was an accident. I suspect that the crash a few weeks ago was a disguised suicide.

But I can change Becca's fate. I could save her life, or I could save my chance at love. I cradle my phone in my hand, unable to decide or act. In my mind, I hear my great-grandmother Veronica's warning. "You may never take a human life, except in self-defense." But Scott's words—"I love you, Cassandra"—drown them out. Yet words are hollow, mostly lies. Only actions matter. To gain human life, I need to take a life. And I know just the person who doesn't deserve to live.

"Hello Brittney, it's Cassandra. I need to see you," I say into the phone.

"What do *you* want, bitch?" I picture the stuck-up sneer on her overly made-up face, along with her acrylic nails and tan as fake as her tears. Worse than her false appearance is the essence of her soul: She's the most selfish creature among any species. She's the blonde-haired, blood-eyed locust of Lapeer High. She consumes everything and leaves nothing except a perfect image in her ever-present mirror. Her list of crimes against my friends is long; her list of good deeds is non-existent. Brittney is sin dressed in cheerleader sneakers by day and red stiletto heels by night.

Before I can even begin to tell her why I've called, she says, "Listen, Cassandra, I've got nothing to say to you. Don't call me again!"

The phone goes dead. Like Robyn. Soon like Becca. I look down again at Becca sleeping peacefully in her bed. Her peace will not last. From my volunteer work at Lapeer Hospital, I know the agony her illness will bring her and her still-grieving parents. She won't live to see nine. By the time her life ends, she might be in so much pain and despair that she would welcome death like a trusted friend.

I could ease that pain by trading Brittney's life for Becca's renewed health, rather than use that energy for my own transformation so I can be with Scott. I've done so many bad things; I must restore balance with good deeds. With my great-grandmother's ability to perform a life-saving miracle, I'd bring joy rather than more sorrow.

Can I sacrifice my chance at human love for Becca's life?

"Cassandra, is everything okay?" Becca's mother asks in a church whisper. She's behind me in the doorway. I've been in this room for an hour watching Becca and considering my options.

I turn around, fake a smile, and lie so easily. "Everything's fine, Mrs. Berry."

"Scott said that you two should get going," she whispers.

She leaves, but I don't move. I stare at this sweet little girl.

Why should Becca have a brain tumor?

Sometimes I doubt my family history and believe there is no God. My friend, Samantha, once asked, "What God would allow so much suffering?" Now I wonder the same. Why should an innocent like Becca die while a selfish sinner like Brittney lives? Will I play God myself and end the suffering He allows? Or will I be selfish like Brittney and use Becca's life so I can feel real love?

Becca is suspended between life and death. So am I, between life as a human or the sorrow-filled existence of collecting tears by causing human misery.

We're studying *Hamlet* in junior English class where people are bored because they can't make a connection to their lives. Normally I'm the same way in all my classes except biology, but something clicked when Mrs. Plumb described the themes of the play: family betrayal, revenge, and decisions about life and death. This play isn't only about a prince in Denmark; it's also about a teenage tear collector in Lapeer, Michigan. Every word rings true as my family's supernatural needs battle my human desires. To be or not to be a tear collector is my question.

Do I accept my fate or do I fight for Scott, for Becca, for myself?

"I need to quit peer counseling," I tell Scott as soon as we're in his car.

It's a beat-up Chevy, unlike the flashy cars that my past cooler and hotter boyfriends drove. For once with Scott, I focused on the person inside, not the outer trappings. Scott is more than a boyfriend; he's my catalyst to becoming human.

"Why would you do that?"

He strokes my long rainbow-colored hair out of my eyes. It falls on my shoulders, which, as always, are bare to the world and all its wretchedness. The skin on my shoulders absorbs human tears in its microscopic pores and converts them into energy. We tear collectors can survive on human food and oxygen, but we only thrive on despair and sorrow.

"So I can spend more time with you," I lie, burying my face in Scott's shoulder.

With my mentor Mr. Abraham's support, I started the peer counseling program where students help other students. This not only lets me soak up tears, but gives me information I need to create drama. Quitting counseling will be my first small step away from my tear collector ways. If I'm to leave my life behind for Scott, I must begin to act more human, less like a tear collector. Maybe like the tear collectors of old, I'll provide genuine compassion, not just fake empathy and concern.

Scott half-smiles. "I'd smile more, but it still hurts."

I wince a little at being reminded of his pain. My cousin Alexei tried to get to me by torturing Scott. His mouth will recover, but I hope his memories of that night never return. I kiss Scott to heal him, I want to feel his pain, but I can't. To do so would be real love. As my cousin Siobhan once said, human love isn't about sharing pleasure, but going through agony together.

I gently kiss Scott's cheek to push the harsh images away. "When you're hurt, I'm here."

"You're always there for me." Scott pulls me closer. When I look into his eyes, I don't see him or me, I see Robyn. When Scott talks to me, he has the same sparkle in his eyes that Robyn did when she talked about her boyfriend Craig, who broke her heart and led Robyn to take her own life. Love isn't a four-letter word; it's a full life sentence.

My shoulders start to tingle. I sense Scott's emotions on the rise. "Scott, are you okay?"

"I'm still a little freaked out. You don't forget a few days of your life. And when you do start to remember, the first thing you learn is that your grandmother has died," Scott says.

"She's alive if you think about her," I say aloud. Inside I think, *Is the same true for the father I've never known?*

"You always look at the bright side, don't you?"

I don't answer. The youngest tear collector female in my family is always named Cassandra. All we see are bad things ahead. If we don't view disaster waiting to happen, then we must cause it, all in the name of collecting tears for the greater good.

"We could sure use some bright days around here," Scott says, turning on the windshield wipers. They move back and forth, I rock against Scott in time. "Michigan's dying, too."

I glance out the window at the vacant stores and foreclosed houses. I've never asked why we moved to Lapeer. Flat, dreary, and desolate, it's an economic dust bowl. A few miles away in Flint, people get shot dead every day, while adults lose their jobs. Maybe we're here to gain the tears that come with so much loss of life and hope.

"Scott, what's wrong today?"

"I'm just thinking about Robyn, about my grandmother, and now Becca up there in her room . . . about all this loss in our lives."

"I understand," I lie.

Tear collectors don't feel loss or love or any human emotions except anger, jealousy, and fear. Those three feelings stoke fires that allow us to manipulate humans for our own purposes, but also to help these humans cry out their pain. We are catharsis machines. I'm starting to feel the stirrings of something like love for people like Becca and Scott, but not enough to understand how humans feel when they talk of missing those they love who have died.

"Do you miss her?" He runs his fingers through my hair, which I grew out and dyed after swim season finished, back when all this madness started. I hate this life; I need to change it.

"Every day," I finally answer.

It's not quite a lie. I'm not capable of missing anyone, but I miss the connection Robyn gave me in school. She was the apex, but like that poem we read by Yeats, the center could not hold. It was Robyn's death more than a month ago that set these events in motion: my relationship with Scott, my friendship with Samantha, my feud with Brittney, and the turmoil in my family. Like the murder of Hamlet's father, Robyn's death hangs over everything.

Chapter 2

Monday, April 20

late evening

"What have you done?" Mom snaps at me when I walk in the door. She's still dressed from work. She runs the local Red Cross. It's a helping profession—a tear collector career.

"Nothing." Mom won't answer my important questions; I won't answer her dumb ones.

Her jaw drops open, and for once a beverage doesn't fill it. "Why did you cut your hair?"

I look in the mirror near the front door. My long black hair with rainbow streaks is gone. Scott and I stopped at the salon on the way home. If I'm going to change inside, I need to change the outside too. My hair's short now, like Robyn's life. It's different, like I want to be.

"I don't like it," Mom says.

The back of my neck itches, while my shoulders miss the familiar tickle of my hair resting on them. They're more vulnerable now, but then again, so am I.

"Why does that not surprise me?" I counter.

I sensed that Scott, who came with me to the salon, didn't like my snap decision either, but he said nothing. Snap decisions are the easiest.

"Where *else* have you been?" She sips her drink, but it doesn't cool her angry tone. With six inches of hair gone, my head feels lighter and cooler despite the decisions weighing it down.

"Out with *Scott*." I throw his name like a punch. She flinches, and her lips curl.

"Where is *Alexei*?" If her lips curled when I mentioned Scott, now my skin crawls at the mention of that name.

"I don't know." I try to move toward my room, but she blocks my way. All she knows—and anyone knows—is that my cousin is missing; they don't know why. It's because after I wouldn't mate with Alexei, he kidnapped Scott. I saved Scott with Samantha's help, and she tried to kill my cousin with her car. But Alexei must have been so energized by Scott's tears of pain, that even the impact of metal on flesh and bone didn't finish him. He must be bruised, but not bloodied. I already found the first news article online as I track him now like I did before. It sits in the printer like a diseased thing. He's regaining his strength; he's biding his time. He wants me to be afraid.

"I don't believe you!" she shouts before she sips her drink.

The cool fluid sooths her throat, sore from years of yelling at me. It's a wonder my ears don't ache from listening to her.

"Then that's your problem."

I know Alexei will return. When he does, will it be to take his place as my mate or to take his revenge for what Samantha and I did to him?

"No, it is your problem." She still stands in my way.

Like me, my mom is tall, thin, and muscular, with a swimmer's build. But when she piles on me like this, I feel like I'm drowning.

"You'd better get it together before you see him again. He'll be back for Feastday on July 12th. All of the family will be there. This is a very special Feastday for Veronica."

"Why is it so special?" I ask.

She sips as her only answer.

"I don't care. I don't want to—"

Mom takes another sip from her drink, and stares at me like I'm the stupidest person on earth. "What you want doesn't matter. You don't have a choice. Veronica's waiting for you."

"I can't help her."

Mom glares and slowly reaches into her jacket pocket. She hands me the handkerchief that I use to collect tears to keep my great-grandmother alive. "I know. You forgot this."

I stare at the six-sided white cloth with the single violet thread that she holds out to me, so innocent-looking but so powerful. The youngest tear collector of the family is always designated to hold the cloth, but Veronica holds the violet veil—the veil she wore that gave her power to save Scott's life by transferring the life force to him from his dying grandmother, the holy relic handed down since the dawn of the tear collectors on Via Dolorosa street in the old city of Jerusalem.

"Take it!"

I do as I'm told. I am the youngest. I'm expected to always obey.

"Did you talk to *that teacher* about setting up a grief group at school?" Mom asks.

I rub the fabric between my fingers, but free of tears, it brings me no energy, just a thirst for tears. It's a thirst I cannot control and cannot extinguish unless I cross over.

Mom claps her hands. "Are you listening?"

"Yes," I lie, which is not easy to do with another tear collector, but Mom believes the partial truth of that one word. I did talk to Mr. A., but not about a grief group. That's the opposite of what I want to do. I'm tired of the drama, the trauma, and being at the center of it all. This center cannot hold either.

"What did that *man* say?" Mom never says Mr. Abraham's name; it's so odd.

"He said no," I say firmly. "I don't need it anyway. I'll do my part as always."

"Veronica's weak because of what she did for you, saving Scott's life. *You owe her.*"

When there is no love in a family, all that leaves is obligation. "I know."

"You've made a mess of everything. She won't stand for it, nor will Simon." Simon is Alexei's great-grandfather, the family patri-arch. "And for what? A school-girl crush. You know you can't feel love; you can only fake human emotion. I know it seems real, but it's not."

I don't say anything. Love sounds like a quenching drink for humans, but all I taste is a longing thirst.

"What are you going to do about *that girl*?" Mom sets down her beverage and crosses her arms. She's maybe an inch taller than me, but her tone allows her to tower over me like a giant.

"Samantha? Don't worry about her. No one believes anything she says."

"That girl knows too much." Mom's tone oozes her disappoint-ment in me. "You've risked too much for *Scott*, a silly crush. You need to focus on your family, not that *silliness*."

"Scott is more than a crush, and we both know it. I think I might be in—" I start.

She cuts me off. "Don't even finish! You know that is im-possible."

I turn on my heel and walk toward my room. Mom shouts after me, telling me how I wrong I am about everything. She might be right about Samantha, but so wrong about Scott.

Mom has never loved; how would she know? She never speaks of my father, and I've never known him. All I've known is the way of the tear collector. Just like the way of the cross that spawned us, it is a path that contains nothing but pain. But I will stray from the road I'm on and the cup I've been handed. Despite what she says, I know from my exiled cousin Siobhan that my growing human feel-ings for Scott aren't impossible. Siobhan crossed over, surrendered being a tear collector for human love. Mom said, "Don't even finish! You know that is impossible." But I'll prove her wrong and risk any-thing to make this love real.

In the tear collector world, love isn't real, but fear is. As soon as I enter my room, I turn on the light and look at the single sheet of paper in the printer. The words stab me like a dagger.

> *Michigan State Police have issued an Amber alert for 12 year-old Elliot Osborne, a 7th grade student at Royal Oak Elementary who was last seen leaving a playground around 5 p.m. on April 19. According to witnesses, he was walking home alone. Law enforcement officials are on the lookout for a black Ford van driven by a young male seen in the area earlier in the day. The male is described as being a tall Caucasian with brown hair.*

There is the fear male tear collectors like Alexei create in their victims, and there is the fear I feel knowing Alexei will return for me. He is my fate; he is my curse. But mostly he is evil—not only because he attacked me and tortured Scott and not because he abducts innocent children off the street and tortures them to take their tears. These things make him bad, but not evil. What makes him evil isn't what he does, but who he is: Simon's great-grandson.

Simon will not rest his weary bones until I obey him, make Alexei my mate, and start the next generation. But if the next generation is like the others, then we tear collectors are doomed. Tear collector rules forbid me from mating with Scott; my own dread prevents me mating with Alexei. A child should not be conceived from duty, but out of love—love I'm never supposed to feel. *"You must never, ever, fall in love."*

But if Alexei can break the rules, then why can't I?

Chapter 3

Tuesday, April 21

after school

"Y ou're sure this is okay?" I ask Mr. A. as I take the buds out of my ears.

He nods and then smiles. It's after last period, and he's letting me use the school pool. With all the drama, I haven't had time or focus to swim. The water refreshes me like nothing else. It gives no energy yet cleanses me. Mr. A., as always, sits by the pool fully dressed, since he never swims himself.

"I'm sorry I'm late. I had a conference with a student who got upset," he says. His voice echoes around the empty pool like I suspect the booming voice of God sounded to Abraham.

"I understand," I say, then leap into the water.

I swim back and forth as my muscles explode with delight. But as I touch the end of the pool with my hand, it's like I cracked my head—a thought enters that won't leave.

This is my life: I swim in the pool of tears, back and forth without any purpose other than survival of my species.

Unable to shake my destiny, I imagine Scott is here with me, his hand reaching out to rescue me from this dismal fate.

"Well, don't think I'm just being altruistic in letting you swim here." Mr. A. laughs.

He doesn't laugh much in class, but then again there's not much funny about evolutionary biology. People think that natural selection is about what a species gains in order to survive, but to me, it's more about loss. Tear collectors started as caring creatures, but we've forsaken that over time. The females fake compassion as we stir up the drama and emotional energy; the males are lazier—or maybe crazier—so they use trauma to feed off tears from fear and pain. These are the creatures we've become.

"Let me guess, you want something in return."

I climb out of the pool, breathing heavily. Since swim season ended in early March, I haven't swum my usual twenty-three laps. He throws me a white towel, but I'll be the one surrendering.

"Somebody you want me to tutor in science?" I ask.

I have a full load of classes, but science and English are the only ones that matter or challenge me. I remove my purple swim cap and dry off as I walk over toward Mr. A.

"No, I heard you might want to stop peer counseling. Are you sure about that?" he asks in that voice I hear often from adults pretending they're offering you a choice, but they're really telling you what you're going to do. My family doesn't even bother faking it. They order and I obey.

I sit by the edge of the pool, the towel covering my shoulders. "It's too hard."

He paces behind me, full of nervous energy despite not having his always-at-hand coffee thermos. "You once asked me about how to make a decision, and what did I tell you?"

"To listen to the silence."

"Right, but now, I want you to do the opposite." More pacing. "Instead, listen to your classmates and the noise in their lives. Noise from hurt, pain, and anger. Many are still hurting over Robyn; many have yet to begin to process their grief. With the end of school almost upon us, and touchstone events like the prom, I suspect that noise will only increase."

"Maybe," I mumble, but he's right. Prom is a drama downpour. Scott and I will attend, and I fixed Samantha up with my gay friend Michael, who is in Honors Bio with us. He's more of a theater nerd than a science geek or a Goth like Samantha. It should be an interesting evening.

"Cassandra, you have a gift for being a peer counselor, and it would be a waste not to use it. Think about Robyn. Would she have wanted you to quit?"

"I don't think about Robyn." I hate lying to him; I often invoke her name for a quick fix.

He stops pacing, and I sense he's standing right behind me like the sun over the earth. "What happened with Robyn was such a terrible ... accident."

I don't ask why he paused before he said the word accident. Does he know that I helped Robyn? That she came to me for a shoulder to cry on like she had so many times, and I soaked up all those tears? But the pressure at home was so great—for both of us. For her, it was to excel in everything, not just for herself, but almost as if she had to fulfill all of Becca's never-to-be-realized dreams. For me, with Veronica growing weaker by the day, it was the push to create and collect more tears. And what could cause more grief than Robyn—the most popular girl in school—dying?

"Are you listening? Do you hear it?" Mr. A. asks. "Think about all the students you know who are hurting—not because of Robyn's death, but from the daily harshness of high school life. If you have a gift, you have an obligation to use it for the greater good. You *owe* her that."

A rare, pure human natural response—goose bumps—invades my naked arms. "What?"

He starts pacing again. "Listen to the noise and please reconsider, Cassandra."

"Okay. For you."

For some reason, Mr. A. is a very hard man to say no to. Maybe it's because I'm conditioned never to say no to adults, and maybe because he's almost always right.

He pats the top of my head. "Thanks. You won't regret it, and I'll be in your debt."

I look at the clock on the wall. "I've got to go. My grandmother's picking me up."

"Taking you somewhere fun?" He laughs. It still doesn't sound right coming from him.

"I'm volunteering at the hospital tonight." I stand up and start toward the locker room. Unlike some of the perv teachers at this school, he doesn't stare at my fine form.

"Cassandra, one more small thing."

I'm laughing now, but hiding it. For a human, that's a very tear-collector move: Once you've convinced someone to do one thing, immediately ask for another favor.

"What's that?"

We walk toward the locker room. Even though he's taller than me, we walk in sync.

"My godson, Caleb, will be staying with me this summer before he starts his second year of Medical School at the University of Michigan in the fall. He chose medicine because he knows what matters most in life is doing not what is best for one, but what serves the greater good."

"And so?"

My hand is on the locker room door. For some reason, it's shaking

"He won't know anyone here. You're a little younger, but mature for your age. You want to go to medical school, right?"

I nod. It's not like I have a choice. If not medical school, then some helping profession where I can help myself to human suffering. The females mostly work in human services, while males like Alexei's grandfather, Asa, own funeral homes and cemeteries.

"Maybe you could give him a tour of the hospital and introduce him. Would you do that for me?"

Before I answer, he places the tips of his fingers on my shaking hand. I nod again and open the locker room door with a now-steady hand.

"Anything for you, Mr. A."

"Let me know when I can return the favor."

"Well, do you know anything about *Hamlet*? I have a paper due at the end of the year."

"Sadly, Cassandra, I'm a man of science, not of the arts."

"You say that, but I think you're just like me," I say. "Just like I said in class once: There's a place for both science and faith. Same thing, there's a place for both art and science."

His expression grows dark. "There's only science. There's only biology. Biology is destiny and duty."

He frowns, turns on his heel, and walks away without saying goodbye.

"Veronica wants to attempt to go out tomorrow night," Mom says when I get in her blue Honda hybrid. I don't ask why my grandmother, Maggie, isn't picking me up, even though I should, since Mom never, ever drives me to or from school. "It's Wednesday night, and there are grief support groups meeting."

"So?" I slurp hard from my water bottle so the noise can drown out Mom's voice.

"So, Cassandra, she needs strength to do that."

Mom's subtle way of reminding me of my duty.

"I tried to call Samantha, but she's not answering and she's not online."

This is not surprising: as steady as Scott is, Samantha is unstable. From what I've learned, she's a cauldron of chaos. Take all the problems that people come into peer counseling with, like depression and cutting, stir in a past full of hurt, and you have a recipe for her damaged life. Until I became her friend, Samantha hid her tears like the scars on her arms and back. I manipulated her to admit her pain to me. She shared her hurt, and because of it, Scott healed.

I continue, "And there just isn't much going on at school. I'm doing my best."

"Why don't you come with us tonight?" Mom says. "You've not been to a support group in a long time. I'm going, and Maggie's going. If we collect enough tears, along with what you bring home, then maybe Veronica will have her strength back."

"If you're doing that, then why do you need—"

"Because we're older, we need more for ourselves. We can't spare as much as you can."

"I have to work, but I'll be at the hospital, so. . . ."

"So?"

I sigh and reach into my purse. I pull out the handkerchief. "So, I'll do my part."

"Remember Cassandra, it's for the greater good."

I drop the handkerchief when I hear her echo Mr. Abraham's words.

"Are you okay?" She merges her Honda out onto the main road.

"Why did you just say that?" I ask. "I mean use those words, 'the greater good.'"

"I don't know, Cassandra. It's just an expression."

I sink down in my seat. It's not an expression; it's an expectation. Before I can ask Mom more, her phone rings. It's something about work. I try texting Samantha and Scott, but get nothing in return. She's vanished, while Scott's back working at his waiter job. He works hard, but then never spends the money on himself, just on me. Always for the greater good.

"So is your prom dress going to be candy-striped like these new uniforms?" I ask Amanda, a fellow hospital volunteer.

I switched shifts so I wouldn't have to work with Brittney's main toady, Kelsey. We're in the locker room putting on these new, horrid, pink-and-white striped uniforms. I preferred the simple black-and-white we used to wear. The old uniforms made us look important; these new ones make us look like walking peppermint sticks. Ugly eye-candy.

She mumbles something and averts her eyes from me as I change.

"I was going to go shopping for prom dresses with Robyn, but. . . ."

Another mumble.

Amanda wasn't in Robyn's inner circle, but they'd known each other for years. Robyn didn't dump her in high school; they just went different ways. Robyn burst like a super nova into the high-school sky, while Amanda stayed this little, unnoticed pale star.

"Amanda, maybe you and I could go shopping for our prom dresses. We could—"

"I'm not going shopping for a prom dress because I'm not going," she snaps.

Like a wild animal sensing prey, my body reacts. The skin in my shoulders opens in anticipation. I'd intended to gather tears from strangers on my rounds, but this is much better. I said I would resist, but tears to me are like drugs to addicts. The need for the fix overwhelms my willpower.

"Why would you say that, Amanda? A smart, beautiful girl like you? For sure you'll have a date."

"That'd be a first." She makes a sound between a laugh and a small cry.

Amanda is smart, but she doesn't take honors classes like I do. She is pretty, but not beautiful like Robyn. She's a like lot Scott: shy, slightly insecure, playing everything safe. She and Scott are as normal as Samantha is strange. My skills allow me to move between polar opposites with ease.

I motion for her to sit next to me. She looks confused, but my deep violet eyes exert their will on her. "I find that hard to believe. Are you telling me you haven't had a boyfriend in high school?"

"I'm not like you, Cassandra, in case you haven't noticed." Amanda dresses in modest clothes with solid colors that make her blend into the bland crowd. "You've always had boyfriends. You're outgoing, popular, pretty. You're everything that I'm not, so can we just leave it at that?"

"Do you know my boyfriend, Scott?"

"I know who he is," she says. "I've seen you together and pix of you two on your page."

"Do you remember my boyfriend before Scott?"

She nods and manages a tiny smile on her plain pink lips.

"Cody. What a tool! But guess what? He was outgoing, popular, handsome."

"What's your point, Cassandra?"

I move closer. "I'm with Scott, not Cody. Scott's like you. He's nice, but shy. You're both so attractive, but in a real way, not like overly-made-up show-offs such as Brittney and Kelsey. You're beautiful inside, too. So my point, Amanda, is that there is someone for everyone."

"You think so."

"You might meet him right here," I say, then tell her the story about my encounter with Scott at the hospital.

When we talked at school for the first time in the library, I sensed a connection in the way Scott smiled at me. But later, when he was here visiting his dying grandmother, I knew Scott was different—not because he was the type of guy every other girl wanted, but because I sensed he was what I needed. After putting up with the Codys of the world, I needed a break. I didn't know Scott wouldn't just be a break. I didn't know that for him, I'd defy family rules and might do even worse. As I tell Amanda the story, her face flips emotions: sometimes she laughs, and then seconds later she looks as if she's going to cry. My shoulders tingle; it's time.

"Listen, Amanda, I know high school is hard, especially if you feel lonely," I say, talking with utter confidence about something I know nothing about. "Do you feel alone?"

She resorts back to mumbling. I reach into my locker and take out my purse.

"You don't need to feel alone." I take the handkerchief from the purse and move it toward her unmade-up face. She squints and sniffs in tandem. "Do you know any Beatles music?"

"Robyn and I used to listen to them," she says, very softly.

I nod knowingly. "Me and her, too. You must miss Robyn. It must make you feel even lonelier, right?"

She barely nods her head, like it hurts to do so. But that's not it; it's filled with tears I'm ready to harvest.

"Like the Beatles sang, Amanda, just 'Cry Baby Cry.'"

And she does.

The ride home with Maggie and Mom is stone silent. Like so many things in my family, I'm not sure of the reason, but there's a tension between these two that never seems to go away, except for when they're ganging up on me. If they are as full of energy as I am, it must be hard for them to sit quietly.

I spend my ride home thinking about Amanda. I don't know her that well, but that's about to change. Everything about her is, as she told me between cries, outstandingly average—except perhaps her capacity to control her tears. I sense in that regard, with my help, she's found an area in which to excel.

When we arrive home, I start toward my room, but Mom cuts me down with a frown. I follow her, and we stand outside Veronica's room on the second floor of this old house. Maggie's inside. I hear them talking, arguing again. Mom says nothing as we wait in silence like two mobsters outside the door preparing to enter and kiss the ring of the powerful Don.

The door opens, and Maggie walks by us, slowly. Mom goes inside, and I wait alone. It seems that all I do is wait. Wait for another girl to place her trust in me so I can harvest her tears. Wait for another swirl of high school drama to feed Veronica's need. Wait with dread for Alexei's return in July. But I wait—with strange, new sensations of delight—to see Scott again. Unlike Cody, unlike the rest, something about Scott—maybe his pure goodness—excites me.

"Cassandra, it's your turn," Mom says.

She holds the door open, and I enter. Veronica lies in bed. On one side of the bed on a silver tray is a tear-catcher bottle from the Middle Ages adorned in silver and pewter. On the other side of the large, ornate bed, also adorned in silver and pewter, is a box holding

Veronica's veil—the veil I must get her to wear to save Becca's life.

I take out the handkerchief, then open the tear catcher. Using the modern convenience of an eyedropper, I place one drop of these tears collected over the years onto the handkerchief. Like an accelerant in a fire, the single drop of old tears interacts with Amanda's fresh ones to create a wet cloth, which I press against Veronica's forehead. In her old age, she can no longer tolerate tears applied directly to her shoulders. Her blue veins quiver as the tears roll down her face and pool on her shoulders. My duty done, I start to leave, but she grabs my hand. Her grip is not that of an old woman but of someone much younger. She pulls me closer. Her cold breath blows in my ear.

"My little Di'mah, one day this will be yours," she whispers, holding my hand tighter. "All of this sacrifice will be worth it to keep our family strong. You'll know what I mean when—"

She starts to cough, not out of sickness, I know, but health. Her lungs breathe in deeply.

"When what, Veronica?"

She grabs my hand so tight it goes numb.

"When it's your turn to be the Veronica."

Chapter 4

Wednesday, April 22

school day

"**W**hat the hell?" I ask Samantha after she drops a note on my desk before Honors Bio starts. The note says, "He's back." She hurries to her seat before I can ask her who "he" is.

All through class, I try to make eye contact with Samantha, but she's having none of it. While her life shifted one hundred eighty degrees because of the events of spring break, this morning she gives me zero attention. Our friendship is new, but I thought it was strong.

As Mr. Abraham leads the discussion on symbiosis with the skill of a maestro conducting an orchestra, I look for opportunities to glance at my phone. No messages from Scott, who isn't in class, so I stare at Samantha's red-ink note.

Who is the "he" that's back?

"Cassandra, would you define mutualism?" Mr. A. asks.

I bury my phone and clear my throat. "Mutualism is any relationship between individuals of different species where both individuals derive a benefit."

"That's correct. Who would like to define another type of symbiosis?" Lots of hands go in the air in this gathering of over-achievers. Samantha's head is on her desk, but Mr. A. lets it pass, again. Some days, she spends more time studying the inside of her eyelids than Mr. A.'s PowerPoint. "Let's see, we've not heard from Michael in some time."

Before Michael speaks, Clark Rogers coughs and then giggles like a little kid. He's the classhole of Honors Biology. I don't know how Mr. A. doesn't notice that whenever Michael speaks, Clark makes this hacking sound. Of course, he's not coughing at all. I hear the words he mutters underneath. Today's it's "fag." Tomorrow will be "coon" or some other racial slur.

"Um, maybe commensalism," Michael mumbles. He speaks so clearly when he's up on stage, but in class he's always unsure of himself. I guess people, like tear collectors, thrive in different environments. When times have been tough for him in the past, I was there for him, so when I asked him for a favor—escort Samantha to the Junior/Senior Prom—he owed me.

"And what is that?" Mr. A. asks.

"It describes a relationship between two living organisms where one benefits and the other is not harmed or helped that much. Is that right?" Michael asks.

Mr. A. nods his head. "Now, how about an example from someone else?"

Mary Nguyen starts to talk, but I'm not listening. I'm too busy staring at Samantha and wondering: What is our relationship? Mutualism or commensalism? I did take advantage of her, learned her secrets, exploited her pain, and used it to break her. She cried rivers of tears, which Veronica harvested for the power to save Scott's life. But now we're bonded because she knows my true self, and I need to trust that she'll never tell a living soul. The fact that Samantha believes in vampires and other such nonsense seems like insurance. Even if she talks, no one will believe her. Still, I can't risk it. I must maintain our friendship to protect my family, its secrets, and Samantha.

"Okay, how about another type. Clark?"

Clark stands up. Like Brittney, he has got to be the center of attention. She's a psychopath—I'm sure of it—but Clark's just a fool.

"Amensalism is where one species is unaffected and another is inferior and completely—and correctly—destroyed." He stares at Michael when he speaks.

"Plenty of examples of that in nature, although some scientists often don't include this," Mr. A. explains. "They would say this is just a form of the third type of symbioses, which is—?"

Many hands are raised, but only one voice: Samantha. "Parasitism. That's where one organism—the parasite—benefits at the expense of the other—the host," she says loud and clear, even though her head still rests on her folded arms.

"Can you give us an example, Samantha?" Mr. A. asks.

She raises her head and turns to glare at me through her thick, black eye shadow. As always, her cut-up arms are covered in long black sleeves.

I mouth the words, "Samantha, no."

Samantha pushes her dyed-black hair from in front of her face, then turns back toward Mr. A.

"Drug dealers and other scum who destroy everything in their path," Samantha says and then puts her head back on her desk.

Maybe *he* isn't Alexei or Scott. Maybe *he* is Mark, her mom's former boyfriend who pushed Samantha through a window, scarring her back, her life.

Mr. A. keeps the discussion going, gathering more examples. As the bell gets ready to ring, he projects a slide up on the screen. We all scribble down the words with gusto.

Mutualism — both species benefit
Commensalism — one species benefits, the other is unaffected
Amensalism — one species is unaffected, the other is destroyed
Parasitism — one species benefits, the other is harmed

"Which of these describes you?" Mr. A. taps his finger hard on his desk after each word.

Although I like Mr. Abraham and this class, it can't end soon enough. The second the bell rings, I turn toward Samantha's desk. But I can't reach her; too many students with overstuffed backpacks block me. "Samantha," I yell, but she turns her back to me and exits. She's quickly swallowed in the controlled chaos that is class change at Lapeer High.

I turn back to talk to Mr. A. about peer counseling, but I see he's talking with Michael. Even from a distance, I sense Michael's distress. As one of the few black kids and out gay kids at LHS, his life is hard, which makes it easy for me. He knows the school—either the administration itself or jerks like Clark—wouldn't let him take his boyfriend to the prom, but he still gets to go by escorting Samantha. Yet another symbiotic relationship; high school is full of them.

As I head to my next class, I ache with an odd sensation for a tear collector: loneliness. Robyn's dead, Scott's not in school, and it seems Samantha is abandoning me. When I broke up with Cody, his clique turned against me. The feeling evaporates when I feel a hard tap on my bare left shoulder. I wince in pain as long, fake fingernails jab into my most sensitive skin. I turn around, and there's Brittney on point. with Kelsey, Cody, and the rest of her acolytes behind her. Craig stands like a statue next to her. I called her in private, but she's going to answer me in person and in public.

"Why did you call me?" Brittney asks, adorned with her perma-smirk as she glares at me through her sea of blue eye shadow. "I have nothing to say to *you* about anything."

"I know," is my weak answer.

It's weak because I can't be strong. In the two short days since I first thought of killing her, I've realized no matter how much I want to love Scott and be human, or want Becca to live, I'm not ready to take a life. Even if someone as shallow as Brittney doesn't deserve to live, I can't take action. Tear collectors have stayed hidden from human view because our actions seeking tears are subtle. Humans don't notice us because through evolution humans and tear collectors have adapted to each other. But to have Brittney die so soon after Robyn. . . . That's a lot of teen death in a small, sleepy town like Lapeer.

"Don't talk to me or about me ever again."

Brittney is shorter, but it seems like her stuck-up nose looks down on me. Kelsey nods like some blonde, bobblehead doll.

"I'd like nothing better," I confess, but I need to make her hurt, if that's possible. "Why should I talk about you, Burnt Knees?" I'm one to talk when it comes to slut-shaming, but I'll use all my weapons where Brittney is concerned.

Craig flinches, but Brittney doesn't even blink.

"You don't exist in this school." She points to her legion of suck-ups. Like that man at my tear collector initiation ceremony, this is a public exile. Her words are the acid. "You're dead to us all."

"You mean like Robyn? That's your fault, too."

You'd think an accusation like this would make someone cry, but she doesn't react. I've touched her tears before; there's nothing there. They're the crocodile tears of a psychopath—full of surface charm and useless beauty.

She smirks. "You've been hanging with Samanatee too much."

"Samanatee!" Behind Brittney, her cohorts echo the insult with glee. It sounds like the laugh track on a bad sit-com. What gives these anorexic egomaniacs the right to pass judgment on anyone?

She continues. "That fat-ass Goth. You weirdos should stay together."

More snickers from her suck-ups. But Brittney's wrong. Samantha only acts Goth. She's not Goth; she's just lost in the darkness of her life.

"Like you and Kelsey did when you killed Robyn?" I counter.

Another flinch from Craig. Still no reaction from Brittney, just silence as empty as her conscience. Maybe she's not a psychopath; maybe she's like me, although I'd sense her tear collector essence if that were true.

"Robyn died in a car accident," she finally says. "How is that my fault?"

"You killed her by stealing Craig from her, by spreading lies."

If anyone knows about spreading lies, it's me. Tear collectors fuel the rumors and drama of high school for our ends, but until Robyn, I tried to obey the rules and keep my actions from causing drastic damage. All gossip comes with ridges which open up small cuts, so that's allowed. But the rapier rumor which cut off Robyn's life put me over the edge. Craig balls his fists, closes his eyes, and grimaces.

Kelsey stars to speak, then stops until Brittney nods her head, giving her permission. "You're one to talk about spreading lies. You're the queen of it," Kelsey hisses.

"And you two are the queens at spreading your legs!" I shout.

Craig gulps.

"*Bitch*! Never speak to me again. Do you understand me?"

Brittney flips her hair from her face. Kelsey echoes the gesture. When I don't answer, Brittney slaps my face. I turn the other cheek. The crowd yells for her to slap me again, but she walks away, Craig by her side. I'm relieved at the idea of never speaking to her; it will help me avoid the temptation of taking her selfish life.

The rest of the morning blurs past with echoes of "he's back" from Samantha in my ears, and images of Scott in my eyes. With Scott missing and Samantha's disappearing act, I head to the library during lunch rather than the cafeteria. Cliques I once joined with ease seem to be closed to me. With my new and growing feelings of love comes the harsh pain of loneliness. Just like everything in nature, nothing comes without price. Nature always demands balance.

As I walk through the library, I scan, not for people in crisis, but for connections. I find a place to sit, open *Hamlet*, and pretend to read. Even as my eyes are on the page, my mind remains on Brittney. In the past, I would have stolen her boyfriend away, but I can't do that because of Scott. Maybe I could manipulate her into suicide, but Brittney is too arrogant to kill herself and deprive the world of her beauty. I don't want to think about her because even though I'm convinced she deserves to die, I can't take her life. That would make me as selfish as her. Tear collectors serve humans by taking their tears, serve our families by obeying the rules, and serve the world by keeping our relationship with humans in balance, transforming their tears into our energy. The deepest human emotion is love; it's also the most selfish.

I scan the library for Amanda—she told me it's her favorite hangout—when I'm startled by a touch on my bare shoulders. I cry out in pain, but it changes to a smile when I turn around. There stands Scott. He wears a John Lennon peace sign T-shirt and a goofy Ringo Starr grin.

"Scott, where have you been?" I rise to greet him

"Rough morning," he says. I hug him and turn his smile from goofy to face-brightening.

"Maybe we can make it a better night," I whisper in his ear as I lean into him.

"You make everything better."

"And you always know the right things to say."

Scott might be lacking in some of the areas other girls seek, but he's perfect for me, even if he's often both too serious and too silly. Maybe human love is another form of symbiosis. Rather than two species adapting to each other in order to survive, it is two of the same kind evolving together to bring out the best in each other.

"As best I can through a broken mouth. Now I have a reason not to talk in class."

"You still don't remember?"

Always checking. Always worried he'll recall how Alexei tortured his mouth with dental tools as a way to get to me. I can't imagine that level of pain.

"Not yet, but I have an appointment after school today to see a psychologist," he says.

"My peer counseling isn't enough?" I whisper.

"You're more for sexual healing," he whispers, then blushes.

That's Scott's life in two seconds. He's a typical, horny teen boy, yet he wants to stay true to our shared Catholic faith. Like me, he's torn between base needs and a faith that denies those desires. He won't let me please him because it makes him feel guilty, but he has no trouble pleasuring me. He says he respects the Church and my rule that we can't have intercourse, yet I know that's what he wants. What I want is a question that leaves me confused and conflicted. I'm so used to just needing, that wanting is an odd sensation.

"Be careful, Scott," I whisper. "Psychologists plant false memories so they can treat you. They'll convince you that space aliens kidnapped you and conducted experiments on your mouth."

"But psychologists are scientists. It's their job to—"

"They're parasites living off the misery of others," says one who should know.

"Cassandra, let's not fight about it, okay?"

"But you need to—" I start, but he finishes my sentence with a kiss.

This is another way Scott is so different than my other boy-friends: He won't fight with me. He always turns the other cheek, which stops me from harming him. I don't want him to hurt. That must be a sign of love.

"I need to see my teachers and get my work, but can I see you tonight?" he asks.

"I can hardly wait."

We kiss again, yet the rush in me still feels like the first time.

After another last quick kiss, Scott starts toward the door. When the door shuts, I re-open *Hamlet*. I know the greatest play ever ends not with upbeat music and a smiling couple, but a bloodbath. Will my decisions result in a happy ending, or with the bodies hitting the floor?

Chapter 5

Wednesday, April 22

after school

"Anybody here yet?" I ask Mary Nguyen when I walk into the school counseling office. The rest of the day was just an excuse to stay after school to do some peer counseling sessions. I can give most of the tears I collect from my classmates to Veronica so she can regain her strength. I keep very few for my own fuel.

"Not yet, but four scheduled. My first should be here soon," Mary answers. Funny she's doing this. Like Kelsey volunteering at the hospital, I'm sure she has some other reason. If there's one trait that humans have adapted from association with us it's this: Everyone has good intentions, but always with strings attached. "It's that time of year. The air is full of pre-prom drama."

"Who is it?"

"Amanda Wilson," Mary answers. "You know her?"

I bite my lip to hide my satisfaction. "We volunteer at the same hospital."

I head into the small conference room and wait for my own appointment with Katie Mason. She comes in looking unsure. Like many girls at Lapeer, Katie looks lost when she's by herself. She is pretty, but works too hard to look prettier. She's smart, but tries to act dumb. It's a bad combination.

After she sits, I explain how peer counseling works, including confidentiality. I talk about how I'll never share what we discuss, even as I'm figuring out how I'll use what I learn. Being a tear collector is exhausting: I need endless tears and the way to get them is by creating drama, but that burns so much energy. I'm stuck in an endless cycle of planting and harvesting.

"So Katie, what can I help you with?" I ask.

"It's my best friend Diana," she starts.

I sense the tears are seconds below the surface. I lean in, open my eyes wide, and let her know I'm ready to take anything she throws at me. "Tell me about it; I won't judge you."

It's the key that unlocks her floodgates.

I hand her Veronica's handkerchief, still freshly-laundered from my morning ritual of preparing for each day of tear collecting by hand washing this sacred cloth to take away all that is not precious to us, such as the mascara Katie spends the next ten minutes leaking onto the white fabric, along with her anguish. I spend my time nodding and echoing back her words. She pours out through sobs how her former best friend, Diana, pounced on her ex, Clark. Now Katie is questioning everything—even her life.

I stop the deluge when the darkness overcomes her. "You don't mean that."

She stares at the floor. "It's the only way out."

"Listen, Katie, it stops hurting," I say softly. "All it takes is time and tears."

"Really?"

"Really."

I fake genuine concern as I pile on the lies. For Robyn, it didn't take time or tears. It just took driving too fast and listening to the wrong people. People like me.

Katie clears her eyes one last time with the handkerchief. "Thanks for listening."

"If you need anything else, you let me know?"

She nods in agreement. "Thanks, Cassandra."

"You need to promise me you won't hurt yourself. You need to look at me."

"I promise." She stares at me through her ruined make-up. This session has helped Katie get through her pain for one more day; it will keep Veronica content for the rest of the week.

"Say it out loud." I beg this stranger to say the words that a month ago I should have made Robyn promise the night before she killed herself. "Say you won't hurt yourself."

"I won't hurt myself," she says. There's no hug or handshake, but my hard stare seals it.

"Come in again next week, but call me if you want," I remind her as I write my number on her hand. We're not supposed to do this, but rules don't mean much to me anymore. "Okay?"

"Thanks." Katie picks up her bag. It's heavy, but life work is heavier than school work.

"You seem like a nice person, but Clark's in bio with me, and he's. . . ," I start. I want to gauge her reaction. How does she define him? But she waits me out. "He's our classhole."

Katie laughs. "Cassandra, I haven't laughed in a week. Thanks for that, too."

"You give it some time and tears, and you'll be good. In fact, I'll see you at the prom."

"I'd like that. Thanks again." Katie smiles for the first time, just before she leaves.

As I'm waiting for my next appointment, I fall into thought. As long as there is love, there'll be loss. As long as there is loss, there'll be loneliness. When there's loss and loneliness, there are tears. The deeper the love, the more the loss, the darker the loneliness. Yet I want it. I want it all.

Before I leave school, I call my cousin Siobhan, but she can't or won't pick up. Like a zombie looking for brains, I walk aimlessly, seeking answers.

I find myself near the far end of the parking lot. Although I know it's not there, I look for Robyn's white Malibu. Everything that happened after I found Robyn crying that first week in March rushes through my veins. I've lived a lifetime in less than two months.

I recall finding her in her car and asking her a question that comes so naturally to me, "Are you crying?" She told me about Craig cheating on her with Brittney, a fact I already knew and had spread like wildfire around school. I seem to recall everything she said those last few weeks, including her tearful "Thanks for everything. I love you, Cassandra. Good-bye." How she said "good-bye" told me what she intended to do, but I was thinking of the greater good. The words said afterward—the ones that pushed me most to action—came from my great-grandmother.

After I told her my best friend had died and I had played a role in her death, Veronica said, "That's just wonderful." It's not as if I hadn't heard those words before. She said them each time before we moved: to New York in September 2001 and to New Orleans in 2005 right after Katrina. But it was different this time. Or maybe I was different. Robyn's death—and my role in it—wasn't the end, it seems it's just the beginning.

One minute I feel Scott's lips, and I'm ready, willing, and able to leave my family behind to experience *real* human love. The next minute, I see Veronica's face, I hear Maggie's words, and I sense my mom's crushing disappointment, and know I can't leave them behind. I complain about them, I resent them . . . they are my family. I've always been a tear collector, so how can I live any other way? With one foot in humanity and the other in my species, it's as if I'm two creatures. Do I act like a human and decide for myself? Or do I behave like a tear collector and accept whatever fate and my family hands me?

As I walk home, a gentle spring rain begins to fall. Each raindrop, like each tear, is different from the others. As the rain soaks into my shoulders, I feel both lost and found. With Scott, I've found something special, but I'm lost as to how to make it real. I need answers that no book or friend or family member can provide. I veer off my path and walk toward St. Dominic's with bright Beatles music filling my ears and dark thoughts weighing on my mind.

I'm damp with rain as I enter the church. I find my usual seat, close my eyes, bring my hands together, and pray for answers. While God is silent, the person behind me is not. I hear a low whisper, then a clicking sound. A smell of cinnamon swirls in my nostrils as I turn around.

Simon. It seems as if every candle in church has gone out at once. I fear this darkness. His darkness.

Black hat in one hand, black cane with a red tip in the other. He taps the cane five times.

"Child, where is Alexei now?" He speaks slowly, accenting each syllable.

I don't answer. I'm cold in his presence, but I don't freeze or fight. I can only flee.

Chapter 6

Thursday, April 23

after school

"So, will you tell me now?" I ask Samantha.

We're sitting on a bench outside of school near where the Goth Tree used to stand. I chopped it down to stir up drama between the various groups at school—an act I thought nobody knew about. However, Samantha found out—or maybe just guessed—although that's far from the biggest secret she knows about me.

"I told you he's back," she hisses.

She's been avoiding me. Maybe she senses me like I sense her. I can tell she's been crying. I'm circling like a shark even as we sit next to each other.

"Who are you talking about?" I press.

"Meth-head Mark." Her words are twisted and garbled. "He's the parasite in my life."

My mind flashes to that night at Samantha's when she told me her mom's druggie boyfriend pushed her through a window, leaving scars on her body, making her back look like a road map of pain. The crosses she now slices into her arms are some sick connection to that childhood trauma. Humans never get totally free of their pain; they just put it in different places.

"What do you mean, he's back? Where was he?"

I lean forward. My beater is white, but even in eighty-degree weather, Samantha wears a baggy, black sweater. Beads of sweat line her forehead. More perspiration puddles under her arms and stains her already-dirty sweater.

She takes a deep breath. "Whenever Mark gets out of prison or jail, he comes back to my mom, and she lets him. He's the Black Death, and mom's addiction is the rat that carries him."

"He went to prison for what he did to you?"

"No, for what he did to me, nothing happened to him. I got the scars; he got nothing," she says. "He was so stoned that I doubt he remembers. And even if he does, I don't think he cares."

"But your mom—"

"I told you, my mom's a junkie," she says. "She's clean for a while, but then. . . ."

"I'm sure your mom loves you, but—"

She cuts me off. "When my mom's high, she's not human. She's like a wild animal. Now that he's back, she's lost herself to drugs again. She's in my house, but I feel abandoned."

"You're really hurting." I lean closer. "What can you do to—"

She denies me for a third time. "How about what you can do for me?"

"Me?" I ask. "Do you need money? Are you planning on running away?"

She rubs her eyes. Her long black fingernails scratch her blacker eyebrows. "I can't."

"Why not? You have a car. After school is over, why don't you just go?"

Samantha leans closer. The pores in my shoulders open with anticipation. "I can't leave my mom behind. I don't know how to explain it, but I need to protect her even if there's nothing I can do. Like you with Becca. You can't save her, but you can't let her be alone."

"But the things you say about your mom, why would you—"

"She's my mom, Cassandra. I hate her, but she's my mom, so I love her."

I shake my head, thinking how complicated the human world is. *Without truly feeling love, how can I hope to understand this kind of conflict?*

"I understand," I lie.

"When she's high, she's a wild animal, but after, she's like a baby or a dying old person, totally vulnerable. What kind of person would I be to abandon someone so helpless?"

Images in my head flash not to Samantha's mom, but Veronica. Without me, would Veronica die? If I leave the tear collectors for Scott, am I sentencing Veronica to death? Every action has a reaction to create balance in nature.

"What do you want from me?"

"I'm afraid," she says as her tears rise to the surface.

"Of Mark?"

When I met Samantha, she wouldn't cry in public, but I broke her.

"No. I'm afraid of what I might do to him," she says.

"What are you talking about?"

"He's got a few guns," she says. "If I don't get out of that house for a few days right now, I swear I'll use one to blow his head off. It's the only way to protect me and my mom."

"Why don't you turn him in?"

"So they can lock him up again for a few years?" she says. "He'll come back. He *always* comes back, and my mom always lets him in. The Angel of Death never passes over your house. That's what he is: an angel of death, except nobody dies, they just suffer. He leaves you alive but wanting to die. I'm tired of suffering and of him ruining our lives. It's a matter of life or death."

"Samantha, you're being overly dramatic," I say, then try to lighten the mood. "And coming from one of Lapeer High's number-one drama queens, I should know."

"You don't get it. It's a simple choice," she hisses. "If he stays in my house, then somebody will die. It's not if, but when. It's not how, but who. That's the only decision."

"You're not serious."

"Deadly serious, Cassandra." She moves her hands in front of her mouth, and leans toward me. She speaks in a loud whisper that deafens me with its content. "The only way—the one and only way to save myself and my mother from him killing us is that Mark needs to die."

"But Samantha, that just means more suffering," I say. "You would be the one who would go to jail. Do you want to spend the rest of your life in—"

"You need to kill him."

It feels as if the temperature drops fifty degrees with the coldness of her voice. She grabs my wrists tightly. Her fingers are like handcuffs.

"I helped you save Scott's life. I risked prison, running over Alexei to save you. I tried to kill your monster; you need to kill mine. I've kept your secrets, and I've asked for nothing. The bill is due. *You owe me.*"

Polonius's wise words to his son Laertes from Act One of *Hamlet* echo in my ears: "Neither a borrower nor a lender be." I might owe Samantha, but this I cannot do.

I shake my head. "I can't kill Mark."

"Yes, you can," she says—each word a nail, her icy tone a heavy hammer.

"I'm sorry, Samantha, that's not possible."

"Why not? You're not human, so you'll have no regret or guilt."

"First, it is against our rules to kill another human, except in self-defense," I explain. "But more than that, it's against the law. I won't go to prison for you. What else can I do to help?"

Samantha releases my wrists and looks at the sky. She keeps looking at the heavens as if they might bring relief, but the answer falls from her eyes. She weeps on my shoulder for a long time. Like her addict mom, I can't resist getting my fix. I reach for Veronica's handkerchief.

After a good cry, she says, "If you won't do that, you need to let me stay with you."

"You can't stay with us. Sorry."

"Why?"

"Listen, my mom—" I begin spinning out my lies, but she won't let me.

"Your mom doesn't run your family," she says.

I walk away six steps, but she follows me. She points her index finger at me like an angry preacher in the pulpit. I'm a sinner in the hands of a vengeful heart.

"Your great-grandmother Veronica runs your family. I could tell that at the hospital. Remember? You had me cry onto her shoulder to give her strength to save Scott. I helped save his life. So don't say your mom runs your house, and don't say you don't owe me!"

"Calm down, Samantha," I say. "You shouldn't be talking about any of this, I told you."

"What if I do?" Samantha fires back.

"Do what?"

"Tell people all I know about you, your family, your species," Samantha continues.

I realize it's not anger or fear running her now; it's power—her power over me because of what she knows, which is *way* too much for any human. She's a friend and a threat.

"What if I told?"

"Do you think anybody would believe you?"

"I don't know."

"You said I could trust you," I remind her. "I thought we had an understanding."

"But I can't understand," she says. "I don't understand enough about you."

"I can't tell you any more."

"If you don't tell me more, then—" she stops, letting her words rest like a line in the sand.

"Then what?" I turn toward her and grab her wrists. Hard. Full of her tears, I feel energy and power racing through my veins. "Never threaten me, Samantha, never *ever* do that again."

"Maybe I'll ditch my vampire novel and instead write about tear collectors!" she shouts.

But I whisper, "If you promise that you won't tell anyone, then I'll tell you more. Deal?"

"I *need* to know," she says, making the word "need" stab like a needle. Samantha seems to have inherited her mom's addictive personality, except my truth is her drug of choice.

"Okay, one thing. I'll answer one question, but that's all." I let her wrists free.

"Okay." A satisfied look overtakes Samantha's face. The silver rings in her nose and ears seem to sparkle. "Why is it only women you live with? Why don't men live with you?"

I pause, then walk back toward the bench. She follows.

"Our elders decided to limit the number of offspring. The more of us, they reasoned, the more likely we'd be discovered. Through evolution, we appear human with few differences in our bodies, except for the part that turns tears into energy. The ways of tear collectors are not written down, for fear of discovery. Elders pass on information as needed, keeping the young uninformed and obedient."

"Something you have in common with us humans," she says. "But why do the males—"

"To make sure the males and females don't reproduce too often, we're kept apart. We don't feel love; it isn't an issue. Both genders survive on their own and only come together to mate, like many creatures in nature. The mating time is limited to our Easter weekend reunion."

"But why Easter?"

"Look, Samantha, I said I'd answer one question, and I did. That was our deal," I remind her. "We're friends, and friends don't break promises, right?"

"So does that mean you're like me—that you don't know your father?"

"That's enough." I stare her down.

"Okay," she says, sounding a little guilty. "But would you ask your mom or Veronica if I can stay there until I figure out what to do about Mark? *Please?*"

"I'll ask." I rise from the bench. "They'll say no, but I'll ask. I need to go."

I get only two steps away before she speaks again. "Alexei is your cousin. Aren't you worried about interbreeding? I mean, not only is it gross, but it's all messed up, you know?"

"No, we're more worried about outer breeding," I say, instantly wishing I hadn't.

"Outer breeding?"

"Through the generations, tear collectors have mated with humans."

"Those things would be freaks," she says, then smiles. "Maybe that explains me."

"No, you can feel; you care about others," I say, smiling back. "You're one hundred percent human."

"So when you and Scott—" she starts.

"That's not going to happen, and Samantha, please, that's enough," I say, almost scolding.

"Enough for today," she says. "But what I don't understand is—"

I return to the bench and sit next to her. I don't grab her wrist; instead I pull her into a tight hug. "I don't understand what it's like to grow up with someone like Mark around. Tell me, Samantha, how does he hurt you? What does he do your mom?"

I go silent as she talks about Mark until she starts weeping again. I pull out Veronica's handkerchief again and hand it over. She smiles for a light second in the depth of her darkness.

"Come in, Cassandra," Veronica says in a whisper.

We're the only two at home. I'm not sure where Mom and Maggie are; they never tell me, yet keep track of me like I'm prey.

The room is dark, as always, but I see her motioning me to sit next to her. I open the tear collector vial and start the ritual to transfer the tears, but I stop. If Samantha has power over me for what she knows, then don't I have power over Veronica for what I possess? Why have I been afraid of her? She needs me. She should be afraid of me. "Di'mah, what's wrong?" she asks.

I hold the handkerchief just out of her reach. "Veronica, who is my father?"

Even in the darkness, her blue eyes pierce me. "He is one who no longer matters."

"If he doesn't matter, then why not tell me?"

She falls back into bed. "You're just like Maggie," she whispers. "Both of you trying to learn things you don't need to know. What you both need to learn is your place in this family."

"Don't you want these tears? They're from Samantha. You remember her?" I'm like some matador, except my red cape is a white, six-sided handkerchief inset with a single holy thread.

She starts to cough, but I realize too late that it's really a snide cackle. She sounds more like Simon than Veronica. She holds the eyedropper in her hand. One drop of those ancient tears carries more strength than a handkerchief full of modern ones.

"Di'mah, don't make me waste one of these on you." Her voice chills me to the bone.

I hand over her boon, and her laughter fills the emptiness of our house. "Don't you *ever* try anything like that again." I can't tell if her words are a warning or a threat.

I look away as I whisper, "I get angry because I can't get any answers to my questions."

She taps my shoulder, and motions for me to continue preparing the handkerchief. "You're forgiven. And do you know why, Di'mah?"

Before I can reply, she does. "Because you are the answer."

Chapter 7

Friday, April 24

morning

"Can I talk to you?" I ask, almost as soon as I walk out onto the back porch at home.

Maggie's on the sun-deck. Mom's at work, while Veronica's up in her room. Against her on my own, I'm powerless. But what did she mean about Maggie not knowing her place? Could Veronica be afraid of Maggie? If so, then maybe I need to get closer to Maggie.

Maggie nods, then sips from her water bottle.

"I don't understand about Alexei," I say.

"Your mother thinks you know where he is. Do you?"

"No." It's not a total lie. I haven't heard from him, but I know he's alive. Alive and up to his old games, if I'm to believe the articles I've found online. He can't change, but I will.

Maggie takes another sip. "He will be back for Feastday. Maybe an exception can—"

"Why does it have to be him? Why does it have to be at the reunion? Why does —"

"You know there are twenty-five other letters than 'y' in the alphabet," she says.

"Why can't you answer just one question?" I sit down.

Talking with Samantha made me realize how much about my own kind I don't know—or rather how much I've not been told. Ours is a culture of obedience, tradition, and respect. In cultures like that, the old always dominate. "Don't ask questions" rules. I shiver at the thought that defiance is a trait I share with Alexei.

How can Veronica say I'm the answer when no one tells me the truth?

"You'll know what you need to know when you need to know it."

"You keep things from me—not just facts, but motives." I wonder—did we learn that from humans? Or did humans teach us to hide evil motives under a veil of goodness?

"What are you talking about?"

"Like the reason you pushed me to mate with Alexei. It has something to do with you."

"It is your turn, Cassandra," she says firmly.

"No, it's not. I'm too young. I have the rest of school to finish, then college, then—" I stop because she's laughing. "What's so funny?" I ask.

"You're right; there's a lot you don't know. So listen: Since your mother obviously hasn't told you these things—which doesn't surprise me—I will," she says. "You must mate six times before you can bear a child. If you start during your junior year in high school—like your mom, like me, and like Veronica—then you will give birth to the next generation around the age of twenty-three. Twenty-three is a magic number: two times three equals six, our holy number, while two plus three equals five, Simon's holy number. The stars have aligned to create a perfect mating, but it must begin now, and it must be with him. This isn't a decision you get to make."

"Why six times?"

"Why does it take a human nine months to bear a child but only takes a rabbit thirty days? Why do most humans have one child while other mammals have litters? It just is."

"That's not an answer," I reply, although she's right. While we're like humans in so many ways, we're different. Human girls get their period; I don't. Human girls feel love; I don't . . . yet.

"The first time you were supposed to experience with Alexei establishes the hormonal bond," Maggie says. "It sends the signal to his body to allow him to give up some of his bodily fluids to this partner, and six times of mating is what it takes to establish that bond."

"That doesn't answer my question: why six?"

"You know the basics of reproduction. Think about what the male of any species must give up in order to breed," Maggie says in her lecture tone.

"What does that have to do with this?"

"Use your brain, Cassandra! The male contribution is mostly made of water," she says. "Much like the ancient tears that Veronica keeps, it is a fluid that must be carefully rationed."

"But why my cousin? Why Alexei?"

"Why don't humans mate with dogs? That's why," she says. "You mate with your own kind. There are so few of us anymore that your mate will always be a relative. It just is."

"Stop saying that!"

"Cassandra, we are from the true Veronica line descended down through time," she says, almost in a whisper. "Alexei is from the Simon line, likewise descended down through generations. Since the beginning, our lines have mated frequently, but also through the years, especially in the ancient times, we've mated outside the species. Other times, because of early death or uneven gender distribution, circumstances have forced imperfect matings such as an older male with a much younger female. Whenever there is a male heir from Simon's line and a female heir from Veronica's line, they must mate, especially when the numerology is perfect. It increases the chances that rather than damaged offspring, you'll produce a strong child to carry out our lines."

"But Alexei is evil. What he did to Scott, what he did do those children—"

Maggie shakes her head in wonder. "That doesn't matter."

"It should."

"It would if we were humans, but we're not humans; we're tear collectors."

"We don't directly cause suffering, and we don't enjoy other people's pain, but he—"

"He did some monstrous things, but his great-grandfather, Simon, and grandfather, Asa, are defending him and angry with you. They don't know where he is or if he's even alive."

"What about his father? I notice you didn't mention him."

Maggie pauses. She looks at the floor, not at me. "Like your father, Alexei's father was exiled."

As if my lungs have filled with water, I struggle to breathe. Whenever I've asked about my father or Alexei's father, Mom—for her usual hidden motives—never answered. If what Maggie says is true, it means both my father and Alexei's father experienced the same torturous punishment—the tear-collector pores on their shoulders dissolved with acid—as that man did the day I learned I was tear collector. What if that man was his father? Or what if it was *my* father? The scent of sizzling skin invades my nose; I feel faint. "What if" pulls me into the deep end.

"Cassandra, are you okay?" Maggie asks.

I put out a hand to steady myself. I can't ask what if, so I'll ask why. I backed down last night with Veronica, but Maggie holds no direct power over me. I will get answers to these questions that I've always thought of, but never asked.

"Why must I follow these rules, this duty?"

"I'm telling you far too much," Maggie says.

"I have a right to know these things if they affect me!"

"In some ways, Alexei is very much like his father, always breaking the rules."

"And what rule did he break?" I ask. "Did he torture children, too?"

Maggie starts to rise, but I put my hand on hers. "Tell me this, and I'll tell about Alexei."

"What do you know?"

"No, you tell me about his father, and I'll tell you what I know."

She stares, but I won't let her break me. Finally, she says, "He broke the rules about mating. He fathered three tear-collector children."

"That doesn't sound so horrible," I say.

A dark look comes over Maggie's face.

"But before he left us, he fathered children with human women as well," Maggie says, her voice walking a borderline between sadness and rage. "He should have known."

"What about his other children? Are they—"

She cuts me off. "Like your cousin Siobhan. You can leave, you can love, you can even steal a soul, but that doesn't make you totally human. What we are never goes away. The children of humans and former tear collectors are the monsters, unable to either feel emotion or relieve pain by collecting tears. Humans would call them psychopaths. That's why we warn you about getting serious with boys and why you shouldn't speak to Siobhan. We're not just protecting you—or our kind—but also humanity from monsters likes the ones Alexei's father created."

"That's terrible."

"It's because his father was selfish. That's why I scold you about being selfish. Obey us, follow the rules, and nature will function as it should. Now, tell me about Alexei."

"Alexei's in the Detroit area; I'm not sure where. I'll show you the only article I found."

"Everyone will be relieved he's alive."

"Everyone but me."

"Didn't you just hear me? This is your role. You must be content to take your turn."

"But you're not content with your role in the family, are you?" I ask. "I've watched you, Maggie. I see your resentment of Veronica. You can fool her—and Mom—but not me. Not me."

"It is *my* turn. Veronica's time has passed."

"You accuse me of being selfish, but you're the one who wants more than she has."

Rather than yelling, Maggie motions for me to sit down next to her. When I do, she takes my hand.

"You can't understand what it is like to be in my position, so you have no right."

"Your position?"

"Part of me wants to take over as family leader, but every cell is programmed to protect Veronica."

She sounds more like a confused teen than a wise, old woman. I always knew Maggie and I were twins under the skin. She, too, is fighting her nature, needing someone to die so she can live as she wants, yet trained to do the opposite. I'm not the only Hamlet in this house.

Chapter 8

Friday, April 24

late afternoon

"Amanda, are you crying?" I ask.

My words lift softly over the sound of Amanda's tears and scattered conversations in the hospital break room. Amanda blends in perfectly with the soft pastels of the floor, walls, and mismatched furniture.

"Mr. Johnson in 127A died." She tugs at her uniform as if it's strangling her.

"He was a really nice man," I say, taking a careful step closer, like a hungry wolf.

"That's the hardest part of this job."

On the other side of the room, a few nursing assistants are smiling and laughing, yet I'm sure both of them knew Mr. Johnson. If you work in a hospital, then death becomes another part of daily life, as common as the carpet.

"I know, I know."

"You're good at this," she says, then sniffs. "You knew him. How can you not cry?"

"I guess I'm used to it."

Because if I started crying, it could kill me, is the real answer.

"Thanks for listening, Cassandra."

"That's what friends are for," I say, tossing out the word "friends" like bait.

"You're right," Amanda says, then finds her smile. "Do you need a ride home?"

"No, Scott's coming to pick me up."

"Oh, that's too bad, I thought maybe you could hang out with us tonight," she says.

"Us?"

"Oh, Elizabeth and Sarah from school."

I know them, but more as Robyn's friends.

"What are you doing?"

"It's Lapeer on a Saturday night, and none of us have dates," she says, then laughs. "So ... probably sitting around watching movies, feeling sorry for ourselves, and eating ice cream."

"No offense, but that doesn't sound like a lot of fun," I say, but I fake a laugh to soften it.

Amanda frowns. "If you eat enough ice cream, then fun, sad, happy—none of that matters."

"Maybe some other time," I say as we head from the break room to the locker room to change out of our uniforms into something appropriate for our nights. She's dressing down for a night in with the girls; I'm dressing up for a night out with my guy.

"You look great," Amanda says.

I catch a glimpse of myself in new jeans and a bright yellow, low-cut blouse. The rainbow ribbons in my short hair blaze in glory.

"Well, it's my one-month anniversary with Scott," I say, the words so alien to me.

While I'd lasted as long with other guys, there were breakups before the final blowout. I'd break up, and the poor fool would crawl back. I'd never move an inch.

"Scott seems really nice," Amanda says.

"He is—unlike a lot of the other jerks I've dated," I say and then laugh. "Listen Amanda, it's better to have no date than waste your time on tools like I have. Like Cody. Please!"

"Then why did you? So you wouldn't be alone?"

Since I can't say the truth, I give her hope. "Because I was weak, not strong like you."

"Cassandra, what's it like?" she asks me, looking at the floor. "To be in love?"

As if she pushed me, I fall back into a chair.

How can I answer her? But more importantly, what is the answer?

I think this human feeling overtaking me is love, but I am desperate to be sure. Only one person can understand. I know only one person who crossed over from being a tear collector into humanity, all in the name of love. All you need is love, but what *is* love? Even as I say a quick goodbye to Amanda, I'm calling Siobhan.

As always, Siobhan resists talking to me, but because she's human now, I easily manipulate her into listening to and answering my questions. No wonder tear collectors lost traits like true compassion through the generations, since it's easier to shatter people's defenses to rubble.

"So, what's it like, Siobhan? How would I know if these feelings are close to love?"

She laughs. "Cassandra, throughout history men and women have been writing songs, poems, plays, and books trying to capture the essence of this most human of emotions. So how do you expect me to describe it to you? I'm not Shakespeare; I'm a damaged human at best."

"How about some signs, then?" I continue. "Like how did you know that Alden—"

"Actually, Alden wasn't the first one that aroused these emotions in me."

"There was another human before him?"

There's a long pause. I don't blame the cell connection, but my lack of connection with Siobhan. Until recently, I've never contacted her. Before, at the reunions, we were never close. I wonder if that's because there might be another human emotion that stirs within female tear collectors on occasion and serves an evolutionary purpose of sorts to make us stronger: jealousy. Me, jealous of her looks; her, jealous of who-knows-what about me?

"Siobhan, you still there?"

"It wasn't a human, Cassandra; it was another tear collector—my intended mate."

I almost drop the phone—not only because I have no emotion except fear for Alexei, but because tear-collector relationships outside of mating are forbidden and, in some ways, worse than those with humans. If you mate with a human, you're exiled from the family, like Siobhan. But male and female tear collectors can be exiled for having any relationship with each other outside of mating. Such a relationship would challenge all tear-collector rules and society. The exile ceremony, like the one I saw as a child, leaves the offenders no longer tear collectors but not entirely human either. They're nothing without any kin or kind of their own except each other. Their love equals almost a living death.

"I guess that's the wrong way to describe him. He wasn't my mate; he was my soulmate."

"And how did you know that?" I must sound like I'm begging.

"It's not big things; it's little things," she continues. "The sound of his voice, the way he laughs, or maybe something silly he says or does. It operates almost on a biological level. That's why it's so hard to describe or define. You'll know when it happens to you."

"I guess that's the case with Scott."

"That's right, Cassandra, you're just guessing because you can't know for sure," she says. "That's the scariest thing about crossing over: not just what you need to do, but that you won't know you're right until you've done it. You know how humans have faith in Jesus, and we don't need to because we know of his supernatural power firsthand? Do you understand what I'm saying?"

"I'm trying to, but it's so hard."

"Of course it's hard to understand, even harder to do." She sounds impatient. "If it was easy to do, then can't you imagine more tear collectors would have tried it? It's a huge leap."

"And what if you miss?"

"That's why you have to be so careful and try to know for sure," she says. "Because if you're wrong, I don't see how you could become a tear collector again. If you risked everything for human love, and the love ended, that, too, would be a fate worse than death."

"I want it to be like science where I can run an experiment and follow a check list."

"That's why poets write about love, not physicists," she says, and I laugh.

She clears her throat. On the other side of the country, I picture her beautiful green eyes narrowing.

"You want a sign? I'll give you a small one. The sound of his voice. If you can easily go a day without hearing it, then you're not in love. There's your test."

I make a quick excuse to get off the phone and call Scott. Even as he says hello, I know that Siobhan's right. Scott, if not my soulmate, is as close as I'll find in humankind.

Chapter 9

Saturday, April 24

evening

"Can I tell you something?" Scott kisses me before I answer. "You're beautiful."

"Thanks," I say, then climb into his car. No sooner does he sit down, than I cuddle up against him. I think how odd it is we're leaving the hospital all smiles, when most of the folks coming in are anything but. "This night, our anniversary, is going to be beautiful."

"That's all I want," he says as we drive into the night. We talked about going to the site of our first date—Coach's Pizza—but decided against it. While Scott never did follow through on telling off Brittney, both of us remember his standing up to Cody that night.

"So where to?" I ask.

"Someplace special."

He turns up the Beatles music, which washes over us like a wave. I lean against him while he drives. The car stops not at Coach's or Paul's Coney Island where Scott works, but in the driveway of a small house on Cypress Avenue in one of the older parts of Lapeer. "For sale" signs fill nearby un-mowed lawns like so many weeds.

"Is this your house?"

"Okay, maybe not so special," he says, then follows with nervous laughter.

"So, I finally get to meet your mom?" I say, half-joking because I think I know.

"No, just you and me," he says as he turns off the engine.

As he walks around the car to open the door for me, I think how right Amanda is: He's so nice. As I try to guess what he's got in mind for the evening, I think how right I am: He's so normal. I told Scott early on that I was more than willing to make him happy, except for intercourse. I'm too afraid of the consequences—pregnancy, exile, or both—and he also seems scared of committing such a sin. He's not deliberately lying when he says sex isn't what he wants; he's just not aware of his truth.

Scott takes my hand as we walk to the door. His palms are sweaty.

"It's the best I could do," he says when he opens the door. We walk into the house, hand-in-hand. Like my house, there are plenty of pictures, crosses, and other trappings of our faith. Unlike my house, there are photos of family: Scott, his mom, and his grandparents. But even if we had photos in my house, Scott and I would share this: no photos of fathers. I know Scott's not one of my kind, but our father-lessness connects us even more. I glance into the smallish dining room. There are three candles, two wine glasses, and one pizza box from Coach's.

"Dinner is served," he says as soon as we enter the dining room. He pulls out the chair for me.

"Thanks." He kisses the back of my neck repeatedly. Sometimes I miss my long hair, but not now. When he finally sits down, I say, "Scott, thanks, but I never drink wine."

"You sound like Dracula!" Scott dramatically acts out putting an imaginary cape in front of his face. It's funny, but it's clumsy; his glass of wine tumbles over.

"Idiot me!" He picks up the glass as the wine soaks the table-cloth and the carpet below. I make a quick run for the kitchen and grab paper towels and club soda. We soak up the wine and leave no damage.

"I'm such a klutz sometimes," Scott says as we pile the used towels on the table.

"It's okay," I say, then pat him gently on the shoulder. "Just relax."

"That's what the wine was for!"

He kisses me: long, soft, perfect.

"Scott, not here," I say gently. We're on our knees in the dining room.

"Do you want to go in the other room?" His voice is so soft I can barely hear it.

"Yes." I look toward the rest of the house. Scott and I have crossed many lines, all new for him, although it seems I've been taking the lead. With most guys, I play strategic defense, always giving them the sizzle, but never my full self. I knew this night was coming despite my warnings, just not so soon. I hate to disappoint him tonight, but until I cross over, I have no choice.

Rather than heading down the hallway toward his bedroom, we go into the living room and sit on an old, green sofa. He puts his arm around me, then clicks on the TV and DVD player. I wonder if it's a distraction or a delaying tactic. Either way, it works for about twenty minutes before we fall into each other's arms, lips, and bodies. Fall is the right word because with Scott, I lose all sense of gravity. As the black-and-white images of the classic romantic film *Casablanca* flash nearby, he runs his tongue down my neck. Things heat up on the sofa while the pizza grows cold in the other room.

"My mom is spending the night out of town at my aunt's house," he says. "It's just you and me until we sing 'Here Comes the Sun.'"

I groan. "Scott, I love you, and I love the Beatles, but please."

"Just trying to fit in." He pulls me closer. "Stay the night."

I gently push him away. "Scott, I can't spend the night with you."

"You're right. We shouldn't give in to temptation." He sounds hurt, but not horny. "I feel guilty even thinking about it. And things we've done in the past—we both know it wasn't right."

I say nothing because, compared to other guys, Scott and I have done nothing more than heavy kissing and light touching. I've always used sex to manipulate guys. Maybe the fact that I don't want to do that with Scott is another of those signs that Siobhan told me about. I need to know.

"Scott, I'm sorry."

"I shouldn't even dream about a girl like you, let alone being here with you tonight, but. . . ."

"But?"

"You know as well as I do, it's a sin. Not just, you know, the big thing, but all of it."

I laugh. "That's why we have confession." I don't mention that I spent as much time on my knees for Cody as I did in confession at St. Dominic's asking God's forgiveness for sinning.

Scott looks at the floor when he speaks. "I pray to be strong, but. . . ."

I slip my hands between his legs. "But still end up hard?"

He coughs, laughs, and blushes in succession, but then moves my hand away. "No."

"Then why did you want me to spend the night if you don't want me to—"

Scott pulls me closer, then whispers in my ear. "I love you Cassandra. I know there are many ways to show that, but I don't know, I thought spending the night was one way. Stupid."

"No, Scott. Sweet. Just like you."

"I'm sorry, Cassandra, I'm just so conflicted. Do you understand?"

Now, I pull him closer like I want him to be part of me. I tell him that I understand, although my conflict isn't between head, heart, and hormones, but something much deeper. "So, we can just watch the movie if you don't want me to, you know, do anything," I say.

Scott mutes the movie and takes a deep breath. "You don't need to do anything for me," he whispers, then takes another deep breath. "Getting pleasure, but not giving it, makes me feel guilty. So what can I do for you?"

I answer by unsnapping my jeans as he falls to his knees. Another first for me.

"It's midnight. I need to go," I whisper into Scott's ear. We're still in the living room—maybe he thinks sexual activity outside of the bedroom is less of a sin? I'm catching my breath. Or rather, he's catching it. I breathe out, he breathes in. More balance in nature.

If any cousin ever asks me what I asked Siobhan—"How would I know if these feelings were close to love?"—I will tell her of this exact moment when something so mundane as breathing becomes an extraordinary sensation.

"I know you can't stay the night, but I want you to stay with me."

"Scott, of course I'll stay with you."

"You're not going to break up with me like you've done with others?"

"I'm sorry about stuff I did in the past, but that's the past. You and me, we're the future."

"Here's looking at you, Cass," he cracks, echoing a line from the movie.

On the way home, it's more Beatles music. The windows are rolled down, and the late spring breeze caresses my skin. But this doesn't seem real; it seems like a movie of my own making, like some perfect love story. For Scott, the love is real. For me—for right now—I feel like those actors on the screen: playing a part, one I do not comprehend. My desire to feel the full force of human love grows stronger; my need to stay a tear collector grows weaker, and my thirst to cross over grows more desperate.

25 April
To: swimmerqueenLHS@gmail.com
From: AlexeiofCyrene@yahoo.com

*You have turned me down twice now: once in your car
and once in my van. You only have three more chances
if we are to be together. I will return for you for Veronica's Feastday on July 12. While we were both babies
at the last Feastday celebration sixteen years ago, I understand that on this day there are no rules, which is
perfect for our predicament. We may mate outside of
the Easter weekend reunion and make up for that
missed opportunity.*

*Before you say no, let me say this: all is forgotten, for-
given. And let me explain myself: I just want to be free,
to be normal. I wanted to do my duty for the family and
then look for a way out. I don't feel sorry—because I
can't—but I know what I did to your friend Scott as
well as the other boys was wrong. I only continued as a
means to rebuild my strength, but I will stop now. For
you. But you crossed a line by involving that girl. And
as such, we are both outsiders; we belong together. I
know everyone is looking for me. I will explain
everything when I return. You think I'm a monster, but
I'm not. I'm someone just like you—stuck in this wheel
of time and tradition, turning not where I want to go,
but where it takes me. Takes us. Let us journey together.*

Chapter 10

Monday, April 26

evening

"Is there anything else I need to know?" I ask Mrs. Berry while her husband helps her with her coat. It hangs on her; she's lost weight—along with hope—since Robyn died.

"No, Cassandra. You and Becca just have fun," she says. The word "fun" sounds like a term in a foreign language. "Just make sure she gets to bed early. She's got a test tomorrow."

"Okay." When a child has a brain tumor, it's never clear if the "test" is at school measuring the child's knowledge or at the hospital measuring the weeks the child has to live.

"I'm not sure how long we'll be," Mrs. Berry says. She's wearing a black dress. Like Robyn, she always used to dress so colorfully, but now, for her, the mourning goes on daily.

"Where are you going?" I ask.

I'm babysitting Becca for the first time in a long time.

"A new support group for parents who lost a child," Mr. Berry says. I sense he doesn't want to go; he's doing it for his wife. Human love is about sacrifice. "I've heard they can help."

"I've heard that, too." I stare at the floor. It's good Mr. and Mrs. Berry are about one step out the door so they won't pick up the lies hiding behind my eyes. Tear collectors know full well about support groups like this. Support groups are great places to harvest tears. I bet the first support groups were set up by tear collectors.

We're an emotional clean-up crew. "Where is it?"

"At the Unitarian church in Flint," she says. I file the information away for Maggie.

"We should leave now. It's about a half-hour drive," Mr. Berry says.

"One last thing," I say. "Could my friend Samantha stop over? We've got a bio test tomorrow. It would be after Becca's bedtime. Is that okay? If not, I understand that—"

"Cassandra, any friend of yours," Mr. Berry says, then he and his wife head to the car.

Becca and I play video games, although she lacks her old energy. Brave enough to face her own death, not strong enough to handle the death of her sister. If you want to harm a human, I'm sure the best way is not to kill that person; instead kill someone they love. Loss hurts more than death because death happens in a few seconds, while loss lingers like cancer.

Between the video games and reading her a story, Becca decides she wants to talk about Robyn. I don't ask questions to create tears; I won't exploit this child as maybe I did in the past. But once she talks about her sister's death, I soak up her tears into Veronica's handkerchief. As always, the crying wears Becca out. She's asleep long before her bedtime.

I call Samantha. She arrives in no time.

"How did you get here so fast? Don't you live, like, ten miles from here?" I ask when she shows up at the door.

"I'm living in my car," she says, and the evidence certainly shows that. Her badly-dyed, jet-black hair looks messy, and she's wearing the same clothes she wore to school on Friday.

"Why would you do that?" I ask as she shambles into the Berry's nice clean house.

"Mark kicked me out. Mom went along with it," she says. "Most people only have nightmares when they sleep. I get those every night, but I also live a fucking nightmare when I'm awake." I recall when I spent the night at Samantha's on Good Friday, how she screamed in her sleep.

"But in your car?"

"I need to go back, protect her," she says. "Besides, without Mom around, I feel empty."

I try not to react to the foul odor coming from her clothes, stained with fresh blood and old tears. *Did Mark hit her?* I also see stains that look like chocolate. "Do you want to shower here?" I ask.

"Really?"

"Just make it quick, okay?"

Samantha smiles "Will you keep me company? I hate being alone in a strange house."

"Are you serious?"

"You've seen my scars. Trust me, there's nothing else I could be embarrassed by."

"Okay, upstairs," I say.

I let her enter the bathroom first. We chat, but when she starts to undress, I head toward the door. Some tear-collector females pretend to be bi to increase the opportunities for tears, but for all my skills at faking human emotion and behavior, that's not one I can pull off. Showing desire for undesirable tools like Cody drained me of energy more than I knew—another reason Scott is such a relief. But at least with the others, there was basic boy-girl attraction to buoy me. I'm not repulsed by girls as a species, but I'm not eager to kiss one either. And since I still don't know if Samantha is bi or not, I don't want to run the risk of giving her the wrong idea.

"Hey, let me see if I can find something for you to wear," I say, then close the door behind me.

I take a deep breath, then walk into Robyn's room; it looks exactly the same: filled with awards and achievements. Mrs. Berry told me that other than picking out a dress for the funeral, they haven't entered the room. As long as the room remains the same, grief haunts this house.

I linger at the closet, remembering outfits Robyn wore for special occasions. I can't find anything that would fit Samantha who's a lot bigger than Robyn. I open a box on the closet floor, containing no clothing except one piece: an oversized University of Michigan T-shirt. I take out the shirt and lay it aside. I look through the items in the box, finding an archive of Robyn and Craig's life together. The shirt was probably his. Maybe he gave it as a gift; maybe he left it here. Maybe she just wanted his smell near her. Maybe that's another sign of love.

I quickly scan a scrapbook filled with photos and souvenirs of their time together. The pages are tear-stained; my shoulders tingle faintly at the ghosts of her grief. Maybe the morning Robyn set out to school—set out to die—she looked at this scrapbook. Maybe she thought she'd never be that happy again; maybe she thought she'd always feel that bad. It's clear that the real cause of teen suicide isn't drugs or depression; it isn't too much loneliness or too much stress. Robyn died not because she lacked love, but she lacked hope and the perspective that things would get better.

I get ready to close up the box that Robyn never could, but decide to take one last look at Robyn's favorite picture of her and Craig together. She's so pretty in her cheerleader outfit with him just as handsome in his football jersey—the perfect couple that everyone expected them to live up to, no matter what. Anything less was a failure. Robyn had a copy of this photo in her car. When she tore it down in anger, I knew it was over between them. I never knew—and maybe I never will—what it is like to love someone so much that without him you want to die.

Although I know it's wrong, I grab the framed photo to take with me. Siobhan told me what love looks like, but this photo can show me every day. I take it out of the frame—easier to sneak out of the house—but when I do, a piece of paper falls like a feather from the sky. So light this piece of paper, but when I pick it up and start to read, it is dark and heavy. It begins, *"Dear Craig,"* and it ends, *"I will love you forever and ever and amen. Don't hate me for my everlasting love. Robyn."* I take the photo for myself, but the note I take for Craig. He should read it, but not now. I'll wait until I require his fresh tears for something important. I've tried many times to reach out to him since Robyn died, but he has refused me. I must rebuild a bridge for when I need him.

I re-read the note as Robyn pours out her sadness and her love for Craig. It reads like great tragedy, but I feel nothing more than I do when reading *Hamlet*. If I was ever going to experience true grief or sadness, this would be the time—reading these words and remembering what I did to Robyn. I thought I really was her friend. I thought I did feel something toward her, but as I read her final words, I question that. Maybe all Robyn ever was to me was a pipeline for tears. Maybe that's why I found Scott and Samantha soon after Robyn died. I think of the dying little girl sleeping down the hall. I say I care about her, but do I? Is she a real person to me, or just more tear ducts to harvest? Can I really help humans or just cause harm? Can I be a real friend or just a parasite?

"Cassandra!" I hear Samantha shout from the bathroom. I race down the hall, shirt in hand.

I knock on the door, then enter. "I found a shirt you could maybe wear."

Samantha peeks out of the shower, "I bet it doesn't say Slipknot on it."

"Not exactly."

"There's something I don't understand about you, about Robyn, about me."

"What do you mean?"

"How could you be friends with someone like Robyn who was so pretty, so preppy, so perfect, and then say you're friends with someone like me? I'm a train wreck," she says.

"I don't know," I say, although the real answer is a tear-collector trait: adaptation. I've always been able to mold myself to be the best friend or girlfriend for all kinds of people.

"I've been thinking about how you live," Samantha says as she turns the shower off.

"How I live?" I pass her a towel.

She stays behind the curtain as she talks. "How the males live apart from the females? From what I've seen in my life, especially with Mark and my mom, it sounds like a great idea."

"Maybe." It's my only response because I don't know any other way.

"He's going to kill her," Samantha says. "But it's Mark who deserves to die."

"Samantha, don't start talking crazy again. I'm not going to kill Mark for you."

"You think I'm crazy, but I'm just hurt," she says, stepping out of the shower. She turns her back to me, then drops the towel. The hot water seems to have made the scars on her back come alive, like a river of small, red snakes sucking her skin. I quickly hand her the shirt.

"I think you just want revenge."

"Maybe I do, but think about how great this could be," she says as she slips the clean shirt over her head, then quickly—and sadly—puts the rest of her dirty clothes back on.

"What are you talking about?"

"Where's the girl? Becca, right?"

"She's asleep in her bedroom. Why?" My eyes narrow in suspicion. What does she want with Becca?

Samantha heads into the hallway. Her eyes looks as wild as her wet hair. "Which way?"

I don't know why I point down the hallway. She takes off in a sprint that shakes the floor. I follow.

"Don't wake her," I whisper outside Becca's door.

"I won't," she whispers back, then cracks open the door. Moonlight shines through the window, almost highlighting Becca's face.

"This is so sad for everybody, but especially her parents. Don't you think it's sad?"

"Of course," I say, understanding the emotion, if not exactly feeling it.

"Do you think a girl like this, so young, deserves to die?"

"Of course not!"

"Now, think about Mark," she says. "What he's done to me, to my mother, but more than that, to every family he's helped destroy by selling drugs. He's not selling drugs—he's selling poison; he's selling death. Does a parasite like that deserve to live?"

I grow silent; I don't need a crystal ball to see where this is going.

"I don't understand what happened that night in the hospital with Scott, other than somehow Veronica saved his life, but in doing so, Scott's grandmother died. Am I right?"

I don't even blink.

"So, we can do the same thing again, don't you see? You could make it happen."

I can barely breathe.

"You trade Meth-head Mark's life for Becca's," she says. "She gets to live; he gets to die."

"I can't do what you're asking."

"Scott was near death. Veronica killed his grandmother so he could live. I was there."

"His grandmother was dying anyway." I don't tell her that it was partly out of self-defense as well. If Scott hadn't been healed, then there might have been enough questions to uncover the truth about tear collectors. Keeping us safe from discovery is part of our preservation.

"We're all dying the second after we're born," she says. "How is it done?"

"I can't tell you," I say. "I can't tell you because I don't really know. I just know that I can't do it. Only Veronica has the power, and she can't do it again. She's too weak."

"I could cry her a river to make her strong."

"No, Samantha. I can't talk about this!"

"Your family has this power, but you won't use it for good. How can you live like that?"

"You have to go." I start to walk away.

She grabs my wrist and squeezes. "I'm begging you, Cassandra, help me."

"Samantha, no! I can't do it. I'm sorry," I say, trying to get my hand free.

"Are you as sorry as you are for killing Robyn?"

"What are you talking about?" I say, lowering my voice, hoping she does the same. I don't want Becca to wake up at all, but I definitely don't want her to hear this!

"She's your best friend, then she gets her heart broken all because of rumors. Don't tell me you didn't spread them, because I know better. But that's not the worst of it, is it?"

"Let me go!" She thinks I mean my wrist; I know I mean her hold on my life.

"So she kills herself. That's what I think happened. Knowing what I know about you, it wouldn't surprise me if you gave her the idea to crash her car and make it look like an accident."

"You're lying," I lie. Robyn's letter burns like acid in my pocket.

"Deny it. Look me in the eye and tell me it's not true."

"It's not true," I say, my voice calm. Tear collectors fib like chameleons change colors, so naturally that nobody knows. It is one of our greatest defense mechanisms.

"Well, I'll let Mr. and Mrs. Berry decide!" She starts down the stairs.

"Samantha, you're talking crazy again." I chase after her. She runs into the kitchen and starts frantically looking through the cupboards like she's lost something. I glance at my cell; the Berrys will be home soon. "Samantha, you have to leave."

"Not until you promise me you'll make it happen." She reaches onto a high shelf and grabs a can of chocolate frosting. A look of satisfaction followed by disgust falls over her face. I sense her mouth watering as she removes the lid, licks it, and then tosses it into the garbage.

"I can't do this."

"If you don't want to do this for me, then do it for Robyn." Her voice, even for Samantha, is agitated. She scoops piles of cake frosting from the can to her mouth with her fingers.

~ 76 ~

I say nothing as I think how everyone wants something from me. I'm overwhelmed.

"Don't you think if Robyn was here—and she knew you could save her sister—that she would want you to do it?" Samantha says between frosting scoops. "You helped kill Robyn, so here's your chance to make it right for her parents, for Becca, for everyone. Maybe you don't owe me anything, but you know what? Seems to me that you owe the Berrys a life. Becca's life."

"Look, even if I wanted to, I can't. It's not possible for me as the youngest member of the family to do it. It's something passed down from generation to generation, and it's not my turn."

"Then get Veronica—"

"I told you she can't."

"What about your grandmother, Maggie?"

"She can't." The truth is I don't know if she can or would.

Samantha throws away the empty can of frosting. She licks her fingers slowly and then messes with her hair like a deranged person. She looks like Medusa, and when she tells the Berrys about my role in their daughter's death, they'll die—not of fright, but fury.

"Samantha, you have to believe me that—" but my words fall under the sound of the garage door opening. "That's them. You have to promise you won't say anything."

"Promise me that you'll make it happen."

"You said if we shared our secrets that you would—"

"You can't have a pact if one person doesn't care," Samantha says. "I don't care; I want this to end. I want that meth-head parasite, Mark, dead. Will you help me or not?"

As the Berrys enter, I whisper the only answer I can. "Yes."

I stare at Samantha, as does Mrs. Berry. Well, she stares more at Craig's T-shirt than Samantha's frazzled look. Does she know it's the one from her dead daughter's room?

"This is my best friend, Samantha." The Berrys nod; Samantha grunts. I hope the "best friend" label saves me from the foul deed I promised, but won't do. "She was just leaving."

"I'm sorry about Robyn," Samantha says. "She was a really

caring person. She was the kind of person who would do anything to help out a friend. Not many people like that."

"Thank you, Samantha," Mrs. Berry says softly.

"Not many like that at all," Samantha glares at me and heads for the door.

"I'm sure that's the kind of friend everybody wants," Mrs. Berry says.

"No, it's the kind of friend they need." Samantha closes the door behind her.

"What an interesting young woman, but I must say, quite sloppy," Mr. Berry says.

"She's living in her car."

"That's terrible!" Mrs. Berry exclaims. "Why on earth would she do that?"

Maybe it's wrong, but somehow it seems right. I tell them about Samantha's life, mostly talking about Mark and her mom. As I'm telling her story, Mrs. Berry makes these little gasps like Samantha's sadness and anger is taking her breath away. When I talk about Samantha's mom's addiction and Samantha's abandonment fears, Mrs. Berry starts the tear-creation process.

"I hope she's doing that peer counseling with you," Mr. Berry says.

"I don't think it would help. She needs professional help," I say.

"She doesn't need professional help," Mrs. Berry says as she walks away from us. She looks out the window toward the street and then turns back to us. "She needs a mother's love."

"She's upstairs," Mother says when I walk in the door. Veronica's attempts to re-enter the world, attend grief groups and funerals, have all failed. She can no longer absorb vapors from a distance like I can. The tears need to touch her face, then drip down on her shoulders to bring her the energy she needs. I bring her Becca's tears; I wonder if she would bring me Becca's life.

When I enter, she rises up and puts a drop from her tear collector into a small bowl. I place the handkerchief in the bowl, and each of the six edges fills with moisture. I squeeze the liquid from the cloth onto Veronica's face and watch it flow down upon her shoulders. My face is expressionless; her face glows like that of a woman growing if not younger then stronger.

"These are excellent," she says. "From that young girl again. Thank you."

"Don't get used to them, Veronica," I remind her. "She's going to die."

"Yes, these are most excellent, but all humans die. Some sooner than others. Good for us."

"You could save her, like you did with Scott," I whisper. "Then you'd have her tears for years to come. I have someone in mind that you—"

"Cassandra, speak not of this again. I didn't want to do that. It is only when your mother told me that you threatened to leave us that I agreed. But I will not do it again, and you will not threaten me again. I have big plans for you, Cassandra, but you must wait your turn."

"My turn for what?"

"What did I teach you to say to people about how to solve their problems?"

"All it takes is time and tears," I answer.

"That's what I'll telling you now. Bide your time, and collect tears for me."

I stand up and look down on her, but her eyes control me. Still, I say, "You didn't answer. My turn for what?"

"I will answer everyone's questions come Feastday." I look at the calendar of saints on her wall. There's no need to circle July 12; everyone knows the occasion. It is Saint Veronica's Day. "On this day, relatives from near and far will come together to learn our fate."

"Our fate?"

"Simon and myself," she says, her voice growing stronger.

"I don't understand what you mean."

"You will, but for now, bide your time—"

"And collect your tears," I finish for her.

Veronica gently places her hand on my shoulder, a rare if false gesture of caring. "We call you Di'mah—Hebrew for teardrop. Do you know why?"

I shake my head.

"Now you are called Cassandra, but one day you will be Veronica."

I can't nod, I don't agree with this. I don't plan to stay a tear collector, but she can't know this.

"One day this will be your family, and then you can choose."

"Choose?"

Veronica points toward the tear collector bottle. "The ways of the past," she says as she hands me back the handkerchief. "Or the way of the future. You will get to decide for all of us."

I run my finger over the single violet thread of the handkerchief. "How will I know?"

She rests the tips of her bony fingers on my young shoulders, opens her mouth, and says nothing. I know what she means: The answer is in the silence that voices the soul's true wish.

Chapter II

Friday, May I

evening

"Scott, why are you apologizing?" I ask, but I know why: his Catholic guilt complex.

"I just had visions of how things would go," he says.

We're whispering about last Saturday night. But the setting couldn't be more different. Rather than Scott's sofa, we're sitting at a lakeside table at one of Lapeer's nicest restaurants in the twilight of the evening.

"It's okay," I reassure him.

"I'm a hopeless romantic."

He touches my hand. My skin tingles, and I feel something. It's like an itch I can't scratch, since I can't replace this imitation of emotion with the real thing.

"And I love it."

"You look wonderful."

"I consider tonight a prom practice run."

While I'm not wearing my sexy, strapless black prom dress, I did spend all my after-school time working on my make-up and hair.

"While you're as handsome as ever, you don't look comfortable."

He laughs, then loosens his blue-and-red-striped tie. "I hate dressing up. I mean I did for tonight, and I'll do it for the prom, but that's it! It reminds me too much of Catholic school."

"I thought you liked Catholic school."

"I did when I was going there, but now I realize how much I missed not being at Lapeer."

I laugh. "Are you serious? What could you miss at Lapeer Get-High School?"

"You," he whispers. "I missed knowing you for two and a half years."

"Scott, please, you're embarrassing me." I try to resist flattery, but it's difficult.

He laughs. "Well, still, I'm sorry about last weekend. I just wanted the best."

"Well, I'm sorry for being late tonight," I say. "So I guess we're even."

"While I mourn the loss of even one minute with you, I understand."

The thing with Scott is: I never can tell if he means these corny romantic things he says. When I told my ex, Cody, that I'd drown in his love, I didn't mean it. If anything, it only showed how much I'd give up myself just to stoke the ego of thin-skinned water-walkers like Cody. But Scott seems so sincere.

"I had two peer counseling crisis calls. I wish I could tell you about them."

"I know you can't," he says, but in a tone that tells me he wants to know.

"Well, one person—let's call her A—is freaking out over the prom," I say after only a slight pause. So many battles rage within me: family vs. love, duty vs. desire, and trustworthy counselor vs. rumor-mill machine. "She just snapped today and had to call."

"It's great you were there for her," Scott says. "What happened?"

"She was driving from school and heard a love song on the radio, and then. . . ." I gesture with an empty hand.

"Then it made her sad because she thinks no one loves her."

"How did you know?"

"I used to feel that way myself," Scott says, then blushes. "Until you."

I lean across the table to kiss him. There are a few disapproving looks from all the adults around us, but that makes me hold the kiss longer. I need practice defying my elders' rules.

"So it was like a last straw for her," I say, moving back toward my own seat.

"Last straw?"

"Not going to the prom makes girls like her sad. They deny it, which makes it worse."

"Give in to the grief. That's what you believe, right?"

"I've got nothing to be sad about, Scott," I say. "Not everybody is lucky like me."

"Cassandra, for once in my life, I got lucky meeting you."

"Scott, stop," I say, not meaning a word of it. My words are as false as my nails.

Scott had suggested we do our post-prom dinner before the prom to re-celebrate our anniversary and the upcoming prom. The problem with humans interacting with tear collectors is that we can almost always tell when they're conning us. As master manipulators, we know all the tricks. Scott is totally sincere, but I know he's got horizontal intentions behind that sincerity. He says he's fighting it—and I believe him—but in my observation, temptation wins every battle. Not just high school guys—kings, presidents, big shots, all of them risk everything for sex. Sometimes I think human men are just as crazed, although in a different way, as some tear-collector males.

Scott takes a bite of his salad, then asks, "Who was the other call?"

"Let's call her K. And it was more of the same, except one of her friends stole her ex."

"Well, you should be able to help her easily."

"Why?"

"You've got some experience in this area."

"Samantha and I were not friends when you two were going out. We were—"

"I mean Brittney, Robyn, and Craig," he says.

"Well, that was a mess."

"I'm sorry I never told off Brittney," he says, looking ashamed. He'd promised to do that right after spring break, but like many things with Scott, his words were not backed with actions.

"You don't need to stick up for me. Don't worry, she'll get hers."

"From you?"

I ponder his question, and imagine the scene. Not taking Brittney's life because I can't go that far, but shattering her ego. She hurt Robyn; she needs to be hurt to restore balance. I don't know how, what, or where, but I know when: on the last day of school.

"I'm not that kind of girl."

He laughs. "Cassandra, what kind of girl are you? I mean, I don't get it. Why me?"

"What do you mean, 'Why me?'" The restaurant is noisy, but Scott's words are all I hear.

"Why me? I'm no Cody. I'm not a jock. I'm not a hot hunk."

"You're more that those things," I squeeze his hands. "Scott, you're everything to me."

"Like I said, I'm not usually a lucky guy. I've had a hard life with my mom raising me, so—"

"Why do you assume this is luck?" I ask. "Maybe it's fate. Outrageous fortune?"

"Beautiful girls like you don't end up with guys like me. You don't need to be in honors classes to know that. You're so pretty, popular, and smart. Everything comes easy for you."

"It doesn't; trust me."

"And I'm not those things," Scott says, looking embarrassed. "Okay, maybe smart, but. . . ."

"Scott, it is not about any of those things."

"Well, opposites attract." I act out his words with another kiss to more disapproving glares.

"It was so nice to come here tonight." I change the subject so I don't let slip the real reason why: *Scott, you're my ride from my past into my future. Both catalyst and catapult.*

~ *84* ~

"Well, after everything we've been through," he says, "we've earned it."

"Amen."

"Cassandra, I bought you something," Scott says, very shyly.

"You didn't need to do that." He pushes a box over to me. "Open it." He gets up from the table and stands beside me as I open the small box from Pandora Jewelry.

"Scott, this is lovely." I take out a gold necklace with a heart charm.

"Let me." Scott helps me put on the necklace. After he attaches the clasp, he kisses me on the neck, then whispers, "I love you, Cassandra. I wanted to show it."

I don't say anything because I can't shut down my suspicious nature of how the world really works—not through selflessness, but selfish manipulation. Without saying it out loud, I sense it in his touch: Scott is saying that I need to show him that I love him in return, despite how much his religious guilt would eat him alive afterwards. We're not opposites—more like opposing forces making trades.

*Is **quid pro quo** Latin for prom night?*

By the time Scott sits down across from me, I've shut out my bad thoughts. He points to the four necklaces around my neck and says, "You have one for peace and one for faith."

"And now one for love," I finish.

"I've always wondered what that tear charm stood for," Scott says.

"Hope." I say, but he looks confused. "Every time a person cries, they release their emotions. They're cleansing their soul. The healing begins, and that brings hope."

"So, once all the tears and hurt are gone, then a person has hope again, right?"

"Sexy and smart," I whisper, touching the charm around my neck.

He blushes. "I think I understand the answer to my question of why me now."

"What's the answer, Scott?"

"We're soulmates, Cassandra," Scott whispers. "We were meant to be together."

As Scott and I fall into each other's eyes, I gently pull the peace sign necklace and wish I had what it represented in my life. Then I touch the cross, knowing I need faith more than ever. The heart charm rests against my chest, signifying Scott's love, while the tear charm speaks of hope. I need all four: peace, faith, love, and hope. But unlike the necklaces that cover my heart and hang together in perfect harmony, these elements of life rage against other. Peace, faith, love, and hope all fight for control, but can any stand up to the strongest force of all? The heaviest chain that binds is fate.

Chapter 12

Saturday, May 2

morning

"Can't you stop picking on me?" I shout at Mom, so loudly that I think my words rustle her black dress. It's Saturday. She's not headed to work but to four funerals. The bigger, the better. Maggie's already left for one in Flint. A young child. Drive-by. A good crowd expected.

"I asked where you were last night," she says, turning on her glare like flicking a light switch.

"Out," I say, filling my water bottle.

"What's that?" she asks, pointing at the necklace Scott gave me.

"It's none of your business," I counter. "Just like where I was is none of—"

"You were out with Scott."

"No," I lie. "I was out with this new friend, Amanda."

"Give me her phone number. I want to check on that," she shoots back.

"No." It's way too early in our friendship to get Amanda to lie for me.

"If you want to leave this house again at night, you *will* give me her number!"

"Why don't you trust me?"

"I used to. I don't know what's happened to you. You used to be such a good child."

"I grew up," I remind her.

"No. You became ungrateful for your family," she continues. "Do you know how sick Veronica is? What are you doing to help her?"

"I bring home tears every day I can."

"She needs more, and it's because of you and that foolishness with Scott," she says. "Why did I ever allow that to happen? What was I thinking?"

"You weren't thinking," I snap. "You were protecting me. It's your job."

"And your job, young lady, is to help Veronica and the family. Now, Alexei—"

"This is warped. Human moms yell at their kids about having sex, but you—"

"Cassandra, we don't have sex or make love; we mate. There's nothing to it."

"That's not what Alexei said," I continue. "He said I need to come to him willingly."

"That's just a legend."

"If you or Maggie would tell me the truth, then I wouldn't believe legends!"

"Each generation knows what they need to know only when they need to know it."

"That's not fair!" I wince at the whine creeping into my voice. I've been hanging around human teenage girls way too much.

"Di'mah, listen to me." Mom turns her volume down. "Veronica is sick because of the miracle she performed, which is why we do it so rarely, but she did it for you. We saved Scott for *you*, and now you owe us. We gave him back his life; you need to let him go."

"I'll go right out of this house!" I shout as I head out the front door.

"Come back here!"

I answer by slamming the door. I try calling Scott because I need to hear his voice—isn't that one of those things that Siobhan said made her know she was falling in love?—but he's not answering. I think he's working. I try Samantha and then Amanda, but no one is answering. It's too early to call Siobhan in California, so I walk until my feet hurt and I reach the school.

I enter the door nearest the pool. From a distance, I hear splashing sounds of an early morning senior swim-aerobics class. School budget cuts have forced them to rent out the pool on weekends. I know I don't belong here, but I need something. I duck into the locker room, put on my swim suit, and head toward the water. The old men and women let out a collective yelp when I jump into the far end of the pool. I hear someone, probably the instructor, yelling, but I don't care. Careful to avoid the elderly folks in my lane, I swim with all the power I can muster. Why are old people always in my way?

"Hey, get out of the pool!" The guy keeps shouting. There's nothing else he can do. My swimsuit is the official Lapeer team uniform. Unscheduled or not, it's what marks this water as more mine than his. I swim six quick laps and climb out.

"Sorry, everybody, I needed to do that," I say as I head toward the locker room.

There's a general murmur, but all I can do is smile. When they get home, they'll have something to talk about. The water refreshed my body but, sadly, didn't clear my cloudy mind.

When I return to my locker, there's a bunch of missed calls from Mom on my phone. One every six minutes. I take a quick shower, dry my hair, then put my clothes back on. Outside, a light rain falls on me. It sends shivers from my bare shoulders down through my newly exercised spine.

I get to the library just as it opens. Not having my backpack with me, I find a copy of *Hamlet* on the shelf and log on to a computer. Despite the madness all around, I still need to fulfill the functions of high school, such as writing papers. Samantha and I have a biology project due in mid-May that we haven't started. Real life draws more Uno cards than homework.

I type at the top of the page, "Major Themes of *Hamlet*." I don't have my notes with me, and the morning's drama has me distracted, so I cheat. I find a site and start the cut and paste: family, revenge, lies, and deceit. I laugh to myself; it all sounds familiar, but that ends when the image of Alexei rushes through me as I read two other themes: madness and death. I quickly close the book, log off the computer, and feel my heart thudding. Almost all unnecessary human emotions have disappeared from tear collectors because they're not needed to preserve the species. Except one, the one I feel more strongly than ever before: fear.

"So?" Samantha says when she finally answers her phone. It's her angry hello.

"Hey, does your car sleep two?" I ask.

"I'm at home."

"Oh, that's great. Is Mark gone?" I ask.

"The police took him away last night," she says. "Why?"

"I need someplace to crash for the night."

"You turn me down when I wanted to stay with you, and now you ask me?"

I suck it up. "You're right, it's not fair to ask, but I need a friend's help. Can you help?"

She pauses, which allows me to think how I've used Samantha, preying not on her tortured past but her ever-present loneliness.

"Do you need a ride?"

"No, I'll walk over," I say. It's a distance, but I need time to flush my mind of the noise from this morning with my mom and fill it with images of Scott from last night. I need the light, spring rain to moisten my shoulders and cool the heat I'm feeling from all sides.

"Okay, but you've got to tell me more tear collector stuff," she says.

"I'd rather hear more about your novel."

"No, I want to hear more, and I've got a movie that—"

I sigh at the thought of a vampire movie marathon. "Can't we just play Uno?"

"No, we need to watch this movie together. It's given me an idea," she says.

"An idea for what?"

"How to kill two monsters," she says, then ends the call.

I turn the phone off to save the battery, which is something I should've done with Samantha. After I drained her to save Scott, I shouldn't have let her back into my life. I knew she was hiding pain, and I used her. But now I'm being paid back for that. What I call fate is really nature seeking balance.

Without my phone to occupy or distract me, I'm lost in thoughts about Scott. The other night he asked, "Why me?" I couldn't explain myself, I guess because I've never had to before. Cody and the other tools I've dated were so full of themselves, they'd never think to ask such a question. They'd just assume they were wonderful, although—as I learned about all of them—most of that was covering up for deep insecurity.

With Scott, it's the opposite. Heck, everything is the opposite. He and I are opposites: I'm outgoing; he's shy. He loves his mom; I resent mine. He's mostly true to this faith; I'm a terrible sinner. He's the opposite of every guy I dated. And it's more than just opposites attract. It's actually something that Siobhan said that I know now is wrong. She said poets explained love, not physicists. But for me, the greatest scientist of all time said it best. Einstein said that to keep doing the same things repeatedly and expect different results is the definition of insanity. How could I find a real love if I kept hanging out with losers pretending to be winners like Cody? When I told Veronica that Robyn had died, she said, "That's just wonderful," and I knew I needed to leave my kind behind. When Scott spoke that day in biology class and said, "All you need is love," I sensed he was my way out of the madness and deceit of tear collecting.

"Who are you?" The skinny, tattooed guy asks me when I arrive at Samantha's door. My tank top is wet from the rain. He can't keep his beady eyes off me, but he's not staring at my face.

"Is Samantha home? I'm her friend, Cassandra."

"I didn't think that fat freak had any friends," he says, then laughs. He tries to smile through the few teeth remaining in his head. "And certainly none as fine as you!"

I cross my arms over my breasts. "Is she home?"

"Sam, get your fat ass down here!" He yells upstairs; his eyes remain on my upper half.

"I'll just go up there," I say, walking past him. I sense in him no tears, like his tear ducts have dried up from lack of use, or all the drugs have messed up his chemistry. The other thing I sense, even more than his sliminess, are his small, black eyes staring at me as I walk by.

"Nice ass," Mark mutters as I climb the stairs while he slithers into another room. At the top of the stairs, I turn back and look at Samantha's house. The bedlam of her life mirrors the chaos here: empty beer cans, full ash trays, and crusty pizza boxes are all strewn about. I try not to wretch as the odor invades my nose. I sip from my water bottle to get rid of the bitter taste that just being here brings, but it's no use. The filth clings to me—and to Samantha—like a leech.

I knock loudly on Samantha's door, but there's no answer. It's locked, so I turn on my cell and call. "I'm in the hall," I say when she picks up.

She opens the door, then retreats into the almost totally dark room. There's an odor here, but it's different. My shoulders, wet with rain, tickle from old, lingering tears, nothing fresh. The only light emerges from a small TV and a blinking DVD player. "I tried to warn you not to come over."

"Sorry, I had my phone off."

It happens fast: the light flicks on. I focus first on Samantha's black eye, then on her bleeding arms, and lastly on her stifled tears. "I won't cry because of him. Or for you."

"What happened?"

"The same thing that always happens," she says. "He gets arrested; Mom bails him out."

"No, to you?"

"Like I said, the same thing that always happens," she continues, gritting her teeth so hard it seems as if she's talking through broken glass. "He gets high. He finds me. He hits me."

"But your arms?"

"That's my contribution," she says. "That's my control."

"Why don't you call the police?"

"He told me and Mom if he ever did that, he'd lock us in the house, set it on fire, and all the police would find is our ashes. He's crazy. He'd do it."

"Here, let's do something about that blood."

"If you were a vampire, we'd make quite the combination." She laughs through her pain.

"I guess I am, just not how you think," I say as I look for something to soak up the blood. "Not how other people think either—and you're not going to tell them, right?"

"Right, I was just angry," she says, then reaches under a pile of books, papers, and notebooks on her desk to pull out some bandages, like they were just one more school supply.

"We all get angry." I notice she even bought black bandages.

"Except we're getting even."

"Right," I say, staring at the fresh cut on her arm. Her skin is an atlas of anguish. She starts to apply one of the bandages. "Don't you have any medicine to put on that?"

"I have plenty of meds." She points toward a cardboard box on her messy desk. I inspect it: Prozac, Ritalin, diet pills, plus other drugs I don't recognize. "And none of it works."

"Samantha, of course it works. All those drugs are based on science about brain—"

"It's not my brain that's fucked up; it's my life. It's my past, present, and future." She puts on the last black bandage. With all of them applied, her arm looks like a chessboard.

"Samantha, why are you so hard on yourself? If you would—"

She cuts me off. "I found this movie we need to watch."

"What movie?" I ask, but she just clicks on the DVD and turns off the light again. The moment the black-and-white image appears on the screen, I can't suppress a loud sigh.

"Don't worry, I won't make you watch the whole thing," she says, laughing.

"Thanks." It's not because I don't want to watch the movie, it's those flickering images. They're almost hypnotic in taking me back to Scott's house. How did I go from that beautiful—if clumsy—evening with Scott to sitting in this gloomy room with this gloomier girl?

"Let me find the part I want you to see," she says, skipping forward.

"What movie is this?"

"It's called *Strangers on a Train*," she says. "And no, it's not a vampire movie."

"I thought that's all you goth girls watched." I regret the words as they leave my lips. Samantha isn't a stereotype; she's a unique person, but one who is so unusual and unstable that it's too hard to deal with her. People dismiss her as a "goth," then think they don't need to know anything else about her. That label makes their lives easier and her life even harder.

"I started reading about vampire movies, which led me to reading about the history of horror movies. It's all so cool." She's excited—as if she were six years old and telling her mom about the first day of school. "And every book talked about this movie, *Psycho*."

"But we're not watching that?"

"No. I watched *Psycho*, and to be honest, I didn't see what the big deal was. Maybe in its time it was good, but compared to movies like *Saw*, it just wasn't that scary or bloody." She continues talking at the same high-paced speed of the DVD advancing. "So then I read about the movie, trying to figure out why everybody thought this boring black-and-white movie was so great. I got this book from the library at the start of the year," she says, then turns the light on.

"Shouldn't you return it?" I ask as she hands me the book, *The Films of Alfred Hitchcock.*

"I always return library books," she says, then laughs. "Eventually."

I laugh. Wow, it's been a while.

"And I thought about my problem with Mark and yours with Alexei. I thought about that little girl dying. A plan came to me when I read about this movie called *Strangers on a Train.*"

"So, what does this have to do with—"

"Here's the part I want you to see. So there are these two guys who meet on a train. They get to talking. The one character named Guy wants to kill his wife. The other character, Charles, wants to kill his father. But they know they'll be suspects if they kill a family member."

"Right. Because if a wife dies, the police would suspect the husband. But I—"

Samantha shushes me, then hits play. I stare at the screen, but I'm distracted for a second by Samantha's movements. She reaches under her bed, and brings out a tin of cake frosting. Just as she did at the Berrys' house, she consumes the contents in minutes as I'm watching the movie. Finished, she rolls it into the corner to join other empty tins. There must be a dozen of them.

"Are you watching?" she whispers. "This is the important part."

I watch as Charles proposes to Guy that they help each other. Charles will kill Guy's wife, and Guy will kills Charles's father, but neither of them will be a suspect because there's no motive, and they'll set up perfect alibis. It's dark genius.

"Criss-cross," Samantha says, echoing a line from the movie. "It's perfect."

"It's just a movie," I tell her, growing uneasy. Uneasy at how interesting the idea sounds.

"It doesn't need to just be a movie, Cassandra."

I want to turn on the light. I'm surrounded by darkness. But the tone of her voice warns me things are about to get a whole lot darker.

"I've thought about this for a while now. I've thought about symbiosis and how species help or hurt each other. It's supposed to be a natural process, but sometimes nature is a mean, unfair fucker. So we have to take action to get results. You know what I mean, right?"

"I can't do that, Samantha." In the beginning, tear collectors were compassionate and benevolent, but over time, as the population grew and the genes thinned, we couldn't rely on human sorrow, so we began causing it. I'm sure it started small, but now our lives are full of creating drama or—as with the males—even trauma to get enough tears to survive. There are many laws in nature, but the strongest is that every species will do whatever it takes to survive.

"I have a plan. You'll think it's crazy, but it's the only solution that makes sense. It's a solution to all of our problems: yours, mine, my mom's, and even Becca's."

"Becca? What are you taking about?"

She points at the paused image on the screen. "You kill Mark, get Maggie to transfer his life energy into Becca, and then I'll kill Alexei for you. Criss-cross."

Time freezes like the screen.

"Samantha, listen—"

"No, Cassandra, you listen," she hisses. "You'll do this not because you're afraid of what I'll do, but because if you don't, my blood will be on your hands, just like Robyn's. Do you hear what I'm saying? If you don't kill Mark, he will kill me or my mother. You let Scott's grandmother die to save his life, so don't tell me you can't do this. *You must do this.* Don't you want to save my life? And since you couldn't save Robyn, don't you want to save Becca?"

Chapter 13

Sunday, May 3

morning

"So does this count as a date?" Scott whispers as we walk together into St. Dominic's for Sunday morning mass. I try not to laugh, but fail. Old women clutching older rosaries turn around and flash their irritation, but it bounces off. Nothing will bother me today.

"Yes, Scott this is a date, but don't get any ideas," I whisper back.

He lets go of my hand as he starts to sit in the back pew. "What? You mean we can't make out? Father Morrison won't see us all the way back here. His eyesight is terrible."

I grab his hand again and lead the way. "No, we can't make out here because we won't sit here." He follows me to my family's normal seats. We always go as a family—until today, when I told them that I wanted Scott to join us. Suddenly, Mom and Maggie's plans changed.

"What is so special about this pew?" Before I answer, the music for the opening hymn starts. The organ blares, and Scott turns to watch Father Morrison enter, but my eyes stare at the stained glass window above us: the Sixth Station of the cross. Veronica wipes Jesus's face, a story I know well from my family's annual re-enactment of the Simon and Veronica stories.

As Scott belts out "Sing to the Mountains" in a surprisingly good tenor, I mouth the words because my mind is elsewhere. How did we tear collectors evolve—or maybe rather *devolve*—from our beginnings? When that first Veronica wiped the Son of God's face, she transferred his tears as well as the blood and sweat. Was it something already about Veronica that made her change? What transformed her from a pious woman to a tear collector?

But even more mysterious, how did our species change so much? How can we trace our beginnings to a Son of God who preached compassion, and yet no tear collector possesses that trait to this day? If we were truly compassionate, we would not prey on the Samanthas, Beccas, and Amandas of the world. The Son of God spoke of love, but we don't know that word, either. These traits washed away because they interfered with our ability to survive. I look around at all these people as they sing about Jesus dying for their sins. If only they knew that from his tears sprang a species that thrives on the damage caused by their selfishness... .

"You must be a terrible singer," Scott whispers when the hymn is over. "You were just faking it. I hope that's not the only thing you fake."

I slap him gently on the arm so he can bruise and blush at the same time. I don't deny it.

Scott is very attentive during mass, much more so than I am. He looks at the Bible as a book with all the answers, but I know it brings nothing but questions and contradictions. When we stand for the reading of the Gospel, Scott gently places his hand on mine.

Father Morrison walks toward the pulpit, kisses the Bible, and starts to speak. "The Gospel according to John 15:1-6. 'I am the true vine, and my Father is the farmer. Every branch in me that does not bear fruit, he takes away. Every branch that bears fruit, he prunes, that it may bear more fruit. You are already pruned clean because of the word which I have spoken to you. Remain in me, and I in you. As the branch cannot bear fruit by itself, unless it remains in the vine, so neither can you, unless you remain in me. I am the vine. You are the branches. He who remains in me, and I in him, the same bears much fruit, for apart from me you can do nothing. If a man does not remain in me, he is thrown out as a branch, and is withered; and they gather them, throw them into the fire, and they are burned.' This is the word of the Lord. Amen."

Before Father Morrison has taken six steps away from the pulpit, I'm halfway out the door. I run, although I wish I was swimming to clear my mind of Father Morrison's reading. In my religion, Jesus is the root vine; in my house, Veronica is. Would I as a branch wither away without her? Would she die without me? It was the Son of God's words, Father Morrison's voice, but it was Veronica's face I saw when I heard: "apart from me you can do nothing."

"Cassandra, are you okay?" Scott says when he finds me outside. He touches my shoulders, but I move his hands to my arms, so he can wrap them around me. "What's wrong?"

Everything, I think; "Nothing" is what I say as I fall into Scott's embrace, wishing his arms were the waves of the ocean and I could sway back and forth in them forever and ever.

"I'm sorry about all that," Samantha says as we pull into the parking lot of the Goodwill store. Scott dropped me at her house before he went to work. On the way over, she apologized for the "crisscross" idea and admitted she just talks crazy. "So, let's just enjoy today, okay?"

"Trust me, Samantha, no one has ever had a day like today," I tell her as we walk from her beat-up, old car into a store that specializes in beat-up, old clothing.

"You mean other people didn't have a date at church with the world's most normal boy and then spent the afternoon shopping for used prom dresses with the world's biggest freak?"

I laugh. "Something like that, except you're not a freak."

"Scott's not normal like most teen boys. He doesn't seem horny twenty-four-seven."

I laugh but don't comment. Conflicted is what he is twenty-four-seven.

"And since it's prom, I figure you two will fuck like bunnies at Easter." I grab her arm and pull her aside. She winces as I drag her away from the front door.

"Samantha!" I shout and then make the whisper motion. "Please be quiet."

"What, like it's some big secret people do that on prom night?" Samantha says. "Well, I guess I won't be. Even if I would've gone to prom with Scott, *that* wasn't going to happen."

I take six steps away from the door back toward the car; she follows. "Why not?" I ask.

"When we went out, he never tried anything. A hot date was a game of Uno with him and his mom. Maybe he knew that I'm as much of a scarred freak under these clothes as I am in life."

"Listen, Samantha, I don't want to talk about this with you. These things are private between Scott and me, you understand?" When she nods, sweat falls from her face. "But I can tell you this. The reason he never tried anything has nothing to do with you and everything to do with Scott."

"So, are you saying he should be taking Michael to the prom?"

I roll my eyes. "No, you know how religious he is."

She nods again, but follows it with a frown.

"In our church, you're not supposed to do things like that before marriage. That's why. It's not you."

Samantha laughs so loud it almost bursts my eardrum. "This is why I tell you there is no God, Cassandra! Or if there is one, he's one sick fucker. He lays down rules against sex with one hand, and he creates teenagers with the other. You tell me that makes sense."

I shake my head in mock sadness. "God doesn't have to make sense if you have faith."

"Or if you're a fool, and I don't think you're a fool. You believe all that stuff, too?"

"Yes, Samantha, more than you could know."

"You believe some long-haired guy walked around, healed the

sick, raised the dead, and all that nonsense? How can you take honors biology and believe that story? Tell me how!"

"Because it's true, and I wish I could prove it to you."

"And how would you do that? Do you have a snapshot of Jesus in your purse?"

I stare at her as those two deep, human emotions of anger and fear rage inside me. I think about the box next to Veronica's bed and the meaning of her name and my middle name, *vera icon*, which is Latin for true image. When the first Veronica wiped Jesus's face, she didn't just capture his tears; she captured his image on her veil—a violet veil that resides in my house.

"Well? Put up or shut up?"

I take a deep breath and walk slowly back toward the store. "Let's find you a dress that is worth taking a picture of on prom night. Let's talk about that instead, okay?"

She grabs my arm, clutching it tight. "Sorry. I guess I have to pick a fight."

"This is a fun day, Samantha. Let's just enjoy it."

I smile brightly, but she just frowns.

"I don't know how to be happy; I just know how to be miserable."

I smile brighter than the sun and speak in an upbeat tone. "Just fill yourself with joy!"

"It will take a lot of joy," she whispers as I open the door. "Because I'm empty inside."

After an hour, we narrow it down to two dresses—black, of course. Both have high backs, but are sleeveless like every other dress she tried on. Her arms don't scar like her back did, and if she doesn't cut between now and then, she should be okay.

She holds one in front of her. "Do you like this one?"

Before I can answer, my phone rings. Amanda's ringtone of

the Beatles' "With a Little Help from My Friends." Samantha's fragile smile turns upside down.

"One second; it's Amanda," I say, then take the call. "Amanda, how are you?"

"I guess you're super busy—I don't see you at the hospital much anymore," she answers.

"And I don't see much of you with Mary at peer counseling," I say. I probably should congratulate her, but what's good for her is bad for me. "She's good, not as good as me, but. . . ."

"It wasn't just the counseling," Amanda says. "I talked to my mom, and I'm on meds."

Anti-depressants are to tear collectors what garlic is to vampires. "That's good," I lie.

"So do you want to hang out today? I've got all this homework to do, and I can't face it."

"Me too," which is true. *Hamlet* and biology projects dangle over me like swords.

"So, maybe we should take a day off. What are you doing now?"

I glance at Samantha holding up her dress and walking away from me. It would be so easy just to tell Amanda I'm shopping with Samantha and rub salt back in those lonely-life wounds that her little white pills closed. But I resist. Before I can achieve human love, I must first demonstrate compassion. I choose Amanda.

"Nothing much, but I should do that homework, I'll catch up with you later," I say as Samantha walks back to me. Amanda tries to keep the conversation going, but I end it quickly.

"How is Amanda?" Samantha asks.

"All smiles and giggles."

Samantha keeps holding the dress in front of her.

"Really?" Samantha says in this exaggerated tone. "She looked like crap the other day."

"Why would you say that?" I ask as I inspect the dress for flaws.

"Oh, I just see stuff at school. Like I saw Kelsey and her going at it. Well, more Kelsey talking and Amanda listening. I overheard some of it, real vile stuff. When Amanda said something back, well, that's when Brittney the Bitch Queen got involved. Like I said, real vile stuff."

"Why didn't you do something?"

"First, Amanda's your friend and was Robyn's friend, not mine. It's not that I don't like her, it just that I don't know her, and from what little I do know about her, she seems pretty uninteresting."

"Unlike you."

Samantha cracks a smile, but it fades with her next words.

"Where was she when Brittney teased me for years? *Years.* Brittney's new thing is calling me Samanatee. How rude is that? She puts me down just to make herself feel better."

I hold the dress up in front of Samantha as we both look into the mirror. Samantha could look pretty if she tried. She'd need to stop eating tins of cake frosting, cutting her arms, and wearing only black—in other words, not be herself. Maybe she does those things because she wants to repel people. If nobody gets close, nobody can abandon her or hurt her. But she hurts only herself, unlike Brittney.

"Between you and me, Samantha, I think Brittney's a psychopath."

"I didn't realize you were a qualified mental health professional. Oh wait, there is no such thing. Those phony doctors push more pills than Mark and cause just as much damage."

"Samantha, what's gotten into you?

"What hasn't? You name the med, and a quack gave it me. Do I seem healthy to you?"

I look at the two of us in the mirror. It's almost like a funhouse show because we're so opposite on the outside, but on the inside, we're more and more alike every day. Samantha is almost like a human cousin. Like me, no dad. Like me, little joy. Like me, full of fear and indecision.

"Come in here with me," she motions, and I follow her into the small dressing room. I sit beside her, and she moves closer. "You might get your fill today. You won't need Amanda."

She rests her head on my left shoulder and the first tear tingles the sensitive skin.

"I wish I could just pop a pill for what was wrong with me. If only it were that easy."

As another tear falls, I whisper. "Samantha, what do you think is wrong?"

"I won't bore you with my fucked-up history because you can figure most of it out by what you know about me, my mom, Mark, and the company he keeps." My right shoulder is jealous as the left soaks up the sadness of her unspoken story. "So the end result of all of that is this: borderline personality disorder. I looked up in the *DSM* I stole from the library."

"*DSM?*"

"*Diagnostic and Statistical Manual of Mental Disorders.* AKA the crazy Bible," she says. "I read a lot about it. They call it BPD for short. It's me, and basically what it means is this: I'm unstable, feel empty and depressed, have obsessive behavior, and I fuck up relationships because chaos was all I knew when I was growing up, so I need to create chaos in my life. No pills fix it."

"What can you do?"

She lifts her head from my shoulder, shrugs, and returns it, dropping more precious misery into my thirsty skin. "The same you can do being a humane and decent tear collector: Learn to live with it, and hurt as few people as you can."

"Really, Samantha, there's no cure?" I ask.

"Well, there's just one cure," she whispers. "And that's death."

"Where have you been all day?" Mom says when I walk in the door well past sunset.

"Out. I'm going to bed," I start toward the stairs. She doesn't know this is a test. If she lets me go without hassle, it will be better for her. Veronica might be the vine; Mom's the rot.

"Come back this instant and answer me!"

I hustle down the stairs, bringing salt for her wounds. "First, I went to church with Scott. Then I went shopping with Samantha for her prom dress. I already have the one I'll wear when Scott takes me. See, aren't you glad you asked?" I hear stirring upstairs over our shouting.

"Sit!" She points at a chair in the kitchen. I resist at first, but surrender to her stare. She follows me, and sits across from me. She hands me a fresh water bottle and then takes hers. "So, it's come to this. We've tried to be understanding about this school-girl crush, but this—"

"If this is understanding, then I'd hate to see what—"

"You can go to the prom with him." She never says Scott's name. "But that's it. We're not going to argue about this. You live in this house and are part of this family. I am your mother, and you will obey me. Do you understand what I'm saying?"

I won't look at her or answer.

She continues. "This is for your own good, and one day you—"

"So is this what Maggie did to you when you had your 'school-girl crush,' as you call it?"

Mom slams her water bottle on the table. "I don't want to talk about it with you."

"Then I will," Maggie says as she enters the room. She looks tired, as if it's a chore just to hold up her ever-present water bottle. Maybe the upcoming Feastday weighs heaviest on her.

"Maggie, there's nothing to say. Just go to bed." Mom's voice drops an octave.

Maggie chortles. "You don't tell me what to do. Remember that, Salome Veronica Gray!"

Mom mumbles something resembling an answer, more like something a teen like me would do after being scolded. Just how ingrained and long-lasting is the obedience gene in tear collectors?

Maggie is dressed for bed, but sits down at the kitchen table. Mom squirms in her seat.

"Do you want to tell her, or should I?"

More squirming from Mom, but Maggie seems to be sitting taller in the chair.

"Well, Salome?" Maggie asks.

Mom answers by leaving the room.

"That you are the way you are doesn't surprise me, Cassandra," Maggie says. "Your mother was a handful at your age as well. Quite the disobedient child, but we broke her of that."

I don't ask how, even though it might be nice to see a glimpse of my future.

"Like you, she had these silly school-girl crushes, and like you, we indulged her because the end result was always the same: a breakup, followed by his tears and lots of drama. Until—"

"Until what?"

"Until her junior prom, a month after the reunion. Until she lied to us."

I sip my water a little faster. "Did she and her date, um, you know. . . ?"

Maggie's face, which was almost smiling at telling the story, sets hard. Her eyes grow small, and her jaw almost locks. "The problem wasn't what she did, but who she did it with."

"I don't understand." I stumble over my words. "Did what with whom?"

She pauses, sips, and swallows. "Mated, of course. What else would I mean?"

"How could you let her back in the family if she mated with a human?"

She sips the drink. The water swirls in her mouth before she swallows. "It wasn't a human. It was a tear collector, Cassandra."

"Who?"

Another sip, another swallow, another pause. "Your father."

Chapter 14

Tuesday, May 5

school day

"Samantha, are you okay? Why did you miss school yesterday? Is something wrong?"

"What do you think is wrong?" She slams her locker door. "Mark."

"Did he hurt you again?"

She pushes her hair out of eyes; there's just the mark of the beast from the other night. "That's all he does. Asking if he hurt me is like asking me if fish swim."

"What now?" I ask as we walk slowly to class. Chaos around us; chaos next to me.

"He told Mom she shouldn't let me go the prom with Michael."

"How does he even know about that?"

"I wanted just one normal thing in my life. I asked Mom to take pictures of my dress, even if it is cheap and ugly. One thing led to another, and she said she wanted to meet Michael."

"How did that go?"

"Michael came to take me to the cast party. Mark was there and drunk," she says. "If you think he's nasty when he's high, you should see him drunk. It's like he grows a second asshole in the region of his mouth."

I hold back a laugh. "So what happened?"

"What do you think happened?" She looks around the hallway. A few people scurry in the halls, but no one comes up to see me. Brittney's branding of me as an exile remains intact.

"He called me a fat, stupid whore for going to the prom with a nigger faggot. It was a wonderful performance. I wish I could've taped it for a drunk douchebag-of-the-year contest."

"What did Michael do?"

"He left and said he wasn't going to the prom with me. I don't blame him."

"That's terrible!"

"Find Michael. You'll get your grief fix from him; then come back to me," she says.

"Samantha, I didn't think you cared about something like prom. I was surprised you let us fix you up with Michael. We thought you'd turn us down, to be honest."

"You're wrong," she says. "I do want to be normal, or at least do some normal high school stuff. But what happens? It's one thing to be on the outside looking in, but to get inside, and then get booted out in front of everyone, abandoned yet again. . . ."

"Samantha, it will be okay," I say, using my calming, peer-counselor voice.

"No, Cassandra, it won't be okay," she says, then walks past me into Mr. A.'s class.

When I finally enter, I see Michael staring at Samantha. All around the room, I sense the remnants of tears—not from hurt or sadness, but stress. Not about school—everybody in this class can handle schoolwork—but the real work of high school, figuring out life. My senses work overtime this morning for another reason: Alexei. No matter what he says—and he can't be trusted—every cell of my body tells me that he is near. That he is here. That he is coming for me.

"Sorry I'm late," Mr. Abraham says as he walks into the classroom. But he's not alone. "Everyone, this is my godson, Caleb."

Caleb looks to be about twenty-three; he's the kind of guy a girl could dream about twenty-four hours a day: a confident smile, engaging dark blue eyes, and a shock of brown hair. I know I'm staring at all six feet of him dressed in a dark blue suit, so I look toward the floor, but it's no use. Like the current of river toward the ocean, Caleb's indigo eyes pull me toward him.

"I know many of you are interested in careers in medicine, correct?" Mr. A. says as he sets his coffee thermos on his desk, pulls up a stool for Caleb, and walks around the room. Caleb sips from a large Starbucks cup as he sits down. Mr. A. continues, "Can I see a show of hands for those who are interested, please?"

Almost every hand in the room goes up, including mine. I force myself away from staring at Caleb to look at Samantha. Her arm isn't raised. Like her head, it's resting awkwardly on her desk.

"Well, that's what I thought," Mr. A. says. "Rather than me asking you questions, I thought I'd let you ask questions for a change. Caleb has just completed his first year of medical school at the University of Michigan. So you can ask him about that experience."

"How much money will you make?" Clark asks. Some people laugh; Caleb frowns.

"It doesn't matter how much money you make or even how much med school costs. I will tell you: once I become a doctor, I know every cent and every second of the journey will be worth it. Medicine is giving yourself over for the greater good." Caleb speaks slowly, making eye contact with many of us..

But it seems mostly with me, which leads to the question that I won't ask: *Why did you stare at me when you said the words, "greater good"?*

I sit quietly, but I'm one of the few. The questions come at Caleb fast; he handles each one with grace and charm. I can't speak. I'm an overloaded sensory outlet, short circuiting from too much information crashing in at once.

"Leave me alone," I hear Samantha hiss. All eyes, even mine, turn to see Mr. A. kneeling next to Samantha's desk. He's wearing the same concerned look I've seen so many times, never more so than after Robyn died. Samantha didn't cry then, but things have changed. Others can hear it, but only I indulge in it. Even from a distance, her familiar essence flows into my skin.

"I said leave me alone!" Samantha shouts. Her head is off her desk, and her feet are on the ground as she runs out of the room. I shoot a look at Mr. A., and he nods.

As I'm about to leave, Caleb walks over to me and says softly, "Cassandra, can I help?"

I'm too shocked to answer.

How does he know my name?

Instead I take off after Samantha. I'm faster than she is, but she's furious. Anger is pure adrenaline. By the time I get out into the commons, she's gone. There's nothing but a bloody, silver-skull earring she must have ripped out in a surge of anger seeking release. She's a self-contained vampire that needs blood to live, but it's her own blood. My shoulders soak in the remains of her trail of tears.

"Cassandra, may I speak with you?" says Mr. A. in the cafeteria. I sit at lunch with Amanda, Sara, and Elizabeth. The school is buzzing about Samantha's scene and the reason behind it. Michael told someone about what went down at Samantha's house, and now it's all over school.

"Sure," I say as I turn to face Mr. A. He's alone. I try to hide my disappointed eyes.

"Let's go back to my room." I gather my lunch and water bottle. We don't talk in the hall. Inside the room, he closes the door. He pulls up a chair by his desk, offers it to me, and sits down. When we're settled, he starts. "So, about Samantha. What do we do?"

"Where do you want to start?"

"Well . . . first, nothing you tell me will I tell anyone unless it's about abuse, which I'm legally obligated to report, understood?" I nod in agreement. "And I don't want you to tell me anything you learned from her through peer counseling."

"She never came in for a session, but we've become friends."

"Girls like Samantha need friends like you. I've seen so many smart girls like her over the years who take a wrong turn somehow. Like Robyn, it's always related to loneliness."

"That's just one of her problems."

"But this morning, what do you think prompted her outburst?"

"The prom."

"Really? Samantha doesn't seem like the kind of girl who would go to prom."

"Well, I actually suggested it, and I was surprised, too," I explain. "But I think if you feel unloved in high school, then not going to prom probably feels like a stake in the heart."

"Appropriate analogy for Samantha," he says with a smile.

"She was going with Michael, but that's off now. So she's feeling hurt and embarrassed."

"And very angry, but that's understandable."

"I'll ask her to come with me and Scott, but who knows if she'll make it until Saturday?"

"For an event that is supposed to be a lot of fun, the prom sure is a big headache," he says and chuckles. "And I ought to know, because I'm one of the chaperones again this year."

"I just wish Samantha could be happy, if for one night," I continue. "She's got so much stuff going on in her life. She's felt like an outsider for so long that this meant more to her than I imagined. She obsessed over it. She obsesses over everything, but I didn't see this coming."

"I have an idea." Mr. A. pours coffee from his thermos into its red cup. "Caleb, whom you met this morning, was probably going to come to the prom to keep me company. What if. . . ?"

"What if Caleb took Samantha?"

"No, that wouldn't be proper, but I think Samantha might be in a real crisis right now," he says. "Instead, what if Caleb keeps her company there so she won't feel alone? Why don't you ask her if she'd be interested? I'll vouch for him. He'll be a perfect gentleman."

"No doubt he learned that from you."

"Well, it would also be a favor for you because I'm sure you must feel responsible in some way. You owe her to make it right. If you hadn't put the thought in her head. . . ."

"Maybe," I say softly.

"And I feel bad that the administration didn't want to do anything about Robyn at the prom," he says. "I suggested a moment of silence, but they thought it would be too sad."

"Have they ever been to a prom?" We both laugh quietly.

"That's true. It seems like every prom I've chaperoned has had as much crying as dancing."

I hide my smile. At an event where everybody has unrealistic expectations, the land between what people want to happen at prom and what really does happen is very moist.

"So what did you think of Caleb?" Mr. A. asks in the most casual tone.

"He seemed really smart." *And attractive.* But I don't say that and shouldn't think it.

Mr. A. blows on his hot coffee to cool it. "You were staring at him, did you know that?"

"Really?"

"You know, if you were a few years older, or he was a few years younger, then—"

"Mr. A., please!" I squirm in my seat. "You're embarrassing me."

"Cassandra, I consider myself a teacher and coach, but I'd like to think you see me almost as a mentor. Am I right?" There's gentleness in his voice that I don't often hear in my life.

I nod in agreement. He sips coffee from his red cup; I sip water from my violet bottle.

"It just seems that someone like Caleb would be better for you than someone like Scott."

His words slam against me like a hard slap, leaving me confused. I shake my head, then say, "I love Scott."

"No, you don't, Cassandra. You probably think you do, but trust me, you don't love him."

I stare up at the clock to see if it's possible for time to stand still, but the second hand moves.

"You sound like my mom!" I laugh when I say it, except he's not smiling. He's serious.

"Cassandra, remember once I told you to listen to the silence to find an answer? Well, sometimes you should listen to the wisdom of your elders. Trust me—you don't love Scott."

"But I do. I would do anything for him!"

"If you love him, then you should want to protect him from all harm, right?"

"Of course."

Mr. A. stares at me for the longest time before he says, "Cassandra, you are that harm."

Chapter 15

Saturday, May 9

prom night

"That's quite the fitting quote, don't you think, Cassandra?" Caleb asks.

He points at the banner at the front entrance to the ballroom of the Atlas Country Club, home of the Junior/Senior Prom, or rather, drama. This year's theme is *A Midsummer Night's Dream* from the play by Shakespeare. The quote is from Puck, Michael's character: "Look, what fools these mortals be."

"Especially tonight," I say.

Other quotes fill banners, while the ballroom overflows with flora: fake trees, bushes, and flowers. There's even a stream. In the corner stands a large maypole, which serves as a backdrop for photos. The ceiling is covered with small lights to look like stars. Like the play itself, the prom creates this dreamlike atmosphere of romantic longing and confusion. I notice there's no banner with the quote that perhaps best fits this night, especially for me as I think about Scott, who has wandered away: "The course of true love never did run smooth."

"So, Caleb, what was your prom night like?"

"Well, I didn't have a Shakespeare theme; that's for sure! I didn't realize Lapeer High was such a literary school."

I laugh. "It's not. It's cheap. The decorations are from the set of the drama club's spring play that just closed."

Caleb laughs, but I don't join him. Michael starred in the play, but he's not here tonight, thanks to Mark. Some mortals are fools, and some, like Mark, are full-fledged evil. Loud music pounds in the background; a louder beating throbs in my chest.

"You're saving Samantha's life," I tell Caleb.

He smiles at my remark, a smile like I've never seen. His eyes are not steely blue; they're all magnet. Even Alexei's scent in the area can't distract me from this perfect evening. The fake stars sparkle, but there's nothing fake about Caleb.

"Cassandra, thanks, but Samantha will be just fine," Caleb says.

We're standing outside the hall leading to one of the girls' restrooms waiting for Samantha. I left Samantha alone to fix the make-up on her arms because the rush was too great in the bathroom. An hour into the prom, and tears are flowing faster than vodka from hidden flasks. The prom theme is a comedy, but I sense tragedy waiting to happen. Every gorgeous gown worn by a smiling senior is a remark, a rumor, or a rude gesture away from becoming a tear-stained testament to this heavy night.

"Well, this was nice of you," I say.

"Where's Scott? Everything okay?" Caleb asks. He seems concerned, almost protective.

"I wish I knew." I glance down to keep from staring at Caleb, the way Mr. A. noticed.

He chuckles. "Trouble in paradise?"

"I don't know," I reply, then look around the crowded room for Scott. He's been acting strangely all evening, especially since we met up with Caleb. For once, I'm not trying to make a boyfriend jealous, but Caleb and I have this amazing connection. He looks so elegant and comfortable in his dark blue suit; I know I look fine in this strapless black dress.

"Well, if there's anything I can do, or if you want to talk about it. . . ." Caleb says.

"Thanks." People are dancing and laughing, but I'm brooding over Scott's behavior.

"I'm ready," I hear Samantha say. She's putting on a brave front, although I sense her discomfort. Not from sitting with Caleb-- although that's part of it—but from the night itself. The style this year seems to be backless dresses, which Samantha couldn't wear. She showed courage going sleeveless—the dark lights and make-up hiding the cuts—but even more so in jamming herself into a place and a dress that don't fit.

"I'm going to look for Scott," I say, then give Samantha a hug.

She returns the favor and forces a smile. Her smile looks as odd as that Goodwill black dress does among the expensive gowns worn by everybody else. It's a fashion show set to bad deejay music.

"And I'm going to learn more about vampires, it would seem," Caleb says.

"I can talk about other things," Samantha whispers to me before I walk away.

I have no luck finding Scott, but go from table to table reconnecting with people. Much to my surprise, I see Katie. After her first counseling session, she only called me once. I'd seen her around school but waited for her to approach me. Now she does, weeks later.

"Cassandra, I've wanted to thank you!" Her words come with a hug. Behind her is some guy I don't know, probably not from Lapeer High. "I'm here tonight because of you."

"I didn't know. You never—" I start. She hasn't let go of me yet.

"I wanted to wait until I actually made it through the night." She finally releases me. She looks stunning in a long green dress. "But you helped me make it through that terrible day."

"Are Clark and Diane here?" I wonder if her dress matches her eyes or her emotion.

"They are, but I don't care. I'm here with Ronny, this guy from my church, and everything is just wonderful! I didn't think it could be just a few weeks ago, but you gave me hope. What did you say to me? Healing just takes time and tears? Well, you were right."

"I'm happy for you," I lie.

"I'd be happy to be you, Cassandra. I know some girls talk bad about you, like Brittney, but you know what? They don't know how caring and helpful you are. You're a lifesaver!"

"I think that's a little—"

"No, really! Until I talked with you, I was ready to do it. I'd written the note in my head."

"Then I'm glad I was there for you." I see Craig across the room; he's oddly alone at his table. This is my chance. "Have a great night, Katie. I'm glad everything worked out for you."

As I walk away, I hear Katie say to her date, "That's Cassandra. She's just wonderful."

The words stop me in my tracks. "That's wonderful," is what Veronica said when Robyn died because of her tear collector friend. But because I'm a tear collector, I saved Katie's life. Balance as always in nature. I make eye contact with Craig briefly, but I can tell he wants no part of me. I'm not Cassandra, a girl he knows; I'm his living reminder of Robyn's death. I decide to try compassion again for the moment and move in a different direction instead of making Craig feel more pain than he probably has from his tuxedo.

"Hey, Mr. A., have you seen Scott?" I ask when I spy him near the dance floor. He's dressed in a black suit, looking more like an usher at a funeral than a chaperone at a prom.

"Probably not," he says, or rather shouts over the music. "I'm only looking at and for people drinking, doing drugs, and dirty dancing."

"With Scott, you're out of luck on all three." He doesn't react when I say Scott's name again. I'd ask him what he meant by his remark, "You are that harm," but I don't want to know for sure. Maybe it's just that even teachers know about the waves of heartache I've left in my wake

"Looks like you're being extra vigilant," I say.

"We've already had one tragedy this year at school. We can't take another."

I don't say anything.

He sips soda from a red plastic cup, then asks, "How are Caleb and Samantha getting along?"

"Fine. Caleb is a really amazing person. You should be proud of him."

"I don't think I could have trusted anybody else I know," Mr. A. says. "But Caleb is very sensitive, very in touch with what people are feeling. He'll make a great doctor. Just like you."

I'm silent as the noise increases on the dance floor. I'm thinking about what Mr. A. said, not now, but earlier this week when talking about Samantha. He spoke about loneliness, yet I don't see anyone with Mr. A. There's no ring on his finger. "So how does this prom compare to others?" I ask.

"In school, I see you as students, as children. But tonight, you seem so adult. Or pretend to be," he says, then points to a couple locked in a lengthy kiss. He heads off to break it up.

I make more small circles around the room, stopping at every table, soaking up gossip. I keep waiting for Craig to be alone again, but Cody and Kelsey stick like barnacles on his hull. He and Brittney, I've noticed, seem to be more jawing than kissing. I clutch my purse. Inside is Robyn's letter. This could be the nail in the Craig-and-Brittney coffin, if I can get to him. Having them break up on prom night, when Robyn was so looking forward to it, would be too sweet for words.

I absorb whatever tears are in the mist until I spot Scott by the door. He's talking with Clark. Even though Clark's a jerk, Scott seems to be getting along with him, for now. But I've watched Clark all year and know he's hateful. It's only a matter of time before he says something mean. I want to break up their conversation to protect Scott, but as I walk over, I make eye contact with Mr. A. His eyes stop me, and his words haunt me. "You are that harm."

I break eye contact with Mr. A. when I clutch Scott's left arm. "What's wrong?"

"I'm just tired," he says. "Maybe we should go."

"Come dance with me." A loud techno song starts, and people race for the dance floor.

"I'm not a good dancer."

"Something else we have in common," I say, touching his

hand. It feels cold.

"Maybe." I expected a laugh; his reaction feels more like a slap.

"Okay, Scott, what's going on?"

"Nothing. Like I said, I'm just tired."

"All night you've been weird. Is it Samantha? Is it Caleb? Something else?"

"It's none of those things," he says very softly.

"Then that only leaves me." I try to get him to look at me, but he won't.

"This isn't the place." He moves away from me, looking pained in his black dress shoes.

"No, but I sense this is the time," I say. "What's wrong?"

"Let's take a walk," he says; then we slip out the exit doors.

We make our way past the smokers, tokers, and drinkers hiding in the woods, then sneak down one of the wooded paths. I try to make conversation, but he's not having it. He walks a step ahead until he finds a bench. We take off our shoes, but I dream for a second about taking off my mask, telling him what I am.

"Scott, talk to me." I press against him. The expected kiss doesn't appear.

"Cassandra, look, there's something I have to tell you," he says, slowly. "I didn't want to do this tonight because I just want us to have a good time, but I can't lie to you. I feel I'm lying every time I kiss you anymore. And tonight, well, I expect a lot of kissing."

"Scott, I don't understand."

"Cass, I love you. You know that, right?"

I clutch the heart necklace as my answer.

"But if you love someone, then you should be honest with them." He sounds as miserable as he did after Alexei tortured him. My shoulders don't lie; the pores prepare.

"What are you talking about?"

"When my grandmother died, she left some money." He bites his bottom lip and coughs, stalling. Finally he says, "I have enough money to go back to Powers Catholic next year."

I look toward the sky. The stars are there, so the world didn't end. It just feels that way.

"You're leaving me."

"I don't know," he says. "I can't decide what to do."

"Scott, you can't go," I say. If only he knew the decision weighing on me.

"I don't want to, but my mom thinks that I—"

"You can't."

"I don't want to do this, but—"

I rip my arm away from him, then stand up. "Scott, you don't know what I'm considering giving up to be with you. I was ready to give up *everything* for you. For you."

"You shouldn't do that," Scott says, but the words don't help.

"Stay with me, Scott. Stay."

His tears recede as I fall into his arms. "That's what I want, but—"

"That's what I need," I whisper, even as I move my lips toward his.

As we come together, there's an ocean of doubt washing over me. I'm drowning because I don't know how to swim in these waters. I break up with people; I break hearts. That's what I do. As I hear faint sounds in the background of the people at the prom and the night creatures in the woods, I grasp at how hard it is to be human. Not fools, these mortal be, but fighters and survivors.

After an hour outside, we head back in. We find Caleb and Samantha at our table, trying not to looking embarrassed by our rumpled clothes. Once again, Scott made it all about me. He's the most unselfish person I've ever met, and I know that's part of what's pulling him apart as he decides about us, about Powers. He doesn't know how to do things for himself.

Back at the table, we avoid physical contact—above the table so as not to make Caleb or Samantha feel embarrassed. But they barely notice us; they're deeply engaged in conversation. Caleb leans in to listen as Samantha, no doubt, fills him in about her empty feelings. At the end of the evening, after all the desserts, dances, and rituals have concluded, Caleb says goodbye to us, and I try not to show him, Samantha, and especially Scott how hard Caleb's departure hits me for some reason. Scott goes to get the car, leaving Samantha and me alone as the prom parade passes us. It's a wave of high school humanity: clicking cameras, jingling jewelry, and limitless laughter.

"Caleb is such a nice guy," Samantha says.

"Don't tell me that you two—"

"He was very upfront about that. I like Caleb too much to put him in harm's way with the shit storm that surrounds me." She touches the bandage on her ear and it reminds me. I reach into my purse and hand her back the silver skull earring she ripped out. She looks down at it. "A real shit storm."

"Meth-head Mark?"

"No, tsunami Samantha."

"I don't think so," I counter.

"BPD, PTSD, ADD, OCD. You name it, and I've got it. I'm an alphabet soup of insanity."

"Don't forget F-R-I-E-N-D." I hug her and feel the scars on her back through the thin fabric.

"Get a room, lesbo!" Clark yells as he passes. I ignore him and start toward Scott's car until my internal compass goes wild and pulls me in another direction. My feet speed up on their own.

"What's the hurry?" Samantha asks at my increased pace. "I can't run in these shoes."

"Look over there," I say, my eyes locating what my sixth sense discovered: a couple in the middle of the parking lot and an argument.

"Is that Brittney and Craig?" Samantha asks.

Brittney is dressed in red, but all night she made people blue. The gossip around prom was that she and Craig were fighting all night, with Brittney taking it out on anyone and everyone with her devil tongue. Her grossly overdone hair hides the horns; her tight, red stiletto heels pinch her hoofs. Brittney's smirk is her bitch fork. I can't hear their words, but their body language suggests they won't be a couple for long.

"How very sad." I suppress a smile, thinking how Brittney's tight, red dress holds down her tail.

"I bet she's mad because Craig came to our table looking for you. He wasn't drunk, but he wasn't himself. I don't know what he wanted. Caleb spoke to him."

"That's odd." I'm listening, but from a distance, sensing Brittney's hollow tears. Craig isn't crying; I sense he's too angry to cry. About what, I have no idea. I'll have to try to reach out again.

"I agree," Samantha says, "but you know the oddest part about this whole night, other than the sheer impossibility of my being at the prom? Talking with Caleb was like talking to you."

She has my full attention now.

"You know, there are nice people in the world," I respond.

"We spent most of the night just talking," she says. "I didn't dance, or even eat much of the dinner other than the cake, but I had the best time. I talked. He listened. I cried."

"Well, I guess once you start crying, you can't turn it off," I say. ""Maybe you two—"

"He's got his own problems," she says.

"He doesn't look like he could have any problems," I joke.

"Well, he didn't get into it. He just said he understood about having a difficult past and growing up without a real father," she says. "He said he understood feeling like an outcast."

"I have no idea how somebody like Caleb could ever be on the outside of anything."

"He said he's got this girl that his family wants him to be with, but it didn't work out," she says. "I told him that his life sounded a lot like high school. He laughed at that."

"Well, you made him laugh; that's great,"

"When he was talking he got really emotional, which got me all caught up in it," she says, then laughs. "Before long, he had me crying on his shoulder. He's a guy, so he didn't cry."

"Well, some guys cry," I say, thinking of how I've made a high school career out of causing those tears. I think how many times I've made Scott cry. Was Mr. A. right? If I love Scott, then I should protect him from things that hurt him, and I'm number one on that list.

"Everybody cries, Cassandra," she says. "Well, everybody but you."

I fake a smile, think of becoming human, and then say, "One day, it will be my turn."

Chapter 16

Tuesday, May 12

school day

"Amanda, did you hear about Craig and Brittney?" I ask, concealing a smile.

"Everybody's heard," she replies. I hide pride in my rumor-spinning skills.

"Do you know what happened?" I ask.

Amanda looks around us. We're standing by her locker just before lunch. She's got this gleeful look, like she's never spread gossip in her life.

"I heard they broke up at the prom."

"Ouch!" I shout. "Well, if you hear any juicy details, let me know, okay?"

"You really hate her, don't you? Everybody I know does. She's so mean."

"Brittney? I'd have to care about her to hate her," I say.

"I don't feel sorry for her. I know I should, but things she said to me for no reason—"

Part of me wants to ask, "Like what?" just to feed off Amanda's reaction, but I resist. Instead I say, "She's a b—"

"Don't say it!" Amanda shouts, then smiles.

I fake a laugh, then head off to meet with Samantha. I'll tell her the breakup stuck. It might help her believe there is a just God and bad people get punished. Sometimes I believe Mr. A. when he talks about how nature is balanced, but then some days I think it's all random. If everything is random, then it doesn't matter what we decide. Maybe the best decision is to let outrageous fortune prevail.

"What's wrong?" I ask. Samantha and I eat lunch outside, near the stub of the Goth Tree. It's a hot and humid May day. She must be overheating in her layers of black clothes.

"After you dropped me off, Mark was waiting for me," Samantha says harshly.

"Wish I could have been there to help."

I wish I would've been any place after prom than where I was: in Scott's cramped car feeling boxed in. We made up, made out, but didn't make love, even though he pushed for it. I thought Scott was special, but it seems the human wheel turns the same way with every guy I've dated. Scott's more caring, more patient, but in my darkest thoughts and doubts, I wonder if that's just an act to get what he wants, which I'm not ready to give him. I can't risk allowing myself to make love until I can make my love human.

Samantha pulls up her sleeve to show her purplish wrist. I can almost feel the tight grip of Mark's hand; I can certainly see the marks he left. I see two fresh cuts on her arm above it.

"Why would he do that?" I ask.

"There is no *because* with a meth-head like Mark," she says. "He doesn't need a reason."

We both fall silent; Samantha is thinking of the hurt in her life; I'm thinking of the hurt all around me. The post-prom drama hovers like a tear-filled cloud, as Brittney and Craig were not the only casualty of the evening. I push my uneaten lunch aside, sip some water, and start to leave.

"We'll do it on July Fourth," Samantha says as she grabs my wrist. "Criss-cross."

"Samantha, are you back to that? The other day you said—"

"Criss-cross." She looks at me with a hard glare. "The Fourth of July will be perfect. Lots of fireworks. Nobody will hear when you blow Mark's head off. Do you want a pistol or a shotgun?"

"Samantha, no!" A few heads turn from other groups and couples eating outside, but I barely see them. I'm staring Samantha down. I move closer to her. "Let me go, or else."

"Or else?" Her grip remains tight.

"You don't want to know," I whisper.

"With what I know, you shouldn't be threatening me." She's in full unstable mode. "Even if you barely give me details about your life, I'm starting to put it together. I heard Scott tell Mary the oddest thing before class. He said you went to church together and you made him sit in a certain seat—under a stained glass window of Veronica. I looked it up. Veronica is the one who wiped the tears from Jesus's face, and your grandmother's name is Veronica, so I got to thinking—"

"Listen Samantha, I'm not making a threat," I say accenting each syllable. "It's a promise."

She blinks, then releases my wrist, but the glare she gives me—not full of anger or rage, but hurt and betrayal—tells me she's not ready to let go of my life until I help her end Mark's.

"You don't scare me, Cassandra," Samantha says without hesitation.

"I should."

"Until you help me—really help me—I don't want to talk to you. Understand?"

I cross my arms. "I won't do it. Do *you* understand?"

"You're on your own, Cassandra," Samantha says. "I don't want to see you, hear from you, or see you online. They call me Death Girl, and that's fine because you're dead to me!"

"What about our bio project? It's due Friday and we haven't even—"

But before I can finish, Samantha's back is all see. My betrayal is just another scar there.

During lunch, I stop by Mr. A.'s room. He's deep into grading papers, but interrupts his flow to let me in.

"Cassandra, how can I help you?"

"I just wanted to thank you again," I say as I walk inside.

"For what?"

"For suggesting Caleb as the one to keep Samantha company at the prom. That was really nice."

"Well, to be honest, I'm getting a little heat for it." We both sit down.

"Heat?" He sips his coffee, while I cool down with water from my bottle.

"Some people didn't think it was appropriate, and they're probably right. There are rules in the world for good reasons, but sometimes you need to look at the greater good."

"I'm sorry if you got in any trouble."

"So, is Samantha feeling better?" he asks. "It's so hard to get a read on her."

"Well, she was fine on Saturday, but it's Tuesday, so she's messed up again."

He chuckles, which seems out of place. "Not the only one, from what I've seen."

"I think we'll set a record in peer counseling this week."

He looks at the papers on his desk. "Cassandra, anything else? I'm a little busy here."

"Well, Samantha and I had a fight, so our project won't be—"

"Your presentation is due on Friday. I'm sorry, no exceptions."

Mr. A. is the one teacher I can't manipulate about grades. I guess that's why I respect him so much. But I wonder if it might be easier in other areas. I take a deep breath like I would before diving into the pool. "I'd like to thank Caleb myself, but I don't know how to reach him."

"Of course, there's no harm in that," he says. "He's not much of an online kid, like all of you. I'll give him your number and tell him to call you once he's in town for the summer."

"I'd like to talk to him sooner, if that's okay with you."

Mr. A. considers my request in silence. I start to imagine a conversation with Caleb, but Scott's voice drowns it out. It's easy to rationalize my desire. If Caleb calls, I'll just ask for his help with my now-solo biology project; there's no harm in that.

"He said he had a good time with all of you," Mr. A. says. "Said he thought all of you were more mature than he remembers people being in high school. You made an impression."

"Thanks," I repeat, starting for the door. I don't need to tell Mr. A. the impression was mutual. Something about Caleb pulls me toward him.

What's wrong with me? I shouldn't think such thoughts.

What's wrong? As always, Mr. A. had the right answer: I am that harm.

Sitting in English, my next-to-last class of the day, I barely listen as Mrs. Plumb leads a discussion about Act II of *Hamlet*. I perk up when she asks how a wise man like Polonius could have so misjudged Hamlet's intentions. As others answer about the play, my mind drifts toward my reality. How did I so misjudge Samantha? Or did I know all along she couldn't be trusted, but ignored that to use her for my own selfish intentions?

It is no wonder tear collectors don't mix with humans; we always know exactly what we need, but humans are too unpredictable, "too human." And if I misjudged Samantha, have I misjudged Scott as well? If so, it's a misjudgment that can alter my life. I need to know.

As in science, I need to run an experiment. In the past, when I broke up with boys, it didn't bother me at all. I just waited until they came crawling back. So, my hypothesis is this: if I break up with Scott and feel anything at all, then my love for him is real and I must decide if I have it in me to do what's needed to be with a human. Mr. A. is right: In the short term for Scott, I will be the harm. In the long term, we might be each other's salvation.

"It's over."

I try not to look at Scott. It's the end of one school day, the end of our world.

"No, don't say that," he replies.

He should have known when I didn't greet him with a kiss or when I sat in his car but didn't close the door.

"Scott, what you want, I can't give you," I say.

"I don't care about sex. I care about you. I want to show that, but not at the risk of losing you. I was weak. I got caught up in the moment. Just forget it, and we'll move on."

"Scott, it's over."

In previous breakups, the plan has always been to manipulate the conversation to cause as much hurt for the hapless hunk as possible. Like everything else in my world since meeting Scott, that's turned upside down. I don't want him to hurt. I will protect him from me.

"I know you don't mean it," he replies, touching my face where there should be a tear.

"Yes, I do," I say softly and then start to leave.

Unlike Samantha who grabbed my wrist like a cop making an arrest, Scott touches the tips of my fingers. "I don't understand why you act this way."

"I can't explain." Never have I spoken truer words to Scott than these.

"I don't accept it," he says as he motions me to join him back in the car. I'm frozen in the heat of this moment. "I believe in you. I believe in us. I'll do anything to keep you."

"Scott, it's over," I say, slamming the door shut first on our love, then on him. I get six steps away from the car, when I feel Scott's hands on my exposed shoulders. I push them away.

"Then at least kiss me goodbye."

"I can't."

"I love you, Cassandra," he says, staring at the ground beneath him. It must feel like it's opening up and swallowing him. Veronica's handkerchief stays in my pocket; his head stays pointed down, but not on my shoulder. "But I know you. I know about you."

"What do you mean?" My heart skips. *Did Samantha tell him in her anger at me?*

"I heard how you break up with guys, get back with them, and break up again," Scott answers. "I can't go through that. So, if you walk away from me now, there's no turning back."

"I understand," I lie. Scott will come back to me; they always do. Boys always say they won't, but every day makes the echo of my voice in their heads seem like a siren song. I need to see if I'll go back to him. That's never happened before; that's the test. A real biology project.

"Cassandra, I'm serious," Scott says. "This isn't temporary. This is forever. This is —"

"Goodbye." I remove the heart necklace and drop it into the palm of his hand.

"What's wrong?" Mom asks as I walk in the door.

"I followed your orders. Scott and I broke up."

"About time," she says. I'm not looking at her, and no doubt the smile on her face.

"I'm going to bed," I announce.

"You know how this goes. He'll be back, but this time –"

"This is—was—different," I say softly.

Mom shakes her head, then sighs. "Every girl your age thinks every breakup is different."

"Every girl my age isn't a tear collector," I remind her.

Another sigh. "Do you think you're the only one of us who ever went through this?"

"I know all about Siobhan and –"

"Don't mention *that* name," Mom cuts in. "She betrayed us. For what? Human love."

"How can you be so cruel?" I slurp from my water bottle loudly.

"Do you think you and she are the only ones who ever were tested?"

I finally take my eyes off the floor and look at her. She's faking a look of concern perfectly.

"Temptation is what keeps us strong," Mom says. "Every-one—yes, even your mother—went through something like this at your age. It's part of the process of growing up."

"Why didn't you tell me this before?" I ask. "Why did Maggie have to tell me about you?"

"I tell you what you need to know when you need to know it," she reminds me. "You're right, though. I did sense something differ-ent about this boy Scott. He was your test."

"No, I really think I love him."

"You know that's not possible. We blend in with the humans, so over time their ways rub off on us, but it's only on the surface. We look like them. We act like them. But underneath, we don't feel like them because we cannot love; love makes us weak. You think you're feeling real human love—I know I did at your age—but it just can't be done. I learned that the hard way."

"But—" I start.

"You must let Scott go now," Mom says. "You saved his life, but you're wasting his love because you can't return it. This is one of the hard lessons of our life. You passed the test."

I look past her, through the window into the open night sky. Scott's gone; I'm alone. This despair, this loneliness ... this must be what it feels like to be truly human.

Mom continues to talk, but I'm not listening. She seems to be saying something about understanding how I feel, but I don't believe her words. It would be nice to think she cared, but she can't. She just said so. Loves makes her weak. She protects me because biology demands it, but that's all I know to be true. I slowly drift upstairs. Maybe she shouts at me to come back, maybe not.

Once in my room, I open my desk and pull out Robyn's final letter to Craig. I read it aloud, but instead of "Dear Craig," I say "Dear Scott." I look out the window and imagine over the miles Scott reading these words and feeling the same heartbreak.

By the time I finish reading the words I could write myself at this very moment, my eyes are burning and my hands are shaking. I feel faint, barely able to hold the single sheet of paper. It drops to the floor as effortlessly as I dropped the necklace into Scott's hand.

I lift my head up high so I don't stare at that piece of paper—a piece of paper that is a fraction heavier and much more valuable than when I picked it up, because on that paper is something quite rare and, for me, quite dangerous: the violet tear of a tear collector.

Chapter 17

Friday, May 15

school day

"Everything okay, Cassandra?" Mr. A. asks as I stumble into class just as the bell rings.

I don't look at him, nor do I search the room for Scott or Samantha. I stare at the floor as I mumble a non-response. Neither of them will answer my calls. The ones to Scott are *not* to get back together, or so I tell myself. My experiment is failing. Only Caleb and Amanda will talk to me. Caleb helped me throw together a project about symbiosis. I'll present after Samantha.

As Samantha walks to the front of the room, I try to focus, but it's hard. It's the seniors' last day, so there's plenty of liquid emotion in the air. I need the energy more than ever. Even shedding that single teardrop the other day almost knocked me out. To cry is to die. Maybe I should welcome it.

"You may begin, Ms Dressen," Mr. A. says, then sips coffee from his ever-present red cup.

"I'm sorry I don't have any posters or PowerPoint slides," Samantha starts. "I was supposed to do this presentation with someone else, but they let me down. They're a real pain in the Cass."

Clark laughs loudly as I sink into my seat. I try to catch Scott's eyes. A compassionate glance is all I need, but he's just looking at Samantha, maybe wondering, "What if. . . ?"

"Now, as some of you know, I have more than a little interest in vampires," she says.

Clark coughs the word "freak." A few people laugh. I'm not one of them.

"I would propose that there is a biological explanation for the vampire mythology, but in order to believe it, I had to question my atheist beliefs. What if Jesus was really the Son of God, as many of you believe? And what if this half-man, half-god creature interacted with humans and somehow in this interaction, his superhuman blood created the first vampire?" Samantha continues. Her voice is sharp as each word cuts at me like a dagger.

"This is sacrilege!" Scott yells. "Do I have to listen to this?"

"Mr. Gerard, that's enough," Mr. A. says to Scott, although for some reason Mr. A. is looking at me. He's probably thinking she's crazy and blaming me for not working on her project with her. "Ms Dressen, continue."

"No, no, no, no, no, no." I whisper to myself.

"Part of the legend of Jesus is that as he carried the cross, he encountered a woman named Veronica. This woman wiped his face-- his bloody face. What if this blood was so powerful and special that it changed this woman Veronica? Maybe it made her—like Jesus—a supernatural creature, gave her supernatural powers. But when the effect of his blood wore off, she needed to seek more blood. Maybe she started with animals, but that wasn't enough, so either she or her descendants needed to collect human blood. These blood collectors became known as vampires. Then, as they evolved, they retained the human shape, but adapted those traits, such as the ability to hypnotize humans, which allowed their species to survive. The story of vampires is another example of evolutionary biology, though in a different form."

"This is just silly," Clark says. "This isn't science. There ain't no Dracula in the Bible."

"This is wrong. Very wrong," Scott says.

Others voice their agreement with Scott.

Samantha stares at the only person not speaking: me. "And these parasites could be among us today—maybe in this very room! Parasites who, for their own selfish reasons, prey on us all."

Samantha performs a stiff little bow to no reaction from anyone except Scott, whom I sense is crying, which means I am taking in those tears, which means I am feeding off him like a parasite.

"Very interesting thesis, Ms Dressen. Very original, if speculative," Mr. A. says. "I'll read your paper, but I'm a skeptic by nature who will look at your evidence void of emotion."

Samantha doesn't say anything to Mr. A., but goes out of her way to pass by my desk. "I told you, Cassandra: don't fuck with me," she hisses.

"Ms Gray, you're next," Mr. A. says.

I wonder if he knows Caleb helped me, but it doesn't matter. I sleepwalk my way through my presentation, mumbling and sounding more like Cody than myself. It's the worst presentation of my life, which fits because it's the worst day of my life. Samantha's right: there's only one cure for some things, and that's death.

As the bell rings, I slowly start out the door like I'm walking with two broken legs. Mr. A. calls after me. "Cassandra, a moment please."

"What?" I snap. The word echoes off the empty chairs.

"See me after school," he orders.

I nod my obedience and head out into the busy hallway.

At lunch, I embrace every senior I can find, but it's like my body has betrayed me. I feel the energy, but there's no rush.

Did that single tear I cried denote some sort of change?

I'm outside in the courtyard where some of the most popular seniors hang out. It's where Robyn would have ruled next year if she'd had a better best friend, or at the very least, one that was human.

"Look at that, Kelsey," I hear Brittney say. Then she snaps her gum. "Where's your pal Samanatee? Feasting on a bucket of fish?"

Kelsey fake laughs so hard it hurts my ears.

"Brittney, Kelsey, don't test me today," I say.

They're silent for a second until Brittney nods in Kelsey's direction. Permission to speak granted. "Or what?"

"You don't want to find out," I reply, punctuated with my best smirk.

"Try us," Brittney says. When I laugh in her face, she slaps my cheek. Hard.

I don't react. Even if something isn't quite right with my body, I still have enough senior tears to withstand this attack. There's no pain.

"Your turn," I say to Kelsey.

She shrugs. Brittney nods, and then Kelsey slaps me, too. Everybody's watching, laughing, but not stepping in to stop it. That's fine with me.

"What's wrong with you?" Brittney says.

I move close to her, right in her face. I can smell her cheap perfume, but not any speck of fear. "Stop calling my friends names, or else."

They laugh in synch. "Or what? You'll let us slap you again." More laughter.

I point to my left cheek and then my right. "No, I already turned both cheeks, so—"

"So?" Kelsey asks, but I answer by walking away for now. For now.

"Sit down, please." Mr. A. says when I come into his classroom after school. "That was a terrible presentation. I expect much more from you."

"Like I told you," I mumble. "Samantha and I ... So I had to do it alone."

He shakes his head, sips from his cup, and sighs. "No, you didn't. Caleb helped you."

"He told you?"

I'd asked him not to. My misjudgment of people continues non-stop.

Mr. A. laughs. "I had a hunch, and you just confirmed it. I'd fail you, but—"

"But?"

"As I may have mentioned, Caleb will doing some work at the Lapeer Regional Hospital this summer. That's where you volunteer, right?"

Caleb. Images and sounds that I shouldn't have flash before me. His voice on the phone. His eyes. His smile. It's more than a twisted human feeling, it's deeper. It's biological in nature.

"Cassandra, are you listening? What's wrong with you?"

"Sorry. Yes, I volunteer there."

"He did you a favor helping with your project, and I'm letting that slide. It seems you owe both of us a favor, agreed?"

I nod as he leans back in his chair.

"I know he would instantly make friends at the hospital, but you already know people. Maybe you could introduce him?" Mr. A. looks up at the ceiling, avoiding my eyes as if they carry a plague.

"I'm just a volunteer; I don't know any of the doctors or anything."

"Cassandra, I know you. My guess is you know everyone there. Isn't that right?"

I shrug my shoulders. As always, Mr. A. is right. "Of course, I'll do it for you."

"Well, Cassandra, it's also for you. I heard you broke up with Scott, is that right?"

I don't say anything. I don't remind him it was partially his idea.

"Now you don't have a boyfriend, and Caleb is—"

"Mr. Abraham! Are you trying to fix me up with your godson?"

"No, that would be wrong for me to do since you're a student of mine." He finally looks at me, wearing a serious expression that suggests, *Don't let me down in this.*

"Good," I lie. I tell the truth. I don't know any more. To my own self, I am not true.

"Totally inappropriate during the school year," he says, but then I watch his face turn like the mask for tragedy into the mask for comedy. "But during the summer, who is to know but us?"

As I round the corner to my house, I spot something odd. In the driveway is a black hearse. Even though it's a sunny May day, it feels like a shelf of storm clouds descend upon me, and not the kind that bring luxurious rain. I start to turn around, when I hear my mother call me from the open door. Like I'm swimming while wearing heavy shoes, I slowly make my way toward the doorway. It is open, but not empty.

Not Mom, but Simon stands there. Balancing on his cane, he tips his black hat like he's some gentleman. There's a red rose in the lapel of his black suit. He removes it and hands it to me. Behind his teeth, he clicks his ever-present cinnamon cough drop. My stomach churns.

"I don't want it." I cross my arms, drop my head, and wait for this storm to pass.

"What you *want* doesn't matter," Simon hisses. "What the family *needs* decides."

I try to walk past him, but he puts his cane up in front of me.

"Let me go, Simon."

He stares at me with his vulture eyes and sneers with a snarling smile. "You will never leave us."

Chapter 18

Saturday, May 16

afternoon

"Is there anything else you want?" I ask Caleb. "I mean, if you want, I could show... you know..."

For some reason, it's hard to talk when I'm around him. The words are in my head, but they get scrambled coming out of my mouth.

"If you decide not to become a doctor, Cassandra, you should consider a career as a tour guide," Caleb jokes.

We stand together outside the hospital under the eaves to avoid midday sun. He wears a dark blue suit, but he drapes the jacket over his arm. I should be dressed in my volunteer uniform, but I didn't want someone as handsome as Caleb to be near something that ugly.

"I don't know about that," I reply, but I'm distracted.

Alexei is near. I sense his presence strongest whenever I'm around males. It's as if he's stalking me from a distance. He's not acting, but preparing. My encounters with males must fuel his jealousy and rage, which makes him stronger. Maybe he only told me I had to be willing to come to him because he knew it would make me run. Maybe he wanted this chase. I shudder, suddenly chilled in the noon heat.

"Well, I'm joking, of course," Caleb continues. "I can tell by the way you talk to patients that you're a natural for the medical field. It's like you're born to it. Is your father a doctor?"

"My grandma, Maggie, is head nurse at the Avalon Nursing Home, while my great-grandmother, Veronica, used to be a hospice nurse," I answer, yet avoid the question. "My mom runs the local chapter of the Red Cross, so we're all involved in helping people, I guess."

"You don't take; you give back. Thinking about the greater good."

"I don't know any other way."

"There was only one thing that disappointed me during our tour."

I pause before I speak. *I wanted it to be perfect.* "What's that?"

"The coffee," he says, then laughs. "Hospitals can be the location of miracles, yet the real miracle would be getting a decent cup of coffee. Is there a Starbucks around here?"

"Lapeer isn't Ann Arbor," I remind him. "There isn't a Starbucks on every corner."

"Well, Lapeer has other advantages." His eyes focus on mine—not a stare, but there's an intensity that's unnerving, yet flattering. Maybe this is how I looked at him that day we met.

I look away, almost afraid. "There is a Tim Horton's I go to with my friend, Samantha."

"Well, maybe sometime next week you can introduce me to the Tim Horton experience." He writes his cell phone number on a piece of paper and puts it in my pocket. "Thanks again for the tour. If there's ever anything I can do for you, don't hesitate to call. *Anything,* Cassandra."

"Thanks. I'll take you up on that coffee. I'd like that," is all I can say.

"So would I, Cassandra. So would I," he says.

As he walks away, it takes more will than I thought I possessed not to follow him—the same will stretched to the limit by not calling Scott. If this raging against fate and emotion is how humans feel all the time, then they deserve to die in peace since their lives are filled with hurt, heartache, and loss must be so painful.

"Who was that?" Amanda asks.

She's taking my normal afternoon shift so I can go to the library and finish my Hamlet paper. I need constant motion and focus to keep from contacting Scott. True to his word, he has not contacted me, and other than my lapse yesterday, I haven't tried calling him. He changed his online status to single. At school, he looks at me with indifference to mask the deeper sadness that only I can sense.

"Caleb. He's Mr. Abraham's godson," I answer. "I first met him at school when he came to talk to us, but then he was Mr. A's guest at the prom."

She flinches as if slapped in the face. "I wouldn't know about that."

"Sorry."

I am. First comes compassion, then love. Then heartbreak, then loneliness.

"It's okay, Cassandra. I know what I'm feeling is nothing you could understand."

"Try me." It's just us and one other person in the hospital break room. "Trust me."

"No, I don't think you could imagine what it feels like."

"How what feels like?" I sip from my water bottle; she drinks a Diet Coke.

"I've seen your Facebook page, and there's a picture of you and Scott. I look at your other friends, and all of them have pictures of them kissing boyfriends and girlfriends."

"I don't understand," I say to her, but I'm thinking about myself. I've yet to take down the Scott photos or change my status. I don't know if I'm in denial or defiant. Or both.

"That's true of everybody," she says, staring at the floor. "And there's me."

"You?"

"You look at my pictures, and it's me, my family, my friends. Do you understand?"

She's repeating herself; that's a good sign. "Not all of my friends have pictures—"

"It's a world full of kissing couples."

"And you're not in one of them."

She's not crying; instead she's at the pre-tear stage. Like Eskimos have a hundred words for snow, tear collectors can describe to each other in detail every aspect of the human crying experience. I want to resist, but biology trumps all.

"Then, at school, I see you and Scott. You look so happy."

I don't correct her. "And how does that make you feel?"

"I think, 'Why can't that be me? Why can't I meet someone like Scott?'"

I reach out to let my skin catch, then absorb, that first teardrop. I feel the energy again.

"Why does everyone else get to be so happy? What's wrong with me?" she asks.

"There's nothing wrong with you," I say. "These are perfectly normal human emotions."

We're distracted by the scraping sound of a chair being pushed in, then the door closing. The last person has left the break room; Amanda's ready to break.

"I don't believe you," she says.

"You're just sad. We're alone now. It's okay to cry."

"I volunteer here. I do well in school. I'm smart." The words pour out with tears.

"And pretty," I remind her. It's not a total lie. Amanda is pretty, but then so are lots of girls at schools. Getting guys has little to do with looks, it's all about attitude and action. I could so help Amanda, but right now, she's got to help me. "I guess it's just not fair."

"It's not fair," she says staring at the table. "I just don't understand —"

"Amanda, there's only way to feel better. To heal, you need embrace the hurt."

Before she can answer, she acts. The tears rush out like a rainstorm. I pull her toward me so her crying cascades on my shoulders. My face flushes, and my eyes almost roll back in my head.

The second I arrive home, I race to my room. There's no time to watch my family rejoice in my loss; there's only time for me to fill it. The test is over: I failed; love won.

But Scott won't pick up the phone. I call; he won't answer. He's like an angry God ignoring the prayers of those in need. I go on-line, but he's not there either. Texting isn't an option. If he won't answer calls, he will just as easily ignore a text message. Downstairs, I hear the faint echo of voices; up here is only the echo of silence.

My fingers, almost out of instinct, start to call Samantha, but I stop myself. I can't use her again, not because it's wrong, but because using her just pulls me deeper into her crazy world. Still, I find it hard to resist, but I find it harder to believe that Samantha's not online. That laptop is her window to the world, and keeping Samantha connected is the one thing her mom does right.

Could they be together?

I think about stealing Mom's car to find the truth, but a larger truth hits me: These feelings are the same story I've heard so many times in peer counseling, a story I've pretended to understand. My empathy has been an act until now. I've always said if you don't mind being alone and don't feel love, then high school is very easy. Now it's not just hard; it's hell. I'm burning in flames of doubt, and I need help from the only person who can answer my questions. Siobhan.

"What do you mean it's over?" I ask. Before I could tell her about my breakup, Siobhan told me her news.

"He wanted to meet my family," she says. "I told him that wasn't possible."

"And that's why you broke up?" I ask.

"One thing leads to another, and before I know it, he's packing," she says.

"He'll be back."

"No, Cassandra, I don't think so." Her voice is barely audible, a loud whisper at best.

"Why's that?"

"When I met Alden, I was a tear collector, so, you know what we do," she says struggling through every word. "After the second or third breakup, he told me that he loved me and it didn't matter how many times I broke up with him, he was always coming back."

"That's good news then, because —"

"But when he ended it this time, he said it was over forever," she says. "The one thing about Alden that was different from any other guy was that he never, ever lied. He's gone."

"No, guys—"

"You're not understanding, Cassandra! Alden wasn't just another guy," she says. "I left everything I knew for him, and now he's left me."

"Boys will—"

"Alden wasn't some boy; he wasn't even some man. He was my life. He was everything. And now I have nothing. I'm empty. No love in front of me, no family behind me. I'm a failure."

Her words echo those in Robyn's letter to Craig.

"There will be others," I say.

"No, he was all that matters," she says, starting to cry. I wonder how much it hurts. Does she cry salty human tears or the stinging acid of our tears? "And now nothing matters."

I go silent. Siobhan helped me, but I'm helpless to help her. I sit here in frustration—not only at my inability to help, but at all those tears I hear but can't collect. My shoulders ache. My mouth feels dry. As always, the things I want seem distant and impossible to obtain.

"You should fly out here," she finally says. "You could get enough tears to keep Veronica alive for another sixteen-year stretch. That would make her about one hundred twelve years old."

"One hundred twelve?" I manage to ask before it feels like I stop breathing.

Siobhan pauses, which gives me time to regain my composure.

"I know, your family tells you what you need to know when you need to know, but listen to what I'm about to say."

I wonder if there's a state of nature beyond surprised.

"You don't know how special you are," she says. I push the phone closer to my ear. "All the rest of us—I mean other tear collectors—live like mortal humans, all except your line. Your line."

"Are you saying that Veronica is immortal?"

"As with all things, the history is clouded. No, your great-grandmother is not the same woman as the Veronica from the creation story," she says. "But she has lived many lifetimes. Generations come and go, but only Veronica and Simon can live beyond human years. The Feastday coming up is when they tell the family if they intend to stay on another sixteen years."

"When Grandmother Maggie says it is her turn she means—"

"It could be, but maybe not," Siobhan says. "Maybe Veronica will stay strong, and Maggie will die off, then your mother. Maybe you! Or maybe you will be the one."

"The one?"

"Maybe Veronica wants you to be the one who takes over the family. Maybe she can hold on for three more generations until you are ready to replace her," she says.

"But why me?"

"Do you understand interbreeding?"

"Of course, in humans it is —"

"Forget humans!" she shouts. "Think about other species, like dogs."

"Dogs?"

"Interbreeding is thought of as passing on the recessive genes, the negative traits," she says. "That's probably one of the reasons all tear collectors are hemophiliacs. Somehow our ability to turn tears into energy thins the human blood that runs through our veins."

"Non-adaptive traits." Somewhere Mr. A. is smiling at his lessons learned.

"Right, that's why female tear collectors don't get their period like humans," she explains. "Because it weakens us. Maybe at first we did. Maybe that's why so many tear collectors had to mate outside the family, because the women died young. I don't know; no one does. I do know that as a species, tear collectors—like their human counterparts—have evolved."

"We've evolved together. It's a symbiotic relationship."

"True, we've adapted to each other but never successfully integrated. So, we've stuck to mating with our own whenever possible. The problem is that when you breed in the same gene pool, and there's nothing to wash out the recessive genes, they multiply and you get birth defects and other undesirable traits. But there are also dominant genes that pass along the best traits of the species. That's how champion dogs come about—through interbreeding, hoping that dominant rather than recessive traits will be the result. In dogs —"

"Stop comparing us to dogs!"

"You're not human, so their rules don't apply either!" she exclaims. "You and Alexei—"

"Don't mention his name!"

"Since his great-grandfather, Simon, is similar to Veronica and has lived many generations, then if the two of you breed, the chances are your offspring will succeed. That's why everyone is so resentful of you and your family, Cassandra. As long as your family keeps breeding with Simon's family, then both of your lines will always remain dominant."

"But Alexei is—"

"But there's the downside," she continues. "In many of the males, for some reason, the interbreeding makes them physically strong but mentally unstable. Not all, but most."

"Alexei's crazy?"

"No, he's crazed," she snaps. "His actions are wrong, but he knows that. He's sane."

"Why hasn't anyone told me this?"

"Because ignorance is bliss," she says. "Do you feel better now? Or do you feel the weight of the world on your shoulders knowing that you live in a house where the oldest generation can live beyond the normal life span and where you have a chance to do the same. That is, if—"

"If?"

"If you don't make a mistake, like I did, and lose everything for human love."

I'm sitting down, but I feel dizzy. "You haven't lost everything."

"I have, and not just because I've lost my family and my traditions," Siobhan says through tears, very human tears. "I've lost my way."

"What do you mean?"

"As a tear collector, your life is simple. You live on instinct and only care about what you need. Feelings of wanting are human feelings. You can mock them, but you can't feel them," she continues. "Your life is planned out for you before you're even born, but—"

"But?"

"But as a human, it's not like that," she says. "Every day you get confronted with things you want and obstacles to getting them. Humans can never get the things they want—like true love—so we're never satisfied, always sad. It's easier to collect tears than to be the one producing them."

"I don't know what to say—" I start.

"The worst of it isn't even wanting things in the future, but regretting the past."

"Regretting?"

"Regretting and hating the things you've done that seemed right and just at the time."

"Oh, Siobhan, what could you have—" I stop because I know what she's talking about. To gain a human life, you must take a human life.

"Cassandra, this is what the other side of love feels like," she says.

She talks more about her breakup, but I'm barely listening. She's speaking about Alden in the past tense, but all I can think about is the future—a future that seems much different than even a few hours ago.

Can I really stand to live forever if I sacrifice my chance at human love? Is a life without love worth living?

Chapter 19

Sunday, May 17

evening

"Why won't you talk to me?" I mouth the words to myself, but they're intended for Scott.

I'm sitting with Mom and Maggie at 5:30 p.m. Mass under the Sixth Station of the cross. I am fighting off fatigue from a long day of loneliness when I see Scott sitting by himself a few pews away. The church isn't that full, so he could have sat anywhere. This is a sign.

The micro-second after Mass ends, I pull away from my family and walk toward him. Unlike most people, Scott doesn't seem in a hurry to leave, but he's a few steps in front of me.

"Scott!" I yell once I get outside.

Believers of the faith pass by us, but today isn't just about faith for me. Alexei was right, I can't fight fate. Scott is my fate, faith, love, and hope.

"Cassandra, I don't want to talk to you," he says.

Yet, he came to this mass and sat in that pew. He doesn't want to break his word; his action shows he does want to unbreak our hearts.

"Scott, I'm sorry." I breathe out. *Will he catch it?* I wait for him to breathe in.

"I'm sorry, too," he says.

I want his smile, but it's not forthcoming.

"I was wrong to break up with you," I say, then go silent. He knows his line.

But he's not speaking; he's using his silence as a wall.

"Talk to me," I say to him.

"I don't have anything to say," he finally says. "I have to go."

I gently touch his unshaven face. "Scott, I'm sorry. Let's get back together, please?"

"No." But when he says it, I don't believe him. He won't look at me.

"How could you say that?"

"I told you, Cassandra, that it was forever," he reminds me.

"You don't know the meaning of the word forever!" My hand presses harder against him.

"I'm not going to be like Cody or those others." He gently removes my hand and places it by my side. His fingers flick my white dress. "I'm not going to be like a yo-yo you play with."

"Scott, you're nothing like Cody."

"Cassandra, don't you get it? It's not about me. It's about you."

"What are you talking about?" I take his right hand and interlock it with my left.

"I gave you a real chance to change."

People are rushing by us to their cars. But just like that morning in the library when we first spoke, it's like we're the only people on earth.

"I have changed."

"Prove it."

"How?"

He pulls his hand away, but our fingers stay twisted like tangled vines.

"It's too soon," he says. "Look, I'm hurting too, but it's too soon to get back together because nothing has changed. We need to give it time. If in a month or two—"

"No, Scott! I can't live like this for a month! Not for another day."

"Cassandra, there's no other way."

I turn around to make sure that neither Maggie nor Mom are nearby. I push up against Scott, then whisper into his ear. "Scott, please, let me make it up to you."

"Summer," Scott says firmly and just as firmly pulls his hand away from mine.

"Summer?" I bury my face in my hands.

"Come summer, if we both feel the same, then we can get back together."

"No, I can't live without you," I say and avoid his eyes. If I meet his eyes, they will pull the truth out of me: First how I saved his life, and now how I am considering taking a life to be with him.

"If we were meant to be together, then we can stand this. If it wasn't meant to be, then we'll know." He touches my bare shoulder. His words say one thing, his actions another.

"Cassandra!" I hear Mom call my name.

"Scott, I need to be with you," I beg as Mom yells my name again.

"No, I told you that—" he starts, but stops when I cry out in pain. "What's wrong?"

I cover my face with my hands, so he can't see the violet teardrop forming in my eye. I grit my teeth to fight the pain as the burning sensation covers me. Pain shoots through my body. I try to speak, but there are no words, just actions. The drop falls, and I collapse into Scott's arms.

Scott catches me and cradles me in his arms. "Cassandra, are you crying?"

"For you, I will." My face stays hidden so he can't see the pain twisting my mouth as another small, violet tear falls from my eyes. "For you, I would die. For you, I would kill." I say the words, hoping I will be sure of them soon.

He stops my words with a soft, short kiss, but I pull him closer and kiss harder, longer, wetter, forever. As our lips come apart, our hands come together, and Scott helps me in my weakened state toward his car. Along the way, we stop, and he puts the heart necklace on me without a word. We walk on as Mom and Maggie disappear like a fading sun into the horizon.

"I can smell it on you," Mom says the moment I walk through the door before midnight.

Scott and I spent the day making up and making out. Mom, Maggie, and even Veronica all wait for me.

"Leave me alone." I'm defiant because I am not alone now. I am with Scott, forever.

"Cassandra, what are we going to do with you?" Maggie says, shaking her head.

I sip from my water bottle, feeling dehydrated and weak from crying so little, then kissing so much.

"Get back here," Mom says as I try to move toward the stairs. My nature and nurture tell me to turn around. To obey. My new self keeps walking even as Maggie shouts my name again. I only pause when I'm in the shadows, able to see without being seen.

"Let her go," Veronica whispers. "Let her be."

"You're supposed to be in charge!" Maggie turns her anger on Veronica.

"I am in charge," Veronica hisses back.

"Act like it," Mom shouts. "Do something about this wild child."

"I know what's going on," Veronica snaps back. "Maggie, I know you think you'll force me aside, but let me tell you something: There's a lot that you don't know."

"Veronica, why would you think such a thing?" Maggie asks.

Veronica says nothing.

As I walk away, I think about Maggie, Mom, and Siobhan all telling me, "You'll know what you need to know when you need to know it." I recognize the look on Maggie's face as one I've seen in the mirror: the look of not knowing. Like the family in Hamlet, in this house, intrigue is everywhere, while truth is nowhere. The only true thing is love. It is real, and it is mine.

Chapter 20

Wednesday, May 20

after school

"Are we going to talk about that little stunt you pulled in bio, Samantha?"

"I've got nothing to talk about with you until you say the words I want to hear: criss-cross. Nothing," Samantha answers, then slams her locker shut at the end of the school day.

"You haven't been online, you're ignoring me at school." I switch tones. "I'm concerned."

"You're not concerned," she snaps back. "You're a tear collector."

"Samantha, please," I whisper, but the sound is sucked into the clamor of weekend plans made and betrayed. "You said you'd never say those words aloud. Friends don't lie to—"

"Well, you said you were my friend, but that was just a lie."

"I am your friend," I remind her. "You're the one who won't talk to me."

"Maybe," she mumbles.

The truth is somewhere in between. I need to stay friends with Samantha to protect myself. I want to stay friends with her because I owe her that. I fear staying friends with her because she scares me. As before with Scott, I can't get myself free of her grasp.

"You only care about me when I'm hurting," she says. "Well, guess what? I am."

"Tell me what's going on."

"What, so you can get me to cry and get your fix? You're no better than Mark or my mom. You're a junkie." She coughs and cracks a smile. "Like I'm one to talk about addiction!"

"Samantha, please, I'm—"

She starts to walk away.

"Look, I have a few hours before I'm volunteering at the hospital. If you want to hang out, fine. If not, that's fine, too. I'm sorry if I've hurt you, but now, I'm here for you, Samantha. Let me in, please. I'm sorry."

"That's hard for me to do." She picks at her silver skull earring like a scab.

"You don't have to be like your favorite card game: Uno, one, alone. Let me in."

"Why, Cassandra, so you can use me?"

"No, Samantha, so I can help you," I say softly. "Let me help you."

"Like I told you: What I got, nobody can heal."

I reach across and touch her scarred back. "All scars heal if you let them."

"Let me guess—all it takes is time and tears?" I notice a smile at the crease of her lips.

"And donuts." I say. She laughs, pretends to drool, and motions for me to follow her to her car to take us to Tim Horton. She's thinking about donuts; I'm thinking about a do not: Caleb. I don't want to want to be thinking about him, for Scott's sake and my own sanity. I'm even willing to re-enter Samantha's intense insanity to distract me from thoughts just as crazy.

"Why are you never online?" I ask as we sit down. I'm drinking from my water bottle, while she sips black coffee. No cream or sugar because there's enough of that in the six chocolate-frosted éclairs I bought for her. She consumes each of them in four bites.

"Mark sold my computer for drugs."

"That's terrible."

"It was wrong for me to compare you to him," she says, stirring her coffee. "You're not a monster, but he is. Funny how that works."

"What?"

"I always knew deep down that things like vampires aren't real, but I wanted it to be true so badly," she whispers. "Then I met you and realized the supernatural *is* real. And then I thought: Maybe how your kind came about would also explain the way vampires emerged."

"Samantha, there's nothing supernatural about me," I remind her. "I'm no more supernatural than any other species on the planet. Think of me that way."

"But I can't," she confesses. "To me, you're like this mythical being. That's why I know you can help me with Mark. I know he's the monster, not you."

"He's not a monster." I say, but I don't know that for sure.

Could Mark actually be the result of breeding between a tear collector and a human? Does he thirst for the tears he causes?

"To me, he is," she says. "That's why he must be destroyed."

"I told you before, I can't sit around and listen to you spin these crazy plans."

"They're not crazy."

The steam from her coffee merges with the sweat on her face.

"I don't think you'll go through with them because I won't help."

"When you needed help, I helped you! Why won't you help me now?" As always, Samantha's raised voice and odd appearance attracts unwanted attention from disapproving adults.

"I have told you to call the police."

"But they don't do anything!" More adults shoot us anxious glares.

"If you don't call them, I will. Or child services—or somebody."

"I'm living in my car again, but I'm not sure how long that will last," she mumbles. "He'll sell it soon enough. You have no idea what it's like to live with an addict."

I let that comment pass. "You can get through this. You're so strong."

"I forget that sometimes." She sips her coffee slowly as if she's savoring the bitterness.

"Like at the prom. Remember how happy you were that night?"

"That was because of Caleb," she says.

I hide my Cheshire smile and pounce like a cat. "So what's he like?" I ask.

Samantha starts telling me what little she knows about Caleb, which isn't much different than what she's told me before. She's answering my basic questions, but it's not really what I want to know. What I want to understand is why I can't stop thinking about him. The only explanation I have is that he filled the void. Just like Samantha filled the void after Robyn, Caleb gave me something to think about after Scott. That's all he is, but even as the thoughts enter my head, something deeper overrides them. I'm listening to Samantha, but the only words that matter are the ones in my head.

That's not all he is, and you know it. He's something more than just another male. What else could explain the connection unless—

"You listening? Do you think he's fine, too? Hey, don't get any ideas!"

But I do have one. "Can you drop me at the hospital for my volunteer shift?"

"Saint Florence fucking Nightingale." She laughs loudly.

I don't tell her I'm working tonight because I know Caleb is going to be there. I'm no saint; in fact, I'm a terrible sinner.

Before I see Caleb, I call Scott. If nature needs balance, then which way will the scales tip? We talk about everything—like his biology presentation on cancer as a parasite—yet discuss nothing that matters. We don't talk about our breakup; we don't talk about his possible future at Powers. It's as if he's too afraid to trust me again. We make plans for later, but something isn't right.

If I keep thinking about Scott, I tell myself, then I won't think about Caleb. Nor will I think about Alexei, whom I sense is already here despite what he writes in his emails. He's not to be trusted—no tear collector is. I've proved that my whole life.

I tell Scott I love him before I hang up; he does the same. Just words. Just words, not actions. I seek out Caleb. Like water finding its level, I seem to know where to find him.

"I wanted to thank you again for your help on my project," I tell Caleb.

He is dressed in full young-doctor mode—so handsome and confident. We're outside a closed door in the pediatric wing. Walking down these halls creates an energy rush even from a distance. There is so much sadness here. There are so many Beccas here: young lives ready to be lost.

"How did it turn out?" he asks. "Did you get an A or did Mr. A. figure out I helped?"

I start in on the details of schoolwork, but it bores me to talk about these things with him. I switch instead to my real work at school: drama creation. He leans closer, eager to hear it all.

"You talk to that guy Craig much?" Caleb asks. His jacket is off, tie loose.

"Craig?" We walk together. "I've tried to, but he won't respond. Why?"

"He's the guy who broke up with his girlfriend at the prom, right?"

I nod. "How do you remember that?"

"Well, just between you and me, I might have had something to do with that."

"What?"

"I asked Samantha how she knew you. She told me about Robyn. She said Brittney and Craig were the reasons that Robyn died. So at the prom, we had words. He's kind of a jerk."

"No, he's a jock; she's a jerk."

Caleb laughs, and I join him. Our laughs sound alike.

"Anyway, I guess whatever I said caused a problem because I heard they broke up." Caleb's smile is big enough to fill his face and mine. "So I guess that's something. They didn't get away with it. I hate when bad people get away with doing bad things. Don't you?"

I'm as confused as I am distracted. In the room near where we stand, I sense sadness. I break away from staring at Caleb's eyes, but he's got the same distracted look on his face. He opens the door for me. I'm one step behind.

Before I enter the room filled with a crying family, I turn to Caleb. "But you don't know Brittney, Craig, or Robyn, so why did you get involved?"

Just before Caleb steps into the room, he whispers into my ear, "I did it for you."

Before all my senses implode and I fall further, I exhale a question, "For me?"

As I listen to Caleb comfort the grieving parents, I hear myself in him. When our eyes lock across the tear-filled faces in the room, a sixth sense takes over, and I feel like I'm drowning.

Chapter 21

Friday, May 22

after school

"Have you decided, Scott?" I ask.

We sit at Paul's Coney Island at the back booth on the same side of the table. Scott is trying to decide what to order for his dinner before he starts working his shift.

"I've eaten everything on this menu, and it all tastes the same."

"Bad." We say at the same time, then laugh together.

These few seconds define Scott and me. We laugh a lot, we think a lot alike, and we can't decide. I can't decide what to do about him, about Samantha, about Becca, or my own future. He can't decide if he's going back to Powers, which to me means he can't decide if he really loves me.

A sudden, scary thought hits me. *If he loves me, he wouldn't leave me. If he doesn't love me, how can I even consider leaving my family to be with him?*

"Well, it's Friday, I guess I'll have the fish sandwich."

"Wow, you are devout! Nobody still eats fish on Fridays except during Lent."

Scott laughs. "Well, we're faithful, and for a while we didn't have much money, so I think we lived on fish sticks and mac 'n' cheese every day of the week. I find it comforting now."

"It sounds awful." I mimic a gagging motion.

"It was! This means they'll probably add it to the menu here."

We laugh again. "No, but really, your faith isn't what you say; it's what you do."

I blow him a kiss, then say in my sexiest voice, "Or don't do." I pretend to pout.

He motions for me to keep my voice down. "You're embarrassing me."

I lean closer. "Sorry, I've never been with a guy who didn't want me to--"

He takes my hand. "I want to, but I need to be true to myself. You understand?"

I squeeze his hand as a response, but inside my mind screams, *More than you can know!*

"But it's not because I don't love you, Cassandra."

With my forehead touching his, I ask a most dangerous question. "How do you know?"

He shakes his head as if he's stunned by the question. "How do I know I love you?"

"Like you said, your faith isn't something you say; it's something you do. Isn't love the same way? We can't do one thing people do because of my rules, and I can't make you feel good because of your beliefs. If we can't show our love, then how do we know for sure?"

"Do you remember the first time we talked, really talked? That day in the library when Samantha made that big scene?"

I nod and gently touch the heart necklace, back in its familiar place. "How could I forget? I thought she was going to kill us."

"And I said something like, 'If love was easy, it wouldn't hurt, and if it didn't hurt, it wouldn't matter.' When I left to go to class, you smiled at me. Remember? Do you know why?"

I nod my head. I will never forget that conversation, but I don't get the question. "Why?"

"Right after that, I started looking online for quotes about falling in love at first sight and I found this one. This is why: 'When I saw you, I fell in love, and you smiled because you knew.'"

After Scott goes to work, I call Samantha to see if she wants to hang out, but she doesn't pick up. Amanda said she needed to study tonight, but that's not different than any other night. I think about calling Michael or some of Robyn's old friends, Sara and Elizabeth, but instead I enjoy the solitary walk home--maybe because I know it's not really solitary. Scott's words are with me, and I can't imagine them—or him—ever leaving me. He might not be able to decide some things, and despite what he says, he is more a man of words than action, but the words he used shook me like an earthquake.

I'm less than a half mile from home when my phone rings. Samantha.

"Hey, Sam—"

"Cassandra, you need to help me," she says, in between sobs. "It's Mark."

"What now?" She doesn't answer right away because she can't speak through the torrent of tears. I could probably guess, since almost every conversation with Samantha is the same: I tell her a little more about tear collectors, and in return she tells me about Mark and her mom, which always makes her cry. We give each other what we need; it's mutualism in motion.

"Samantha, are you there?"

"I'm afraid."

It's hard to hear her. There's a lot of noise in the background.

"Why don't you call the police?"

"He told me and Mom if we ever did that, he'd lock us in the house, set it on fire, and all the police would find would be our ashes. He's crazy. He'd do it."

"Then just leave!"

"My mom won't go, and I can't abandon her to him with what he's—"

"What is he doing to her?"

She sniffs, coughs, cries. "It's not what he's doing that's killing her; it's who he is!"

"What?"

"A psychopath," she hisses.

"Listen, Samantha, I think you should—"

But that's as far as I get before I hear a slapping sound, followed by the phone crashing onto the floor.

"Samantha! Samantha!" I scream, but she doesn't answer.

I think about running back to tell Scott, but I'm not sure he'd know what to do. I think about calling the police, but I remember what Samantha said he'd do. Maybe Mark *is* crazy and would rather burn the house down with all of them in it than go back to prison. Who can save Samantha? Who can help me? Who would do *anything* for me?"

Caleb arrives in a white Dodge Charger in less than ten minutes. I told him the situation on the phone, including what Mark said he'd do if the police showed up. As we drive to Samantha's house, I try to come up with a plan, but there's nothing I can share with Caleb since he doesn't know what I am. The best plan would be to get Samantha out of the house, get her head on my shoulders, and, if she's got any tears left, take them all. Then, unless Mark has a weapon, I could take him down since I'd be energized. But how would I explain that to Caleb? How would I explain when Samantha's tears flow through my skin and into my veins making my eyes roll back in my head? In that moment, I'm sure I look like a junkie who has just shot up and is feeling the warmth of nature's chemistry working its way through the bloodstream. There is no mundane way to explain tear collector chemistry.

We get to her house without a rescue plan in place.

"Stay here!" Caleb says. When I start to get out of the car, he locks my door. It won't hold me physically—I can unlock the door from the inside—but it does send me the clear message he wants to handle this. I decide to just watch . . . for now.

"Samantha, Samantha!" he yells as he walks toward the door.

Caleb is six feet tall and well-built like Craig, but I suspect Caleb is a healer, not a fighter. I get my phone ready in case I need to call the police no, matter what the risk. One person who thought I was their friend already died from my inaction. I won't have another set of bloody human remains on my hands.

"Samantha! It's Caleb!" he shouts at the door.

I don't know how much she told him about her home life, but even from a distance, I sense no fear in Caleb. Despite what he told me, I get out of the car. I don't know what to do, but I want to be ready just in case.

"Caleb!" Samantha runs out the door. Her face is bloody, so Caleb strips off his white shirt to clear away the blood. I get closer. Maybe Mark has left. Maybe this is over.

"It's okay," Caleb says once he wipes the blood from her face. He pulls her head onto his shoulder, and she cries, no doubt tears of relief since her tears of terror must be gone.

They walk together toward the car, her face buried in his shoulder. They're about five feet away when the front door opens. A scary-skinny woman wearing a bloodied, pink beater stumbles from the porch onto the lawn. She trips and lands face-first in the grass. Behind her stands Mark.

"Who the fuck are you?" Mark is shirtless: beer in one hand, a studded belt in the other.

Caleb doesn't answer, look up, or turn around. He just keeps comforting Samantha, while I head toward the woman in the grass. I assume it's Samantha's mom. Just as I've hidden my family from Samantha—other than the night we saved Scott—her mother is just a name to me, not a person.

"I said, who the fuck are you?" Mark steps off the porch and staggers toward Caleb.

Still Caleb doesn't respond. Instead he pulls Samantha tight, like he's trying to squeeze her inside himself to protect her. She keeps crying, but then I notice something odd when Caleb finally lifts his face. He's smiling, and his blue eyes seem almost ablaze.

Mark stumbles another step toward Caleb. "That's it, you're so—"

This is as far as Mark gets before Caleb pushes Samantha away from him, turns on his heels, and dives into Mark, knocking him to the ground. Caleb throws two quick punches against Mark's jaw. Something flies out. Maybe Mark's last tooth? Mark pushes Caleb off and starts to crawl away, but Caleb dives on his back and locks his arms around Mark's neck. Mark's eyes roll back in his head as he gasps, and oddly, so do Caleb's eyes.

I run over to Samantha's mom to comfort her—and to feed Veronica. As I'm taking the handkerchief from my purse, I sense a shadow over me. I look up, and there's Caleb. His eyes now look as peaceful as the ocean between tides.

"What are you doing?" he asks.

"Nothing, just trying to help."

He looks down at me like the sun over the earth. When he smiles, something chills and warms within me at the same time.

"Something is different," Veronica says as I sit next to her.

I've prepared the handkerchief as always, but she's right. The tears I captured from Samantha's mom were those of pain and terror, more like Alexei would collect. By the time I got to Samantha, she had cried herself out.

I tell Veronica the story. Even as her face comes to life from the tears revitalizing her, there's a darkness in her expression.

"No, something is different about you."

"No, Veronica, everything's okay. It was just a little scary."

She grabs the heart necklace Scott gave back to me. "Liar!"

"I don't know what you're talking about."

"You met with him. I knew it." She pulls the heart necklace from my neck.

"I know you're scared for me, for you, but you need to trust that I'll do the right thing."

Veronica hands me back the necklace. "You've met him. Your soulmate."

"That's why it's so hard. I know you can't understand. Trust me, Veronica."

"How can I trust you when I see you conspiring with Maggie? I might be old, but I know what is going on—exactly what is going on. Maggie wants to take over, right?"

"I don't know anything about that." I try to re-attach the necklace, but it's broken.

"Once you mate, the next generation starts, and there can be no more than four. That means either I die or Maggie does. Who would you choose?"

"Veronica, no. It's not like that."

"I asked you, Cassandra: who would you choose?"

"Don't make me answer that!"

She lies back in the bed, then lets out a big sigh. "You will do what you are supposed to do. You will mate with another tear collect-or and start the next generation. As for Maggie, well, as there can be no more than four generations, she needs to be very careful."

Her room—and her words—have never seemed darker.

"Why do you say that?"

"There can be no more than four, but I can decide if there are less," she whispers. "Maybe we could have only three generations for a while. I know she is trying to force me out."

"How do you know that?"

She sits straight up in bed, grabs my wrist, and squeezes it. "Because I did the same!"

"Let go, please."

She squeezes so tightly it feels like the blood supply is being cut off.

"Remember this, Di'mah, there are many tear collectors," she says as she releases her grip. "But there is only one Veronica."

Chapter 22

Monday, May 25

afternoon

"Becca, do you want to take a walk?" I ask softly, the way you're supposed to speak at a cemetery.

She stares ahead at Robyn's grave, silent as the stone with her sister's name.

I've joined the Berrys at the cemetery. Becca stands with her parents at Robyn's grave. I'm right behind her; behind us are a few of their relatives from out of town. Maggie is with us, too.

"Whatever you want, Short Stuff," I say, placing my hand on her shoulder.

She finally turns to me and says, "I want Robyn back."

I bend down and hug her, then say "Me too, Becca. Me too."

Mrs. Berry turns around and glances at us. Her eyes are red, yet more tears still come.

"You won't leave me," Becca says.

"Never."

We each lay a single white flower on the grave. The flowers are courtesy of Simon's son, Asa, who owns this cemetery. To get more visitors on Memorial Day, Asa offered free flowers. People must have thought he was so generous. If only they knew his true motivation.

"But I'll leave you," Becca says, very softly. Less than a whisper.

"Don't talk that way."

"I know what's going on," Becca says, softer yet.

"Stop."

"I'm so sorry."

"Sorry?"

"I'm going to make everybody feel bad, just like we all do for Robyn," she says. "I don't want to die and make everybody sad. I want people to be happy."

I hug Becca, not to squeeze out her tears, but to try to make her happy, even if it's only for this second in this place where happiness rarely visits. The emotion of the afternoon has stolen her hope and strength. My hugs can't give her either; only my actions can.

"Thank you for coming out today, Cassandra. It means a lot to Becca," Mr. Berry says.

"I'd hoped Samantha might be with you. How is she doing?" Mrs. Berry asks.

I answer by telling them about what went down the other evening, leaving out the part about how Caleb choked Mark unconscious. Unlike me—unlike Scott—Caleb is a person of action.

"That poor, poor girl." Mrs. Berry shakes her head. "No one deserves that fate."

"She doesn't know what to do, and to be honest, I don't either."

They think I'm talking about Samantha; they don't know that I'm talking about everything in my life right now.

"How could a mother let a child suffer that way?" Mrs. Berry asks me, but I wonder if she asks herself the same question about Becca.

I could stop all this suffering with one decision.

"She's tough. What's the saying? What doesn't kill you makes you stronger. I think—"

Mrs. Berry cuts me off. She holds her chin high, almost defiant. "Suffering doesn't make you stronger, Cassandra. It makes you numb. Sometimes I wish I couldn't feel anything."

"No, Mrs. Berry, you don't want that. You want to feel. Especially love, right?"

"The more you feel love, the more you feel loss." She takes Becca's hand, squeezes it tight, and then falls to her knees in front of Robyn's grave. She's overwhelmed, and so am I. If there were no love in the world, there'd be no grief. If there were no grief, I wouldn't exist.

"The little girl seemed upset," Maggie says as we return to her car, a silver Toyota Prius.

"Becca," I say. "Her name is Becca. She's the one who's dying. I told you about her."

"How much longer?" Maggie asks in the tone a vulture would use if it could speak.

"I don't know. Less than a year?"

"You really like her, don't you?"

"It's more than that," I say. "I told her parents I'd be there, but I can't do it. I'm so busy with everyone else, but it's more than that. I just can't face seeing her, knowing—"

"Knowing she's going to die," Maggie says.

"Why do you have to say it like that?" I fire back.

Most of the other cars have pulled away, but we're still sitting. Maggie rolls the window down so we both can absorb the tear-filled mist. "She doesn't have to," Maggie says.

"But Veronica can't," I remind her. "She's too weak. And Mom said—"

"Your mother doesn't know everything," Maggie says.

"What do you mean?"

Maggie starts to speak, stops, and then whispers, "Maybe I could help."

"But I thought only Veronica had the ability to perform miracles."

"So it is said, but I think that's something we've all been led to believe by Veronica."

"I don't understand." I lie often, but truer words I have never spoken.

"If I could perform this miracle, then that would show everyone, including Veronica, that it is time for her to surrender her place to me."

"What if she doesn't?"

"Don't act so dumb," she says. "I'm not some boy you need to hide your intelligence from. You know what happens."

"I don't. No one tells me anything," I protest.

"That's because everyone wants to protect you," she says. "And themselves."

"Themselves?"

"What will you think of your mother when she comes to you and tells you that your grandmother Maggie must die?" Maggie says. "What will you think of her then?"

"But why?"

"When you mate—when you start the next generation—then one generation must depart. There can be no more than four generations. It has always been; it will always be this way," Maggie says. "But if Veronica refuses to surrender her spot, then I'm the one who will die."

"Then I won't start the next generation," I say.

"It is a biological imperative that our species continues. You don't have a choice. You must mate with Alexei. Once that begins, then Veronica must announce at the Feastday celebration if she plans to continue living for another generation. If she does, then there is no hope for me."

"So you're saying that when I create another life, I'm ending yours?"

"Yes, Cassandra," Maggie says.

"There has to be another way!"

"The only chance would be if Veronica knew that I have the power to perform miracles," Maggie says. "I could save Becca just like Veronica saved Scott."

"You would do that for me?" I say. I know, of course, she's doing it for herself.

"Yes, but in return, I would expect something," she counters.

"What?"

"If that girl's life matters so much to you, then you wouldn't need to ask what."

"That's not fair!"

"Nothing is, Cassandra. You're old enough to know that by now," she says. "Well?"

I answer by swinging open the car door and running. I can run, but to what end? I know what I am running from, but what am I running to? Or am I running? Maybe I'm being pulled.

"Cassandra!" I hear Maggie shout my name, but I hear only darkness and shout back silence. She's somewhere off in the distance, probably standing next to her car.

"Cassandra! Get back here!" Maggie shouts again, but it's softer. She's fading.

Like some silly, middle-school boy, I'm engaged in a game of hide-and-go-seek in a cemetery. Night is falling, and the wind is picking up, but I walk on until I find Robyn's grave again. I see the empty green grass next to it. I imagine myself less than a year from now in this same spot with more flowers and Becca's name on a stone next to her sister's.

I hear Maggie yell my name in the distance as my skin absorbs the tiniest molecules of tears floating in the air. Sitting on the increasingly cold cemetery grass, I'm not thinking about life and death, but love and hate. People always talk about the destructive power of hate. Hate has nothing on love when it comes to destruction. Without hesitation, I make the call.

"Hello, Cassandra. I was hoping you would call."

"I'm sorry to call you like this, but I need help. Will you help me?" I ask.

"Of course, Cassandra, I'll do anything to help you. What do you need?"

The answer to that question is vast, and seems to change every second. I thought I knew what I needed, but somehow it got all mixed up with the human notion of wanting.

"I need a ride home." I say.

"Where are you?"

"I'm at Cyrene Cemetery." I start to give directions, but he cuts me off.

"I know where it is. I can be there in about ten minutes."

"Thanks," I say. "You've done so much for me. How can I return the favor?"

Can you hear a smile through the phone? Can you see blue eyes flash in delight on wireless signals through the air? Can he see me melt when his words reach my ears?

"Cassandra, I think there's a lot we can do for each other."

I start toward the front gate of the cemetery when I hear that sound: five taps of a cane. Simon's cane.

At the front gate, Simon stands stone silent dressed in black except for the red flower in his lapel and the red strip on his fedora. The tapping of his cane against the wrought iron gates echoes like thunder. His son, Asa, and two of Asa's cousins stand behind Simon. All are dressed the same.

"Tell me: where is Alexei?" Simon asks.

I want to run away, but wonder if Caleb could find me. Instead, I hold my ground and wait for him to rescue me. I've never relied on anyone else before, but I need Caleb. I won't answer Simon's question or look at that snarling smile. His voice and eyes drown me in fear.

"Answer my question, or else!"

I feel the tip of his cane against my chin. He pushes up, but I knock the cane away. In a flash, one of the cousins retrieves it for him. Simon grabs it.

"I know everything. Trust me." His dark eyes pierce me like a silver sword.

The cousins stand next to me now. One pins my arms behind my back, while the other pushes up my chin, exposing my neck. Like me, they're full of tears and energy. I could fight one of them, but not four male tear collectors.

In the swirl of his snarl, Maggie's deceit, and my panic, clarity arrives like a beam of light.

"I'll never, ever mate with him! I won't bring another tear collector into this world, this madness."

"You don't have a choice." Simon is the calm in the eye of my storm.

"Yes. That's the first choice: knowing I have a choice."

I stare him down. His small eyes become almost pinpoints: black laser beams shooting through my eyes into my heart.

"You will mate with Alexei."

"Never!"

We all hear a car coming closer. I pray it's Caleb; they have no clue who it might be, but they don't want witnesses to what surely comes next. Simon motions for the cousins to let me go. They release me and walk back behind Simon. Simon shakes his head and laughs that bone-chilling cackle. The sound echoes through the empty cemetery filled only with souls.

Simon raises his cane again and rests it on my shoulder. I try not to show my pain.

"Do your duty, or else."

I don't ask what "or else" means because I know. Death.

Chapter 23

Wednesday, May 27

school day

"Can't we talk about this?" I gently touch Samantha's hand as I ask the question.

"No." She stares at a huge book on the table between us. We're in a small study room in the library. It's the first time we've spoken since Caleb rescued her. Her face still shows Mark's marks.

"I reached out to help you, but you—"

"Caleb saved me, not you. Besides, you reach out to help yourself."

"Listen, stop that," I counter. "I don't need you, Samantha. Don't you get that? If you were just some other girl, I would have collected your tears and moved on. But you're not. You're my friend."

"Like Amanda?"

"Samantha, you're impossible!" I shout, grateful these study rooms are almost soundproof. "I spend time with you, and you accuse me of having only evil intentions. I don't spend time with you, and you sound like some jealous boyfriend. I can't deal with you anymore! I'm *your* friend, but you don't act like a friend to me."

"Friends don't lie to each other."

"I had to lie to you," I remind her. "'I have to protect myself.'"

"No, not about that," she says. "You lied about helping me with Mark. You saw what he's capable of, but then again, you're used to watching human misery. You wallow in it."

"I won't commit murder," I whisper.

"You killed Scott's grandmother." She's talking way too loud. "How is this different?"

"I didn't kill his grandmother, and Veronica didn't either. She was dying."

"We're all dying the second after we're born!"

"Samantha, you know what I mean. She was sick. Her body was there, but whatever part of her that was Scott's grandmother was long gone. It was a mercy killing."

"And this would be too!" She slams her fists hard against the table.

"It's not the same."

"How can you say that?" she counters. "Show me some mercy."

"You're reaching."

"I thought I knew what pain was," she says, her anger trumping any tears. "The pain of how Mark hurt me. The pain of feeling empty and alone, like a freak. But I was wrong."

"Wrong?"

"You know how Scott talked about watching his grandmother die a little bit every day?" she asks. "That's how I feel. Every day that Mark lives in my house, I watch both Mom and myself die a little more. Mom's slipping away, and there's nothing I can do to stop it. You could help."

"Samantha, no."

"One day, rather than grabbing me around the wrist," she says, pulling up her sleeve to show me the still-bluish skin on her wrist, "he'll grab me around the throat!"

I'm silent in the roar of her screaming; I'm expressionless in the face of her pain.

"You have to decide right now: are you going through with it?" Her black eye make-up starts to run. "Tell me now that you'll help me, and I'll help you. If not, I'll put so much fucking fire on the bridge between us that it will burn forever."

I take a deep breath, soak in her tears from a distance, and sip my water bottle. I don't know what to decide: Mark does need to die, but I can't kill him. I'm not ready.

"No," I say.

She opens the big book in front of her. "When you needed me, I was there, but now that I need your help, you're absent. You're not a human or a tear collector, you are a *parasite*."

"Please, Samantha, don't talk this way."

"You leech off people in pain. I hate you! I never want to see you again."

"I'm sorry you feel hurt."

That's all Samantha is now: sorrow and hurt feelings.

"You disgust me with your lies," she says. Rather than slamming the book in front of her shut, she instead starts paging through it. "And that's all you've ever told me: lies!"

"That's not true," I lie.

"You must think you're real funny, real clever," she says. "You knew I'd believe all this bullshit about being a tear collector. But I know now that's all a fucking lie as well."

I'm silent again. Part of me wants Samantha to believe in me, the other part is relieved to hear her question everything I've said, and more importantly, everything she's seen.

"There's no such thing as tear collectors. That's just a sick story you told to use me for some reason. 'Oh, get freaky Samantha; she believes in vampires; she'll believe this bullshit.'"

More silence from me; more righteous anger from her.

"And I did. I'd ask you questions, and you always had some bullshit to feed me, to keep me hooked like Mark does to my mom with meth. How could someone be so cruel?"

"I'm not cruel," I finally say in my defense. "I'm a caring person who—"

"You don't care about anyone, but you do a better job of hiding it than your cousin, Alexei. He's crazy, but that's not the worst of what he is—what you are, too."

"And what is that?"

"You're not a tear collector; neither is he! You're psychopaths," she hisses. "Look, here."

I say nothing. She pushes the book in front of me and points at the page.

"Go ahead; read it!"

"This is crazy." I start to gather my stuff to leave.

"You're afraid of the truth. This is you and your cousin to a T."

"I'm leaving," I announce.

"Listen to me!" She grabs my wrist with a vise-like grip.

She must have learned this from Mark.

"You're superficial, lacking remorse, guilt, or empathy. You're deceitful and manipulative."

"Let go!"

Her nails dig deeper into my wrist. I must escape before she rips open the skin and I start to bleed. Once I start, I may never stop! Now I'm wishing this study room didn't block out so much sound.

"Here are some good ones: shallow emotions, impulsive, and poor behavioral control." Her voice is as unhinged as the look in her eyes. "Do you feel like you're looking in a mirror?"

"Stop it, Samantha! Just stop it."

"You waltz around this school breaking hearts, betraying friends, and telling lies. Oh, and this one: constant need for stimulation! I thought I needed chaos to not feel empty, but that's why you spread rumors. You don't need tears. You need the drama because you're bored."

"You're hurting me," I tell her.

One drop of blood drips from my wrist, and I feel faint.

"You hurt everyone, and you don't fucking care," she says as releases me. "I'm done with you. If you won't help me, I've got no use for you. You're not a friend. You're nothing, because you feel nothing—not because of some supernatural bullshit you thought I'd swallow, but because you can't. You're wrong about Brittney. She isn't the psychopath. You are!"

I grab my things, but before I can leave, she hurls her book at me.

"You might want this!"

The huge book bounces off my back and falls to the floor with a thud: the DSM IV.

As I run away from Samantha, I wonder if I'll cry again—tears of relief knowing I don't need to worry about Samantha telling our secrets or tears of anger for all the terrible things she said about me. Maybe tears of loss knowing we'll never be friends again. Or even tears of truth—for I *am* all that she says I am.

"Cassandra, what's wrong?" Scott asks as he taps on the glass.

I ran right from the library to his car. I'm curled in the backseat with a makeshift bandage wrapped around my wrist. Like this cut, things with Samantha will mend. Yet I sense that means more blood will flow.

When I don't answer, he sits down next to me, pulling my head into his lap. He gently strokes my hair.

"Whatever it is, let me help."

"I hate myself," I say, then bang my fists against my face.

"You can't hate yourself," Scott purrs. "Because I love you."

"You shouldn't."

"Does this have something to do with Samantha?"

"Why?"

"Well, the two of you left class for the library together, but she's the only one who came back," Scott explains. "And she had this strange look on her face."

"What?"

"Like she was happy," Scott says, then laughs. "Well, it looked strange on her."

"We're done being friends. I'm sorry."

"Do you want to talk about it?"

"No." I bury myself in Scott's arms.

"I wish I knew what to say," he says softly. "That's one of the things I love about you, Cassandra: You always know the right thing to say when somebody is feeling bad."

I swallow hard.

"When Robyn died, you were so helpful. I'm sorry I don't know what to say."

"There's nothing to say now," I mutter. "Samantha said everything."

"What? What did she say to you?" He pulls me tighter.

"She's crazy," I say, starting to spin the web. "I guess we've both always known that Samantha was a little odd with the vampire obsession and everything, but it's worse than that. She has worse problems than I can help with. She's unstable and has lost touch with reality."

"Given the reality of the past few months, that's not a bad idea," Scott jokes.

I sink into myself like a black hole collapsing.

"Cassandra, whatever it is, it will go away," he says, then leans closer. "Let's go back to my house. My mom won't be home from work for a few hours. Maybe we could—"

"No, Scott, no!" I pull away from him and sit up on the other side of the car.

"I'm sorry, I just don't know what to say," he says, reaching out for me.

I turn my back, then open the door. "I know you don't," I say as I leave Scott behind. "You don't know what to say because you don't know the real me. And Scott, you never can."

Scott doesn't follow me, and I don't blame him. He must have skipped seventh period because as I'm walking into school to get my things, everyone else is leaving. I sort through the sea of Lapeer High humanity to locate the person I need to see, but not for tears: Amanda.

"Hey, Amanda!" I call out.

She's talking with Sara and Elizabeth but shoots me a wave. A few seconds later, she joins me out in front of the school.

"You working tonight?"

"No, I asked to take off some shifts to study for finals," she says. "You?"

"I guess I'm working for you, then. Could you gimme a ride?"

"Sure thing," she says, and we walk to her car.

Along the way, rather than talking with each other, we grab our phones and check messages. None from Scott or Samantha. Or Caleb.

"I've been thinking about you," I say once we're in the car and on our way.

"Really?"

"What you talked about before, about not having a boyfriend," I say, very slowly. "Well, I think you don't know how lucky you are."

"Lucky?"

"Trust me, for all the pain it causes, it's just not worth it."

"That's easy for you to say, Cassandra," she says, although she doesn't sound angry. "It's easy for a person who's had boyfriends to say it's not important."

"No, Amanda, just the opposite," I counter. "I'm telling you because I've had these experiences. I know what I'm talking about. You're not missing anything."

"That's nice of you to say." I want her to hurry, but she drives exactly the speed limit.

"And I think I know why you've been so lucky," I say.

"You keep using that word," she says, then laughs. "I sure don't feel lucky."

"But you are because you've avoided all this stupid, wasteful drama."

"Well, maybe I haven't met him," she says as she brakes for a yellow light.

"Who?"

"My soulmate, that one perfect person who was meant for me," she explains. "That's why you've broken up with so many guys, Cassandra, because they're not your soulmates."

I am silent; the universe shouts at me through this shy girl.

"I mean that one person in your life who understands you and knows everything about you even before they meet you. You don't need to explain yourself. You just know," she says.

"By that logic, the fact that you haven't had a boyfriend in high school means nothing," I say. "It just means you haven't wasted time or given the most secret part of yourself to the wrong person."

"So I just have to wait as I look for that right person?" She lets out a small laugh.

"It shouldn't be so hard," I say.

"Why's that?"

"Because he's looking for you, too."

I feel faint again, but not from blood loss.

"Are you okay?" she asks as we pull into the hospital parking lot.

"I need to go," I say.

Taking a deep breath, I head for destiny's waiting, open door.

"Cassandra," Caleb says when he sees me standing in the hospital hall.

"What did you mean, 'There's a lot we can do for each other'?" I ask.

He motions for me to follow. We walk in perfect stride until he finds a vacant room. We go inside. He locks the door on us and dims the light. We sit on the edge of the bed. He removes his jacket and loosens his tie.

"Cassandra, I think you know exactly what I mean," he whispers. "And I think you know exactly who—or rather what—I am."

"You are..." is all I can say. He touches not my face, but the tear charm necklace.

"No. We are," he responds.

Every cell within me tingles, and then we say the words together. "Tear collectors."

"I sensed it from the first time I saw you, but I thought it couldn't be true. I thought it was another one of us, my cousin, Alexei, stalking me. Do you know him?"

"I wouldn't believe anything he tells you. He is known among the males as a habitual liar."

"Why? What do you know?"

"So much of what we know is passed down, and much of it can't be believed. The elders manipulate us like pawns on a chess board." He moves closer to me, and takes off his shirt. "I was raised with Simon's family, but then my father was exiled. My younger brother and sister stayed behind, but I knew I needed to leave, too, even though I am a pure-blood Simon."

"And if we are both what we say we are, then—"

He places my hands on his shoulders. I sense the texture and know for sure he is one of us.

His voice comes at me huskily. "If a male from the Simon line and a female from the Veronica line are about the same age, they must mate. You know why this must be and that we must be together."

"Because we are soulmates," I say, before he covers my mouth in a moist kiss.

Chapter 24

Saturday, June 6

afternoon

"How is Becca doing?" I stand with the Berrys outside Becca's hospital room.

"Not well, not well," Mrs. Berry answers. Even though I'm wearing my volunteer uniform, I'm here as a friend. "Some sort of infection."

"I'm sure the doctors will—" I start, but I stop when I catch Mrs. Berry's eyes. It does no good for us to lie to each other anymore.

"Sometimes she's strong, and other times . . . ." Mr. Berry says, then trails off.

"What can I do?" I ask.

She sighs. "Pray for a miracle; that's about the only chance."

"Honey, don't talk like that," says Mr. Berry.

"All that's left are prayers and hope, and I don't think I have any more in me," she says.

"You have your faith," I remind her. I point to the cross around her neck, just like the one I wear.

"Cassandra, dear, even that is slipping away, just like my baby."

"Becca's strong," I say.

"But I'm not anymore. I'm not," she says, collapsing into my arms.

Mr. Berry comes to comfort his wife, but I won't let go. Even through the fabric of my uniform, the tears absorb into my skin, and I feel a rush. Her weakness gives me strength—strength I'll need to sort out all the decisions that keep rushing into my life—decisions not just about love and fate but, as I think about Becca and about miracles, choices of life and death that can no longer be avoided.

After taking every tear Mrs. Berry produces, I continue my rounds. Little do the nurses know that letting me in this hospital is like letting a vampire into a blood bank.

When I pass by one room, however, I stop outside. The person inside is sleeping; there are no visitors. Less than two months ago in this room, Veronica was inside with Scott and his grandmother. All that mattered to me then was Scott.

Back in April, I told myself I would avoid tears. I'd take only what I needed to survive and to keep Veronica alive. I wouldn't live as a full tear collector but live as a human, experience love with Scott, and, once I discovered the secret, turn human. It was six weeks ago, but it seems like a lifetime with all that's happened to change those plans.

Now I crave grief to make myself strong for the action I must take. Because of Caleb, doubts about Scott wash over me like a flood. But about Becca's fate, I now am sure. She is a beacon of innocence and light in a world of darkness. I must spare the Berrys their grief and keep Becca alive. I helped Robyn die; I must help Becca live. That is more than balance. It's love.

"How many days are you volunteering for this summer?" Amanda asks.

"Probably a few more, but I do another volunteer job in the summer."

"Where?" she asks. We sit in the break room, just the two of us.

"At the Avalon Nursing Home," I explain. "My grandmother works there."

"I don't know if I could do that . . . ." As her voice trails off, my senses spike.

"Why's that, Amanda?"

"No reason," she deflects.

"It's okay, Amanda. You can tell me," I remind her. "Did one of your grandparents—?"

"My grandfather," she says sadly. "I don't want to talk about it, okay Cass?"

I take the rejection in stride with her use of the word "Cass" as acceptance of our growing friendship.

"Sure. I'm sorry. You know me: I just like to help people."

"Me too," she says and then laughs.

Amanda laughs a lot—not so much when people say something, but when she talks, like she's laughing to deflect anxiety. She's wound too tight.

"So if you're volunteering here, I assume you want to be a doctor like me?" I ask.

"No, a nurse," she says, then again, the nervous laugh.

"Really? Why not a doctor? You know there are women doctors now, right?" I joke.

"I guess for the same reason I don't take honors classes."

"I wondered about that." I gently lean toward her. "You seem smart enough."

She pauses; this is a breaking point. I look open, friendly, and accepting. I wait her out.

Amanda chews on her nails. She wears no nail polish, little make-up. She's pretty, some boy needs to tell her.

"It's okay. Everybody has reasons. Everybody has secrets, but you just seem, I don't know, a little smarter than everybody else. Trust me; it helps to talk about it."

"It's just—" she starts, then takes the corner of another nail.

"It's just? Go ahead, Amanda. Tell me."

"I just don't think you'd understand. We're so different, you and I."

"Maybe not. At least I can listen, and that would help you understand," I respond. "Problems become a lot worse if you keep them in. Just unwind, relax, and talk to me."

She has no more nails to bite. She finally says, "I'm afraid to fail."

"So if you don't take honors classes or plan on being a doctor, then what?" I ask.

"I'd rather succeed in something easy than fail in something hard. It's how I am."

"That's okay. Didn't it feel good to say that out loud?"

She pauses. I wait for tears that seem close to the surface. They're not tears of sadness, but rather odes to joy.

"You're right; it did," she says. "How did you get me to do that?"

"Because that's how I am."

"I guess I'm lucky we became friends," she says.

"Luck is just another word for fate."

"Well, either luck or fate, one day my prince will come."

"Not the prince of Denmark, I hope. Hamlet didn't kill Claudius, but he's killing me."

Amanda laughs. "I guess that's another reason I don't take AP classes: They're hard."

"It's regular English. My *Hamlet* paper is due Monday, and I still don't have an idea."

"I wish I could help, but I have never understood that play. It's too long, if you ask me."

Now I laugh. "I didn't realize you were a Shakespearian scholar! Why is it too long?"

Amanda shrugs her shoulders. "Well, I'm not super-smart like you, but it seems Hamlet didn't need to go through all that and have all those people die if he would have just done one thing: He shouldn't have tried to kill Claudius; he should have forgiven him."

I pause for a second. I don't want to correct Amanda, but she's got to learn some hard truths.

"It's not an easy decision to take a life," says one who struggles with the same choice. "It sounds fine to forgive, but if someone hurts your family, you fight back."

"Eye for an eye?" Amanda asks. "I thought you believed in turning the other cheek."

"You have two cheeks but only one family," I say sadly, yet also proudly.

Amanda laughs that nervous laugh, then shrugs again. Her phone rings; it's her mom. So while she talks, I race over to the bulletin board on the break-room wall. I pull down an old flyer for a blood drive, pick up a stray pen, sit down with my back to Amanda, and start to write.

"To forgive or not to forgive: the role of fate, family, and forgiveness in *Hamlet*."

As I work out the thesis in my head, I know I'm not writing a paper, but my statement of purpose. Through the lens of the play, I'll discuss why Hamlet had no real choice but to seek vengeance, just like I have no real choice but to help Maggie in order to save Becca, and why I know I can never leave my true destiny for Scott. Your family is your fate; your fate is your family. They are both past and future.

"I love Scott. I mean, I want to love him," I tell Caleb as I sit next to him.

He's giving me a ride home, but we're still sitting in the hospital parking lot. I have so much to say to him that I don't know where to start. But somehow, I know he already knows everything about me.

"He seems like a fine young man."

"Or I thought I loved him," I say. "That's silly, I know."

"You're young, Cassandra," he reminds me. "Mature for your age, but still young."

"So what are we going to do?" I ask. "I thought I had everything figured out."

"What else is bothering you?"

I pause as a thousand images race through my head. "Becca."

"Not Scott, not your family, not your other friends?" he asks.

"I can't explain it, but I just think if somehow I can help save Becca, then everything will be all right," I say. "Somehow, everything got out of balance. This will set the scales right. It all started when Robyn died, so if her sister lives, maybe everything will be how it was before."

"But you don't really want that, do you, Cassandra?"

"In some ways, yes. But then if Robyn hadn't died, all these events wouldn't have brought us together. You never would have found me."

"Yes. Yes, I would, because we've always been together, if not in the same place."

"I just don't know what to do, what to decide."

Caleb touches my arm, and I feel a rush like a thousand tears.

"Leave everything to me."

Chapter 25

Tuesday, June 9

evening

"Can't I see you tomorrow at school?" I ask Scott.

We're talking on the phone. He's on break at work; I'm at home waiting for Maggie. This is the calm before the biggest storm ever. The last day of school is tomorrow, and I have my unfinished business with Brittney. Although I've avoided her at school, I can't get her—one thought of her—out of my mind. Whenever I pass by Robyn's empty locker, it reminds me of how unfairly the universe unfolds. Robyn dies—no doubt in great pain—while Brittney struts around, walking unhurt and untouched between the raindrops. Nature should balance itself, but sometimes it needs a push. I need to create an excuse for just that push.

"It will be a crazy day tomorrow," Scott shouts over the clatter of the dinner rush.

"Last days always are, especially if it's *your* last last day."

He pauses. Restaurant background noise fills the empty space. "I haven't decided."

"You mean, your Mom hasn't decided," I say, knowing that's not fair. I'm sitting here waiting for my family—my grandmother—to make decisions for me. I'm not one to talk.

"Even if I go to a different school, that doesn't mean we can't still be together."

"No, some rich chick from Powers will steal you away."

"Hey, it didn't happen my first two years, so I doubt it will happen now."

"But you've changed. I've changed you," I say.

The only constant for me is change.

Scott pauses again, considering the truth of that statement. What he'll never know, of course, is how much he changed me—how close I got to changing myself forever for him. I still don't question these human feelings of love for Scott. I question my judgment and ability to make decisions.

"Well, I go to confession a lot more since I met you," he says, then laughs.

"I hope I'm more than that to you," I snap.

"I'm at work. I can't talk," he says. "Can I come over after work?"

"You can't. You know that," I remind him.

While I know his mom is no fan of mine, I've at least met her. Scott *has* met my family. Of course, he just doesn't remember.

"Why not?"

"You just have to accept it. If not, then maybe you should go back to Powers and never see me again." I smack him with another verbal slap.

How many cheeks can one man turn?

"Why are you doing this?"

"What?"

"Picking a fight with me. Is it just for the make-up make-out?"

I laugh. I don't want to, but I do.

"I'm sorry, Scott. I've got a lot on my mind."

"Cassandra, you're the only thing on my mind," he says, laughing again. "Okay, that and my boss yelling my name. You're sure I can't see you tonight?"

"I'm positive that's a negative," I say.

"I'll be thinking of you."

He's waiting for me to say, "And I'll be thinking of you," but I can't because I don't want to lie to him any more than necessary.

"Scott, I'll see you tomorrow," I close with an empty kiss and hang up the phone.

Maggie is at my door less than ten minutes later. I finish chatting online with Amanda, and head downstairs. Mom is still at work, and Veronica is in her room. She rarely comes out anymore, and I only see her after I've worked at the hospital and collected her tears.

"Well?" Maggie asks when I walk in the room.

"I haven't decided," I say.

"The problem with you, Cassandra, is you *want*," she says. "You covet."

"But what I want isn't something for me, but for someone else," I remind her. "I want Becca to live. I want her parents not to have to suffer. That's not coveting, that's not selfish."

"You fool yourself." Maggie sips from a bottle of water. "This is about your guilt—your foolish, childish, human guilt. Why you have any human feelings, I'll never understand."

"It's not guilt!"

But she's right. I know perfectly well why I feel guilty; it is because I feel at all. Once Scott tapped human emotion in me, others trickled out. Love came with hate, and joy came with guilt.

"Whatever your reasons, it doesn't really matter to me," she says. "What matters is—"

"You're the one who covets," I snap back. "You want power. You want immortality."

"Do you want my help or not?" is her non-response.

"Why won't you tell me what I need to do?"

"Because we need to rebuild trust in this house," she says. "Your silly infatuation with that boy, Scott, makes me *not* want to trust you. The way to earn that trust is to trust me. I wouldn't ask for anything in return that would harm you. You are family."

"You want me to give up Scott? If I break up with Scott, then you'll save Becca?"

"No. That needs to happen either way. You need to end things with that boy once and for all," she says. "Consider that a pre-condition."

I pause and say with defiance and regret, "But I love him."

She slaps my face. Hard. "He is a human, Cassandra. You *don't* love him because you *can't* love. You're like a deaf person pretending to hear. You know what you must do."

"If I don't?" I challenge.

"Not only will I not do this for you, but I will make your life with us impossibly difficult!"

"Then maybe I'll leave!" I shout back.

"And go where? And do what?" Maggie calls my bluff. "Go live with Siobhan? From what I've heard, she's made quite the mess of her life. And for what? Temporary human love."

"I hate this!"

"It doesn't matter, Cassandra. You will accept it," Maggie says. "You have no choice."

"Yes, I do," I shoot back. "I have lots of choices."

"Just one: Will that girl live or die? Her life is in your hands," Maggie says, then stares.

I break the stare, grab my purse, and run for the street, phone in hand.

Caleb and I talked long enough on the phone to decide to meet in person.

"That's a lot of weight to be carrying," Caleb says.

We're sitting in his car out in the Holly Lake Rec Area, watching the twilight fade.

"And I've had no one to tell," I remind him.

"You're special, Cassandra," he whispers. "No one can totally understand you."

"Except you," I say, pushing closer against him.

"Except me," he says, letting my weight lean against his strong shoulders.

"This is wrong," I whisper. "Scott—"

"Cassandra, listen to me. I'll make everything right. Trust me."

"I do," I say, falling back into our shared silence.

For the past hour or so, however, this small, shared space has been anything but silent. I told him everything about Robyn dying, about saving Scott's life, about involving Samantha. I told him about Alexei's threats, Maggie's schemes, and Siobhan's agony. Caleb listened patiently to me—as I have listened so many times for so many others—while I poured out my doubts, my fears, and mostly my indecision. As I was telling him, I sensed that somehow he knew it all. When he looks at me, he looks *in* me.

"Can I ask you something?" I say, turning to face him.

"Maybe."

"How have I never seen you at any reunion?"

It is the first of so many questions. Even as I know better than to ask about his past, I can't resist. His smile vanishes.

"My father was exiled, and I went with him, but my brother and sister did not," he says calmly. "As you know, once you leave the family, you are never allowed back in."

I shudder at the memory of the exile ceremony I saw at age six. "What did he do?"

"Cassandra, that's all the past," he whispers. "What matters is the future. Our future."

"Our future," I repeat the words.

"I knew I would find you. It was only a matter of time."

"Except your timing couldn't be worse," I say. "Everything's a mess."

"No, the timing is perfect because I'm going to help you. You shouldn't have to decide these things alone. We've all spent too much time alone and apart."

"I guess I didn't know what it was like to feel lonely until Scott," I confess.

"You never have to feel lonely again. I'm here now," he says. "Let me help."

"I don't know what to say."

"Listen to the silence," he says, and I let out a small laugh.

"That's something Mr. A. said to me once."

"I guess that's where I got it from," he says. "He's a very smart man."

"How did your father know him?"

Caleb pulls me closer. "Cassandra, look ahead, don't look back," he reminds me. "About Becca—"

"I told you what Maggie said. I don't know if I can trust her."

"What do you think she wants you to do?"

"I don't know," I reply.

"Then think about what she wants," he says.

"She wants to be Veronica," I say.

"And what needs to happen for that to become a possibility?" he asks.

"The next generation has to start." I almost whisper.

"And how does that happen?" He moves closer.

"I start it."

"With Scott?" he murmurs softly.

"No," I say, as the veil of confusion lifts in the light of Caleb's warm, knowing smile.

"With another tear collector. You should do this because it is right for you, for us."

"Us?"

"I don't want us to be together just to help Maggie, or even to help Becca. I want more."

"More?"

"Cassandra, I want everything," he says. "And not just once a year, but always."

"But Caleb, you know the rules."

"These rules are meant to keep the young dependent on the old—to keep us separated. But I don't care about those rules anymore. All I care about is us and our potential."

"It's just so much."

"We can stand up to Simon and Veronica and tell them we are the next generation. We—not they!—have the power. If they want the tear collector line to continue, they must listen to us. We are done listening to them," Caleb says. "I will make a stand if you are by my side."

I fall into his arms, knowing he's there to catch me now and forever.

"Tell Maggie yes," Caleb says. "Trust me; you'll get exactly what you want."

Chapter 26

Wednesday, June 10

school day

"**D**oes anyone else want to sign up to be a summer swimming coach?" I ask as I look around the room. Everybody wears that last-day-of-school look of exhaustion and excitement.

"If you have me next year, I might extend extra credit," Mr. A. adds.

"In that case!" Michael reaches for the sign-up sheet.

"Anybody else?"

I'm directing my words to one person: Samantha. Since that terrible day a few weeks ago, not only has she not spoken to me, she hasn't even looked at me. She's back with her head on her desk, shutting out the world. If I lived in her fresh hell, I would do the same.

"Let's hope next year won't be as hard as this year for all of us," Michael says as he signs. He puts the sheet on Samantha's desk like an olive branch, but she pushes it away.

The last few minutes of class dissolve into a free-for-all of summer plans, although with this group of students, most of them are talking college essays and school visits. Like Amanda, they're wound pretty tight; they just do a better job of hiding it from each other—but not from me.

❦

Before I meet up with Scott for lunch, I wait for Amanda by her locker.

"Hey, Cass!" she says when she sees me.

Even on the last day of school, Amanda is dressed in her usual jeans and dark-colored polo shirt. Today is navy blue day.

"Hey, I wanted to thank you for that ride the other day," I say as my excuse to speak with her. "Maybe next year when I'm a senior, I'll get to drive and give you rides."

"I'd like that," she says.

"Or maybe this summer you'll meet your soulmate and won't need me anymore."

"Cass, I promise you: I won't be one of those girls," she says. "I hate those girls."

"It happened to you," I say, already knowing that part of her history. In addition to spreading rumors, I'm just as adept at gathering information, sometimes trading one for the other.

"How did you know about that?" She looks embarrassed.

"I won't be like Jen," I say, evading her question.

"I'll never understand her," she says. "We were best friends since, like, eighth grade. Then this year she starts going out with Adam, and it's like—"

"Like you never even met." I say it so she doesn't have to re-live it.

"Well, I don't think that's going to happen," she says with a melodramatic flair.

"Trust me: you never, ever know who is going to walk into your life."

"I guess I need to trust you, right?"

I nod, hiding both my smile and my frown. "You going to the bonfire?" I ask.

There's a big bonfire at Morgan's farm on the last day of school. I went the past two times, and I know there's enough alcohol to guarantee fireworks.

"I'm not a big party person," she says. "I think Sara and Eliza-beth are going."

"Tell you what: We'll get together this summer and have our own party," I say, trying to pump her up. "You supply the place, and I'll supply the fun. Deal?"

"Just don't invite Brittney and Kelsey, okay?"

When she says their names, her tone changes and tears form. She confesses what I'd suspected: The two of them insult Amanda just as they do Samantha. As I listen, my anger grows and a plan begins to take shape—one with actions, not words. I can't avenge the dead like Robyn; I can protect my living friends.

I take a quick detour into the restroom before meeting up with Scott. This restroom is down by the gym and a little out of the way, but I know I'll find the Queen B holding court here. As I open the door, I see Brittney moving to leave with Kelsey two steps behind her. I've avoided this psychopath as best I could, even as I've harvested from the people she's hurt. Caleb might have helped break up Brittney and Craig, but I'm going to break her. This is step one: add fuel to the fire.

"Well, Cassandra, how is life in deadland?" Kelsey says.

Brittney just stares at me.

"Life is just fine," I say.

Although they made good on their threat to make me "dead" to much of the most popular crowd, there are plenty of Amandas in the world.

"How is life with you, Kelsey? Why don't you volunteer anymore? Did you bag your medical student?"

"No, I have a life," she snaps.

"Hey, Brittney, how's Craig?" I crack.

Brittney doesn't react.

"Too soon?" I ask in mock concern.

"Bitch," Kelsey answers for her.

The B-word seems to silence the room. A few people wanting to avoid a scene on the last day of school slip out. Others stay to enjoy the show.

"It was you," Brittney says. "You spread lies about me to Craig."

"Brittney, I don't need to spread lies about you," I counter. "Your truth is harsh enough."

Brittney nods to Kelsey.

"Shut up," Kelsey says.

Brittney beams like a proud dog-owner whose puppy just performed a trick.

"Hey, I didn't tell anyone about you, Brittney," I say. "I didn't tell anyone that you're a stuck-up selfish bitch because everybody knows that."

"I said shut up!" Kelsey shouts.

Brittney is glaring, but I'm staring. I won't blink.

"You two are perfect for each other," I say. "Kelsey, your nose is up in her ass, and Brittney, your ugly, bent nose is always up in the air."

"I hate you." Brittney speaks at last.

I call her a bitch, and she doesn't react, but I question her deluded self-image of physical perfection, and she finally speaks.

"I'd hate you, too, but I don't have the time or the inclination," I reply.

"This is all because of Robyn, this—" she starts.

"Don't you mention her name again," I spit. "You don't deserve to mention her name."

"Don't tell me what to do." Brittney points her fake-nailed index finger in my face.

"Robyn was a saint!" I shout. "And you're just a—"

Kelsey pushes me, but I don't move.

"Come on, Brittney. Try me," I dare her.

Afraid to break a nail, Brittney swings her over-sized purse. It hits me in the face, but it doesn't hurt. It just makes me thirsty. I block a second shot with my arm, and head for the door. Before I exit, I take a last glance at Brittney's smug face. She turns away and stares at her favorite sight: her perfect self in the mirror.

Enjoy the view while you can, Brittney.

Energized by last-day-of-school tears, I push past Cody and get in Craig's face at his locker. For months, he's avoided my calls and messages. This is my last chance. I need him.

"What do you want, *Cassandra*?" He almost hisses my name.

"Same thing I've wanted for months: just to talk to you," I answer softly.

"Back off, Cassandra!" Cody shouts. He grabs for my shoulder. I swat his paw away.

"We have nothing to talk about!" Craig doesn't sound so much angry as afraid.

"I understand you don't want to talk with me, but I want you to listen to somebody else."

He looks down at me in all his power and strength, which I'm about to shatter. "Who?"

"Robyn."

When I say her name, his anger deflates and sadness rises.

"Robyn? What about Robyn?" I sense the tears forming deep within him.

"We'll talk in the library. Five minutes. That's all this will take."

"Five minutes?" he asks.

Cody starts to say something, but Craig shuts him down.

"Craig, give me five minutes today and you'll never hear from me again," I say.

He pauses, looks away.

I deal from the bottom of the deck. "You owe Robyn that much."

I turn and walk toward the library, but he doesn't immediately follow. Two boys I don't know are in the small study room, so I flirt with them enough to convince them to vacate.

What fools these mortal boys be, indeed.

I stand by the door and wait for Craig. He walks across the library as if each step hurts.

"What about Robyn?" Craig says again as he enters the room.

I close the door.

"Sit down there."

I point to the chair with the back facing the window and door.

"This is stupid," Craig says, but he sits anyway.

I sit across from him.

"I want to show you something of Robyn's." Craig flinches. "And I want to tell you that I forgive you. I want to tell you that you should forgive yourself. I want to tell you—"

"I have to go!"

I grab his hand. He has the strength to throw me across the room, but I intend to even the odds.

"I don't want to talk about this. Robyn's dead. Why are you—"

"Read this." I take out Robyn's good-bye letter and slide it across the table. He hesitates, looking back and forth between my eyes and Robyn's words until I shout at him, "Read it!"

Dear Craig,

> *I told Cass today that I don't have a self anymore. When you dumped me for Brittney, you took it with you. My body might be writing this, but it's only the empty shell.*

> *The majority of me is gone, but what's left is spazzing out in pain. I need it all to stop.*

> *I've always had this crazy need to be successful. I worried that if I wasn't doing well at whatever I did, I would disappoint someone. I guess this was the*

perfect recipe for success, because I supposedly never failed.

I was perfect. I was a well-behaved, popular cheerleader who got good grades. I was a good, Catholic girl and a good role model for my little sister.

I lived the perfect life. But you were the only part that was really perfect. The rest was fake. I was fake. I created the "perfect" world for myself. Nothing was ever supposed to be wrong in my life. But in reality, you were the only thing that was right.

I was successful, and you were the center of my perfect life. But I wasn't me. I faked a lot. My perfection was a lie.

And now that you're gone, I can't fake it anymore. But I can't disappoint anyone either. I can't really do anything anymore. I need everything to stop.

I've always been successful, but now I've failed. I've failed at everything. I need to leave behind my failure. I need to avoid disappointing myself or anyone else again. I know this is the one sin that will surely land me in Hell, but I probably deserve it. God is probably already disappointed in me anyway. I wish I could've been better for him, for you, for Becca.

And I know you do, too, Craig. I don't blame you for taking the easy way with Brittney. I know she's like the devil offering you an apple. You're strong, but not that strong. I forgive you.

I'm so sorry for everything. This is all my fault, but it's not your fault, Craig. Don't hate yourself, Craig. Forgive yourself.

I will love you forever and ever, Amen. Don't hate me for my everlasting love,

Robyn

I say it again. "It's not your fault, Craig. You didn't know what would happen, what she would do. You loved Robyn. She loved you."

He stares at me, then through me. "I know." His voice cracks.

"It wasn't your fault." I kneel next to him. "You need to say it."

"Cassandra, look. I can't . . . I don't . . . I need—" His words tumble randomly.

"I forgive you. Robyn forgives you. All you need to do is forgive yourself."

"No. I can't."

I sense the tears forming. His eyes start to water, and the first few drops fall on my hands. I push his head into my left shoulder, but shield my eyes so he can't see them rolling in my head. The tears come harder, faster.

I press his face against my shoulder and stroke his head as he says through sobs, "I miss her so much. It was my fault."

I repeat my words, his new mantra for unleashing tears. "I forgive you. Robyn forgives you. All you need to do is forgive yourself."

"I can't," Craig says as tears continue to rush like water from a burst pipe.

"Just say it," I say, but I can hardly speak. The tears rush into my body and through my veins. I feel their energy almost lifting me off the ground. "Say it, Craig, say it!"

"It wasn't my fault," he says, just before he bell rings.

I take Veronica's handkerchief and wipe away the last few drops. They'll be enough to last her a week. I have all I need for my task today.

"You did good, Craig. We'll both feel better now."

I whisper this rare truth, then head off.

"Ms Gray, you are late. I know it's the last day of class, but—"

This is as far as Mr. Lane gets into his little speech before it's interrupted by the sickening sound of my smashing Brittney's face hard against her desk and her nose breaking. With the energy of Craig's tears fueling me, I'm surprised that I didn't splinter the wooden top. "That was for Robyn."

I yank at her perfect blond hair, pull her crying, bleeding face up, and then slam it against the desk again.

"And this is for me, Amanda, Samantha, and every other girl you insulted."

It looks like I'm wiping away the blood, but I touch one of her tears with my index finger and bring it to my mouth. Unlike those empty drops that fell from her eyes when Robyn died, these tears of pain from Brittney are real. For the first time, I start to understand why Alexei acts as he does. Getting tears this way is so much quicker and easier My revenge took a while, but for Robyn and every other person Brittney hurt, I hope it was worth the wait. I dab Brittney's tears and put them not on my shoulder, but on my tongue. My whole mouth sizzles as the energy rushes into me. Yes, these tears are very real and quite tasty.

Brittney's mom, whose fake tan is more orange than a basketball, shows up just after the police. The METs arrive quickly, and get Brittney to the hospital. I wonder if her dad is at the hospital, and if not, then why isn't her mom there with Brittney instead of here at school?

My mother is out of town, or so I tell the principal. I say I'll call Maggie, but instead I call Caleb. As the final bells rings, I sit alone in the office, while the adults confer behind closed doors. I sit right in front of a big window, and as other eleventh graders pass by, they either give me two thumbs up or one middle finger. I don't keep exact score, but it's pretty clear the thumbs are winning. I pull out my phone, which earns me a nasty scowl from Principal Carlson's secretary, so I put it away. I can at least pretend to look repentant in this moment.

"Oh my God, Cass, I heard!" Amanda says way too loud when she enters the office.

The scowling secretary becomes the shusher. Amanda sits next to me. I don't think I've ever seen her happier. Maybe that's my challenge. Rather than making my classmates miserable, I'll choose one of them—Amanda because Samantha's way too messed up—to make happy.

As Amanda chats on and on about what other people are saying about what I did to Brittney. I'm pretending to pay attention. Using all my active listening skills from peer counseling, I nod my head and say "that's right" a few times to keep her going, because I'm lost in my own thoughts.

I took decisive action today to avenge a wrong, but when will I take one to set myself on the right path? I thought maybe by prom night I'd know for sure, but then Scott complicated things. I thought breaking up with him and being unable to sustain that would prove it, but it didn't show strength—on either of our parts—just weakness. I need to act from strength.

So maybe tonight is the night I decide. Scott and I plan to attend a big end-of-year party . . . if I'm not spending the night in jail, that is. I'll be surrounded not by the tears I need, but by the laughter and happiness I want. I once thought that Scott was the only person who gave that to me, but could a human ever suffice? Can a human be my soulmate, or is it Caleb?

"Why did you do it?" she asks, breaking my reverie, and I have to answer.

"I did it for you, for Samantha, for Robyn."

"That's just like you, Cass: doing for others. You should really think about yourself more."

I smile. "Amanda, I intend to do just that."

After Amanda heads off for her car, I check my phone for messages—despite the secretary's renewed glare—but there are none. I thought I might hear from Alexei again since it is the tenth, a multiple of five, the sacred number for all male tear collectors. As I get ready to make a call, the scowling secretary leaves her desk. I hear the door open. Caleb walks in, dressed in a suit and tie.

"So what did you do now?" Caleb asks. When he says, "now," he smiles.

I tell him about smashing Brittney's face and breaking her nose. He came in smiling, but he totally lights up the room as I recount each detail.

"Well, a broken nose shouldn't be too bad. She should be in and out."

"No, Caleb, trust me. I crushed that thing. Maybe it's because it was on such an odd angle— you know, always stuck up?—that the break was so bad." He laughs, smiles, laughs. I mirror him.

"So what's going to happen to you?"

I point at the door. "They're deciding my fate."

"And you're not involved? That doesn't seem right," he says. "But then again, from what I remember about being your age, the adults decided everything, and all I did was obey, right?'

"You don't know how right you are."

"Well, what you need is someone to argue your case. Do you know a lawyer?"

I look up at him, my eyes begging for his help, his strength, his soul.

"Why not me?" He points to himself, then straightens his tie.

"What? You're not a lawyer!"

He laughs again, then puts his hands gently on my shoulders, barely touching them because of how sensitive they are.

A human could never not-touch my shoulders like this, yet still bring me this warm feeling.

"I'm not a lawyer. However, except for Mr. A. and a few kids not in that room, nobody at this school knows me. And Cassandra, I can be very, *very* persuasive."

"I bet," I say, trying but failing not to fall into his blue-eyed trap.

"Trust me, Cassandra." He walks over to Mr. Carlson's office, ignores the newly-returned and now-sputtering secretary, opens the door, and starts talking.

Chapter 27

Wednesday, June 10

evening

"What do you think?" I ask Scott.

He needs to think tonight—not feel—for the sake of both of us.

Scott and I have circled the area around Morgan's farm three times already.

"I don't know, Cass, it's your call," Scott says, handing this decision over to me as well.

"Will you protect me from the angry mob?" I ask, almost mockingly.

"Only if you can run as fast as me," he cracks. "I'm joking. But no, I can't fight off the whole football team. Where the heck did you get the idea to do that to Brittney?"

"I didn't think. I acted."

I knew the second I saw her in the bathroom—and I chose that bathroom because I knew she'd be there—that she'd give me both a reason and an excuse.

"What's going to happen?" Scott asks.

I tell Scott how Caleb pretended to my lawyer. Whatever he said worked because the police didn't press charges, Brittney's mom won't sue, and I got off with just in-school suspension for a week at the start of next year. Scott looks pleased by the story except for the mention of Caleb.

"What about Brittney?" he asks.

"Pardon me, but fuck her." Scott looks shocked. "She hit me first. I have witnesses."

"Cassandra, there's never a dull moment with you," he cracks, then kisses me.

"Let's go," I say.

"Sure you just don't want to stay in the car and—"

"No, let's find the fire."

We exit the car and follow the sweet smell of burning wood. As we get closer, it's hard to tell which is loudest: the pounding bass coming out of SUVs parked close to the fire, the crackling of the logs in the flames, or the endless chatter interrupted by raucous laughter and friendly shrieking. Both Scott and I pass up the beer-filled cups thrust our way and look for some of his friends over by a clearing. They appear to be the few not drinking, smoking, or toking. No wonder some call our school Lapeer Get-High School. I wouldn't be surprised if tear collectors helped spread alcohol across the globe, as few things have caused more tears over time than drink.

Scott and I can barely walk two feet before somebody else—often someone I don't know that well—comes up to tell me how great what I did to Brittney is. Like Katie messaged, "I don't condone violence, but in Brittney's case, I'm willing to make an exception." If Brittney, Kelsey, and their kind thought I was dead to the school, it seems as if tonight I'm born-again popular.

"It's Karate Cassandra! Don't hurt me, please!" Clark says, getting down on his knees.

"Don't piss her off, and you'll be fine," Scott jokes.

"Is Brittney here?" I ask.

"Not her, Kelsey, Cody, or any of that crew," Clark answers. "They're probably still at the hospital trying to repair her broken nose."

"You mean her broken ego," I say.

"I don't think they have operating tables that big at Lapeer Regional," Scott jokes.

Clark laughs, and I pretend to join in the fun. I let Scott and

Clark joke around, mostly at my expense.

Elizabeth and Sara stumble over, either because they wore high heels to a bonfire or they're drunk or both. I meet them halfway.

"Is Amanda with you?" I ask.

Sara shakes her head.

"Cassandra, man, you did it!" Sara says.

I've never heard her say "man" in her life.

"About frickin' time," Elizabeth adds. "Everybody hates Brittney."

"For what she did to Robyn, stealing Craig away," Sara says. "That was wrong."

"Well, I made it right," I say.

They talk about me—not *to* me, but about me—for at least five minutes while I'm standing right there.

Finally, I say, "I made it right, except it can't bring Robyn back."

Sara stumbles toward me. She smells like that bottom-shelf whiskey that Cody and his pals used to steal and slam back.

"She's gone," she slurs, her breath loaded with booze and grief.

I knew I'd have a good time tonight; I didn't know I'd have a feast.

"It's okay," I say as I step closer.

Despite the cool breeze, my shoulders are bare, willing, and able. Sara sheds far too few tears before Elizabeth taps her on the shoulder and Sara pulls away from me.

"Watch it, Sara! Maybe she'll break your nose," Elizabeth cracks. She laughs too loud.

"Or steal my tears," Sara says.

"What did you say?" I ask.

"Just kidding," Sara says. "Everybody knows how you're, like, Miss Shoulder-to-Cry-On for the losers. I mean, man, you even hung around with that filthy, freaky Samantha chick."

"Frickin' head case," Elizabeth says.

"Hey, lay off her!" I say.

"Maybe she gets Mr. Gorgeous to fight her battles," Sara says. "Why a hot guy like that was talking to that fat freak at the prom, I'll never know. You think she paid him or what?"

"Paid him all right," Elizabeth says then makes an obscene gesture.

"What did Samantha ever do to you?" I ask.

"She's a freak. I bet she's not here because she thought we'd throw her into the fire."

"A witch! A witch! Burn her!" Elizabeth cackles.

"I'm leaving," I say, turning my back.

I start to walk away, thinking how mean they are to talk about Samantha that way—and also how mean I've been to her. I need to make amends. Tonight. I need to make everything right. I've passed every test, except one with Scott. School's out, but this is my final.

I walk by the fire that seems to be growing as people throw whatever they can find into the inferno. Even though the heat's rising, I step closer and put my right foot at the very edge of the firepit. As I stare into the flames, it's as if I'm looking into my essence. Within me, so many fires burn, and I can't control any of them. The answer is to let the fire burn, let fate rule. I know where my fate resides, so I must follow that true path, no matter the consequences. With Scott, I have walked through the fire—not as an end, but as a means to find Caleb, my true soulmate.

"It's time," I say to Scott.

We walk hand in hand back to his car. He's looking forward, and so am I. The fire and the past are behind us; it's time. Scott is so smart—you'd think he would have figured that out by now—but when humans love someone, they also trust. That's their biggest mistake.

"Everybody seems to think you're the new Queen Bee taking down Brittney," Scott says.

"I don't want to be the center of attention."

"Well, you're the center of *my* attention," Scott says as we climb into his car.

I'm silent as we exit. The fire shrinks the distance. Beatles in my ears; Yeats in my mind.

> *Things fall apart; the centre cannot hold;*
> *Mere anarchy is loosed upon the world,*
> *The blood-dimmed tide is loosed, and everywhere*
> *The ceremony of innocence is drowned;*
> *The best lack all conviction, while the worst*
> *Are full of passionate intensity.*

I queue up the Beatles song that Scott will need as he stops—as always—a block from my house. It's symbolic: he could be close to me, but never really in my life because he, unlike Caleb, is not my kind. He may love me; I may have thought I loved him, but we are not alike. We shared a moment in time, a wave of emotion that drowned our innocence and left us lying broken on the beach.

"Scott, I don't know how to say this," I start.

"Not again," he sighs.

"This time, Scott, I'm sorry; it's for real," I say.

I still can't look at him. All this started with my finding Robyn crying in her car, betrayed by the one she loved. Now, I'm going to leave Scott in his car this same way. I'm bringing back balance; I'm completing the circle.

"You say that, but tomorrow you'll want to get back together!" There's more anger than sadness in him.

"I know, but this is for the best for both of us now," I say. Here's where the "we can still be friends" card gets played, but not here, not now, not this time, not ever again.

"Why? Why now? We have all summer, and about next year, I still don't—"

"Scott, I know how things work when people need to decide between family ties and heartstrings," I say, knowing this hard fact—harder than ever of late. "Family always wins."

"So?"

"So, that means you'll leave Lapeer. You will meet somebody at Powers, and your life will be better for it," I say. "This is really what's best for you. I'll only bring you more harm."

"I can decide what's best for me, thank you, and I still want to be with you."

I want a life with sound effects; I want thunder and lightning. "No."

"But Cassandra, after everything we've been through, everything we've done, I don't understand why you would do this," he says. "Is this really what you want?"

The imaginary thunderstorm intensifies into a tornado's path of destruction. "Yes."

"I don't believe you," he says. "I know you lie to others, but look me in the eyes right now, and tell me that you don't want us to be together anymore."

I swallow, take a breath, and stare at his soft brown eyes for the last time. "We're over."

"Cassandra, please," Scott says. "Tell me this isn't happening. Stop it."

"Breaking up is a little like dying," I say, trying to appeal to his intellectual side since I've sliced his emotional insides to shreds. "Remember when Robyn died, we talked with everyone about the stages of grief? The first is denial. You'll accept this. You have to. Let it be."

And with that, I cue the song. The sad piano starts, the words of comfort soon to follow.

"Why should I accept it?" he asks over the music.

I grab the handle to exit the car, but when he sees me make my move, he clicks the lock.

"No, you can't leave until you tell me why."

"Scott, let me go," I say. "Let me out. Let it be."

"What did I do wrong?" Scott asks. I just shake my head. "Why, Cassandra? Why?"

His few teardrops feel like acid, not nectar.

"Because, Scott, you are not my soulmate."

15 June

To: swimmerqueenLHS@gmail.com
Fr: AlexeiofCyrene@yahoo.com

    Cousin, why do you ignore me still? I told you I would return; I am closer than you think. But I am not the same; I am changing. If you've followed the news—as you like to do—you'll know that. What I did was wrong. I have told Simon, and I have begged him to let me return: the prodigal great-grandson. I will be there at Feastday, and I will save you a seat next to me.

    One day, I will be Simon, and you will be Veronica. We will live forever as it was meant to be, just like we once were. Remember? I do. I'm coming for you, Cassandra, coming to take what was promised me, what is owed. This time, I will not take no for an answer. This time I will not fall for your tricks or let these humans stand in the way of our destiny.

    So far, it seems all these words have not mattered. But if you do not answer, then you will have refused me five times: twice in person and three times in these messages if you do not respond within five days. You will not do it a sixth time. I will be watching you. I will not wait until the Feastday for your last chance. You will be mine.

Chapter 28

Monday, June 15

morning

"When did you know?" Caleb asks.

I pause and look out across the almost empty Lapeer High School parking lot. I told my family I was going to help Mr. A. teach summer swimming, but first I'm swimming in Caleb's blue eyes, and for the first time, I'd be fine either to just float or even to drown in them. My family can't know about us for a hundred reasons, but only one that matters: Caleb asked me not to tell them. When I asked why, he said what he always says, "Cassandra, trust me."

"When did you know?" He touches his fingertips on my shoulders, and I feel faint.

"Know you are a tear collector, or know that we're soulmates?"

"Either."

He breathes in, I breath out. A step in nature beyond symbiosis.

"When I first saw you at school, there was a sensation—that knowing we females get when we're around a true male tear collector, but I thought it might be my cousin Alexei," I answer.

He doesn't react to the name. While Caleb has asked me many questions, he evades mine, or—as he must have done that day in Principal Carlson's office—turns the conversation around until he gets what he wants. And what he wants is to know everything.

He knows that other than over Easter weekend, I don't see male tear collectors. I was barely born for the last get-together to celebrate Veronica's Feastday. The Feastday is every year, but only every sixteen years do both sides of the family come together. He's as starved to hear about my life as I am to tell it, scars and all.

"I sensed it, too, but I also spotted you because you were the most beautiful girl in the class, maybe the most beautiful girl I've ever seen," he says, touching my cheek.

"You realize I'm not susceptible to flattery," I crack, and he laughs.

"It's not flattery; it's the truth."

I can't blush, but I would if I could. Instead of turning red, I turn toward Caleb and bury my face in his chest. He strokes my short hair. Eventually, I look back up at him to say, "But that day when you saved Samantha and her mother? That's when I knew for sure, but how could I ask you? I knew when the time was right, things would reveal themselves."

"Fate," he whispers before he kisses my face.

"No, Caleb. Call it outrageous fortune, and I'm all done fighting it."

When we see Mr. A. arrive, we walk together—although not hand-in-hand—toward the pool. He opens the door for us, lets us in, but says nothing other than hello. The class I'm helping teach starts in an hour, but Caleb and I start our first week together. There's a lot to figure out—in some ways even more decisions than I had with Scott. The difference is that we can make them together because we both know how high the stakes are and how great the risks. I feel a tingle of missing Scott, but deep down I know I was fooling myself; it could never be like this. I have found love like Siobhan, but in the opposite way: She started with a tear collector and found a human. I can't tell her that she's wrong in calling Alden a soulmate; she can't tell me I'm wrong about this because I won't tell her about Caleb. Only one person knows about Caleb and me, and that's Mr. A.

"You two have a good swim," he says.

Maybe it's because school's out, but Mr. A. looks different: more relaxed, almost happy. Caleb has improved both our lives. Mr. A. stands, arms crossed, hands lightly touching his own shoulders, looking like a serene monk.

Caleb and I head into separate locker rooms and emerge a few minutes later. Once in the pool, our strokes somehow seem in synch. Our heads rise above water simultaneously; our fingers touch the end of the pool together. Am I swimming harder, is he holding back, or are we naturally in time? We do twenty-three laps until Mr. A. blows a whistle to let us know time is up. As we reach the end of the pool, we look at each other, and all I want to do is kiss him, but I can't. Mr. A allows us—even encourages us—to be together, but not where others can see.

"Caleb, you'd better go," Mr. A says.

Caleb nods in obedience and heads toward the locker room. I watch each step he takes.

"Cassandra, you can take a break, too. I'll open the doors for the class in a few minutes. Thanks for helping me out."

"Happy to do it."

What kind of person wouldn't want to help young children learn to swim? It's so much fun for them—except for the ones who are afraid. They put up quite a fight. Some scream, but other young children can only cry.

"I'm not scared," Becca says as I dip her head in the water.

Like many of the other children, she's wearing a bathing cap. Others cover their hair; she covers her balding head.

"I'm so glad we get to spend this time together, Short Stuff," I say—and mean it.

"Me too!" She's not really swimming, more floating in my arms. Her life in my hands.

While I'm nowhere near as good with adult women as I am with teen boys, I was still able to convince Mrs. Berry to let Becca take swimming lessons with me as part of this class. It's not all selfish. Becca hasn't shown she's afraid to swim, just as she has never said she's afraid to die. I told her mother it would give Becca something to look forward to. She said the only thing Becca should look forward to is a miracle. Mrs. Berry doesn't know I'm ready to make a miracle happen.

I tried to warn Maggie that Veronica knows something is up, but she won't listen to me. I even told her about Veronica's threats, but if anything, that seemed to make her more determined to attempt to perform the miracle that Maggie believes will convince Veronica that she is ready, willing, and able to take over the family. I sense that Mom is the source of Veronica's information; it's the two of them against the two of us. They have Veronica's power and Mom's iron will. We have Maggie's cunning, and I have a reason: a soulmate.

"Come on Cass, dunk me again!" Becca shouts.

"Not once, but six times!"

I do as I say, and she screams in delight, but a few feet away there is another young child, a boy, who is screaming. Michael looks scared at the child's distress.

"I got it!" I swim over.

"You're sure?" Michael asks.

"Helping scared young people is my specialty."

"Be careful, he's a crier."

I nod, purse my lips so I don't smile, and grab hold of the boy. He looks to be about six.

"My name is Cassandra. What's your name?"

"Keef," the boy says.

"Keef?"

"Keef," the young boy repeats. I turn toward Michael.

"Keith. His name is Keith," Michael says.

I nod, and Michael swims toward Becca.

"Okay, Keith, sorry I didn't understand you. Maybe I have water in my ears!"

He doesn't laugh; instead he just looks more upset. "It's my fault."

"It's okay. I can call you Keef or Keith. It doesn't matter as long as you follow my instructions. Everything will be okay. But it's okay to be scared; it's even okay to cry."

He nods. "Come on, Keef! Let's see a big, happy smile."

He frowns instead. "Come on, Keef! You can smile for me, can't you?"

Normally a child's smile makes other people smile, but when Keith gives in to my request, it feels as if someone has filled the pool with ice.

His mouth is almost devoid of teeth, but full of stitches. I spin around the pool so quickly, I'm dizzy. Now Keith isn't the only one afraid. No dentist pulled Keith's teeth. There's only one person who would torture a child like this: Alexei.

Chapter 29

Friday, June 19

evening

"Cassandra, you know you made the right choice, don't you?" Caleb asks.

He's right—even giving decisions over to fate is making a choice.

We sit on the hood of Caleb's car in a secluded area at the Holly Rec Area. We can't go to my house, of course, and while Mr. A. looks the other way, he wants—for the sake of appearances—us not to be seen at his house or in public. Other than that, he's our biggest fan.

"But I didn't think it could be like this," I say, pushing against him.

"I think we've become more and more human through the generations," Caleb says. "The more human we become, the more likely it is we'll have not only the physical traits of a human, but also the secondary traits such as emotions. You thought you were in love before."

"But Mom kept telling me it couldn't be real," I say.

"We're conditioned to manipulate humans. Our mock emotions are like a spider's web."

"What about you? Did you ever feel anything close to human love before?"

"Not until you," he says and kisses me. "There's a rush I can't describe; perhaps it is best compared to a fire consuming everything in its path. But even that falls short; nothing compares."

"But this is forbidden."

"I knew when I saw you that morning at school that nothing else mattered. I don't care if you're sixteen; I don't care if this is wrong. I care about you, Cassandra. You trust me, right?"

"I do."

"You can trust me because you trust your instincts. When did you realize what was happening with us?"

"I knew you were special; I knew I couldn't stop thinking about you," I confess, but I realize again that my words fall short. I'm not lying to Caleb; I don't have the ability to describe something I've never experienced before. "I tried to avoid you because of Scott."

"Because you didn't know for sure about him."

"I told myself Scott was different, that I was going to act differently," I explain. "It wouldn't be like Cody or the others, when I was always looking for the next one. I didn't want to look." But in the end, I wound up looking at you, even when I wasn't looking for you. This is real. That was just some kind of shadow.

"Being with you is destiny," Caleb says.

"When did you know?" I ask.

"I sensed a connection deeper than what male tear collectors experience around female ones," he explains. "It wasn't like those feelings I had faked for humans to collect the tears I needed to survive. But I was confused because tear collectors don't feel. I was attracted to you like any tear collector, male to female, but it was—*is*—more than biological urges."

"Much more."

"I tried to deny it, then explain it, but nothing made sense except one thing."

"One thing?"

"That you were the one," he whispers into my ear.

My body shakes like the leaves on surrounding trees would in a windstorm."I denied it, too."

"Because of Scott?"

"I'd caused so much hurt, and I didn't want to—"

"Hurt Scott," he finishes.

"I think that's what makes us different from others of our kind. You and I have what humans call a conscience. Although we're built to cause human suffering, over time—for whatever reason—we're troubled by it. Then when Robyn died and Veronica said it was 'just wonderful,' something changed in me. I started thinking that I couldn't keep on delighting in suffering."

"But you didn't delight in it," he reminds me.

"Unlike Alexei," I say. He gets a hard look at the mention of that name.

"Maybe because my father left the family," Caleb explains, "I knew I was different. I always felt like a freak. I still do, except ... except when I'm with you."

"What are we going to do?" I ask.

"Tell me more about Samantha."

I recount how I met Samantha, how our friendship grew, how she helped save Scott's life, her plan to kill Mark, how our friendship was over, how she said she didn't think I was anything other than human anymore, and how I am not so sure I believe her.

He does like I do in peer counseling and practices active listening as I speak, then says. "No wonder you're not friends anymore."

"Because she knows I used her."

"No, because she has power over you," he suggests. "She knows something about you. Because of that, she thinks she can control you, get you to do what she wants."

"But she can't," I say. "I won't help her with her crazy plan. I can't kill for her."

He kisses me deeply, then whispers in my ear, "How about for me?"

I take a step back. "What are you talking about, Caleb?"

"I've been looking for you, and now I've found you. But if we stay as tear collectors, we can't stay together. We might defy Veronica and Simon, but in the end, I confess that I know they'll prevail."

"Why?"

"Because they always do," he says. "But there's another way for us to be together."

"I don't understand."

"You mentioned the one who left," he says, and I nod. "You spoke with her, right?"

"Yes, I know it was wrong, but I was so confused about everything. And Siobhan—"

"That's the past, and the past stays buried," he says. "But she told you how she crossed over? She told you how she rejected her family and her intended mate to become human?"

"She did."

"The only way we can stay together is to cross over together. We must transform."

"Then you're suggesting that we—"

"Look at me, Cassandra," he says, turning me to face him.

The sky above doesn't appear as blue, as inviting, or as infinite as the possibilities in Caleb's eyes.

"Think about that girl, Samantha, and what a liability she is to our family. If we leave the family, we must still protect them. Samantha can't be allowed to live; you will need to take care of that."

"She's my friend," I say.

"She was your friend," he says. "Now she's your enemy because of what she knows. She is a threat—not just to you, but to all our kind. She will talk, and someone will believe her."

"But she said—"

"Even if one person believes her, that's enough. She's dangerous."

"I know."

"There are some humans who help us by creating tears here and there. People like that guy Mark might as well be tear collectors for the pain they cause. But he is *not* one of us, and he hurts everyone."

"Caleb, this is too much." I put up a hand. "I need to think."

"No, Cassandra, you need to feel," he says, then kisses me so perfectly and deeply it's like I've been swallowed into his soul. "What do you feel?"

"I can't trust those feelings," I say. "I thought I loved Scott, but—"

"What you felt was probably as close as you could get to love," he explains. "And you know why you felt that way about him?"

"Because he—"

"It has nothing to do with Scott," Caleb whispers. "You knew I was next. You knew somewhere deep down that your soulmate was coming closer. Scott was practice."

I say nothing because I don't know what to think. Or what to do.

"I've thought this through," Caleb says. "You have to trust me, Cassandra. We can keep our love hidden and forbidden, restrained by the ways of our elders. Or we can feel human love deeper than we can even imagine now. We can be human. We can be—"

"Be together." I complete his sentence; he completes my life.

"Humans always ask, 'Will you die for me?'" he says. "But Cassandra, I'm asking if you will kill for me. Because I will kill for you."

As always, Caleb drops me off a few blocks from my house. Our final kiss burns within, even as his words chill me.

Would he kill for me? Could I kill for him?

As I round the corner toward my house, I'm blinded by a flash of headlights. I step off the sidewalk as a car drives closer, then stops. A door opens, and there are footsteps: one set of feet, but a third sound as well: a cane tapping five times.

"What are you doing now?" Simon asks.

Does he know about Caleb? What is Caleb's relationship to Simon? To Alexei?

It feels as if the roots of my family tree wrap around my throat and strangle me.

"Leave me alone, Simon."

The headlights dim. He's nothing but a shadow. Simon lifts his cane and brings it up toward me. It rests on me: first on my chest, then my shoulders, and then against my throat.

"But Cassandra, you are alone," Simon whispers.

I know I shouldn't make him mad, but I can't help myself. I am tired of living by family rules, most of which haven't been revealed to me. I say, "No. I won't be like you, like Veronica, like my mother. I won't live without love."

Simon sniffs loudly and then pops a fresh cinnamon cough drop in his mouth. He keeps his mouth moist, but his words are so dry and brittle. "Then maybe you should die."

"No, Simon, it is you and Veronica who must die so tear collectors can change back to—"

"Do your duty, or else!"

He presses his cane against my throat but then pulls it away. There's a clicking sound. I stare at the end of the cane; I'm transfixed by the glint of the blade.

Chapter 30

Monday, June 22

morning

"So, Keef, how do you feel?" We're in the shallow end of the pool.

He starts to talk, but he's so hard to understand.

I nod as he goes on. He tries not to smile with his broken mouth, but I'm making that very hard for him this morning. Rather than causing tears, I'm earning trust. There are enough second-hand tears in the mist to meet my needs, although with Feastday in just twenty days, I'll need to find a more direct source. Veronica is determined to attend her own celebration. I wonder for a second what Amanda is up to these days, but then remember I said I'd use her to learn compassion. While it can't help me as a tear collector—and I no longer plan on crossing over to become a human for Scott—it seems to be a trait that Caleb possesses. I'm not sure how he managed to develop it, but I'm afraid to ask him.

"Keef, do you know what the word trust means?"

He shrugs his small shoulders.

"You trust me, right? You know when I put you in the water that I won't let you go and I won't let you drown? That's trust. Understand?"

"I fink so," he mumbles through a closed mouth.

"Well, another way you trust people is to tell them a secret. One way we could trust each other more is if we told each other secrets. I know you know what a secret is, right?"

He nods.

"So, I'll start. My secret is that I have a boyfriend nobody knows about, and I could be in big trouble. Do you know how big a secret that is? The biggest I could tell," I lie.

He starts to giggle.

"So I want you to tell me a big secret. Can you do that?"

After another nod, he starts to talk, but I put my finger up by his mouth.

"I bet you have so many great secrets, Keef. You don't know which one to tell me, so how about this: I'll ask you a question about something I want to know, and you answer. You have to answer, okay?"

"Okay, Cassanfa!"

"Keef, what happened to your mouth? Did your dentist do this?"

He shakes his head, then drops it so our eyes don't connect. I gently touch his chin and lift his head up.

"If a dentist didn't do it, your secret is to tell me who did."

He starts to shake his head again, but I hold his chin tightly—not so much that it hurts.

"I bet your mom or dad told you it was a secret, right?"

I help him nod his head.

"I bet it's the biggest secret you know, isn't it?"

Another nod.

"Well, I told you a big secret, and you owe me a big secret. So who did this?"

He starts to shake his head, but I won't let him. "I don't know."

"You mean you don't know the person or you don't remember?"

"Boaf."

"Let me help you remember," I say. Then I describe Alexei and what he did. Before I can finish, Keith is in tears, sending me in two directions—flying to Heaven and falling straight to Hell.

"Is it true?" Amanda says, the second she sits down. We're at the Tim Horton's near my house where Samantha and I used to hang out. "I heard that you and Scott broke up. Did you really?"

"Heard from whom?" I ask.

"Well, rumors spread," she says, but doesn't laugh.

How could she not know she's sitting across from Lapeer High School's number one shit stirrer? I'm the TMZ of LHS.

"I've heard that rumor about rumors."

"What happened?"

"Very complicated." I'm not sure which way to play this. "Amanda, can I trust you?"

Amanda looks both puzzled and pleased by my question.

"We're friends, right?"

"Right." She sips from her coffee, which is filled with cream and sugar, unlike Samantha who drinks her coffee like she views her life: bitter and dark.

"Can I ask you something?"

When Amanda nods, I ask, "What do people think of me?"

"I don't understand."

I can't tell if she's stalling, socially awkward, or something else.

I say, "We don't really hang with the same people. You hang with all those smart, dedicated students. What do people think of me?"

"Honest?"

"Honest."

She pauses again. These early conversations in friendships are baby steps; sometimes you walk, and sometimes you fall.

"Well, most people I know are really jealous of you."

"Really?"

"You always have a boyfriend," she continues. "You were always hanging out with Robyn and those types of people. We all said we didn't care, but deep down, we did."

"Care?"

"About being popular, about having boyfriends—everything you had. We'd tell ourselves: Just study, please our parents. We said those things were not important, and in my head I know they're not."

"But in your heart?" I ask.

"In my heart, all the time I was saying those things, I didn't really believe it."

"Having a boyfriend isn't all it's cracked up to be. I've had enough. I know."

"Easy for you to say," she says, adding that nervous laugh of hers.

"Amanda, it doesn't solve anything. It complicates everything."

"Again, easy for you to say." She laughs again. "You're popular. You've had boyfriends in the past, and no doubt you already have another. Do you —"

"What about Robyn? You knew her since grade school, right?"

"Robyn. . . ." Amanda whispers.

"She was more beautiful than me, more popular. She had everything, but—"

"It wasn't enough," Amanda says.

"Just the opposite," I explain. "Everything was wrapped up in those things. She'd lost herself to all of that, so when Craig broke up with her, there was nothing left."

"It's so sad," Amanda says. "What a terrible accident."

I decide it's time to strike.

"Amanda, I can trust you, right?" I ask before I put her words to the test.

Again she nods, smiles, looks hopeful.

"Robyn's accident was no accident. I think she killed herself."

"No!"

"I'll trust you, and you'll just have to trust I'm telling you the truth."

"Robyn had so much to live for!" Amanda says. "Everybody loved her."

"It's very sad," I say and wait just the appropriate amount of time to let that thought sit there between us. Then I add. "But we need to focus on tomorrow, right? It will get better. Trust me."

"Right. Tomorrow," Amanda says, but with this news, even

today is a struggle for her now.

I must try harder to make Amanda my test to see if I can be a real friend. If Caleb is right—and how could he not be?—we're evolving toward becoming more human. Amanda is a test of my growing humanity.

Can I finally treat her as a friend, not a feast?

"She lost her head," Amanda says. "She let her heart rule her life."

"Ruin her life," I correct her.

"No, loneliness ruins your life," she says.

"You're not alone. You have me, but I know it's not the same as having a boyfriend."

"You know the worst feeling?" I lean in to listen. "It's wanting and not having. If I could just turn off my heart and not *want* to fall in love, I'd be fine. But I can't."

"Never turn off your heart. Never lose hope."

"One day my prince will come, right?" Amanda says. Then she laughs, short, sharp, and bitter.

In her words, I find the answer key to this test. If Amanda and Scott hook up, then I won't feel bad for Scott, and Amanda won't be so sad. If I make it so she's not so sad, then I will be a friend, not the creature that my natures compels me to be. Amanda stirs her coffee while schemes stir around in my head.

Caleb and I spend the twilight hours swimming at the beach at the Holly Rec area. In between swims, I tell him about Robyn's death, the aftermath at school, and Veronica's words. I tell him everything except how Simon is pressuring me to be with Alexei, using threats of violence that I know he can't make into actions because that would defeat his goal of getting me to mate. I finish by saying, "That's why I decided I didn't want to be a tear collector anymore."

"You don't feel that way now, do you?"

"No. I want to be a tear collector so I can be with you."

"Like I said the other day, we could become human together." He pulls me tightly to him. "I'm confident I know how to cross over, but we still need to decide two important things."

"When and where?" I ask.

"Those are the wrong questions." He presses against me. "The question is who?"

Chapter 31

Saturday, June 27

afternoon

"**D**o you want to take a break?" I ask Amanda.

"I could use one," she says with a tired-looking smile. "Extra long shift."

"Tell me about it," I add. "I'm working here and over at Avalon for my grandmother."

"That nursing home, right?"

I nod.

"I've changed my mind, Cass. I'd like to volunteer there with you," she says as we walk outside. There are some small picnic tables behind the staff area. We're going to get some sun, while the smokers come here to hide.

I say, "That would be great, except—"

"Except what?"

"You'll be too busy."

"I think I can leave Farmville for a while," she says as we sit down.

"How about Loveland?" I say.

She looks confused.

"I think I have a date for you."

"Really?" She lets out that nervous laugh.

I can't believe what I'm about to say. "Scott."

"Scott?"

"I've thought about it," I say. "It's the only thing that makes sense to me. I care about Scott, so I want him to be happy. I care about you, so I want you to be happy."

"I don't even know him!"

"Neither did I," I remind her. "That's the best part: getting to know one another, but from what I can see, you'll be very compatible."

"This is too weird," she says in between another bout of stress-induced giggling.

"No, this is right," I say. "It's what Samantha did for me."

"Samantha?" Amanda asks. No two people could be more different than her and Samantha.

"She and Scott used to be a couple. She could've been a jerk about it, but she let it go. Scott was even nicer. He knew that Samantha was hurting, so he encouraged us to be friends."

"That's so sweet."

"I know, that's the kind of guy he is," I say. "So, what do you think?"

"I don't know." Another nervous laugh. "But, Cass, would we still be friends?"

"I would insist!"

"It seems so weird," she says, although I notice a smile rising like the sun. "How?"

"You leave that to me," I say.

Although I have plenty of experience breaking couples up directly or indirectly, bringing them together will be a first. My life is full of firsts now.

"Are you sure?" she asks. More laughter—not nerves, but anticipation.

I make sure she's looking at me before I bat my false eyelashes. "Trust me, Amanda."

After my shift, Amanda drives me by the Berrys' house. Becca and I play video games for an hour, but it drains her. She has so little energy, so little life left within her. I know there's not much time before her game is over.

Mrs. Berry catches me before I leave. "Thanks for coming over, Cassandra."

"Any time you need me," I say, punching every word.

"You're so caring."

I hope she doesn't see the handkerchief sticking out of my pocket, moist with her dying daughter's tears—tears I'm taking not to Veronica, but to Maggie.

"Are you still attending the grief group?" I ask.

"We just went that one time," she says, sounding ashamed.

"If you want to go again, I'll take care of Becca."

"They're not meeting again until after summer," she says, stopping, afraid of the next words to come out of her mouth. I want to coax out the words, but I show her mercy for once, leave the words unsaid, and offer help instead.

"If you want to talk with someone, my grandmother, Maggie, is really helpful."

"I don't doubt it," she says, trying to force a smile.

"No, I'm serious, Mrs. Berry," I push. "She's a trained grief counselor. What you're going through, it's just too much. She's coming over to pick me up if you want to meet her."

"It's okay, Cassandra, I'm fine," she says.

"Mrs. Berry, you're not doing okay." I step toward her, arms out. "You should let Maggie help."

"Caring about others must run in the family," she says, and now I'm hiding my smile.

"It does, Mrs. Berry. It does." I lock her tight in my arms, probably like Robyn used to do.

"Thanks again," she says, but I won't let go.

"Listen, everything is going to work out," I say, almost in a whisper. "Trust me."

I finally let go of our embrace, and she quickly changes the subject.

"Cassandra, how are things working out for your friend, Samantha?"

I pick up my backpack and start for the door. "I don't know. We had a falling out."

"That happens between friends, but no matter what, you've got to make it right."

I put my hand on the doorknob. "Why's that?"

Mrs. Berry looks not at me, but at the photos of Robyn on the wall. "Because you've already lost one friend, Cassandra, and I know you don't want to lose another. Am I right?"

I nod in agreement, even though Samantha is more than a friend; she's also a threat.

"From what you've told me, that girl is all alone in the world, and that's a terrible place to be. You can fall into a pit of despair and never come out of it. Like Robyn."

I turn before I leave and say very softly. "Robyn was strong. She would've come—"

"No. Robyn wasn't strong because she never had to be. Everything came easily for her, so she didn't know how to handle the hard times, and that's why she—" Mrs. Berry starts to weep.

"That's why she?" I prod. Maybe she's finally figured out the true nature of Robyn's death.

Mrs. Berry's tears are her answer, since she can't finish the sentence with the truth.

Maggie is waiting in the car looking upset with me, or maybe just the world.

"So?" she says.

I sit down while pretending not to hear her.

"I broke up with Scott," I remind her. "What more can I do?"

"Your duty," she says. "Keep your promise to me."

"But it's not Easter," I remind her.

"Cassandra, yes, that's considered mating season," Maggie says, stumbling over her words. "But that's when biology overcomes all. Off season, it's possible—if there's a connection."

"A soulmate," I whisper to myself, but loud enough for her to hear.

"Maybe."

"You don't believe?"

"No. Your mother believed, and that was almost her undoing," she says.

"What are you talking about?"

"Nothing."

"If you want my help, you need to tell me what you mean," I protest.

Maggie pulls off to the side of the road so she can face me. "Your mother thought your father was a soulmate. They wanted to break the rules—stay together—but I talked her out of it."

"No wonder the two of you don't get along."

"We don't get along because I was right. He wasn't a soulmate. He was just a mate, but he didn't stop with your mother; he mated plenty of others." Maggie is almost spitting out her words.

"You mean?"

"You have several half-brothers and sisters," she explains. "Some of them part human."

"Why didn't you tell me this before?"

"I'm telling you now so you'll be careful and not make the mistake your mother did."

"And then you'll help me?"

"If you mate with Alexei and start the next generation, then I will be ready to take over from Veronica," she reminds me, as if she has to say it again to make it real. "She'll see that I'm ready when I perform the miracle, and she can leave the family in my hands."

"But Alexei—" I start.

"This is not about sex or human ideas of love. This is species survival."

I fall into silence disguised as blind acceptance. "I understand."

"You know how the miracle works," she says. "A life for a life."

"I know." Few words leave my mouth because my mind is too busy with thoughts racing.

Maggie starts toward home, but I ask her to change direction. I ride in silence until Maggie stops the car.

"So, you'll really do this? Transfer a life force into Becca from someone?"

She nods.

As I exit, she asks, "You've decided?"

"I don't know yet," I say, the truest words I've ever spoken. "And I don't know who."

"I don't care who," she says. "I need to know when and where so I can prepare."

Sounds and images of fireworks and Samantha fill my head. "Fourth of July."

"There's one important thing you need to remember," she says. I turn to face her, and her cold eyes freeze on me. "Make it look like self-defense."

"What do you want?" Samantha says when she opens the front door.

It's 80 degrees outside. Her clothes are black; one eye is bruised blue. I sense the tears; I smell the sweat.

"Can we talk?" I ask.

Metal music is pouring out of the house.

"I told you: I don't want to talk with you until—"

"I'm going to help you," I say, trying not to smile.

"You're going to break Mark's face like you did Brittney's?" she asks. Then she laughs.

I join in. "I've missed your laugh, Samantha."

She shrugs. "Me, too."

I look behind her. The house seems filled with more garbage, perhaps because it contains almost nothing else. No lamps, chairs, tables, or mirrors. A living ghost town.

"So, Cassandra, you're really going to help me? You're going through with my plan?"

"Really." She closes the door behind her, and points at the road. "Let's get out of here."

"Where to?" I ask.

I turn and look for her car in the driveway, but it's missing.

Samantha licks her lips. "I'd give you a ride, but Mark sold the car. We're walking."

"I'm sorry."

"I'm not. It proves that I'm right. He's like a cancer. He needs to be cut out of my life."

I let the remark go; it's too perfect. We will cut Mark out of Samantha's life and erase Becca's cancer. The guilty will be punished, and the innocent will be set free. Balance always.

We start down the road.

"Little vampires," Samantha says as she swats a mosquito off her bruised face. "That's the title of my new book, you know."

"You're writing a new book?" I pull her back into my life. "Tell me about it."

As we walk in the sun, Samantha explains that in her book, vampires are evolved mosquitoes, and mosquitoes are nothing more than little vampires. It's an intriguing idea, which plays nicely on the idea of adaptation. But the best part of the idea is that she doesn't mention tear collectors, nor does she accuse me of being a psychopath. Samantha's OCD, ADD, PTSD, and BPD serve me well. We're at end of the block when she finishes telling me the first chapter.

"That sounds great! Can you tell me—"

She puts her hand up as a stop sign. "You're in for sure?" she asks.

I nod in agreement. "Criss-cross."

"Is Alexei back?"

"I can sense it, but he hasn't shown his face," I explain.

"We'll flush him out. I'm not sure how, but we'll figure something out," Samantha says calmly. "But first you need to take care of Mark. Then later, I'll take care of Alexei."

"Okay, but about Mark?"

"You'll shoot him on the Fourth of July. It'll sound like just another firecracker."

Her sweat hits the pavement. Steam rises.

"So, we're seriously doing this?"

"What choice do we have?" Samantha sneers. "For both of us, isn't it just a matter of time before something bad happens to us? If we don't kill them, one day they'll take our lives."

"You're right. There's no choice, so I guess it's fate."

We discuss how I will kill Mark, making it look like self-defense. A few days later, we'll lure Alexei into a trap, and Samantha will strike, also in self-defense. Making it look like self-defense is no act; that is exactly what killing Mark and Alexei means for both of us.

"I don't know what to do about Samantha," I say.

Caleb looks embarrassed. He picked me up outside of Tim Horton's after Samantha left. She can't see us together; nobody can.

"It's complicated," he says.

"Humans have it so hard," I say. "Always having to decide things. I had it easy."

"I'll make it easy for you."

Our fingers touch, and it's like sparks under my skin.

"How?"

"I'll figure it out. I'll fix everything. I'll make everything right."

"Everything?" I ask.

"Everything, Cassandra. Just trust me."

Chapter 32

Wednesday, July 1

afternoon

"What are you doing here?" I ask Scott in a not-so-chance encounter at the hospital front door.

"I'm here to meet Amanda," Scott says. I can't tell if he's angry or proud. Or both.

"I'm happy for you." I think I should add, *Happy you are safe from harm, from me.*

"I'd like to say the same about you and your *soulmate*, whenever you find him." He spits out the word soulmate.

"Scott, I'm sorry."

"Saying it doesn't make it any better, Cassandra," he says.

I motion for him to follow me, and we walk over to one of the benches.

"I didn't mean to hurt you."

"We were supposed to be together. You said you loved me, or was that just a lie?"

"I guess it was," I say.

I thought what I felt for Scott was love, but it was nothing compared to the connections I feel—really feel, not faking, not imitating, but really *feeling* through skin, muscle, and bone—with Caleb.

"I didn't mean to hurt you," I say again.

"That's funny, because you did a very good job," he says. "A *very* good job."

"I said I'm sorry," I say. "And I encouraged Amanda to get in touch with you. I don't know what else you want from me."

"You. I want you," he says, reaching for me.

I pull away.

"Scott, don't do this. Amanda will make you very happy."

"Do you remember what I answered when you asked me what my type was?"

"Someone like you," I whisper it away.

"That's still what I want, Cassandra."

"I'm sorry, Scott, there's someone else."

"Your soulmate," he scoffs.

"You can't understand what it's like," I say.

"To be lonely?" Scott says. "Everybody gets lonely."

"It's not that," I say, realizing I'm talking too much but unable to stop. "There's a lot you don't know about me. I can never tell you about who I am, where I've been, what I've done."

"I would listen."

"But you wouldn't understand."

"Try me."

"You don't know what it's like to be an outcast from society."

"Outcast?" Scott says. "You were one of the most popular girls in school. You—"

"You don't understand," I repeat. "Only an outcast could accept me, could love me."

"I love you!"

"But it would never be enough," I say as gently as I can say such harsh words.

He just stares at me—daggers of hate, eyes of hurt that are ready to weep.

I need to walk away from him, this, us.

"I'll tell her you're here," I say, but Scott is silent.

"Who is it?" He stands, turns, and looks down at me like an angry judge.

"I can't tell you."

Scott grabs my bare shoulders and I cringe in pain. The skin on my shoulders is so sensitive, like the nose of a dog. Caleb knows this; Scott could never understand.

"Who is it?" Not a question, but a plea. A primal scream.

"Please, Scott, you're hurting me!"

"That's enough!" a voice shouts. A male voice. Alexei's voice.

"Is that him?" Scott hisses, then releases his hold on me.

"No!" I shout at Scott's question and Alexei's presence. Even from a distance, Alexei's eyes lock on me like a missile on a target. He's dressed in black except for red All-Stars. When his coat swings open, I see something else that's not black: the silver glint of a pearl-handled knife.

"I know him," Scott says as Alexei draws closer.

"No!" I run from Scott, from Alexei, from my past, toward my future, and into the hospital.

"Where's Caleb?" I ask the nurse on the third floor.

"Pediatrics."

My shoes smack the hard floors of the hospital almost in time with the beating of my heart. I know he's not with Becca; she went home this morning.

I push the button for the elevator, but it takes forever. I race for the stairs, but almost as soon as I open the door, I see Alexei waiting for me, as if he could read my mind.

"Cousin, stop this running," he says.

"Alexei, just leave me alone!"

"I wish I could, but we both know I can't, Cassandra. I have my family duty."

"You don't care about the family."

"You're right, Cousin," he says. "We can't lie to one another, can we? I don't care about the family. The family doesn't care about us. About me. About my father."

"You broke the rules."

Alexei scoffs. "Let he who is without sin cast the first stone."

"I never kidnapped children. I never tortured people. I never—"

"By degrees, Cousin, by degrees," he says. "You don't think your manipulative heart-breaking way causes just as much pain? What I did to that boy downstairs has already healed, but what you did to him—he'll carry that scar forever. Don't lecture me."

"I was never cruel to innocents like you are," I insist.

"It's all I know," he counters then advances on me. "You think I want this?"

"What?"

"You think I want to be like this toward you? You think I want tears of terror and pain? I don't, but it's how I was made. You think I like hurting people?"

"Yes, I do."

"You're wrong, Cassandra, but this is what we are like."

His voice is calm, but his eyes glow with something like insanity. A sudden thought chills me to the core.

Would the painful tears of another tear collector be the ultimate rush?

I need to keep him talking until I can figure out what to do, how to escape, and how to stop him for good. Is he willing to do anything, break any rule, including that of killing one of his own kind?

"You don't need to be like this. Not all male tear collectors are evil. Caleb is good!"

"Ah, Caleb," he says, then frowning. "What makes you think he is any different?"

"I know." I regret saying his name to Alexei, but I need to understand their connection.

"You believe," he counters. "We're all alike! Cousin, you seem smart. How could you be stupid? You think he cares about you? He wants only to do his duty, then move on."

"You're wrong!"

"You watch: Once he takes what he needs, he'll leave," he says. Then he laughs, not a cheerful sound.

"No, you need to leave me alone. Now."

"You want to be rid of me?"

"Yes."

"Then it's simple: Let me fulfill my duty." He steps closers.

I can feel his cold breath on me. The only thing colder is the steely blue of his eyes staring through me—as if I am nothing.

How can I mean so much and so little to him at the same time?

"Let go!" I shout, but he's too strong.

He's dressed in black because he probably went to several funerals to fuel up for our encounter. He's got the strength of grief; I have only fear.

"Don't. worry, Cousin. I won't harm you," he says, yet waves the knife in my face.

"Let go!" I shout again.

He laughs. His near-cackle sounds just like Simon's laugh.

"I want to let go!" He twists my arm. "I want to be free of rules, of family, and of you, Cassandra. You are my curse! You are my duty. It is our time to be together. It is your turn."

He pulls me toward him with arms like steel cables. I can't escape, so I start shouting at the top of my lungs. He tries to silence me, but I bite his hand. He doesn't even flinch until he sees the skin is broken. A few drops of blood splatter the floor and dot my teeth. He must be full of energy because even this small blood loss doesn't faze him; it would make me faint.

"You dare refuse me this sixth time?" he asks, as he puts his mouth next to mine and suddenly has the blade to my throat. "If you deny your duty, you deny your life!"

"Let her go!" I hear Scott yell from the bottom of the staircase before I can even figure out how to respond to Alexei.

Scott isn't alone. Standing next to him are two hospital security guards and a cop with his gun drawn. Alexei says nothing as he lets me go. I fall to the ground unharmed but shaken as he runs up the stairs like a spider scaling a wall with the officers in rapid pursuit. Just before he bursts out the door one flight above, he turns to look back at me. His mouth says nothing; his eyes say everything as they stare right through me, telling me something I already know: This isn't over between us.

"Do you want to come in with me?" I ask Caleb when we pull into the church parking lot.

Even though Caleb consoled me and told me not to fear Alexei, I know I deserve Alexei's wrath and my terror for the sins I've committed. Nature demands balance; I've sinned too much to escape punishment.

He shakes his head. "I'll wait here."

I know him well enough already not to ask why. Caleb shares so much with me, yet there's a big part of him—including his history—he keeps hidden. Unlike Samantha who wouldn't respect my boundaries, I resolve to accept Caleb's silence.

I sit in our customary pew under the Sixth Station, but I can't help looking up at the Fifth Station: Simon carries the cross. The Gospel tells us that Simon did this willingly, but no one in Simon's current family, except Caleb, would do anything to help anyone but themselves. If male tear collectors once eased people's pain, now all they do is cause it—for humans and tear collectors alike.

As I walk into the confessional, my back feels as heavy as Simon's must have that morning as he carried the cross. I kneel down, take a deep breath, and wait for Father Morrison to begin.

"In the name of the Father, the Son, and the Holy Spirit. Amen," he says.

"Bless me Father, for I have sinned. My last confession was six months ago. These are my sins." I unleash a torrent of truth, trauma, and tears. I tell him everything, not why I did these things—it is my nature—but all the people I have hurt: Cody, Robyn, Samantha, and Craig, mostly Scott. I confess my lies, my betrayal, and all my evil deeds. Male tear collectors leave physical scars, but Alexei is right: The scars I cause don't heal with time or tears.

If all my words are lies, then how can I be true to myself?

I must trust Caleb, since I don't trust myself.

"You must seek forgiveness from those you hurt, not just from God," he says.

"I know."

And I know where I must start: Craig. All these events began with him. If he and Brittney hadn't hooked up, none of this drama would've occurred. The world is an ocean, yet one small drop of deceit rippled and wrecked many lives. Tomorrow night, I will help end a life for the greater good: I will save Becca, and I will save Samantha.

After Father Morrison gives me my penance, I recite the final prayer. "My God, I am sorry for my sins with all my heart. In choosing to do wrong and failing to do good, I have sinned against you whom I should love above all things. I firmly intend, with your help, to do penance, to sin no more, and to avoid whatever leads me to sin. Our Savior Jesus Christ suffered and died for us. In his name, my God, have mercy. Amen."

As I leave the confessional, I feel lighter. It lasts a second, then I hear the tap of a cane.

Under the Fifth Station of the cross in his black suit sits Simon in the flesh. I want to look away, but I can't. Simon flashes that snarling, twisted smile before he stares at me with those vulture eyes. His eyes echo his great-grandson's dark glare: this isn't over yet.

Chapter 33

Saturday, July 4

evening

"Are you sure this will work?" I ask Caleb.

We're in his car outside Samantha's house. The ruckus of bright fireworks, dark metal music, and stoned laugher envelops the white Charger.

"If everyone behaves as they should," Caleb says as he pulls me close. "Trust me."

"But you'll be here?" I ask.

I think how many times I've told someone "trust me" when that was the worst choice they could make. Now Caleb wants my trust, and I give it to him.

"I'll know if anything's wrong."

"I have my phone." I show him.

"You don't need a phone. I'll know, trust me."

"It's like we're connected," I say.

"You should get going," Caleb says.

"You'll protect me?" There's fear along with the smell of firecrackers in the air.

"Forever," Caleb whispers. "If you want Becca to live, you need to take a life. Mark causes nothing but hurt for everyone. Is Maggie really going through with this?"

I nod. "They'll take Mark to the hospital, then we'll get Becca. I'll call Maggie. At the hospital, you'll create a distraction so we can perform the miracle and she doesn't see you."

"Remember, Mark can only be wounded," he says. "Aim for his shoulder or leg."

"I've never fired a gun before," I remind him.

"Get close, and it will be easy," he says. "Just remember what's at stake."

Images of Becca not sick in a hospital bed but running, playing, and laughing fill my head.

"Do you think Samantha will go through with this?"

"She gave me her word," I reply.

But I also wonder. Unlike me, Samantha doesn't lie all the time. Her words I trust; it's the instability of her personality and actions that bothers me.

Caleb looks concerned. "She's a human. Do you really think we can trust her?"

"She's all I have," I say. "I'm doing this for her, but I'm also doing this for me. And for Becca."

"And Samantha swears she'll do her part."

"She thinks Alexei is a monster. She said she wants to kill a monster," I explain.

"He's not; he's just twisted," he says, and I give him a hard look. "I'm not defending what he's done; I'm just explaining. You don't know what it's like to be a male tear collector. You females thrive on sadness, but we're programmed to thrive on tears caused by pain."

"The pain of humans, not of other tear collectors," I say. "He wants to hurt me."

Caleb's jaw grows tight, just like it did when I told him about Alexei trying to attack me the other day. "I know, Cassandra, but we need Samantha to do it. I can't protect you from him. Taking the life of another tear collector is against all our rules."

"Our rules make us all monsters. Maybe Alexei was right: It is all by degrees."

"We're not monsters—not even Alexei, although some of his deeds are monstrous," he says. "Others have had his experiences, and it has not twisted them. It has made them stronger, more able."

"That's what these past months have done for me: Made me stronger."

"Good, because it's your turn to take control of your fate," Caleb saysbefore he kisses me goodbye.

"Hey, it's fat Sam's hot friend," Mark slurs when I walk into the house. He's shirtless and shit-faced. There's a party going on. "That other guy's not with you again, is he?"

I take a deep breath. "No, I didn't like how he jumped you. Can I get a drink?"

"And how!" he says, stumbling just a few feet away.

He hands me a red, plastic cup, then offers me a cigarette. I take the cigarette, but only so I can drop it. I bend over to pick it up, and I feel his eyes peering down my white, button-down shirt. I need to stomp out this insect.

"Where's Samantha?" Somehow I make that simple question sound sexy.

"Out," he says, taking a step closer.

Samantha, of course, only pretended to leave. We talked just before I came in the door. She's up in her room waiting for us.

"Is she watching the fireworks?" I ask.

Behind the house, Mark's stoner friends are shooting off M-1s, creating a sea of light and an ocean of sound—a celebration. It's just a few minutes early.

"I don't know. I don't care," he says, clearly only caring about looking down my shirt again.

"Well then, maybe I'll just have to party with you," I whisper in his ear.

My skin crawls being this close to him as my nose fills with the stink of smoke, whiskey, and evil. I let him brush against me. It has probably never been this easy for him. His drunken mind can't keep up.

"Maybe. . . ." I let my drawn-out voice draw him in.

"I'd like that, Mark," I lie with my mouth and my hands as I touch his studded belt.

"Shit," he slurs.

I wrap my fingers around one of the loops of his faded jeans.

"If she's out, then she's not using her room."

I pull on the belt loop like reins on a horse.

"Shit, girl! You get right to the point!"

If he's got even one male chromosome still functioning in his addled brain, he'll follow me. I take my time walking upstairs, letting him enjoy the view. We're at Samantha's door.

"Let me get ready." I open the door, step into the dark room, and lock the door behind me.

"Are you here?" I whisper into the blackness.

A small light emerges in the corner. Samantha has tears in her eyes and a pistol in her hand.

"Give me the gun," I whisper as I put out my hand. She can't see that it's shaking.

The energy from her tears starts to course through my veins. I rip off my blouse to expose my skin and plant the evidence of Mark's attack. The buttons scatter like blood from an open wound.

"I changed my mind. I want to do this," she says. "This is my problem."

"No, we agreed." Mark pounds on the door. "We would make this look like self-defense, and it's better if I do it. Fewer questions. I have no other motive. Give me the gun."

She stares at me through a mask of silent tears, but then complies.

"Don't be playing with me, girl," Mark calls through the door.

"I'm getting ready."

I nod to Samantha, then she opens the shade. The room is filled with the spotlight of the moon and the strobe-light of the fireworks. I take a deep breath, open the door, then retreat to the middle of the room, gun behind my back.

This isn't for me. This is for Becca, for Samantha. This is for Robyn.

"Let's go." Mark mumbles as he stumbles inside.

I try not to gag at his tattooed, skinny chest, which is sunken because he has no heart. His black eyes devour my white bra.

"Close the door," I say, and he does.

He's a puppet, and I'm pulling the strings. I motion him with my finger, calling him to me. "So, Mark, are you really ready? Let's see."

Mark's heavy, studded belt and chained wallet hit the floor with a loud thud when he drops his pants.

"This is gonna be sweet," he mumbles as he struggles to walk toward me.

"You're gonna get it," I say, but my change in tone doesn't register. "If you're man enough," I sneer, and that *does* register.

"Shut up!" He struggles to pull up his pants. "You fucking tease, I'll teach you!"

"Shut me up," I say, bracing myself for the blow. "Or is your fist as limp as—"

The slap coincides with an explosion outside. Light fills the air; stars fill my eyes. I step away from the window. He walks closer until I pull the gun on him. His mouth opens in shock.

"Mark, this is for Samantha!" I say as I pull the trigger.

The blood splashes across my face as the bullet lodges in Mark's shoulder. His knees buckle, then he hits the floor and rolls on his stomach. Blood oozes from underneath. I glance outside; nobody has noticed a thing.

I open up my phone to call 911. Once Mark is on the way to the hospital, I'll call Maggie to meet us there. We'll pick up Becca on the way. We arranged with her parents earlier to take her to watch the fireworks tonight. I drop the gun and take a deep breath before I punch my own face and slap my chest, trying to raise bruises as signs of Mark's attack while being careful not to break the skin. My pain distracts me from the sounds of Mark's agony.

"Fuck you," I hear Samantha say.

I turn on the light. Mark is breathing, but just barely. She holds something metal, shiny. The glint almost blinds me. A knife.

"What are you doing?" I ask her.

"Criss-cross," she says. Then she slashes the knife across Mark's naked back. Blood spurts in the air like some gusher, covering her arms. She makes another slash. "Criss-cross!"

"Stop it!" I yell, but she doesn't listen, slicing Mark's back again with the knife.

She stares at me, but doesn't drop the knife. Instead, she smears some of Mark's blood on her face. "No, Cassandra, this is pay-back!" Blood and tears mix in a stream of rage down her face.

"It has to look like self-defense!" I shout. "You're ruining everything!"

"I want him dead," she hisses. "I want him to suffer first. I want to watch him die."

"No!"

I grab her hand. Although her tears don't touch my skin, they are powerful enough for me to absorb them through the air. They give me the strength I need. I wrestle the knife away from her, although halfway through the struggle, she gives up. Samantha and I are breathing deeply, but Mark's breathing is growing shallow. I call 911, give the address, and collapse into the corner, the bloody knife by my side.

"Samantha, are you okay?" I ask.

"It didn't feel like I thought it would," Samantha says, pausing as if she's waiting for something. I look across at her bloody face and back to where Mark's crimson-soaked body lies. "It felt better."

With the knife in my hand, I crawl toward Mark. "I don't know how we'll explain those cuts."

"Justice," Samantha says as she joins me next to Mark's prone body. "Sweet jus—"

It happens fast. Mark grabs the knife from me, plunging it into Samantha's chest. She screams. I knock the knife from Mark's hand and smack him hard across the face. He collapses. Samantha lies a few feet away, screaming in pain, clutching her chest as blood pumps out.

"Cassandra!"

Caleb rushes into the blood-soaked room. I pull myself off the floor and rush toward him. He holds me, wiping the blood from my face and shoulder. "What happened?"

"She lost it," I say, pointing at Samantha. "Look at Mark's back!"

Caleb doesn't speak; he acts, checking Samantha first and then Mark. He grabs some of Samantha's T-shirts lying on the floor and creates a makeshift bandage for her chest. She's crying and screaming, but Caleb is calming her down. Or maybe taking her tears for strength.

"I called 911," I tell him, gasping for breath. "I don't know how we'll explain it."

"They'd better hurry," he says and crawls over to look at Mark. He checks Mark's pulse and shakes his head. "He's lost a lot of blood. He's going into shock."

"This is bad, really bad," I say, rocking back and forth.

Caleb crawls over to me, pulling me into his arms, and I rest my head on his chest.

"Cassandra, listen to me," he whispers. It's hard to hear his words over the noise outside, Samantha's sobbing screams, and my head pounding with sensations. "This is our chance."

"What?" I look into his blue eyes, but he directs them toward the two bloody bodies.

"The two of us," he says, still whispering. "We could cross over—become humans. We have these two lives. Mark *should* die. Samantha's wound is deep. She might not make it anyway. This is our chance to be together—maybe not forever, but as long as humans live."

I can't answer; my mind is exploding like the fireworks outside. My sense of danger increases. I don't hear an ambulance; instead I sense something wrong, very wrong.

"I don't want to let her die. She's my friend."

"So was Robyn, but this is for the greater good. She knows too much about our kind. Don't just think about us, think about all tear collectors. One death might save our species from discovery."

"Samantha was right. We're not really tear collectors; we're just psychopaths."

"I want to be with you, Cassandra, no matter what. We can be together as humans and defy our nature, or be together as tear collectors and defy our family. You need to decide now."

Before I can speak, the door swings open, and it feels like cold air enters. Alexei.

"What happened here?" he asks as he enters the room. He locks the door behind him.

"Alexei, what are you doing here?" I ask, stunned at his appearance.

"I've been following both of you. Us purebreds can sense each other, no?"

"Alexei, stay out of this," Caleb says, stepping in front of me.

"Here is our chance," Alexei says. "Take these lives and be on our own as a family."

"No," I shout at Alexei. "I won't join you—"

"I don't mean you, Cousin," Alexei says, pointing to Caleb. "I mean you, Brother."

My heart is as ripped open as Samantha's chest, as shredded as Mark's back.

Brother? That means Caleb is also my cousin. They share the same father, but does that mean that I—?

I snap out of my thoughts as Alexei slowly walks toward us. "How could you not tell her, Caleb? Doesn't it make you wonder, Cassandra, what else he hasn't told you?"

"Stay out of this!" Caleb turns away from Alexei and me to return to Samantha's side. She's still screaming, crying, and probably dying.

"It is not my fault your mate ran away with a human. Siobhan was such a silly girl."

"Don't talk about her!" Caleb hisses.

"What? Cassandra doesn't know about you and Siobhan?" Alexei says. He turns to me, his face like that of a five-year-old with a secret. "They were to mate, but she left Caleb for a human, leaving him without a mate and making them both outcasts."

"Just like Cassandra left you!" Caleb shouts as he attends to Samantha.

"No, she's mine!" Alexei snarls, grabbing my left arm and pinching it in his vise-like grip.

"Let go!" I shout to no avail. Alexei is too strong for me once again.

"It doesn't work that way, Alexei," Caleb says with his back to us. "Those are the old ways. We're free to choose: Choose to live as humans or tear collectors and choose our mates."

"She wouldn't choose you," Alexei counters.

"You're right; it wasn't a choice," Caleb says over Samantha's tears of agony. "It was destiny. Cassandra and I were meant to be to-gether—not you and her, not me and Siobhan."

"Choice is how you ended up alone when Siobhan rejected you as her mate and became human," Alexei says. "Now you must be alone the rest of your life, like our father. Cassandra is to be my mate. Brother, get out of my way!"

"No," Caleb says as he presses against Samantha's tear-streaked face.

When he turns around, his eyes are wide, almost rolling back in his head. He dives at Alexei, knocking us both down. Alexei rolls away and reaches for the bloody knife. I try to grab it, but he gets it first with his left hand and makes a slashing motion toward me. When he misses, Caleb leaps on top of him, catches hold of Alexi's left wrist, and starts squeezing. Alexei cries out as the knife falls from his hand. Caleb scrambles over Alexei to snatch the knife, which allows Alexei to rise to his feet. Before I can react, Alexei is behind me, his right arm locked around my throat. I feel the painful pressure of his grip give way to the sting of the knife—his knife—he holds at my throat.

"Let her go!" Caleb shouts over the sound of approaching sirens.

"No, Caleb! *You* let her go. She is mine!" Alexei chokes me harder, presses the knife more firmly against my skin.

Caleb turns back to Samantha and presses down on her wound. She shrieks in pain, but Caleb doesn't care about her pain, only her tears. He touches his fingers against her face, then advances on Alexei, his eyes afire. Alexei squeezes me tighter, and hangs on even as Caleb jams the knife into his brother's right leg. Alexei loses his grip on me and his knife, his blood flowing like an oil gusher. His face flushes as he grimaces with pain.

"I will kill you both for this," Alexei says as he pushes me down.

My skull cracks hard against Samantha's desk. The blood spurts from Alexei's leg like a rain shower from crimson clouds, while more blood oozes from my head. My vision swims. Before Caleb can reply, the sirens stop outside.

"Brother, I will kill you!" Caleb shouts, advancing on Alexei.

Alexei moves toward the window, but there's no place left to run. The house almost shakes with the footsteps of police entering and running up the stairs. Seconds later, they pound on the door.

"Open up! Police!"

Alexei's eyes dart around the room, first at the bodies on the floor, then at Caleb, at the door, and finally at me. "This is your fault, Cassandra! You will be the first to die."

Caleb moves between his brother and me. "Cassandra, I will protect you."

Alexei takes one step toward us, but as the door frame gives a loud crack from the officers trying to break it down, he quickly turns to the only exit remaining: he crashes through the window and down onto the grass below.

I'm still gasping for breath from Alexei's choking. The pain in my head is unbearable, made worse by the thudding kicks splintering the door frame. Another kick, and the door starts to shatter. Caleb turns to look at me.

"We're not safe with Alexei alive. He's weak now, and I'm strong. I will defy the rules, and I will kill him!" Caleb shouts, and he leaps out the window to chase Alexei into the night.

"Don't—" I start, but Caleb can't hear me; he's deep into the darkness.

I try to stand, but fall backward, joining Samantha and Mark on the bloody floor. The blood of humans and tear collectors mixes together on the soaked carpet. As the door bursts open, bright light soars into the room, and the police enter.

"Jesus! God! It's a bloodbath!" I hear one of the cops say.

I see the face of a young black man, leaning over me. "Just stay with us. You're going to be okay."

"Really?" I ask. He grabs my wrist with one hand, the other goes against my throat.

"Trust me," he says just before I black out.

I come back to consciousness in the ambulance. The police officer is with me. When he starts asking me questions, I pretend to black out again.

Once in the hospital emergency room, I just lie there, low man on the triage totem pole. The nurses and doctors scramble around me tending to those in immediate danger of dying. It's still the Fourth of July, and burn injuries flood the unit. In the bed next to me, someone loses the fight, and the weeping relatives fill the air with my ambrosia. I don't even have to touch their tears to feel the potency of fresh grief coursing through me, speeding up my natural healing process. Soon my head is feeling clear, and my pain has vanished. I wait until I'm left alone and slip easily away into the night, an anonymous girl who was never checked into the hospital.

Outside, I call Maggie and tell her everything, except about Caleb.

"Who is hurt worse, Mark or Samantha?" she asks.

"I don't know. I blacked out."

I wish I could black out the whole evening—not just the physical violence but the truth-attack from Alexei. Caleb never denied knowing Alexei, but he never told me they were brothers.

How could two brothers be so different? Or are they? Alexei's deeds hurt my head, but his words shattered my heart. What else is Caleb hiding?

"The Berrys called looking for you. They're waiting for us to come get Becca. I lied to them and told them we had a flat tire."

"Tomorrow night. We'll do it tomorrow night." I know Mark and Samantha both might die before then, but I need time to sort out my thoughts.

"I'll smooth things over with the Berrys," Maggie says. She sounds wired.

"I'll be home soon."

"Do you want me to come get you?"

I feel the bandage around my head, which the EMTs applied in the ambulance. With the burst from the tears of the hospital to fuel me, there's no wound beneath this cloth now. I start to remove it and say, "No, I want to walk."

"It's a long way. You're sure?"

I'm sure of nothing except that the long path that brought me here is filled with lies, hidden agendas, and broken trust by everyone. Everyone is guilty, yet only one can be punished.

"I need the time to decide," I say. "Decide who lives and who dies: Mark or Samantha?"

Chapter 34

Sunday, July 5

early evening

"We'll call if we're going to be late, okay?" I say, but we're already a day late.

All the complications from last night have delayed the plan for a day. One day's wait is worth it to save a life. Since we didn't pick up Becca yesterday, we're doing it tonight. Fireworks for the Fourth were last night, but tonight is the end of the county fair. There will be fewer fireworks—I hope in every regard.

"Cassandra, what happened?" Mrs. Berry asks. I have a bandage on my right hand where I skinned my knuckles. I can't risk a cut.

"I fell down. But when you fall, you get right up again. Isn't that right, Becca?"

"You're always right, Cassandra!" Becca says, grabbing hold of my left hand.

"Is Samantha coming with you?" Mrs. Berry asks with a rare hopeful smile on her face.

I wipe it off quickly when I tell her about Samantha fighting for her life in the hospital, giving her some version of the truth about Mark's attack.

"I pray she'll be okay, just like I pray for Becca. I believe in miracles," I say.

"I bet Samantha's a fighter," Mrs. Berry says. "She's had to be all her life. She'll make it."

"You should visit her, Mrs. Berry. Just having someone there would be a comfort."

"No, I don't know her. If she's that bad, she needs to spend time with her mother."

"Her mother is gone. I went over to Samantha's house this morning, and it was stripped bare. Either looters or Mark's friends, maybe one and the same. Her closet was empty."

"As empty as her heart. Who could abandon their child?" she asks the universe.

"You never would; I know that. I wish Samantha had a mother like you."

Mrs. Berry smiles, hugs me, her daughter, and me again. "If you can talk to Samantha, tell her we're thinking of her. And please say hello to your grandmother for me. If she ever stops being a nurse, she could become a top-notch therapist professionally, instead of just a volunteer grief counselor."

"I'll let her know," I say as Becca and I head outside and climb into Maggie's car.

The end-of-fair fireworks at the fair are bright, but I'm not looking up in the sky; I'm looking out into the woods. I have not heard from Caleb since last night. He's out there. He found me once before; I have faith and hope that he will find me again. But then again, so did Alexei.

Becca spends the entire fireworks show looking up the sky and clapping her hands in delight. I spend the time looking backward at my life, in particular the last few months, and staring in wild wonder at how much I've lived, learned, and survived in such a short time

After the grand finale, Maggie starts us walking back to the car. "We should go."

She sounds tired, and it's no wonder. She spent the day at the nursing home using my handkerchief to collect every last tear from the sick and dying in order to heal the sick and dying. I'm tired, too—not just from Alexei's attack on my body but from the day spent answering questions after the police tracked me down with my cell phone number. I answered every question, not once telling the truth, never once mentioning Alexei or Caleb. I told them that Mark had tried to rape me and Samantha tried to stop him first with her knife, but then I found the gun. They believed every word. What fools indeed.

When we leave, we head in the opposite direction from Becca's house. At first Becca doesn't seem to notice, but finally says, "When are we going home?"

"We have a surprise for you," Maggie answers.

"I like surprises," she says, and I try to contain my smile. She has no idea.

"You need to be quiet," I say. "And you can never, ever tell anyone about this. Promise?"

"I promise."

"If I find out that you told anyone about this surprise, then we can't be friends anymore. You don't want that to happen, do you Becca?" I say, laying it on thick.

"No, never," she responds. Then she hugs me as tightly as her frail arms can manage.

Becca keeps asking questions, but I just deflect them. Maggie says it's doubtful she'll remember much about this time, anyway. Something about the transfer process sends the body into temporary shock, which short-circuits the memory. Or so she says. She's never seen it done before, only heard what Veronica has told her—which is very little—and of course the legends and stories. It's a long shot, but it's Becca's only chance. I have a little more faith, given how Scott forgot everything from his ordeal, which was only a few months and forever ago.

We have no trouble getting into the hospital. I tell the nurse a story about Becca wanting to visit one of her sick friends. Maggie helps, and we get the nurse to break the rules and let us onto the floor. Once there, I wait until no one is around and look at the computer.

Caleb, of course, isn't here to create a distraction. I called Amanda several times in hopes she could meet me here. I'd thought to start a huge screaming match with her, which would give Maggie time. When she didn't answer, I called Scott and asked him to have Amanda call me, but he didn't answer, and she hasn't called. I even called Amanda's house, hoping to get her mom, but without success. They must be out together, maybe with Scott's mother. The four of them happy, laughing, and full of life, just like Becca will be again very soon, thanks to me. I helped kill one Berry girl; I'll do anything to save this one's life. It's bad but, ultimately, for the greater good.

"Intensive Care Unit, one floor down," I tell Maggie.

We take the back stairs. Without Caleb to provide the distraction, we need to bide our time. I tell Becca we're playing a special game of hide-and-seek, making up new rules as I need them. Seconds turns to minutes, but eventually the hallway of the ICU clears during shift change, and the three of us make a silent, mad dash for the room.

"Now!" signals Maggie, and we duck into the room.

Maggie pulls the curtain by the bed so Becca and I can't see what's going on. My ears overdose with the beeping electronic sounds of modern medicine.

"What's my surprise?" Becca asks. "Why are we in the hospital? Who is that?"

She starts toward the curtain, but I hold her back and then close the door tight. We need to be quick.

"If I tell you, then it's not a surprise," I say.

"It's not my birthday."

I think, *No, it's your re-birth day.*

I say, "It's just for being you," and pull her towards me in another hug.

"I'm ready," Maggie says, sticking her head out from behind the curtain.

"Okay, Becca, time for your surprise," I say. "We're going to put a blindfold on you, and then we're going behind this curtain. Don't be scared. Everything will be fine. Trust me."

"Everything's always fine when I'm with you, Cass."

I fake a smile because she doesn't sound like herself, she sounds like Robyn, who started all of this in motion.

"Let's go." Maggie sounds beyond impatient.

"Okay, be very quiet—like we're in church," I tell Becca.

I put on the blindfold and lead her behind the curtain. Maggie sits silent as machines beep like a computer game, keeping the baby on the bed alive.

"Sit her down here," Maggie says softly.

Becca sits at the table next to the bed. Maggie opens up her purse and pulls out Veronica's handkerchief, which she presses against her face. She lets out a loud sigh, almost like she's been punched. She sets the handkerchief down. Next, she pulls out Veronica's violet veil and places it over her head.

"Leave the girl here, but you can't see this," Maggie hisses. "Out!"

I do as I'm told. I unlock the door and stand guard in front, pretending I belong here—acting natural while the supernatural occurs behind me.

I run my fingers across the chart outside the room with the patient's name. I wish I could erase the print on the paper and wish this wasn't the only choice to make. In the room behind me rests—if only for a few more minutes—the human life known as Samantha Dressen.

Why didn't Samantha understand that "trust me" are words never to believe from a tear collector?

What was it that Samantha said was the only thing that would cure her? Death. As always, a tear collector is ready, willing, and able to help with the healing process. As with Scott's grandmother, it's another mercy killing—although God will have no mercy on my soul for any of this. All my guilty sins are worth it for the life of one innocent.

Welcome back, Becca.

Chapter 35

Sunday, July 5

late evening

"Where is *she*?"

My heart almost stops when I hear that chilling, familiar voice echoing off the tiles of the ICU hallway. I turn, and there is Veronica—not sitting in a wheelchair, but standing tall. Mom is next to her.

Before I can answer, or rather decide what to answer, they act. Mom pushes me aside as she and Veronica go into Samantha's room. I stand frozen in time, but everything melts in a few seconds when Mom emerges from the room with Becca in hand, blindfold still on her face.

"This—*this* will not be allowed," Mom hisses. "Stay here."

Mom returns to the room. Becca is next to me. I allow her to see again—see everything but how frustrated I am that I have failed to save her life.

"Is this my surprise?"

"Well, Becca, it's such a big surprise that I wanted to have all my family here."

"I wish all my family was here," she says sadly.

My shoulders tingle, but my ears burn as inside the room I hear raised voices—mostly Veronica and Maggie; Mom is muted.

"I know! Tell me, Becca: What's your best memory of Robyn?" I say to distract her. "You tell me yours, and I'll tell you mine. Deal?"

We shake hands to seal it. She starts to talk, but I'm not listening to the little girl's memory. I crack open the door gently to hear the grown women argue.

"Don't think I don't know what's going on. I might be old, but I'm not senile!" Veronica says in a whispered shout.

Samantha must be in a deep sleep or maybe even a coma. But even if she wakes up, maybe she'll just think it's another one of her nightmares, a nightmare that's all too true to life—and death.

"You are old—too old!" Maggie counters. "You have outlived your usefulness. It takes too much of our time and energy to keep you alive yet another generation."

"You're just trying to save yourself, Maggie!"

"As are you, Veronica. As are you."

"What I'm doing is none of your concern," Veronica says. "What you have done tonight—stolen my veil and tried to perform this miracle—is the most serious of sins, Maggie."

"No, I did it to show you that I'm ready to become the true image," Maggie says.

Mom remains silent. She sides with Veronica, I know, but why she does I do not understand.

"That is for me to decide, and for you to accept my decision, your fate," Veronica says.

"So I should just stand here, and watch you take my life?"

There's a slight commotion. I peer inside, but they're all behind the curtain.

"Yes, your mother did it, and so did her mother and her mother before. It is your turn, Maggie."

"No, Veronica, it is your turn to die."

"That, Maggie, is her decision, not yours," Mom says.

"Quiet, Salome. This doesn't concern you," Maggie hisses at Mom.

"Once Cassandra starts the next generation, you must go, Maggie. There is nothing more to say." Veronica's tone has changed: not arguing, but stating facts as she foretells the future.

I'm distracted when one of the nurses comes my way. I know her. She likes me. They all like me here. I smile and lie through my teeth. When she asks about Becca, I distract the nurse by removing the bandage and showing her my skinned knuckles. I ask for a new bandage, which sends her on her way. The skin itches from healing. I resist scratching it.

"Becca, would you like a pop? I know I would." I reach into my purse and hand her a few dollars. "There's a vending machine real close. Go down the hall, take a right. I need to stay here, but you come right back."

She nods and heads on her way. How I'm going to explain all of this to her parents is beyond me. All of this is beyond me.

The best-laid plans. . . .

I turn back toward the door, but jump back when it opens. Maggie walks out, head down.

"What's going on?"

"I'm leaving."

"But what about Becca?"

"Not what about Maggie?" She clutches my wrist. "Never mind, I'm leaving."

The tone in her voice is odd, and then I look up. There is one small, violet tear dangling from her left eye. It must burn like acid. Her knees buckle, and I help her stand.

"Are you going home?" I ask with best intentions, even as I fear the worst.

She looks at the floor, then at me. "No. I have no home any-more."

"Maggie, what are you saying?"

She lifts her face. Another tear forms in the right eye, then falls on my hand.

"I'm not just leaving the hospital, Cassandra. I'm leaving the family. Veronica has exiled me. Forever."

Maggie starts down the hall. I follow.

"Wait! There has to be another way."

She says nothing as she walks, head down in her own darkness under the bright lights. I look down at my skinned knuckles where Maggie's tear landed. The skin has healed perfectly.

I return to Samantha's room, where the door remains open. Seconds later, Veronica and Mom emerge. Veronica clutches her veil with both hands. Mom stares at me like I don't exist.

"Cassandra, we're leaving," Mom says. "Where's the girl?"

"I sent her away," I mumble. "Does that mean you're not going to save her?"

Veronica and Mom glance at each other. Mom frowns, while Veronica almost seems to smile. It's the same twisted smile I recognize from after I told her Robyn had died.

"Not tonight," Veronica whispers.

"But you will save her? You will perform the miracle?" I beg.

"Cassandra, I will not." Veronica looks at the floor and then stares at me. "It's your turn."

Chapter 36

Monday, July 6

afternoon

"So, Craig, are you ready to talk?" I ask. I'm not wasting any time. Veronica wouldn't tell me why, but she did tell me I would need the most potent tears I could find by tonight. I have to work fast.

The fact that Craig agreed to meet me tells me he wants to talk, not *to* me but *about* Robyn. We're at his house in the big living room. It's as if his parents built a shrine to their living son: framed photos and painted portraits adorn every wall. His parents are at work; so am I. He needs to tell the truth; I need his tears. Honors Biology is over, but symbiosis remains heavy in my life.

"I've wanted to do this for a long time," Craig starts, but he's struggling.

"I tried, but you didn't seem interested," I remind him. "You blew me off."

"Cassandra, look, you don't know what it's like," he says. "At first, I was just in denial about it all, but I know you. I knew if I talked to you, I'd have to face it. You were like this dark cloud hanging over me. I was too afraid. Like Robyn said in her letter: I wasn't that strong."

"You're strong enough. Show me."

He breathes deeply, then leans forward. While I don't touch his hand, I lean forward as well. My white strapless summer dress is perfect for the occasion. I position myself so when—not if, but when—he starts to cry, my left shoulder is ready, waiting, and more than able.

"I don't know where to start."

"Why did you cheat on Robyn? She loved you so much. You knew that."

He shakes his head back and forth, like he's been punched in the face and is trying to shake it off. "I know you won't believe me, but it really wasn't my fault."

"You're right, Craig. I don't believe that. How is cheating on her not your fault?"

"Look, only two things mattered to me in high school: Robyn and sports. Without them, I didn't have a reason to attend Lapeer. Heck, without them, I didn't have a reason to live!"

"And yet, it's Robyn who's dead, not you."

Another head shake, like I'm giving him an emotional concussion. He can't see straight.

"Okay, listen—and I want you to know that I'm telling you the honest truth," Craig says almost without opening his lips.

He's trying to keep it together, to appear strong even as he admits his mortal weakness. His male weakness. They all have it, even my most pious Scott.

"Do you remember the end-of-season basketball party?"

I shrug. Before Scott—when I hung with Robyn, Craig, and Cody—I went to so many parties that they all blur together.

"You got into a fight with Cody," he says, but still I register nothing. "I mean, I'd seen you do this before with Cody, with some of my other friends. I thought you were a real bitch."

"Would I be here now if I was?" I ask. "Would I have shown you Robyn's letter so you could know that she forgave you? Would I forgive you if I was a bitch?'

"Well, you did used to be a bitch, but then I saw a change in you. After Robyn—"

He stops, so I finish it. "After Robyn died."

Craig goes silent. I sip from my water bottle and lean another inch closer.

"Well, Cody got real upset and called you a bitch, and I agreed, and then Robyn and I started fighting about it. We were fighting about you. I think all this mess is your fault."

"So Robyn's death is my fault?" I ask, but wonder, *Is it really?*

"No, I'm just saying that was the start of it," Craig answers. He doesn't seem like the big, popular jock right now. He seems like a lost little boy trying to find his way home. "So, we got in a fight, which was hard to do with Robyn since she was such a gentle person. Robyn got a ride home with someone and left me there. I was pretty upset, and I guess she noticed that."

"She?"

"Brittney. Like I've seen you do with so many people, she came over and tried to comfort me. And 'southern' comfort me as well," he says, lifting one eyebrow significantly.

"So she came on to you?" He nods. Then, another head shake. I take it as a sign and put my hand on his shoulder like a friend. "Keep going, Craig. Tell me everything. It's okay."

"I don't want to talk about it. I don't want to relive it."

"Craig, it's the only way to let the healing begin. Time, tears, and now *truth*."

"Okay, Cassandra. Can I trust you?"

"Of course," I lie.

"I got really drunk and . . . well, Robyn was pretty strict about stuff. You know, sex?"

I nod and sip my water bottle a little faster.

"And, well, Brittney was quite the opposite." I would expect him to laugh or smirk here like most guys, but instead he still looks sad. "I knew it was wrong. I knew I messed up. So I thought I'd man up and ask Robyn to forgive me. I didn't know if she would, but I loved her so much."

Now, I shake my head. "If you loved her, you wouldn't have hooked up with Brittney."

"In the heat of the moment, people do stupid stuff. Like you've never made a mistake."

I stare at Craig, but my thoughts are elsewhere: Scott.

"So, did she forgive you?"

"She never got the chance," Craig says, his words more deliberate now. "The next morning at school, Brittney told me I needed to break up with Robyn and be with her."

"Why?" I ask, even though I know the answer: She's a psychopath, and all that matters to her is hurting others. I hurt because I must; she hurts others for the thrill of it.

"Do you mean why did she do that, or why did I go along?" he asks.

"Same thing."

He pauses to lean back on the sofa, almost sinking into it. "I had no choice."

I laugh. Then I stand up, take six steps away, and walk back. "How is that?"

"She had photos of us," Craig whispers. "I don't know if she took them or had someone else do it—maybe Kelsey? Like I said, I was really drunk. My first time, and I don't even remember it—although it seems I'll pay for those few minutes all my life."

"But still, Robyn might have forgiven you."

"You don't get it, Cassandra," Craig says as he leans closer. He puts his right hand on my knee, and I notice it's shaking. "Brittney said she'd not only show the photos to Robyn and everybody at school, but that she'd also send them to the Mr. Baldwin, the athletic director."

"So?"

"You were on the swim team, Cassandra. You know the code we all sign. You get caught drinking, and that's it; you're gone. Zero tolerance."

"So you choose sports over Robyn?"

"No. It's not like that." He pauses, takes a breath. "I didn't know what else to do. And Brittney knew how to play me. I was this naive kid who'd never had sex before, and—"

"Spare me the details," I say, putting up my hand to cut him off.

For someone who sounds as if he regrets the whole thing, he seems a little too eager to share this part of the story. The male weakness is so very strong.

"But I never thought it would come to this," Craig says. "I didn't know that almost immediately rumors would spread about me and Brittney—rumors she started, I suppose."

I nod. I'm sure she started them, but I spread them like a disease for my own needs.

"And then everything—well, everything just got out of control," Craig says. "After Robyn died, I was lost, and Brittney was there for me. It was too easy. That's what I know now. I took the easy path. I didn't stay strong. I let myself be weak, and because of it—"

"Because of it, Robyn died."

My shoulders tingle. He's almost ready to harvest.

"Say it, Craig."

"And because of it, Robyn died," he whispers. "I've read her letter a hundred times, and I still can't figure it out. Was it just a letter, or was it a suicide note? I mean how she died—she'd driven that road many times. So why on the morning after she wrote that did she crash? Why?"

Before I can answer, the gentle sobbing starts. I move closer. "It's okay to cry."

"Why, Cassandra? Why?"

The now fast and furious tears are a mix of sadness, anger, pain, and confusion. He's a full pallet of human emotion unleashed. The tears flow into my skin, and I feel the surge of energy. I hold him close so he can't see my eyes rolling back in my head.

"Why, Cassandra? Why?"

The second tidal wave crashes into my skin. Feeling full, I reach into my purse and hand him Veronica's handkerchief. He wipes the tears from his eyes and hands it back to me. It's good for now, but not enough for later. I need more. I need them all.

"I don't know why, Craig, but I know there's someone else you need to tell."

He sniffs and wipes his nose with his sleeve. "Who?"

"You need to tell Robyn's parents. They need to hear you say you're sorry, like you said to me at school. Spare them the details, but you need to tell them to their face. Let's go now."

"No, I don't think that's a good idea."

I grab his hand and look him in the eye.

"Craig, listen, trust me. Her family needs to know. You need to tell them."

He shakes his head. "I don't know if I can do that."

"You said all this happened because you were weak," I remind him. "So to make it right, you need to show that you're strong. You need to face them. You need to tell them."

"Won't that open up old wounds?" he asks. "Won't it just make them blubber like me?"

I touch his face. "I'll go with you in case Mr. or Mrs. Berry needs a shoulder to cry on."

Chapter 37

Monday, July 6

early evening

"Craig, can I ask you one more thing?"

He nods, but it's not because his head is heavy. It's lighter thanks to another explosion of emotion in front of the Berrys, who responded in kind. Becca must have been listening upstairs because as the Berrys and Craig filled my shoulder with tears, Becca's tears trickled down from a distance. He gave them the note, and the Berrys read it together. They knew what it meant, but they denied it. Suicide is a sin, and they want to believe Robyn left the world as she entered it: innocent. If the Berrys are guilty of anything, it is denial. Sometimes believing the lie is best.

Now we're in front of their house, and Craig awaits whatever question I have for him. What could be worse or better than what I've already put him through today?

"At the prom, what did Caleb say to you?"

We stroll toward his car. "How do you know about that?"

"You don't remember? He was sitting with Scott, Samantha, and me?"

"I try to forget everything about that night," Craig says softly.

It's twilight, and the air is starting to cool. I don't need more tears; I need answers.

"He came out of nowhere. I was by myself. Brittney was off pouting in the bathroom."

I can't tell him that Caleb must have sensed his pain.

"So what did he say?"

"Well, I had come over to talk to you. Just to say hello. I know—stupid. But when I got back to the table, Brittney was all jealous and talking about you the way Cody did. Suddenly I realized everything with Brittney was wrong."

"So you fought?"

"Yes, but then she started to make promises like she always did. I believed her until—"

"Until?"

"Until this Caleb guy comes over. He says he knows all about me and Brittney, and I ask him how, but he won't answer. Instead, he winks and says he knows more about Brittney than I do. I ask him what he means by that, and he says, 'She was the best I ever had.'"

I try not to react as I remind myself that all tear collectors lie to stir up drama. Caleb couldn't have known Brittney—let alone been with her.

"Did you believe him?"

"It didn't matter because I knew she was with someone when we hooked up. I knew she cheated on him with me. So then Caleb asked, 'So don't you think she'll cheat on you, too?'"

"He's right. That's how Brittney operates," I add.

Craig nods in agreement. "When she came back, we had it out, and I realized that she didn't care about me. Brittney cared about Brittney, and she'd use me, dump me, and move on."

"I'm glad Caleb helped you see that."

Craig looks at his watch. "Sometimes you get so close to something, you can't see it."

"Because you only want to see what you want. You only want to see your dreams."

"I don't have those since Robyn died." Craig grunts and opens the car door to start his journey back home, back to himself. "Now, Cassandra, all I have are nightmares."

"She seems different," I tell the Berrys once I'm back inside.

Mom and Veronica will be over very soon. Then we're headed to the hospital. Like me, Mom collected tears from some powerful sources and also used her Red Cross connections to arrange things at the hospital.

"I know. It won't be long. The doctors say—"

"Just the opposite, Mrs. Berry," I say. "Last night during the fireworks she seemed like her old self. Did she tell you anything about that?"

Of course, it's what happened afterward that I need to make sure Becca didn't tell. Mrs. Berry shakes her head in the negative.

"I'm telling you—you should get her checked out tomorrow or the next day," I say. "She seems to have more spirit."

"Maybe that's just because you're around so much," Mrs. Berry says.

"Well, thank you for sharing her with me."

"You're a good friend, Cassandra. No, more than that. You're a good person."

"I try to be," I say, and I smile—not at the lie, but the truth in that statement.

As I wait for Mom and Veronica, Mrs. Berry asks more about Samantha. I can't tell her how Samantha is now—why make her worry when it will all be over soon?—so I tell her Samantha's truth for her whole life: she's getting better physically, but emotionally she's a wreck.

"I wish I could do something to help her." Mrs. Berry shakes her head in sorrow.

I put my hand on her shoulder. "Why don't you pray for two miracles?"

It's odd to be in the car without Maggie—odder still to see Veronica outside two days in a row. Either Mom must have worked

overtime, or Veronica must have dipped into the tear collector vial because she seems, if not young, then at least younger. Maybe it's having Becca in the car with us, or maybe it's something more. With
Maggie gone, maybe Veronica thinks she's safe and secure, which is
the opposite of what I think I am with Maggie in exile.

All morning, I tried to get them to tell me what happened and
where Maggie went, but they refused. Veronica just kept repeating
that until Maggie understands her place, she's exiled from the family.
I'm not sure if the exile is permanent, like with my father, Caleb's father, and Siobhan, or if there is something Maggie can do or say. As always, the one thing I'm sure about is: Veronica and Mom won't tell
me any truth they don't want me to know. Truth is rarer than even
those ancient tears.

After we take Becca for ice cream to make the lie true, we go
to the hospital. Again, I get Becca to swear she won't tell about our ad-
venture tonight. Unlike me—unlike most humans even—Becca is
trustworthy. She keeps her word, and tonight, I'll keep mine.

We enter the hospital and head for an empty office that Mom
secured to use for the evening. Like me, she can talk herself into anything she needs. Once inside, Veronica sits in one chair, and I sit in another. Mom starts to leave with Becca.

"Mom, where are you going?"

Mom motions for Becca to walk ahead, then she turns to me.
"Veronica needs to talk to you, in private. She'll tell you what you
need to know, but ask her no questions. Understand?"

I nod in obedience as I've done a thousand times before. Mom
shuts the door and leaves. Veronica is silent at first, then she puts her
aged hands on mine, holding them down. My hands shake, but hers remain perfectly still—just like this night, just like time itself.

"Cassandra, everything depends on you—not just that girl's
life, but our lives. Our kind." I stare at her.

She squeezes my hand more tightly. "Cassandra, he has found you, hasn't he?"

I start to fidget, but she clamps down. "Caleb has found you, correct?"

I nod. His name used to make me smile, but now all I can do is worry. The hospital is abuzz over his disappearance, but my phone doesn't buzz or ring. I haven't heard from him since he followed Alexei out the window at Samantha's house. But how does Veronica know about him? About us?

"Listen, and you'll understand all you need to know."

Her grip on my hands loosens, but I sense her grasp on my life about to tighten like a steel vise.

"As he probably told you, Caleb was to mate with Siobhan, but she left us. Before I could bring her back, Caleb ran away after his father was exiled. It is vital that Caleb mate with a tear collector. Like you, he is very special."

"I know he is."

Veronica makes a sound that mocks human laughter. "Not in the way you think. As you know, Caleb is from the Simon line. He was the first born to his father, before his sire turned on us as well. Caleb's mother is from our line. So that makes him the most pure."

"Our line? Who is his mother?"

"What did your mother say? I will tell you what you need to know and nothing more. Do not ask me more questions, Cassandra. I will not answer, and it saps the energy you will need if you are going to save that girl's life. Do you understand me?"

My obedient nod returns.

"When tear collectors began, we were a compassionate race. Over time we've evolved into something quite different," Veronica says slowly. "The only hope for our species is to return to the old way. As in past generations, the women must act with compassion, and the men must inspire empathy, not fear. That is how it once was and can be again. There is something about you, Cassandra—like Caleb, you are special. He is not like other male collectors."

"You mean like Alexei? His brother?" His name sets my

hands shaking.

"Half-brother—different mothers, and that is the difference," Veronica explains. "Somehow, it is as if Caleb became a more pure tear collector, while Alexei became—"

I cut her off. "Evil and crazy."

She nods her head in agreement. "Simon insisted that despite that fact, the two of you must mate as it has always been done. I said no, but Simon wouldn't listen. Alexei wouldn't listen."

"He attacked me! You knew that, and no one did anything about it."

"Alexei had no choice. The two of you—biologically—were meant to be together," she explains. "He couldn't *not* want to mate with you any more than the earth could stop orbiting around the sun. It's nature. But you did not have that same biological drive to him, did you?"

"No. All I felt around him was fear. I knew he was evil."

"I expect that came from nature and nurture under Simon. But Cassandra, despite some of the things you have done, you are like Caleb. You are more pure than most tear collectors. If you and Caleb were to mate, I believe that child could start a new era of tear collectors. Maggie knows this, too. It is why she sided with you against me. She wanted to use you to assume my place. She is right. It is time for me to let go, but not until I know that the family is safe. I do not trust Maggie, and I do not trust your mother. Cassandra, it will soon be your turn to be the true image, the Veronica."

I cannot breathe.

"You will start tonight by performing this miracle. I will show you the way," Veronica explains. "But afterward, you will be tired like you have never been before in your life. You will feel near death yourself, but it is the only way to prove to me—to everyone—that you are worthy."

"I will not let you down."

She squeezes my hands so tightly that pain shoots through my body. Even though I'm full of energy from Craig's and the Berrys' tears, she seems stronger. Maybe it's because she's in control.

"I thought we lost you with Scott, but you passed that test. As you gave me tears, I sensed what you did to collect them. I sensed everything you went through for me, for this family. It was so long ago when I was your age. I cannot imagine how difficult it was for you, but you did as you needed to, even though I sensed you were fighting it—fighting your fate."

"What is my fate, Veronica?"

"When you told me about Robyn's death, I saw a real look of hurt in your face, and I knew you were not like us. I said it was wonderful that she died, just to push you. Another test. You will be the Veronica; I will see to it. You have nothing to fear."

"Except Alexei."

He face grows hard. "No, Alexei is a pawn. Simon is the one we should fear. I am far too old to transform us back into a compassionate species, but you are not. Simon does not want us to change. He is content with what we have become; I am not. You are not my pawn. You are my queen."

I try to ask Veronica more questions, but she refuses to answer. We wait in silence until the door opens. Becca comes in first, all smiles. Mom backs into the room, pulling a wheelchair behind her. The life we're about to take sits in the chair. She spins it around.

It's Mark, not Samantha. I told them about Samantha—about her knowing too much, about her threats. And yet they chose Mark. He's either asleep or unconscious in the chair. Either way, he's already seen his last waking moment.

"Mom, why didn't you choose Samantha?"

Mom looks at Veronica and then says to me very softly. "No mother should lose a daughter."

"Her mother is a junkie! She's doesn't care about Samantha."

Mom touches my shoulder even more softly than she speaks. "Of course she does. She must. For it's her daughter."

Chapter 38

Monday, July 6

late evening

"Are you ready?" Veronica finally asks me.

Mom stands guard in front of the door. I don't how to answer because I have no idea what is expected of me—either now or in the future. I just know that whatever cross I thought I carried revealed itself to be much heavier. Like the first Simon, Caleb must help with the burden to carry out Veronica's design to save the tear collectors.

"Can I have your tear charm, Cassandra?" Veronica asks.

I hand it over. When I unclasp it, the sound kicks me back to the night I handed Scott his heart charm back, the night I handed his heart back to him, broken but soon to be repaired by time, tears, and Amanda.

"Becca—it is Becca, right?" Veronica asks, and Becca nods. "Do you like this charm?"

"It belongs to Cassandra!"

"But it could belong to you, if you do exactly as I say. Would you like that?"

Becca nods again, but soon her head is moving in a different direction—back and forth as Veronica whispers words into Becca's ear. About a minute later, Becca's head tilts forward as if she's asleep.

"What did you do?" I ask, but Veronica puts her left hand on my lips to silence me.

She motions for me to hand over her bag. She takes out the tear collector vial and her veil and then whispers for me to give her the handkerchief. I remove it carefully from my purse. Becca isn't moving, nor is Mark. Veronica moves slowly while my heart races laps around all of them.

Veronica positions me to stand between Becca and Mark. As I have done hundreds of times for her, she moistens the handkerchief with ancient tears and hands it to me. I press it against my face and almost fall backwards. When I press the cloth against my bare shoulders, my knees buckle, and I start to breathe heavily.

"What is happening to me?" I ask.

Veronica says nothing as she motions for me to kneel between Mark and Becca. She carefully places Mark's limp, tattooed hands directly on my left shoulder. On my right shoulder, she rests Becca's head. Beneath the skull lies the tumor that will take her life. There's no hair left on her head, few days left in her life.

"Say my prayers, Cassandra. Say both of them," she whispers.

I nod, and then whisper the familiar words, "Saint Veronica, you gave Christ your veil on His way to Calvary which He used to wipe the Precious Blood and Tears from His Holy Face. In return for this act of kindness, He left you His Most Holy Image on your veil. Pray for us, Our Lord, that His Holy Face may be imprinted on our hearts so that we may always be mindful of the Passion and Death of Our Lord Jesus Christ. Through the same Christ, our Lord, Amen."

"And the other."

"O My Jesus, Saint Veronica served You on the way to Calvary by wiping Your beloved face with a veil on which Your Sacred Image then appeared. She protected this treasure, and whenever people touched it, they were miraculously healed. I ask her to pray for the growth of my ability to see Your Sacred Image in others, to recognize their hurts, to stop and join them on their difficult journeys, and to feel the same compassion for them as she did for You. Show me how to wipe their faces, serve their needs, and heal their wounds, reminding me that as I do this for them, I also do this for You. Saint Veronica, pray for me. Amen."

"Both of them again," she says. Then again and again. After the sixth time, she places the holy veil over my face. The image within the veil seems to come alive, and the room starts to spin. I start to cry out in pain as a burning sensation like acid on my skin rips through my left shoulder, but Veronica clamps her hand over my mouth. The burning sensation is countered on the right with a flush of pure energy like a million fresh tears falling directly onto my shoulder. The room continues to spin, and I shut my eyes. When I do, I don't see blackness. I see before me the face of Jesus, Son of God.

Then it happens. All the energy whisks away from me, taking with it the burning sensation in my left shoulder. Veronica grabs me around the neck to keep me from falling, while still clamping down on my mouth to stifle my screaming. As a different surge of energy enters my body, I start to shake. The room grows black as my eyes fill with tears that fall like violet rain down on Becca's head. From my right, I hear Becca taking deep breaths. From my left—from Mark—I hear nothing.

When Veronica removes the veil, I open my eyes. Veronica is hugging Becca to her chest; Mark's drooped head is hugging his own chest. I reach out, touch his wrist. No pulse, no life.

I turn to look at Becca. She clutches the charm as she breathes in deeply, almost like some new-born taking her first breath. While still holding tightly to Becca, Veronica releases me, and I pitch forward, falling toward the ugly, blue floor. It's as if I'm diving into the ocean.

I block the fall with my hands and try to rise, but I'm too weak to stand. When I try again, I find myself facing the side of Mark's shiny wheelchair. I stare at my distorted reflection, and for a split second I see not Cassandra Gray, but my true image. I am the Veronica.

Chapter 39

Wednesday, July 8

afternoon

"How do you do it, Cassandra?" Amanda asks. Scott is by her side, holding her hand like he used to hold mine. As if through some sense memory, I can still feel his skin against my skin.

"Do what?" I ask.

They stand, but I barely have the energy to sit in this hard hospital chair. I spent all day Tuesday in bed, unable to move. Today only feels a little better, but I needed to be here.

"Talk people into things!" Amanda sounds upset about breaking the rules.

Samantha is still in the ICU. Only family is allowed, but I got one of the nurses to break the rules when I explained that Samantha had no family. Helping me get in to see Samantha made the nurse feel better. That's all most people want: to do good in the world, which presents one of the biggest obstacles for tear collectors. We always struggle to break down basic human decency. Rather than fighting it, we need to accept it and own it. I keep having to remind myself that things are about to change for our species and, by extension, for the humans with whom we come in contact as well.

"Does she know yet?" Amanda asks.

Amanda has heard through the hospital grapevine that Mark was found dead in his bed, although the cause of death, she said, is yet unknown. Veronica told me it will look like a heart attack when he is examined. I don't think anyone could believe this about Mark since his heart didn't function at all.

I shake my head in answer to Amanda and say, "No, I want to be the one to tell her."

Scott finally speaks. "Shouldn't her mother—"

"Did you ever meet Samantha's mother?"

He shrugs; Amanda does as well. They look like twins.

"If she had to choose between her drugs and her child, she'd choose her drugs. I think she has abandoned Samantha for good, but we can't tell anyone until I figure out how to help her."

"I guess it's a good thing only God gets to choose who lives and who dies," Scott says.

I'd like to tell him how wrong he is, but he doesn't need to know. He has his faith; I have my certainty. He believes in his loving God with life everlasting; I know that for a few seconds, I was God's instrument to save the innocent, punish the wicked, and serve the greater good.

When it looks as if Samantha won't be waking up any time soon, Amanda and Scott excuse themselves. Before they leave, I ask Scott to stay in the room for a second. Amanda shoots me a funny look as if she's jealous, and an even funnier look at the realization that she's jealous of me. She's in a very good place right now, and I put her there. I try to give her the most reassuring look I can muster as she leaves the room.

"Scott, I don't want to make a scene or anything. I just want to tell you how sorry I am about how things turned out between us. I'm sure you see now it was the right thing."

"I don't know," he whispers.

"You two are perfect for each other. You're much more alike than you and I ever were."

"What about the whole opposites attract idea?" he asks, still whispering.

Is he afraid that Amanda will hear these words, or just unsure of what he's saying? I can't tell; my senses short-circuited on Monday night. I can only hope they will return soon.

"I mean if you can't believe in science, Cassandra, then I—"

"Hey, Scott, there's a sweet spot between science and faith, between nature and emotion, and there will always be a sweet spot in my heart for you. But it just wasn't meant to be."

"I know, I know. I'm not your soulmate." He sighs, staring at his shoes.

"You're right. You're not my soulmate. And do you know why?"

"Because I'm not good-looking enough? Or because—"

"That's not it," I whisper. "You're not my soulmate, Scott, because you are Amanda's."

After Scott leaves, I check my messages, but there are none from Caleb or Alexei. I want to learn more from Veronica, but I don't have the energy. Even if I did, I doubt she would tell me more. When Veronica thinks I need to know more about Caleb, his father, or mine, I now trust she will tell me. She needs to tell me because it's obvious that she needs me more than I will ever need her again.

"Cass?" Samantha says through her chapped lips.

"Samantha!" I shout, which causes her face to tighten like the sound hurts her ears.

Almost like a baby being born, each part of her starts to come to life. First she moves her fingers, then wets her lips, and finally manages to open her mouth again.

"Cass, where am I?"

"You're in the hospital."

You would think the smell and sounds would tell her that.

Her eyes open and close in rapid fire, blinking as if her brain is working overtime to recall details. Her mind is asking itself a million questions, but lacks the power to keep up. Just like I felt the other night, Samantha's consciousness seems as if it's about to short-circuit.

"Why?"

I breathe deeply. This is important.

"You don't remember?"

She shakes her head. More rapid eye movement. More licking her dried lips. I reach over for a large, plastic cup of water and put the straw in her mouth. She swallows; I do the same. We look and sound like twins. We're not, but we're connected even more deeply now.

"It was the Fourth of July. There were fireworks," she mumbles.

And how! I think, but I say nothing other than another prompt. "What else?"

She shakes her head. "Sometimes I can't tell my nightmares from my daily life."

"That, Samantha, is about to change."

She tries to sit up, but fails. It's okay because I stand up for her. I push my chair closer, and the effort almost exhausts me.

"The monster from your life is dead."

Samantha closes her eyes, and when she opens them she looks around the room. She starts to speak, then stops as her eyes inspect each inch of the room, every piece of equipment by her bed, and those on the wall. She stares at everything in her line of sight until she reaches me. Her dark stare, the one I first recall from that day in the library with Scott, returns.

"Monster?"

"Mark's dead," I whisper.

Like an old computer starting up, I see her load the data slowly.

Samantha doesn't look like herself without make-up—her special effect. She looks like nobody I know. But she sounds like Veronica as she smiles and says, "Cassandra, that's just wonderful."

"You're sure?" I say into the phone.

There's a long pause as Mrs. Berry tries to catch her breath. I left Samantha for a moment—the second she ran out of questions and asked if I had Uno cards—partly so I could make this call, but also because I'm confident she doesn't remember anything other than something happened on the Fourth of July, and now she's in the hospital. As with Scott, trauma wreaks havoc with memory. The big difference is that Scott had very little in his life until Alexei kidnapped him, and until that fateful night, she'd had nothing but trauma

"I guess all those prayers worked," Mrs. Berry finally says. We're separated by this phone, but never closer. "The doctor told us she's cancer-free. He can't explain it."

"I told you not to give up hope! I told you miracles were possible!" I remind her.

"I thought I'd lost it after Robyn, but this . . . this is . . ."

Sputtering, she can't find the words, so I say them for her. "Just wonderful."

"Everything is great," Mrs. Berry agrees.

On my end of the phone, I nod. I think about the Berrys, Scott, Amanda, and Samantha. Yes, for them, things are good. But then I wonder about Maggie and Caleb, and I fear for them. As I say goodbye to Mrs. Berry, I think I know whom I need to call next: Not Craig, although I'll get to him. I'll call Mr. A. and tell him I listened not to the silence but to my better self and did the right thing for the greater good. There are some fates you can fight and others to which you must surrender or they will crush you. You don't get to decide your ultimate fate, but maybe you can modify its direction.

It's not, "To be or not to be?" Life is a gray area somewhere in between.

Chapter 40

Sunday, July 12

morning

I watch in silence on the wet grass, awaiting Veronica. Even though it is her Feastday, she refused to come to the park with Mom and me, telling us only to await her arrival.

I know now that every sixteenth year on her Feastday, Veronica must reveal if she plans to remain in charge of the family. As Simon was never beatified, he has no Feastday, but he will reveal his intentions this morning as well. That they must reveal their intentions is the only tear collector rule we follow on this day. All the attention is on the elders and their life-and-death decisions. Nothing else matters; no other rules apply. It is a day we can act our best or be our very worst.

With Maggie exiled, I doubt if there's a decision for Veronica to make, especially since I have refused to start the next generation with Alexei and never had the chance to do so with Caleb. Where they are now, I do not know. No one does. For that—and no doubt other sins—Simon's tiny, dark eyes stare at me like round vultures from across the dirt path.

"Cassandra, don't be afraid of Simon," Mom says, pulling me close to her.

"I'm not," I say.

It is the last lie I will ever tell. From now on, I will speak only the truth. All those lies and rumors and all that manipulation brought me other people's tears, but at what cost to myself and to the humans we're supposed to serve? We were intended to help humans, not harvest them. My experiences over the last few months have shown me that tear collectors can feel emotions like humans—and not only fear. With Becca and Samantha, I showed compassion. With Scott, I know that my love was real because I let him go to protect him—and to help him find his own happiness. I helped him by doing him no harm. That I can begin to feel emotions other than fear is perhaps the scariest thing of all.

"He won't hurt you," Mom reassures me.

Simon walks slowly toward us. The red tip of his cane stirs up dust. He wears a blood-red tunic like Alexei wore the day he and I became tear collectors.

"Di'mah, where are the boys?" Simon asks as if he is speaking to a child. The pet name that always brought me comfort from my female relatives drips like an insult off his lips.

"Leave her alone." Mom stands in front of me.

"This is not your concern." He taps his cane five times at her feet and takes one step closer. Even as he speaks to my mom harshly, his face twists into his usual snarling smile.

"Simon, haven't you done enough harm to my family?" Mom asks.

"The harm is *your* doing." Another step; five more taps.

Mom stands tall. "Today, I know Veronica will choose to stay on another generation. But you, Simon—you have outlived your usefulness. Your heirs have shamed and endangered us. Why don't—"

Simon lifts his cane with great effort and points it at me. "The blame is with Cassandra."

"She knows her role in the family," Mom says. "She will perform it. She has no choice."

Simon's snarling smirk seems to cover his whole face. A light rain falls. Dressed in our re-enactment garb, my shoulders thirst for the healing moisture falling from the sky.

"That is not the truth," Simon says.

He raises his cane and moves it closer to me until it rests heavily on my left shoulder.

"I will do whatever Veronica asks of me," I say, ignoring the pain

Simon shakes his head in disgust before he snarls, "So, *she* is our future."

"Yes, Simon, I am the future. But you? You are of the past—you and your ways," I say. "Why did you not teach Alexei the rule of do no harm? Why did you not allow Caleb to—"

"Silence, you insolent, wild child!"

"I've been silent too long!"

I quickly shrug my shoulder. He groans as if in pain when he drops his cane. He motions for two of his nephews to help him. One picks up the cane; the other brings his ear close to Simon's mouth. Simon whispers something. I can't hear a word, but I smell the foul odor of cinnamon in the damp air.

The nephews help Simon undo his tunic. He reaches into his pocket and takes out a small vial, but he lacks the strength to open the container, which I suspect is filled with ancient tears. One of the nephews takes it from Simon, uncorks it, and sprinkles a drop on each of Simon's shoulders. The other nephew hands him his cane.

"Sinners suffer for their sins."

I watch his small, black eyes roll back in his head. Simon's pupils expand as the energy runs through his veins. He points the cane in my face and flicks his thumb. The small blade touches my flesh. Like Hamlet who was too unsure to act, I'm too afraid to move. Unable to flee or fight, I freeze in the heat of the moment.

"You must know your role!" Simon swings his cane with full force, not aiming for my shoulders but rather my head. "Cassandra, Veronica cannot protect you!"

"But I can!" Mom grabs Simon's cane in mid-air.

Simon struggles to wrestle the cane from Mom's grip, but she holds on tight with her right hand. With her left, she pushes me back, out of harm's way. I fall to the ground.

"Out of the way, now!" Simon shouts.

Everyone watches; no one moves a muscle.

"No," says Mom, "As you say, Simon, all sinners must suffer for their sins. It is now time. You exiled my soulmate because you knew he was different from you. He was better than you."

Simon pulls hard and finally wrenches the cane from my mother's hand. He lifts it again, pointing it, not at me, but at Mom. He moves it up against her throat.

"None are better than I."

"He was my soulmate, but you—" Mom starts. Her eyes grow wide at the clicking sound. Still, she continues. "He and I could have started a new way, but you wouldn't allow it. I won't allow this!"

"You broke all my rules." Simon words come as sharp as the blade in the cane's tip.

"And you broke my heart."

I try to pull her away, but she won't move.

"Today is the Feastday, and there are no rules. I will defy you, Simon. I won't listen to your rules any—"

"There are no rules, indeed."

"Simon, you will—"

The red tip of Simon's cane grows redder with the blood trickling from Mom's throat, slashed by the blade embedded in the end of Simon's cane. A trickle quickly turns to a torrent.

"There are no rules, indeed," Simon repeats.

Mom falls, clutching her throat as Simon walks slowly away. All the males follow behind him like sheep behind a shepherd.

"Mom!" I shout as I dive toward her. She tries to speak but cannot.

"Salome!" I hear a man's voice cry from behind me—a familiar, yet out-of-place voice.

I turn. It's Mr. Abraham. Next to him stands Veronica. Mr. A. runs toward my mother. Veronica walks behind him slowly as she moves through the misty rain. I try to speak over the shouting, but Veronica silences us with a wave of her hand.

What is Mr. A. doing here? How did he know?

"Move away, Cassandra. Let them be together *at last*," she says.

"Together?" I ask, but I already know: Mr. A. is my teacher, my mentor, my coach, and my father.

Veronica looks down at my mother. Mr. A. holds her head in his lap as he cries a river of human tears that mix with the violet drops now flowing from my mother's eyes.

"There is little time," Veronica says.

Mr. A. removes his white shirt and presses it against Mom's throat. It slows, but he can't stop the bleeding. Although Mom's blood taints the air, Mr. A.'s scarred shoulders fill my nose with the scent of death itself.

No wonder my swim coach never swims!

Like the scars on Samantha's back, the scars on Mr. A.'s shoulders remain. He was the man I saw exiled: my own father.

He sees me at last and says, "I was prepared to sacrifice myself, but fate has intervened. Grab her!"

Mr. A. pulls my mother to her feet. I drape her left arm over my shoulders, while Veronica shoulders her right arm. With her arms in a T-shape, Mr. A. bends down so his left shoulder is directly under Mom's weeping eyes. Mom's expression of agony subsides as her tears fall on his left shoulder and—after he moves—his right. As the violet drops quench the damaged flesh, Mr. A. begins breathing deeply. Mom breathes out; he breathes in as his skin begins to heal.

"You were my soulmate, Alexander." Mom garbles through her cut throat.

"No, Salome. You *are* my soulmate," he whispers.

Her eyes closing, her breath fading, Mom reaches for me. She clutches my wrist. She starts to speak again, but can only produce a gurgling sound as if she's drowning. And she is.

"Mom, I'm sorry."

She clutches more tightly, and I press my ear against her mouth. Her tears fall on me, but they can only heal my body, not my heart. They can't wash away what I'm feeling now. The hurt. The loss. The love.

"Cassandra," she whispers. "Listen, there's something you must know."

Each word takes such effort, even with her lips against my ear almost in a kiss. She opens her eyes again. She looks at me, at Mr. A., and then back at me.

"Life without love isn't worth living."

She lets go of my wrist, and Mr. A. pulls his soulmate tight against his healed body.

He breathes in; she doesn't breathe out.

My mother is dead; my father is reborn.

Chapter 41

Wednesday, July 15

morning

"He's one of us?" I whisper to Veronica as I stare at Father Morrison at the pulpit.

She nods her head slowly. We're all moving slowly, worn out by the events of the past few days, but even more by the fear of the events to come. Along with Father Morrison, Mr. A. is the only male tear collector at Mother's small funeral. No friends, just family: The family.

"Why didn't you tell me?" I whisper again, but she silences me.

"I will tell you what you need to know when you need to know."

She nods her head; I nod my head slowly, a mirror image.

After Father Morrison speaks, he invites Veronica to say something. As Mr. A. and I help her toward the pulpit, I flash back to my last funeral: Scott's grandmother. She died so that he could he live; Mother died so that Mr. A. could be reborn. The bleeding might not have killed her. Perhaps it could have been stopped, but once she started to cry, her fate and his were sealed.

I return to my pew, but Mr. A. remains with Father Morrison, supporting Veronica. She lifts her violet veil off her face and starts to speak softly.

"Family, today we give to God the soul of Salome, who died so that another could live, just as Jesus died for all of our sins."

"Amen," we all say.

"Salome reminded us that we are a species of sacrifice, not selfishness. Our actions on this Earth should help, not harm. We must reclaim our true heritage. We must restore the old ways of true compassion, actual sympathy, and providing humans with comfort. We must still collect our tears to thrive, but our ways must change, for our own good and that of humanity."

"Amen."

"It is hard for the old to change their ways. Therefore we turn to the young."

When she says this, I feel everyone's eyes on me as if Veronica's words are a spotlight.

"Earlier this year, Cassandra told me Robyn had died. Her tragic death created an environment for Cassandra at school and at Robyn's home that could give us many of the tears we need to thrive. But when she told me Robyn died, I replied as only I could: 'That's just wonderful,' for I knew the human grief that such an event would cause. It was the only way I knew to respond. It is my nature," Veronica says.

"Amen," everyone says—everyone but me.

"But Cassandra did not react that way. She did not smile or rejoice. She did not see her friend's death as an opportunity. She felt the stirrings of something else, something like regret and sorrow and maybe even a little grief at her friend's passing.

"In her reaction, I first thought she was—as many of our young are prone to doing—becoming too human, too caught up in the drama she so often created, and no doubt, like all of us, beginning to feel under the surface something that seemed like genuine human emotion. But then I knew: It was not human emotion, but the reactions of an authentic tear collector."

"Amen."

Mr. A. seems to say it the loudest. He wears the same suit he wore to the prom, but this is no midsummer's night's dream; this is a midsummer morning nightmare.

"And I knew. I knew the only chance for our kind was to take a new direction, which is, in fact, an old direction. I would have too much to unlearn, and so would Maggie."

An already silent church grows somehow more silent—a vacuum of noise.

"Maggie feared too much about her role in the family. Her fear led to impatience, and that led to her exile. But if she wishes to return to be with family, it should be allowed. She left without the scarring ceremony, but if she returns, she must undergo it and serve the rest of her life as one who collects tears without feeling the benefit of them herself. I forgive; I do not forget."

"Amen." Again, I do not join in.

"Salome had great potential," Veronica starts.

She stops to balance herself. Mr. A., who is holding on tight, seems to hold on tighter, like no force could remove him from Veronica's side. His strength gives her the will to continue.

"Perhaps. But her anger at Simon never left her. It defined her; it destroyed her."

"Amen."

"Cassandra, child, please come up here."

I do as I'm told; that still comes naturally.

Father Morrison stands aside, and I take his place supporting Veronica. She seems more frail than usual. I haven't seen her stand for so long; I've never heard her talk for so long. Veronica conserves everything as if she is afraid it will all be taken away from her one day. She held onto her position all this time out of instinct but also goodness; Simon holds on out of avarice and greed.

"From the day you told me about Robyn, I knew this day would come. I watched you as you navigated through the minefields of adolescence. As you felt the stirring of human love, as you took actions sometimes to change your fate and other times accepted what fate allowed. So today, fate and action come together once more. Cassandra, you have proven you possess true compassion."

I look at Veronica. She glows almost as if she's stronger than ever. She slowly removes the violet veil and holds it up for all to see. Mr. A. holds on to her with one hand, while the other now steadies my trembling shoulder. Veronica's hands shake as she holds the veil out to me.

"Take it, Cassandra." I obey. "I will remain beside you to guide you if you need me."

"Guide me? What do you mean, Veronica?"

She smiles for the first time in recent memory. "I am not the Veronica now. You are."

"I am the Veronica," I whisper.

I'm barely able to speak or stand as I put on the violet veil.

"Say something, Daughter," Mr. A. says.

His hand stays on my shoulder, strong yet soft.

Before I speak, I think, *Despite the blood and betrayal, my life isn't Hamlet's after all. I acted but also let fate act upon me. I fought against the wind, and I went with it.*

Chapter 42

Wednesday, July 15

afternoon

"How are you feeling, Samantha?" I ask.

She sits up in the hospital bed. It's so odd to see her in the white patient's gown rather than something black.

"Better, physically. Emotionally? I'm a wreck as always." She snickers.

I pull the chair up close. "Time and tears."

"And more therapy." Another laugh.

I join in vaguely, but I'm distracted. I glance again at the clock. Visiting hours end in less than an hour, but they're still not here. Maybe while my family was marking the death of my mother, the Berrys were celebrating their new lease on life and their cancer-free child. The doctors called it a miracle, and for once, they were right.

"No word from your mom?" I ask.

She shakes her head. Her dye-job is fading.

"What are you going to do?" I ask.

Another head shake, this time with a shrug.

"I mean, does anyone know she's missing? Like the police or social services or anybody?"

"I lied to them. You taught me well." A short, cynical laugh.

"Those days are over," I begin. Then I tell her about the morning, about Veronica putting me in charge of the family, and about her staying on to guide me.

"What are you going to do differently?" Samantha asks.

I think about the scars on her back; I think about the scars on Siobhan's shoulders.

"For starters? Invite back to the family all those who have been exiled. Rather than removing them, we should have learned from them, just like I've learned so much from you. We need to embrace our humanity, not exile it from ourselves."

"What have you learned from me—other than about vampires and meth-heads?"

"Resiliency."

I touch her shoulders—mine more sensitive, hers so much stronger.

Exhausted from the morning, I sense that Samantha is growing tired of talking. She suggests we play Uno. I sigh but agree. She grabs the cards from the table next to her while I stare at the clock. Almost right away, Samantha finds herself deep in cards, yet she's smiling.

"What's going on?" I ask. "You know the object is to have no cards, not all of them, right?"

She laughs so loud it echoes around the room. "You said I'm resilient; that's why."

"I beat you in Uno, and that somehow makes you stronger in life? I don't think so."

"No, what you said about my being resilient," Samantha says. She holds her card-packed Uno hand in front of me. "Listen, life is just like a game of Uno: It hands you cards. Have a druggie mom? Take three cards. Get scarred for life? Get four cards. Choose to fuck up your life with bad habits? Take six more cards. I got a full hand. But you know what? Somehow, slowly but surely, I will get rid of these cards. I'm strong because I've been beat up so much that I don't think I can hurt anymore. I've lost everything, so anything is possible."

"Anything?"

The smile on her face responds better than any words ever could.

Before we can finish the hand, the Berrys enter. Becca runs to me, while Mr. Berry stands near the door and then walks slowly toward the bed.

"Samantha, how are you?"

"I'm feeling better. Thanks for coming, Mrs. Berry, Mr. Berry."

I stand and offer my seat to Mrs. Berry, who wears a bright orange dress. She sits down; I stand behind her.

"Samantha, Cassandra has told us all about you and your situation."

Samantha glares at me—her eyes dark even sans her normal black eye shadow and thick mascara. "She had—"

Mrs. Berry cuts her off by raising her hands, palms out. "Now, before you get mad, let me tell you that nothing Cassandra told us about your past matters. What matters is your future."

"My future?" Samantha asks.

I take a step toward the bed. "Nature needs balance, Samantha, right?"

She nods in agreement, but I can tell from the look on her face that she's confused. My senses, now fully recovered, tell me she's afraid. My tear collector instinct pulls me one way; my new nature pushes me the other.

"So we thought since no one knows that your mother is missing, and you don't have a place to go that ..." Mrs. Berry starts to say softly, slowly.

I take a deep breath and squeeze Mrs. Berry's shoulders. "Finish it," I tell her.

"You need a mom," Mrs. Berry says. "Becca needs an older sister. We need another daughter."

Samantha pushes herself toward the edge of the bed. Mrs. Berry meets here there.   "Really?"

In just that one word, I sense a hundred emotions running through Samantha. My shoulders tingle, my mouth waters, but the handkerchief—my handkerchief—stays hidden.

"Really, Samantha. Really."

Mrs. Berry leans over to hug Samantha, who almost falls into her arms. Mrs. Berry's arms wrap around her, but when they do, one of them slips through the opening in the back of the gown. As her hands touch Samantha's scars, I watch the wave of expressions on Mrs. Berry's face as she feels the scars: shock, sadness, and, finally, simple compassion.

I turn away, look in the mirror, and see the same expression on my face, but the image soon changes as a single tear forms in my eye. I transfer the tear onto my finger and return to the bed. I place the violet drop on Samantha's exposed back. The skin starts to heal immediately—as do I.

Samantha touches my hand. "Cassandra, are you crying?"

I don't correct her. I'm not Cassandra. I'm Veronica, new matriarch of the tear collectors, fated to create a more compassionate species, even as my own kind work against me.

I close my eyes to stop the tears and shut out the darkness that I found online this morning.

Michigan State Police have a lead on a series of child kidnappings in the Detroit area. A witness described one suspect as, "Having a shock of brown hair." The other has dark blue eyes. Both look as if they have recently been wounded. They were last seen driving a white Dodge Charger.

𝕸eet the 𝕰lsinore 𝕼uills

Jordan McMullen

To be honest, this project has meant more to me than I ever thought it would. I have fallen in love, not only with the book itself and the people involved, but with the entire world of publishing. I now know that publishing/editing is the field I want to go into after high school, which is a pretty freaking huge deal to me! Even though this project had its down moments of stress and crazy frustration, it has also had more hilarious, screwed-up, and touching moments than I can count! I loved all of our meetings at IHOP, and I cannot believe how close I am with these people now. I roped together a small part of this team, and I can honestly say they have amazed me beyond words—in talent, as well as dependability. I would like to thank the other members of this team, my dear mother for driving me everywhere, and Spring Lea Henry, without whom none of this would have happened. I love you guys!

Jessica Stonebraker

Upon hearing about this project, it caught my notice instantly. My older sister's friend, Spring Lea Henry, had cooked up a wonderful idea to have teens edit one of the novels she was publishing, and my sister was among the teens chosen. I immediately wanted to be part of it, and my great choice is one I didn't regret. I met wonderful people such as the author, other teens, and the adult editors. I have been blessed with this opportunity because I have always enjoyed reading, writing, and books, so this chance to help out and learn was really awesome.

Chika Zuri

Working with the Elsinore Quills on this project was a privilege among the best I've yet to receive. Not only did we edit an awesome book, we ravenously pillaged the IHOPs of NoCo, launched a full blown assault for the rights to bloggers' photos, and persistently scoured maps to locate hidden conference rooms to then overthrow and establish as our headquarters!

*Please acknowledge the above note by Chika Zuri should be read in a ridiculously over-the-top pirate accent of any nationality you should deem appropriate.

Linnea Ren

The Cassandra Project has been . . . an interesting experience, to say the least. Our meetings were half-filled with goofy conversations, inside joke after inside joke, and pancakes and half-filled with serious conversations about Patrick's book. We talked about everything—from his first book in the series, to character development, to the plot itself. What we wanted, what we didn't want, how we wanted to see it, what we liked and didn't like, and what advice we could give to him. It actually wasn't easy—especially since I'm an introvert, and the majority of the group are extroverts. The table was loud and rambunctious, and sometimes there were days when I just wanted to scream at everyone. But we managed to pull through and get our work done.

*Being a writer, this was an excellent experience for me. I got to see how the editing and publishing process works, almost from beginning to end. Granted, it terrifies me. There's no way I'm good enough to get published. But I'll keep trying. Patrick did with this story. The final version we have here is so different from the first draft. I almost don't recognize it because it's been helped, morphed, and changed.

*So, not only did I get to learn about the whole world I want to enter, but I made new friends and new connections. My life has just been better because I was roped into this project.

M. Hawkins

The elusive M. Hawkins is elusive. <_<

Intern Editor and Cover Designer's Note

Working on *Cassandra's Turn* was, in a word, ambitious. Admittedly, I had my doubts when I was asked/volunteered to stand in as Intern Editor on this project; I think I partially took the job just to see if it could be done . . . with an admittedly more-than-casual interest to observe the forthcoming chaos that was sure to unfold. I certainly agreed to help where I could and do everything in my own power to make the project a success—whatever power is bestowed upon a common intern (ha ha)—but my mental popcorn was already in the microwave.

My first surprise was in not being treated like a common intern. I had opinions, feedback, suggestions, and people cared. The author cared. And they listened! Suddenly, I found myself committed to this project as much as any of my own projects.

Mr. Jones was completely open to feedback and criticism on a level that was practically saintly. Every suggestion proposed was considered carefully, every paragraph cut was taken in stride—even whole concepts that we scrapped and started from the beginning he thoughtfully considered because, ultimately, his goal was the same as everyone else's: to tell the best story possible.

Each of the Elsinore Quills had something genius to contribute. Their level of professionalism and dedication is not met by most adults. That's not to say we didn't have our moments. It's a fact that the amount of tension is directly proportional to the amount of people added in a mix. But even for all our diverse opinions and personalities, it was awesome to be a part of that creative collective.

Designing the cover was a different set of challenges. Once we finally got to cover art, my professional training in graphic arts took over and the intern badge came off. We were working under a very tight deadline and slim budget. I tried to remain open about concepts and ideas, but everyone who had ever heard of the project ever had an opinion on how the final should look . . . except for Mr. Jones! Good ideas were hatched, took flight, and then quickly grew talons and breathed fire. Life as I know it is this: If a final product looks easy, it wasn't. If it looks hard, it was near impossible. But I am proud of the book—both inside and out—and consider myself lucky to have been part of such an innovative team.

So, sit back and enjoy your mental popcorn.

The Cassandra Project: An Adventure in Editing

For me, this project began back in 1999 while I was in graduate school for a master's degree in library science and had started a course in young adult literature. I can still feel the uncomfortable plastic chair beneath me as I sat at a desk staring down at an intimidating volume: *Connecting Young Adults and Libraries: A How-To-Do-It Manual (Second Edition)* by Patrick Jones. Amazon.com says this tome weighs only three pounds, but to me, it seemed to weigh so much more because of all the information, wisdom, and practical advice within its 400+ pages. I wasn't alone in my thinking. My whole class consulted that book so often that we started calling it "The Big, Pink Bible of Teen Services." I owe much of my success as a teen librarian to Patrick's brilliance.

Flash-forward to July 17, 2011, a normal workday. Up to my ears in editing Shawn J. Gourley's book, I took a quick Facebook break. Patrick Jones had posted about his publisher not being willing to "go there" with his latest project because it was too edgy. Just seeing him in my Facebook feed was something of a novelty to me, even though we'd friended up in 2009. Although we had worked together in small ways, including my contribution of a bibliography to his book on building core collections, I felt like a celebrity stalker. Maybe it was my lack of sleep from 20-hour editing stints or just a wild impulse, but I sent him a polite Facebook inquiry about his book, billing my company as a young, up-and-coming indie house with a flair for experimenting with new ideas. His book didn't sound too edgy; in fact, the concept excited me, and I hoped he would consider us. Alas, that conversation petered out, and I got back to business as usual.

Now we jump to November 11, 2011, a big day when Shawn's paperback edition came out with a strong burst of sales. I also received an email from Patrick Jones on Facebook. He wasn't pitching the edgy book to me, but his sequel to The Tear Collector was up for grabs and he wanted to know if I was interested. As gutsy as I felt back in July when I had emailed him, I found my nerves giving out when faced with the actuality of being his publisher. Life saved me from an instant decision by giving me the flu, and during that time, I questioned myself constantly over the same issue: What if I had to tell Patrick Jones, one of my heroes, that his manuscript needed work? No manuscript has ever come to me pristine, and helping him with revisions would likely be my reality. I would have to be brave enough to do the job of a good editor and help him tell the best story possible. The way I was feeling, it seemed impossible to achieve.

In late December, this thought came to me: "I wish Patrick was a teen. I never feel this nervous around teens." In one of those flashbulb moments, I had my answer. I would find some teens to do my dirty work! Teens are not afraid to speak their minds, even if they are overly blunt. I knew that if I got a group of teens together, taught them the language of editing, and set them loose on Patrick's work, they would be able to tell him what I wanted to say, but couldn't. They would form my safe buffer zone, making me comfortable enough to open my own mouth as well. Like me, Patrick "gets" teens at a deep, abiding level. Working with teens would give us common ground, and I knew he'd be on board.

I wasted no time in contacting Sue-Ellen Jones (no relation to Patrick), a librarian at Poudre River Library District in Fort Collins, Colorado, with whom I had often worked on teen events. She loved the idea and thought her co-worker, Diane Tuccillo, would also be interested and might be willing to write an article for *VOYA* (*Voice of Youth Advocates*, a journal for young adult librarians), about teens acting as editors. She also thought her library teens would be happy to participate.

Then I called Cathi Dunn MacRae to see if she'd be willing to join us as a real-world career mentor for a series of talks I envisioned. I wanted professionals to relay to our teen editors the ins and outs of being an editor in many situations. Cathi said she could speak about freelancing, and we discussed other aspects of editing for which we would need instructors.

Our professional roster of helpers included Nina Hess, an editor at Wizards of the Coast, who talked about life in a big publishing house; Melissa Powell, a freelance editor for *Colorado Libraries* and *Publishers Weekly*, who spoke about how to juggle a busy schedule and the work that goes into periodicals and web content; Victoria Hanley, author of young adult fantasy novels *Healer's Keep* and *Violet Wings*, among others, who taught the teens how to give healthy critiques; and Dori Eppstein-Ransom, owner of The Writer's Elf editing services, who talked about how to present one's skills professionally and deal with clients one-on-one. I asked my friend and writing partner, Teri Stearns, to become the Grumpy Dragon intern editor for this project, helping me to teach the editing process and also give me feedback on my own work, giving me course corrections like a good ship's navigator.

Finally, there were the teens themselves. I already knew two of them, Jordan McMullen and M. Hawkins. Jordan found the other players: Chika Zuri, Linnea Ren, and Jordan's sister, Jessica Stonebraker. Each of these young people brought something special to the table. Linnea was our super-critic and the one who wrote the prologue. Chika gave us ideas for the cover art. M. and Jordan formulated questions for the professionals to answer during the mentoring sessions and questions to address in the VOYA article. Jessica will be the primary reader for the audiobook. Collectively, this group calls themselves The Elsinore Quills.

As I put all these pieces in place, I suspected there would be so much awesome energy in this project that existing technology wouldn't be able to measure it! When I brought the whole bundle as an offer to Patrick during a phone call in January 2012, I felt my feet leave the earth when I heard his reaction. He caught my glee at working with teens in this new way and joined right in. Knowing that we would be facing this project as equal partners with the teens as our common bond gave me the courage to keep moving forward with this challenging experiment. Every action I took was fueled with a mix of hope, faith, and my love of connecting teens with caring adults.

During our initial phone call, I told Patrick about a Victorian tear bottle that my matron of honor, Lisa Benwitz, gave me as a wedding gift, which I still displayed on my mantelpiece. I sent Patrick a picture of it, suggesting that he might want to use it as an artifact in the story. I am delighted in the way that he did so, and happy to see it on the cover of this book. That little bottle got us off on the right foot, and I am forever grateful to Lisa for her gift.

We all worked hard throughout 2012, and much of it happened on Facebook, where many people live these days, myself included. I created a private group with all the players in a safe, shared workspace where we could discuss the manuscript, upload files, set up meeting schedules, and even get a little silly sometimes. With Patrick in Minnesota and our Grumpy Dragon staff, teens, and consultants in Colorado (except Cathi in Maryland and Nina in Seattle), technology was our friend. Patrick Skyped into our initial meeting, and Nina used Skype for her mentoring session with the teens later that summer. In addition to written critiques, some of the teens used audio or visual recordings of themselves to give feedback, which capitalized on each of their expressive styles.

Our real-life meetings mostly occurred at the IHOP in Fort Collins, where pancakes became an essential part of the editing process. I had no idea how important pancakes could be! The work never began until the short-stacks arrived at the table. What fun it was to learn and laugh with Teri and the Quills! The teens' insights helped me to sharpen my editing skills, and Teri helped me develop better ways of communicating ideas. It was truly a collaborative process.

The real magic happened during a July weekend in a conference room when Patrick and the editing professionals joined us in Fort

Collins. We came to call it the Mega-Meeting because of the two long days and all we accomplished in those precious hours. Saturday was devoted to Patrick's novel itself. We hashed out major issues, talked about solutions, helped Patrick plot the last three chapters, and set up a project timeline for all that had to be done to launch the book. Then we all trooped over to the Olive Garden, where the editing professionals joined us for a casual dinner. In both locations, Patrick sat at one end of the table, and I sat at the other, which seemed to physically represent the relationship between author and editor with our support staff between us, helping us connect in the most meaningful way.

The second day of the Mega Meeting was devoted to the editing professionals, who answered the teens' questions about what their jobs entail. It was also a very special experience for me. In Library-Land, I had the benefit of graduate school and many professionals to help me learn all I needed to become an accomplished teen librarian. By contrast, the publishing environment is extremely competitive. The few editors I had approached with questions had played it very close to the vest. I had felt rather alone and sometimes lost as I tried to figure out how everything works, what I wanted to adopt for myself, and what needed changing in the industry. Being able to ask questions of other professionals helped me experience collaborative energy, and I continue to communicate with them and learn from them. I gained what I'd been sorely lacking: colleagues!

After that key weekend, the work of wrapping up the writing happened quickly for Patrick. The editing process, however, proved to be much slower as the teens dealt with the start of school, and allergens from a nearby forest fire provoked a month-long migraine in me. New lessons in this juggling act of producing a book on schedule are resulting in changes in how I handle workflow.

In addition to participating in the Mega-Meeting, Cathi Dunn MacRae served as copyeditor for this project, and I am immeasurably grateful to her for adding her brilliance to this book. As she tweaked and tightened, I learned much from her marks and comments. I also owe thanks to author David Boop for his advice on clearance issues for the quoted material at the front of the book, and Reb Irwin Keller for his knowledge of Hebrew in developing the term "Di'mah" as a name of affection that Cassandra's female relatives give to her.

In the end, learning is this project's central theme. I can say for certain that the teens learned a great deal. From the changes between Patrick's early drafts and the tight, well-chosen words that you see on these pages, I can venture a guess that he learned more about his storytelling craft. I hope Teri and the other editing professionals learned what a kick it is to work with young people. I learned so much about myself as an editor and leader during this project, and I'm still learning.

As I write this note, the copyediting for the book itself is being finished across the country, Patrick is awaiting the final draft for approval, Teri is finalizing the cover image, and Diane's *VOYA* article is on its way for the April 2013 issue. There is much left to do between now and April 6, 2013, when the book will launch at the Colorado Teen Literature Conference in Denver. As I reflect on the process from this brief resting place, I know that surprises and lessons are waiting for me in the months ahead.

But a beautiful book also waits for me in the future. My multiple passes through this story did not make me weary of it. I never wanted to throw the laptop across the room because I couldn't bear to read the same sentences again. What happened instead was the magic of seeing deeper and deeper layers of meaning with each reading. Patrick's story often touched my heart to the point of tears. I'm not sure how Cassandra would use such happy teardrops, but I would hope they would feed her in some way.

Cathi Dunn Macrae had this to say about the project, "Enlisting the insights and feedback of teens in the editing process — especially teens who savor reading, writing, and their own creativity — takes the young adult novel to a whole new level. Everyone involved in the Cassandra Project can be proud of their contributions to this book by Patrick Jones, who himself is a rare model of insight and inclusiveness with the youth for whom he writes." I cannot agree more with this sentiment. I am full to the brim with gratitude for everyone's hard work and dedication.

Ultimately, despite bumps along the way, this journey has been perfection. Perfection on a pancake.

~~Spring Lea Henry
January 2013
Colorado Springs, Colorado

About the Author

Patrick Jones is the author of books for young people ranging from the supernatural (*The Tear Collector*) to the superstars of the pro wrestling ring (*The Main Event*). His first novel, *Things Change*, was an American Library Association Quick Pick for Reluctant Teen Readers, while his third novel *Chasing Tail Lights* was a Minnesota Book Award finalist. In 2006, he won lifetime achievement awards from the American Library Association and Catholic Library Association. A former librarian for teens, Jones has trained librarians in every one of the United States. The Michigan native now lives in Minnesota, on the web (www.tearcollector.com), on Myspace (www.myspace.com/connectingya), and on Facebook (www.facebook.com/TearCollector).

Other Great Books
from
The Grumpy Dragon

The Cadence
Casey Hays
Emma King's life is fairly ordinary, with the exception of one extraordinary aspect. She is plagued with the rare ability to feel a person's emotions with a simple touch. Any sensation she feels becomes amplified to almost unbearable levels. Emma has learned to keep her hands to herself and her emotions under wraps. But when Gage Parmer moves to town, everything changes, and for the first time in her life, Emma loosens the chains that hold her emotions in check and prepares herself for the whirlwind that is to come. Mysteriously lacking in emotions, Gage tells Emma an incredible story that pulls her into his world of impossibilities. At first, she refuses to believe. But when she puts his words to the test, she discovers that his world is also hers. Soon, she will be forced to use her ability in an attempt to destroy an ancient evil that has defied death and ruled the centuries in a reign of terror. They are called... The Cadence.

ISBN: 978-0-9881880-0-6 **List Price:** $19.95
Also available for Kindle and Nook

Shatterwood I
Mello Yello
Chael is new to Shatterwood and right away things are looking pretty weird. His roommate is nowhere to be seen when Chael arrives. The other students all have an air of mystery. And even the faculty gives him the creeps. Before too long, Chael hears a strange word, "casters," in the dining hall, and he is told to forget it. But how can he forget it when odd things keep happening around him and to him. Who are the Leaves of Mendell? How do the students from the past play into the present? And what is Chael's role in all this? These are the questions that await you, dear reader, on the pages inside...

ISBN: 978-0-9790084-8-1 **List Price:** $9.99

Other Great Books
from
The Grumpy Dragon

Macabre: Quirky Poems for the Morbid Soul
Claudia Amiel Harrington
Written by a teen for teens (and adults), *Macabre* is a quirky exploration of human angst in poetic form. *Macabre* is particularly suited to the Goth audience and to anyone who has ever had difficulty "fitting in".

ISBN: 978-0-9790084-2-9 **List Price:** $9.99

Dragon's Horde 1
Edited by Spring Lea E. Henry
Dragon's Horde 1 is the first in a series of teen art and writing collections. Inside are the works of the winners of The Grumpy Dragon's first Dragon's Horde Teen Writing and Art Contest. The Grumpy Dragon congratulates all the contest participants for daring to dream big.

ISBN: 978-0-9790084-4-3 **List Price:** $9.99

Coming Soon
from The Grumpy Dragon

Breeder by Casey Hays

The first book in the
Arrow's Flight Trilogy

Colophon

The original source of the book was produced using Scribus 1.3.3.13 and exported to PDF.

The fonts used are Arial, Cardinal, FreeSans, FreeSerif, Princess Lulu, Times New Roman.

CPSIA information can be obtained at www.ICGtesting.com
Printed in the USA
LVOW081442180613

339153LV00003B/65/P